Sing Down the Moon

"There is so much to admire in Robert Gwaltney's new novel—how it is both intensely Southern yet also reminiscent of the magical realism of writers such as Gabriel Garcia Marquez; its appealing heroine caught between the demands of her community (both the living and the dead) and the desires of her own heart; its delightful blend of colloquial and lyric language—all of which make *Sing Down the Moon* a remarkable achievement."

—Ron Rash, *New York Times* bestselling
author of *Serena* and *The Caretaker*

"*Sing Down the Moon* is a wholly original, ambitious, and lyrical southern gothic fantasy that is both tantalizing and immersive. Gwaltney's imagination soars in this epic story centered around a young girl named Leontyne Skye who struggles to come to terms with her birthright while navigating the complex environment of a mythical Georgia barrier island where trickery, lies and deceit are as abundant as quicksand and moonbeams. An enchanting and alluring read—I loved it."

—Donna Everhart, author of
The Saints of Swallow Hill

"Robert Gwaltney's sophomore follow-up to *The Cicada Tree* is Southern Gothic at its finest. With beautiful prose and an artist's eye, his descriptions immerse the reader in the beauty and fairy-tale magic of coastal Georgia. Characters who are wounded both physically and emotionally populate this story of family legacy and the price of betrayal. This is the perfect read for fans of Southern fiction and magical realism and for those who enjoy savoring every word."

—Karen White, *New York Times* bestselling
author of *That Last Carolina Summer*

Robert Gwaltney's silver pen spins a Southern Gothic tale of spangles and shadows that drape over the history of this haunted island and the fabulous family that lives—well, mostly lives—there. With nothing short of glee, Gwaltney bestows fates and furies upon his beloved and tortured characters as artfully and soulfully as he names them, and beneath the swirling poetry, writes a simple coming-of-age novel that examines the hard truths about life and death. A rambling fever dream, *Sing Down the Moon* will sweep readers away on a fickle wind and a wild tide and deliver them softly on a benevolent shore, gasping with wonder. Be prepared to love this book.

—Kimberly Brock, bestselling author
of *The Fabled Earth*

"*Sing Down the Moon* is a brilliant fable written by an extremely talented man. It is a dazzling performance about the distance between life and death on a haunted island off the coast of Georgia. Incredibly inventive and unexpected at every turn, this novel shines with talent. You will love it."

—Philip Lee Williams, author of twenty-one volumes
of fiction, poetry, and essays and a member
of the Georgia Writers Hall of Fame

"Tender, wistful, and poignant, *Sing Down the Moon* is a novel of profound beauty that mesmerizes with lyrical prose and earthy Southern magic. Gwaltney woos and sings you on a redolent journey through the Lowcountry marshes, where haints seek redemption and a trio of uncommonly charming young people grapple with the sins of the past, false memories, and secrets left unburied. Lush, haunting, and completely unforgettable."

—Paulette Kennedy, bestselling author
of *The Witch of Tin Mountain*

"There's an almost Dickensian denseness to Robert Gwaltney's lyrical writing that invites a savor-every-turn-of-phrase reading. Happy to report, his *Sing Down the Moon* is no different. This lavish, beautifully-told ghost story is populated with characters who hover between the living and the dead in a dimly-lit world that is both frightening and funny. His characters want what they want with a mighty need, always tempered by Gwaltney's hand with a tender humanity. One can't help but root for them as they journey through this tale that sits, uniquely, at the intersection of Southern Gothic, Magical Realism, family drama, and coming-of-age story-telling."

—Jeffrey Dale Lofton, award-winning
author of *Red Clay Suzie* and
Georgia Author of the Year

Sing Down the Moon

A Novel

ꟹ

Robert Gwaltney

MERCER UNIVERSITY PRESS
Macon, Georgia

MUP/ P734

Published by Mercer University Press
1501 Mercer University Drive
Macon, Georgia 31207

30 29 28 27 26 5 4 3 2 1

Books published by Mercer University Press are printed on acid-free paper that meets the requirements of the American National Standard for Information Sciences—Permanence of Paper for Printed Library Materials.

Printed and bound in the United States.

This book is set in Adobe Caslon.

Cover/jacket design by Burt&Burt.

ISBN 979-8-89736-009-3 (Print)
979-8-89736-010-9 (eBook)

Cataloging-in-Publication Data is available from the Library of Congress

Foreword

Magical realism is an amazing way to tell a story with depth and complexity. Southern magical realism adds another exquisite layer to the building of an intricate world. The opening line of *Sing Down the Moon* brings a ringing bell of truth to this fantastical story imagined in the Lowcountry.

"We are all dead here on Good Hope."

There are so many ways to be dead and still walk this earth in a body that breathes. This golden-threaded tale took me back to when I was eleven in my great aunt's high-ceiling living room in Appalachia, where I listened to these women weave stories about haints on many Sunday afternoons. Readers will be drawn to this island off the Georgia Coast as if they have always known of its existence. I love a good story where place becomes one of the main characters in the telling and whisks me away. This book didn't disappoint me but inspired me to keep reading.

"My name is Leontyne Skye. Fourteen years I have lived upon this sweet Lord's earth righteous and blue."

Leontyne tickles my Appalachian soul, though she has never seen my mountains. Her narration of the events ring of a sassy determined young woman. This is what an author with great artistic passion provides for his readers. He immerses us in familiarity as if somehow, we have walked into our childhood memories. Good Hope feels nothing like a fictional island. Yet, it is. Robert Gwaltney opens the door to the existence of good and evil and how shrouded the lines between the two can become. And whenever this journey begins, we are bound to learn more about who we are than about the subject itself.

Not since I followed Lucy into the wardrobe and emerged in Narnia have I encountered a story so absorbing and layered. As adults we need the challenge of questioning worn out assumptions about the world we live in. *Sing Down the Moon* makes us pause and do just that. Good Hope, with its ever-present full moon hanging in the sky, magic hidden in the most tantalizing places, and Redemption, the sweet cure, that promises to save all wandering souls cuts a new path into magical realism accompanied by lyrical language, the pure music of storytelling. So many have forgotten how to tell a story just for the sake of telling one. This is an art that is threatening to retreat into the past if brave artists don't put pen to paper, brush to canvas, and notes into music. Robert's effort places him in the same league as Appalachian storytellers Lee Smith, Silas House, and Ron Rash, who write to tell the truths of their places and whose work remains within the mind's eye far out into the future.

Sing Down the Moon promises to stay put in my mind for years to come. I will return back to this novel for the pure pleasure of visiting the language and living in this beautiful but challenging story.

Ann Hite
An Appalachian Writer

For Daddy.
To the Forever Moon,
The Island, the River, the Forest, and Sea.
To all the unspoken words buried deep-deep.
And for Timothy, always.

MERCER UNIVERSITY PRESS

Endowed by

TOM WATSON BROWN
and
THE WATSON-BROWN FOUNDATION, INC.

“I am the daughter of Earth and Water,
And the nursling of the Sky;
I pass through the pores of the ocean and shores;
I change, but I cannot die.”

—Percy Bysshe Shelley, “The Cloud”

Good Hope, A Georgia Coastal Barrier Island
The Marsh

Chapter 1

We are all dead here on Good Hope.

The itch of these words, this chitter of memory troubles my tongue. I hurry behind Eulalee, my mama, cradling this rusted coffee can in the crook of my puny, no-hand arm, hankering to fire these words into the air like buckshot. To rip loose the past. A clue.

My name is Leontyne Skye. Fourteen years I have lived upon this sweet Lord's earth righteous and blue. Like a psalm, I speak these words to myself to niggle memory, to trace over the things I remember as true.

Good glory, glory, Eulalee sings, making her way to the Sarah Fig that has come aloose from a salt-jeweled branch of old Damascus Tree and fallen into the Marsh. "Fine a one as I ever did see," she says, admiring the velvety, lilac fruit swole up to the size of a cabbage.

The retreating Sun casts uncanny embers upon the Marsh, upon the lowly fact my Eulalee is naked and shameless as a jaybird. I listen to the cordgrass basket knock against her shin, the clack of her oyster shell necklace keeping time with her chore, keeping time with my frantic heart. My Eulalee has lost her mind. Her decency.

Pluff mud slithers between Eulalee's toes riling the stink of rotten eggs and the remembrance I am sixteen years old. *Not fourteen.* And the plain awful truth I might never be myself again. That I shall never mend from the tragedy I suffered on Tribulation Day two years back. The loss of my memories, of the *me* I was before. And the end of Mirabelle, my severed hand, resting upon a scrap of old wedding lace sealed up tight in this here dented coffee can.

Inside my apron pocket, my teensy marsh rabbit stirs. "Mind yourself, Darkly," I say. "Damascus bears a gift." Damascus bears anything but gifts, but Eulalee will have no part of me disrespecting that witch of a tree. A tree, no doubt, she loves better than me.

"You there. Tie your wings on," Eulalee says, hurrying me along. "And leave that damn mudlark be."

"Be nice, Eulalee. You will up and hurt sweet baby's feelings." I poke my hand into my pocket fiddling with and loving on my Darkly's ears.

"Call me by my rightful name, stupid girl. Do you not know who I am?"

"Yes, ma'am. I surely do." Of course I know who she is, only in this moment she has forgotten herself. We both have forgotten things, Eulalee and me. Tending Damascus has wrung the life from Mama while Tribulation Day has near abouts knocked all the good sense loose from me.

"Can you not hear, stupid girl? I asked you a question."

Eulalee has turned crueller this last year, fraying into a dreadful thing, a Eulalee I can hardly love. "You are Eulalee Skye. You are the Great Redeemer."

"Ain't that something? The Great Redeemer," she says. Her bones lament, sounding every bit like the slow chirp of crickets. She stares at me. Looks down at her feet gobbled to the ankles in muck, the wide brim of her cornhusk hat stealing her face. "And who are you?"

Here, in the clutch of one of her forgetful spells, I might tell Eulalee lies. Tell her she is not my mama. That I am Armageddon, an angel flown down vengeful from the firmament on reaping-hook wings to topple down Damascus Tree and chop Eulalee in two. Know this: Damascus will be the death of Eulalee. Damascus will be the death of me. The bittersweet pill I swallow is that without Redemption, life as we are accustomed to here on Good Hope would cease to be. No means without it by which to earn our keep.

My name is Leontyne Skye. "I'm your daughter. Your Sister Girl," I say. *Sixteen years I have lived upon this sweet Lord's earth, righteous and blue. And one of these here days I am going to leave this stinking Marsh and you.*

A breeze peels the brim of hat away from Eulalee's face. The look of her shocks me. Seems to me her skin was once smooth. Polished pale as pearl. She is withered now, an ancient estuary carved of river and stream. This is not the Eulalee I remember best. This is not a Eulalee I can love. She is the wreckage that comes from bootlegging this commodity, this drug we call Redemption.

Eulalee squints, her head rotating slow and sneaky as a hoot owl's. "Sister Girl, you say?"

"Yes, ma'am. Sister Girl."

"You is that gal that fell the long-long ways. You was dead once."

"Once, I reckon," I say. If ever I was dead, I cannot recollect the sorry occasion. There are pockets full of things I cannot remember since the great fall I took on Tribulation Day, but Avery tells me it is so. That it was he who resurrected me with his reading of a stanza from a poem by Mr. John Keats. It is his twin sister, Rebecca, I believe. That it was she who did it, played me back to the living with a song from her violin, a Chopin nocturne she favors best. One of these here days my Rebecca and me are running off beyond the River to far-far places. *My dearest Rebecca, sleek and tall. You are the one I love best of all.*

Eulalee's eyes give off a slow blink of recognition. "Of course, you is my Sister Girl," she says, her voice confounded with tremors. "Who else might you be?"

"Not another soul but me," I say. If I were a lucky sort, I might be any other girl. I might be Anna Karenina from the book I just read, smart enough to know when enough is enough. I am put off by every kernel of this disgusting business, furious Mama's memory is ruined from years of making Redemption. Furious she remembers me easily as she forgets. That she is not what she was. That I will one day be just like her if I stay here on Good Hope to tend Damascus.

Sure as the Forever Moon shines ever-loving day and ever-loving night, never moving in the ever-loving sky, I am destined to turn plum cruel and pitiful as Eulalee, as all the Skye women come before, a sickness Eulalee calls the Worsening. An ailment sure to wilt my memory more fragile, cracking my body open easy as a terrapin egg. Leaving behind nothing but a puddle of goo.

This Worsening is the levy paid for tending Damascus, for harvesting life and death. For distilling Sarah Figs. Making Redemption. Long as there has been the Forever Moon, there has been Damascus beguiling haints across the River with her wind chime song, wooing these ghosts to the sweet-warm pulpy-womb of her Sarah Figs. And long as Sarah Figs have had their way with haints, Skye women have made and sold Redemption, have crawled off to the Doldrums to tumble apart and die when the drug-making is done running poison through their blood.

Eulalee pulls off her hat. A tuft of thundercloud hair lets loose from the roots. Drifts silvery and angry into the Marsh. Once she was towheaded as me, curls spilling gracious and plenty to her waist. I imagine gathering up and mourning my own fallen-out hair, a remembrance to braid about and comfort my Mirabelle. Just how much more of me might I squeeze alongside my cutoff hand inside this coffee can when the Worsening comes to shuck me loose like Mama? My teeth? The last five of my fingers? Every last one of my ten toes?

The fallen Sarah Fig mewls, rocking back and forth upon the muck like a sickly kitten. The haint inside is near abouts give out and gone, dissolved within the fruit's womb. A curious affair it is the dead can die again. That this gobbled up haint will be squeezed into a tincture of Redemption, and the fools we call Sinners shall follow. Always they follow, begging to ease the pain of living by drinking themselves a drop.

Darkly sniffles inside my pocket. Like me, he holds a tender heart for suffering things, for haints dim enough to be bamboozled by Damascus across the River to wheedle their way into a sweet-sweet Sarah Fig. "There now, Darkly," I whisper. "The haint will be gone soon." I set down Mirabelle next to the toe of my rubber boot. I pull Darkly from my pocket, lift him up to behold the scandal of the Sarah Fig finishing off the haint: vibrating, bucking. Moaning intimate in the pluff.

Eulalee spits. "What dang fool tied a ribbon about that marsh rat's neck?"

"You stop calling Darkly a rat, Eulalee." The fool is Avery Longwood, the one that adorned my baby's neck with this ribbon. Avery possesses a gift for turning lovely things lovelier. There is something to be said for that, do you not think?

"Darkly.... Queer name for a white rat," Eulalee says. "Sinful waste of a ribbon, if you ask me."

"I do not give a snail's trail what you think, Eulalee." True it is my Darkly is near abouts the size of a rat, but he is a rabbit just the same, a color so blinding white he gleams. I cuddle Darkly beneath my chin, smelling the scent of Rebecca and Avery Longwood clinging to the ribbon's ends. *Black licorice drops and peel of Christmastime orange.*

"Sassy mouth you got for a gal that was dead once. For a one-hand gal that fell the long-long ways." Eulalee drops her cornhusk hat and starts singing her haint-dying-song to the fallen Sarah Fig, to the haint trapped inside.

On across the River,
To where you ought go,
Way off beyond Zion,
Fields plentiful with gold.

Eulalee is more improved now than just a spell back, her words coming easier. I sing along, pretending a funeral song might rouse the living. As if it might bring my old Eulalee back.

The Sarah Fig sputters. Then, a final piteous gasp. And woe, the haint is gone, dissolved by the Sarah Fig. This is the way of things, the commotion of a fig gobbling the last bit of a haint.

Eulalee sets down the basket. Her skin labors, pulling taut across the lattice of crackling bones. I want to run back to the house for her shawl, to cover up the sorry sight. She sings, lifting the Sarah Fig to her chest, her bosom flattening to hoecakes.

With all I can muster, I try my darnedest to focus upon pleasant things: Darkly's good-smelling ribbon, the book borrowed from Avery Longwood hidden beneath my mattress waiting to be read.

Eulalee sways side to side as if sparking a beau, whispering sweet-sweet nothings. Seeing Eulalee turn tender, a teensy wound tears aloose inside me, and I wish I could be that Sarah Fig in the care of Eulalee's arms. Pacified with secrets and love songs.

Eulalee spits a rotten tooth into the pluff and grins. "Put that jewel in your chicory can, you one-hand gal." Before my very eyes, Eulalee comes apart. I imagine her carcass picked clean, a feeble pile of bones and scatter of teeth. I am not ready to be left here on my own, to take up where she left off. To become what I aim never to be. *The Great Redeemer.*

The smell of death, of simmering collard greens grows strong, and I know in the coming darkness the Sarah Fig turns pale violet and soon will go off to ruin if Eulalee is not quick. "That Sarah Fig will not be fit for a batch Redemption," I say, "If you do not get on with it." Sarah Figs do not last long once they have eaten up their haint and fallen away into the Marsh.

"Keep away from my affairs, you one-hand gal," she says. "I know what I know." Eulalee presses her ear to the fig. Gives it a listen, a thump, and a sniff. "I have me plenty of time left to do what I need to do with this Sarah Fig. This one ain't anywhere near close to turning off to rot."

In the distance, from Morningstar way, a dreadful note howls from the River, the sound scraping grim from my ankles all the way to my shoulders. McKinley Longwood, Rebecca and Avery's father, plays the note on his small steamboat's calliope, a rattletrap vessel he calls the Undine, a signal he is departing across the River for Abraham's Bluff. McKinley Longwood is owner and master of Good Hope, and on his way to fetch Miss Hushabye Byrd, the Singing Prophetess. She is the one who sells our Redemption from the back flap of her revival tent in the world beyond this place.

Undine's screech seems to shake aloose good sense in Eulalee. She bends down, *crackling* and *popping*, placing the Sarah Fig into the basket gentle like she is tending a newborn. "That damn Hushabye Byrd comes to reap our harvest."

"How much Redemption do you have bottled and ready to go?" I say, afraid there will not be enough, terrified of Miss Hushabye Byrd's wrath. Eulalee and I must earn our keep and do our part to keep the Longwoods and Morningstar afloat. Skye women always have earned their way here upon Good Hope. I also worry for my Rebecca and Avery, the twins. Hushabye Byrd is forever trying to steal away my friends from me to lands far away.

"I ain't gonna tell the likes of you. You got a tricky look about you. Like you might run off and peddle the whole kit and caboodle of Redemption for yourself."

A suck of wind lifts Damascus's feathery branches frosted crystalline with salt. With life stolen from the Marsh. How those branches quiver and chime.

From Eulalee's basket comes a rustle of tatters, shreds of something Eulalee has put down to cushion the fig. These tatters and tufts of her thundercloud hair drift quiet upon the place. I shut my eyes, imagining a fierce cold, air so chill it summons true wintertime flurries. *Snow.* A wonder I long to one day see.

The Undine crows another foghorn note, and I open my eyes to the darkening sky in time to catch a passing tatter. I almost release it to the Marsh, but I notice it is a shred of paper. I land my eyes upon a sentence, reading it aloud to any soul bothering to listen.

"Every trail has its end, and every calamity brings its lesson." Right off, I know the awful thing my Eulalee has done.

"How could you?" I scream. She has plundered my mattress. Ripped apart Avery's book, *The Last of the Mohicans*, and I can think of nothing perfect and vile enough to holler at Eulalee. I search the ground for something hard to throw, but next comes a whisp of memory. Something I heard someone say once before. *You are no better than that whore down by the Marsh.* The ground rumbles. The tide comes. Damascus drinks, her banyan roots roaming mile upon mile into the Good Hope Marsh clear out to the Doldrums. Hump-backed and thirsty.

Eulalee picks up the basket. "I will do as I please, and you will do what I tell you," she says. "I am the Great Redeemer."

The Undine howls again. I collect Mirabelle. Head off toward Good Hope Forest to see about the twins, to try my best to keep them safe from that Singing Prophetess who will be here soon for Redemption.

"Where you going, one-hand gal? I need your help."

"Call me by my name," I say.

"I do not rightly remember. What is it?"

"I am Armageddon," I holler, running toward the Forest.

"Say again," she laughs. "No need to worry. One hand is better than none."

I am Leontyne Skye, and I am sixteen years old. "I was dead once," I scream.

I fell the long-long ways....

The Forest

Chapter 2

Damascus sings, the lull of her wind chime song aiming to wrangle me back to my burden, to surrender myself a handmaid as all Skye women are ordained to do.

Far as I know, Damascus cares not one tiny bit if we pestle a drug from the haints squeezed from her fruit. All she requires is that we clear the rotting haint-filled wombs of Sarah Figs from the base of the tree. From seeping deep-deep into her roots to wound her. I suspect we also keep Damascus from being lonely. I hardly can hold a grudge against that, not wanting to be alone.

This is a thing I will tell you my Eulalee said to me not too far back before her mind took a turn for the worse. "What would become of this sorry world, Sister Girl, filling up to the brim with haints, if it was not for Damascus?" Still, I hate that tree, regardless of the fact she weeds out the dead, her Sarah Figs devouring haints like a rat snake keeping watch over a barn.

And what of this drug Redemption? Best I can tell, it is a gainful pursuit grown from necessity, from Damascus's purpose of putting an end to haints, to those come back around from the grave. Why toss a perfectly good Sarah Fig swole up with haint adrift down the River when you can cook it up into a batch of Redemption? It is a simple matter of commerce, really. Of survival.

I keep thinking on what Eulalee said, imagining the world and all of Good Hope swallowed up with haints if Damascus up and quit her wind chime song. And I wonder how that first Skye woman figured out how to make the first batch of Redemption. And how it is that folks figured out heaps of other things from the beginning of time. Like which mushrooms are safe to eat, and which ones are not. Or if the world is flat or round.

I ponder these things, but mostly I plot how I might escape Damascus, Eulalee, and this business of Redemption, biding the time until I am almost to my destination, the Chapel of Abundance—a place I sometimes hide my Mirabelle from Eulalee and Rebecca. They take dim views of Mirabelle, neither one of them bearing a scrap of patience for me toting around my hand inside this can.

The final steps of the way, I sing a stanza Avery taught me, a bit of poem written by that poet fella named Keats.

I met a lady in the meads,
Full beautiful—a faery's child,
Her hair was long, her foot was light,
And her eyes were wild.

At last, the roofless ruins of the Chapel of Abundance rise a glory before me, a gleam of pale, sharp-shelled tabby walls. I sing the last of the stanza, my voice floating misty through the bricked arches of empty window frames. *And her eyes were wild....*

Mirabelle will be safe here tucked in a hole within the crumbling wall. The only Longwoods about this place are dead ones dug deep-deep into graves across the way yonder in the chapel's cemetery. Rebecca, Avery, and their father never visit, and Eulalee never wanders far from the Marsh. I envy the Longwoods this lonesome resting place. There are no such final gatherings for Eulalee and me, or any Skye woman come before. Just rusty, dented coffee cans, and the fall away of tooth and bone into the Doldrums, the farthest side of the Marsh sucked dry and left to ruin by Damascus. In equal measure, Damascus saves. And Damascus kills.

I raise up Darkly to give him a look. "This here is our place," I say. It is a lie. Nothing here belonged ever to a Skye, though we were squatting here long before the Longwoods came. All of Good Hope, every gator and palmetto frond—swindled by a long-gone Longwood in a drunken game of cards. Eulalee says never to trust a Longwood on account of them living off the backs of others, but I trust my Rebecca and my Avery, my Longwood twins. They are my friends. *They would never harm me.*

I pretend the Chapel of Abundance is a palace with a fine, shined-up floor. Roof pitched high-high above the live oak trees, and a cut-glass chandelier dangling down the middle burning bright with flame. Sometimes I coddle myself with stories. Weaving things pretty the way I want them to be. Rather than the sorry way they truly are.

Damascus sings louder, and I imagine I am a two-handed girl. I lift Darkly to kiss, my finger tangling in his blue ribbon. "I am Anna Karenina, and you are my Count Vronsky."

I put down my coffee can, and quick as a split, Count Vronsky and I take off spinning, careful not to venture to the dangerous center of the room. Truth be told, I rather be dancing with my dark-haired Rebecca. I call Rebecca my Blue Heron on account of she is elegant and proud. *Rebecca-Rebecca, sleek and tall. How I love you best of all.*

Outside comes a commotion. A rustle of palmetto and rile of leaves. A snort. And a deer leaps wild through the window knocking Count Vronsky and me to the well-shined floor. A shuffle and another snort. A leap. And through the other window the white-tailed deer flees.

And the floor is dirt. And Rebecca is my Darkly. And I lay here, my breath near knocked out, gawking up into the Forever Moon, sorrowful my cut-glass chandelier is gone. *Five fingers are better than none.*

I run to the other side of the ruins to see about that deer. Right off, I recognize the deer to be the one named Babylon. In the garden of dead Longwoods, atop a tabby stoned grave, this deer stands pretty as you please with the nerve to be staring them harlot eyes right back at me. She cannot be trusted, not that Babylon. Always taking up with this buck or that one. *Always watching me.*

"You stupid hussy," I holler to the deer.

Babylon taunts back, tapping her hoof on a grave I know well. The grave of Constance Rose Longwood, the mama of Rebecca and Avery. *My Longwood twins.* That white-tailed hussy sniffs the next grave over, one much teensier and slim. All that is bothered to be carved into the stone is:

Baby Girl Longwood
Gone Quick As She Come

Avery's poet, Mr. John Keats, wrangles his words back into my thoughts. *And her eyes were wild.* I sing along melancholy with Damascus, staring at that impertinent deer, then at that teensy grave. *Tribulation Day. Two years back.* For the life of me, I cannot recollect if Constance Rose Longwood's eyes went wild when she done the thing she done. If she spoke a single word, screamed a single scream when she killed herself and that poor baby girl. When she tried to end me, too. Dragging me down treacherous with them from the Up-Up There.

There are many things I cannot remember about Tribulation Day, about Constance Rose Longwood trying to murder me. About my life before. Rebecca says it is for the best. I do my darndest to pay my Blue Heron mind. She is wise on matters such as this.

Beyond the wall, someone sings along with Damascus, the duet coming upon the place sonorous. Eerie. *And her eyes were wild. . . .*

Darkly and I go still. Babylon, the hussy, hitches her tail. She has the good sense to get gone. Through the gape, where a door once was, a man enters the chapel, his foot tipping Mirabelle over. He appears stupefied in the full wash of Moon's glow. Dazzled by the glare of limestone and layers of seashell sneaking out from the walls.

I step backward. Hide my no-hand arm behind my back. No doubt, this man has come for Redemption, a Sinner like all the rest, looking for a sip of something to ease his worry, the misery and ecstasy distilled from the dead. *To forget.* Long as there has been living, there has been woe, and only fools travel Good Hope seeking Redemption.

This island is full-up with danger. With lures, and tricks, and snares to keep us safe from Sinners swimming across the River too impatient for the Singing Prophetess to bring around to them what she is peddling. Already, this Sinner is dead close to a snare. And stupid to the fact.

Into the sky he stares, the Forever Moon glossy in his eyes. "What strange place is this?" he asks, a world of wonder turning his voice gentle.

From the get-go, I know he is different from the others. Not bald in patches. Not stinking treacle-sweet from the innards of a Sarah Fig. His eyes do not glow golden or look anything like a goat's, an unsettling side effect of taking too much Redemption. He also appears in possession of every last one of his teeth. For the life of me, I cannot imagine why Sinners do it. Why they would rather fall apart for just a few drops of bliss. Is it not better to make your way through the pain? Through misery?

Unlike the others, he does not chase after me pleading to see the Great Redeemer. *Lordy be! Where is she? I will soon be dead without her. I am begging you, please!* I step back, laying space between us, but there is only so far I can go.

I say nothing. He asks once more. This time he sets those moon-dazzled eyes upon me casting a spell, and I have no choice but to speak. "This here is the Chapel of Abundance on the island called Good Hope," I say.

"Abundance," he says, fondling the resurrection fern turned brown and clinging lifeless to the walls. "You all alone here?"

It is a dangerous question asked of me by many a Sinner before, except he is not nearly ravenous looking as they in the eyes. No lips cracked and bleeding. No filthy fingernails scraping desirous at sores for a drop of Eulalee's elixir. Or hankering to love up on a towhead girl. I am proud to say nary a sorry Sinner ever has caught a hold of me yet.

"No, sir. I am not alone. I have Darkly here. Then there are the Longwoods," I say. "Those that is living. Those that is dead." I point over to the graveyard deciding not to tell him Eulalee is my mama or about Mirabelle knocked over yonder in a can. "Then there is the queer matter of our Willadeene. She is a haint."

"A haint you say?"

"Yes, sir. Willadeene is a fearsome sight, and she sure is mean." I tell lies to scare this Sinner.

"Does she not look like every other haint?"

"You would probably keel over dead if you got one look at her." Know this: Willadeene is beautiful to every sort of eye. From what Eulalee has told me, there is not another one like her. She is near abouts a human creature. A womanly form with arms, legs, and bosom. Evergreen skin and flowers for hair. And she is the only specter ever to escape a Sarah Fig before it could do her in.

"Why do you reckon she is so mean?"

"I imagine she is not one bit happy she is dead and gone," Much I might tell this man about our Willadeene, that she come around two years back with not a lick of memory of who she was before. That it was Eulalee who raised up Willadeene from a ghostly babe, teaching her to speak and walk. I will keep it to myself Eulalee broods bitter our Willadeene up and run off to Morningstar to take up with the Longwoods when she first saw the chance.

"What about your mama? Where is she?"

"Dead." She is near abouts dead, so I regard it mostly true.

"Your Daddy?"

"Never had me one." Much as I yearn to run clear of Good Hope with my Rebecca, I ache to know the truth of my daddy.

"Well now, there had to be a Mr. Somebody kicking around one time or another. Everybody has a daddy." He takes two steps forward, the sole of his right boot come apart and flapping.

"Stay right there," I holler. "Not one step more." Sure as sure, beyond a few more flaps of that worn out boot, death awaits my Sinner. Why shoo things along? There is something about this one I like.

"I do not aim to harm you," he says.

I possess a keen sense he speaks the truth. "Just stay put, and I will tell you a secret. A secret about what I know of my daddy."

"Sounds like a thing worth knowing. I promise not to tell another living soul."

He speaks the truth. Poor thing will never have the chance. "Yes, sir. I believe it is," I say.

"Go on then. But first tell me your name."

I stand here staring, liking the way he looks at me, those eyes filled to the rims with Moon. Right now, right here, I desire to be anybody other than I am. *What name shall I give him?*

"Okay, then. I will tell you mine first. I am Ewell Day Higgs from across the River," he says. "Out Abraham Bluff's way."

Ewell Day Higgs. Never have I known the name of a Sinner. Never cared to ask. Never cared to know.

"Alright then," Ewell Day Higgs says. "If given a guess, I reckon I just might know your name."

"Well, get on with it then."

"Starshine," he says, smiling, his sweet-talking mouth bragging with teeth. "If ever there was a Starshine, it was you."

Starshine. What a beautiful name. "How ever did you guess?" I ask, smiling right back at Ewell Day Higgs, showing him he is not the only one blessed with a complete set of teeth. Showing him I have not begun to fall apart like Eulalee. Somewhere near abouts, there is a *clickety clack.* "Hear that?" I ask.

"The wind chime waltz? Is that the sound you hear?" he asks. *Flip flap.* Ewell Day Higgs takes another step forward.

"Stop. I done told you to stay put."

"You promised me a secret, Miss Starshine."

"Yes, sir. I reckon I did."

"Well now," he says. "I am listening."

Why I confess this next thing to him, I will never know. "I suspect my mama once lay tender with a haint," I say. "There is no trace of me ever having a daddy. Not hide. Nor a hair." I want to tell him aside from missing my hand, there is something else gone missing from me. What it is, I cannot say. Cannot remember. Centuries I wait for my Ewell Day Higgs to speak.

"Your daddy was a haint, you say?" That world of wonder still drifts like clouds in his voice, and I can breathe again, grateful he has not given me a piece of his mind for being half-haint.

"I am afraid it might be so."

"And your mama? What did she ever say?"

"She never has confessed. On the business of my daddy, she speaks in riddles," I say. "I do not much care for riddles, sir."

"Go on now. Just what did she say?"

I spin around once like Eulalee does before telling me the riddle.

You are a child of the Forever Moon.

You are of the Island.

You are of the River.

One more time around I turn slow, hiding my no-hand nub in my pocket with Darkly.

You are of the Forest and the Sea...

Ewell Day Higgs looks up into the sky and back at me queer. "Not just anybody can boast such a thing, to be a child of the Island and Forest. The River and Sea. A girl named Starshine, a girl every bit pale and bright as you would have to be the daughter of that Forever Moon."

"That is a mighty kind thing to say." Never has a body, living or dead, unwrapped such sweet lollipop words for me. And for the life of me, all I want to do is lick.

"Folks says this place is damned, that Good Hope is only for the dead and fools. But just look at your Moon, Starshine. Just look at her," he says. "Tell me, how is it in this world that you can have this Moon here and a different one across the River? My moon over Abraham Bluff's way goes and comes. Why is it you reckon Good Hope's Moon misbehaves, never changes?"

"There are many peculiar goings-on here I cannot explain. Forever Moon does what she always did. Least as long as I have been living." I refuse to tell him I can only remember far back as two years, that a gal named Starshine only ever has seen this one stubborn Moon.

Clickety clack-clack. The sound, same as before, rattles upon the place. This time I detect it venturing somewhere from over Mirabelle's way.

"Ewell Day Higgs, do you mind telling me why you come all the way across the River to Good Hope." I suspect I know the why, but I want to hear him say it. *Lordy be! Where is she? Where is the Great Redeemer and her bottles glistening Redemption?*

He smiles, bragging a king's ransom of teeth. "Why, I come to see the Forever Moon."

No sorry Sinner ever has come to see the Forever Moon before. I find it quite a quandary. Before I can speak a word, he speaks again. "And pay my respects to the Great Redeemer."

I will soon be dead without her. I am begging you, please! Ewell Day Higgs is like all the rest, only he is not. "Why not just get on away from here, sir?" *Before it is too late.* Only it is too late.

"Do you mind if I ask you a question, Starshine? Before I get to moving on."

"I do not mind one bit, I reckon. Long as I know the answer."

He speaks soft and sad, as if paying a final respect. "Where did your hand get off to?"

He has noticed my no-hand arm. I eyeball Mirabelle tipped unladylike, spitting distance from us. Ewell Day Higgs should hear a pretty story before what comes next. I decide not to tell him Mirabelle got infected and sawed off by my sweet Rebecca. I will not tell him Mirabelle was salted up fancy as an Easter ham and plunked into that can. *Tribulation Day.... Two years back....*

Flip-flap. Ewell Day Higgs comes my way, stepping safe away from the path of calamity yawning wide and hidden before him. I stay put, unable to move a toe, a prisoner of them moonbeam eyes.

"My hand run off to marry the Prince of Arabia," I say. "Now she puts on airs from inside that Prince's pocket while the two of them ride a camel upon the hot-hot desert sands."

He shuts his eyes and smiles, making me believe he believes it is true. "The hot-hot desert sands. A mighty fine place to be."

Ewell Day Higgs stands close enough I can smell him. *Pine tar and swirly river water smells.* The wind wrestles my skirt. Taunts my hair. Stirs a fight inside me to either tell him to stay or tell him to go. Gentle, he takes my no-hand arm and gives the nub a kiss, shooting off a glory of good-feeling tingles across my skin.

The drizzle of rain swells shimmery to the size of rock candy drops, delighting the crumple of brown resurrection leaves lifeless upon the walls. From way off in the distance, I hear Rebecca's violin sing. The sonata she plays drifts from Morningstar's Cupola by the wind to me here in the Forest. *Rebecca, Rebecca, sleek and tall. What is it you want most of all?*

Yard upon yard of resurrection fern scratches the tabby, swelling and turning green. The walls bloom lush. Fronds unfurl. Reach and swoon. Ewell Day Higgs keeps ahold of my arm, his eyes appearing stupefied by the Moon. I make no attempt to pull away, dizzy from and wanting another kiss.

Behind Ewell Day Higgs comes a ruckus. C*lackety, clack, clack.* The coffee can shimmies. Rights itself from its dented side. Darkly squeals. *Have mercy.* My Mirabelle has come alive. Ewell Day Higgs pays no mind to the miracle come about, his eyes taking turns looking at the Moon, the fern-draped walls. And me.

Ewell Day Higgs seems startled by the effect. He turns me loose. Steps back. *Flap.*

"Stay put," I scream.

"Starshine." He looks all about. Back at me. His eyes glittery with quick swelling tears.

"Be quick," I say.

The ground crackles. *Flap.* Another step.

"It is beautiful here," he says, taking slow to his knee. The ground gives way. Loose boards. Dirt. Leaves. And my Ewell Day Higgs is gone.

Gone....

I will not go over to him. Will not look down into the stake-lined pit into which he has tumbled. I am too frightened of all the carnage I might find, my Ewell Day Higgs butchered, his innards spilling out. "I told you not to take another dang-fool step. Now just look what you did."

A sound of confusion lifts vaporous from below. "Starshine," he says, the world of wonder ebbing from his voice. "What have you gone and done to me?"

"Forgive me. But I tried my best to get you gone from here." What is there for me to do for him but stay until the end? Until Moon's gleam blinks gone from his eyes. "You are not like the others," I say, mopping tears with my sleeve. I wait to hear him say my name again, to unwrap another sweet something for this towhead gal to savor. Nothing comes but a gurgle.

"You are not alone, Ewell Day Higgs," I say, weeping for myself. For Ewell Day Higgs. For Darkly, and the deer. *We are all alone here. All of us. Each and everyone.* Resurrection fern treads silvery across the ground beneath the ever-lasting Moon, the Moon my Ewell Day Higgs come across the River to see. "Look up," I say. "Look up." Here—at the dead end of things, I speak a dangerous truth the way a Miss Starshine should.

It is beautiful here....

Morningstar
The In-Between

Chapter 3

Lantern light dances a slow hoochie-coo, reflecting in the Cupola's windows beneath its copper Byzantine onion dome. I gawk at the Longwood house called Morningstar, this eight-sided, unfinished place. Avery brags it was inspired by an Oriental palace his dead Great Granddaddy Longwood saw once in a picture book. With its Moorish windows and verandas on every side.

I stay this way, listening to Rebecca play Salome, her violin, jealous of how darkness and firelight caress and sketch my Rebecca in charcoal silhouette. I feel a smidge guilty thinking of my poor Ewell Day Higgs while I watch my Rebecca, remembering the tingle of his kiss, leaving me to wonder why I feel such a way as this.

More.... More.... More.... A haint yowls in the distance. Haints always are bellyaching for more earthly pleasure. *More* is their only word unless you are our gifted Willadeene. She knows many words. Weaves them smart into sentences.

I smell the haints, seawater mingling salty with the sweet-ripe aroma of persimmon. Eulalee says this is the odor of intimacy. Of *More.* The smell turns me sheepish. Lightheaded.

Three haints come into view, lured by Damascus's wind chime song. Each one is no bigger than a freshwater bream, swimming the sky feverish, glowing purple with desire. The haints' skin, prickly as puffer fish, swells expectant. Throbs shameless. *More.... More.... More....* Only two haints ever come along at once. Tonight, three smell the place up with yearning.

"My name is Starshine," I say, watching them pass above me on their way to the Marsh. "And just who you might be?" I ask out of politeness. These fool haints never possess the sense to remember who they were before. Not even Willadeene knows who she was back when. "Tell me. Where you been? What you seen?"

Just one of them haints pays me one bit of business, tipping down, puffing up, and letting loose a skirl. *More....* This haint is presumptuous, and I have the mind to slap him if he were not out of reach.

"Get on away from here. You deserve what you get," I say. "By the way, not a single one of you looks near good enough for Willadeene." Always, I am on the lookout for a sweetheart for our Willadeene. For a haint smart acting enough who might figure out a way to stay. To escape the Sarah Fig. To grow up from a fishtailed runt to something resembling a person. To lay down roots like our Willadeene done.

Rebecca's violin goes quiet, but she is not idle for long, picking up to play a different song. Right off, I know the piece. *Lord, Rebecca, no. Do not do it. Do not play that song.*

From inside Morningstar comes a scream. "Agamemnon..." It is Rebecca's brother, Avery.

I take off running for the house. I am up the stairs quick, through the doors, the scent of persimmon and seawater rushing in behind, wind tangling in the great crystal chandelier, the distant echo of haints beckoning into the gallery. *More.... More.... More....*

"Rebecca means to murder me dead as Agamemnon," Avery screams. Avery is forever shrieking the name of the murdered King of Mycenae, an exclamation he brandishes when he throws a fit. "Make her stop. Make her stop playing."

I holler Rebecca's name into the Up-Up There. She stops. Her bow screeches—the sound of a hog dragged off to slaughter. Avery turns loose another dying howl, leaving us reeling in a chorus of butchery.

An anxious moment passes. I collect myself. Gather my bearings. From the windows of the Cupola, three stories up, Forever Moon drapes a bluish mourning veil across the vast, desolate place, this unfinished hull of a house. Unplastered bricks. Scaffolds and beams. The only other light weeps from a smatter of tapers set about the floor and from Rebecca's kerosene lantern from above.

Willadeene scampers into an empty gallery niche, pressing herself against the wall, covering her ears. She is fine and lovely as any statue might ever hope be. And Avery is a glory in his dead mama's ball gown shimmering wild-eyed and beautiful atop the abandoned Stieff piano crate. Sometimes Avery and I squeeze inside that old empty wooden box, pretending it is the great Pyramid towering majestic over the foreign land called Giza, the two of us playing Egyptian queens buried alive with our two dead kings.

Avery weeps. "Leontyne. Rebecca is a fiend. An assassin."

And Avery is a millstone, every bit fragile as his dead mama, Constance Rose Longwood. Rebecca says the two of them were forever teetering the edge of a powerful emotion. But I shall always remain in his debt. He is the one that taught me to read. All I know of this here world, I know from the books borrowed from the Longwood's Celestial Hall of Books in the Up-Up There. From sneaking about and peeping in and listening at Morningstar's windows. From dying confessions of Sinners hung up in traps.

"Do not speak ill of your sister," I say. "She is anything but a fiend." Rebecca is everything good. Like Avery, I owe her heaps of thanks—working with me like she done to quilt back scraps of memory torn away on Tribulation Day when I fell. I would have no sense of myself from before if it had not been for her. If she had not told me what I was. Who I am.

"I should have known you would take up her side. How could you?" Avery says. "You heard the song she was playing. Or have your ears fallen off now along with your hand?"

Avery's hair has grown longer than his father's liking, cascading lustrous in dark waves to his shoulders. He tends the hair falling across his face. Sweeps it across a chisel of cheekbone and behind his ear. He is the spitting image of his sister.

"Avery Longwood," Willadeene says, nervous. She plucks a violet growing purple from the top of her head. "Calm yourself down. What a dreadful thing to say." Though she has made no such confession, I possess the impression Willadeene is frightened of Rebecca.

"Leave me be. You are all treacherous. The whole conniving lot of you will not be happy until I am dead," Avery says.

Rebecca should know better than to play that Chopin nocturne forbidden by her brother, the one reminding him of their young tutor that went away. I am not allowed to say the tutor's name, but I suspect Avery drove Rebecca to it, grounding her down until she could not bear him a lick longer. Avery is young for his sixteen years, at times behaving like an infant. While Rebecca is wise and serene as King Solomon.

"No one means to murder you," I say.

If given the chance, I imagine his daddy, Mr. McKinley Longwood, might give murder a go. Love is not lost between Avery and him. Both are a grave disappointment to the other. Murder is no stranger to Morningstar, it is a ticking heartbeat true as the *clack* of Mirabelle alive in her can. I should know. *I fell the long-long ways....*

"Where is Darkly?" Avery asks. "He is the only one that loves me. The only one that cares." Darkly does love Avery, and I must admit, though he does not pave the path smooth, I am fond of him, too.

"Right here, Fiddler Crab," I say, putting Darkly on the floor. My nickname for Avery is Fiddler Crab on account of he is a fidgety thing and nervous most of the time.

From the vastness above, Rebecca plucks a note. Then another. I fear she might not be done with Avery, that she might start up that nocturne again. Or worse, mention the dreadful thing Avery done to his mama, Constance Rose Longwood. A thing hinted at. But never told. A thing I long to know.

Willadeene tugs another flower from her head. This time, a white dogwood bloom. Poor Willadeene suffers nerves when Rebecca and Avery rip at the other's throat. Darkly hops quick, gathering the flower from the floor, and off to Fiddler Crab he goes.

"Enough of that, Willadeene," I say. "Take a hold of yourself." Already a new flower blooms where the last one grew. In many ways she is dead, our Willadeene. Many ways she is not.

Stair treads creak. Rebecca starts up humming along with Damascus who can be heard through the walls. My Blue Heron is coming, winding her way down-down the well of stairs from the high-high up, from the place we call the Up-Up There. *Sleek. Majestic. Sure and tall. My Rebecca could never-ever fall.*

Darkly uses his back legs to try and scale the sawhorses propping up the ancient Pyramid of Giza. Avery bends, pulling him up. He takes the dogwood bloom. Sniffs it. Works it behind his ear. Avery gazes up into the skeletal expanse, his dark-river eyes glossy and brimming with the Forever Moon. I still cannot see Rebecca.

Avery speaks. "The Assyrian came down like the wolf on the fold. And his cohorts were gleaming in purple and gold."

Avery quotes Lord Byron, I think. He is forever wielding verse like sorcerers spin spells. A poem for this. A poem for that. His gift for recitation might only be contended by the beautiful and stupefyingly fragile look of him, a porcelain figurine to be shelved and admired careful from afar. Rebecca appears every bit fragile as her brother, only she cannot be broken.

Pluck. Rebecca threatens her brother again.

Avery slaps back. "And the sheen of their spears was like stars on the sea."

At last, I see hint of my Rebecca, the ancient arch of a high-buttoned boot. Mirabelle flutters from inside the can. The stairs squeak. The train of Rebecca's gown, a trail of slithery satin, *hisses.*

When Avery speaks the last of Lord Byron, he says it slow. "When the blue wave rolls nightly on the deep Galilee."

Avery's spell is meant to bully Rebecca, to threaten her into retreat. I feel the effects, the sense I should turn around. Hightail it to the Marsh.

Fiddler Crab is stock still, bewitching as ever I have seen. I am grateful there are no looking glasses about, anything within which he might spy a dazzle of himself. Avery is susceptible to beauty, even his own, swooning when the light falls a certain way. Overcome by the unending vista of the Sea.

Pluck. Willadeene and I both wince.

"Do you not believe me now, Leontyne?" Avery yells. "She means to assassinate me."

Poor Fiddler Crab. If my heart did not beat sure that my Blue Heron is good and kindly, I might think her bad. "Fiddler Crab, this is pure foolishness," I say.

"You do not know her like I do," he says. "She is…."

Hiss…. Rebecca is in full view at the top of the last curve of stairs, the train of her gown puddling behind. She has discarded the pins from her hair, a freedom Avery decrees forboden. Rebecca's hair floods her tiny waist with midnight ocean waves, her defiance near about drowning the room.

"Look. Look what she is up to now," Avery screams.

We all see clear what his sister has gone and done, who she conjures into the room. When her lovely hair tumbles down-down, Rebecca bears an uncanny resemblance to their late, murderous mama. Or so Fiddler Crab has told me. Fiddler Crab misses his mama some kind of awful. Mourns her deep as I grieve my Eulalee coming apart. I imagine he thinks also of his poor, dead sister, Baby Girl Longwood. *Gone quick as she come.* That he regrets the thing he told his mama that sent her jumping through the air to her death. Pulling me down with her when I tried to stop her. I wonder what might have been the awful thing he said. Fiddler Crab has sworn his sister to secrecy, and Rebecca promises never to tell. The tide is high in this room with gone-away mamas. A dead baby, and secrets. And Rebecca's jealously of the tether her brother and mama shared.

"What has she up and done?" I ask Avery, staring at Rebecca, playing dumb to the awful mess.

Rebecca speaks at last. Her voice is deeper than Avery's—the somber sound of someone calling up from down deep in a well. "Perhaps you should ask my brother what it is he has done."

This is an ear of corn I refuse to shuck, so I keep quiet. We all stay put, Avery holding tight to Darkly. Rebecca cradling tender the violin she calls Salome. Me clutching my coffee can.

The rising wind wriggles cool through the crannies and cracks to meddle, stirring the flames burning from the tapers on the floor, mixing the air with good Longwood smells. With the smell of *More.... More.... More....* With the unmistakable scent of Willadeene, the earthen delight of rain fallen fresh upon the soil, a perfume Avery calls *petrichor.*

A cat-scratch fever comes over me, and I am near abouts toppled with desire from the smell. I ache to be alone with Rebecca regardless of anything she might have done, any forboden song she has played. I long for Ewell Day Higgs and his sweet-sweet tender kiss. I hanker to traipse down into the Pyramid of Giza with Avery to lay there queenly, cuddling warm and near.

Willadeene wobbles, appearing half-drunk like me, intoxicated from the smell. Petals dither from the hem of her velvet dressing gown discarding a trail of violet in her wake, the gold-tasseled curtain chord fixed about her waist dragging the floor. The curtain chord is nothing more than a fancy leash. Avery treats poor Willadeene like a prize cow, though he says the leash is meant only to keep her near and safe. But I think it is to keep Willadeene to himself and away from Rebecca. Avery wants everyone for himself.

"Come here, Willadeene," Avery says.

Willadeene ignores Avery and comes straight for me. "I will tell you what he has done," she says, taking hold of my arm. She leans into me to whisper, her pale green hand brushing my cheek, her rose petaled lips tantalizing my ear.

"Avery broke our rule," Rebecca says, before Willadeene can speak. "He said *his* name. Claimed our tutor as his own. And now see what has happened." Rebecca's voice vibrates in the catgut strings of her violin.

There is only one name that cannot be spoken here at Morningstar, and it seems our Avery has said it. It is not that the name cannot be spoken. Rebecca reserves the right to speak it anytime. And Avery holds the same condition for his sister.

"Do not dare say it, Willadeene," Avery yells. "The name is meant for only me. He loved me best. He was mine."

Avery has broken the rule, and Rebecca has punished him by playing the forboden Chopin nocturne, the one taught to her by the man whose name we are not allowed to speak. When Salome sings this song, she sings it good, sawing Avery with beauty, and memory, and jealousy. Clean down-down to the pulp of his Longwood bones.

Willadeene fiddles with the belt of her leash, and when she whispers, it is not so very much a whisper but verdict. "Rushworth L. Wintergarden," she says, stretching the letters like pull-taffy with her tongue. *Rushhh … worth…. Win … terrr … garrr … den.*

"Murder," Avery shrieks.

The whisper, the memory of Mr. Rushworth L. Wintergarden roils into a plume of fog. Turns dark. Hovers between Willadeene and me. The meddling breeze curls about my ankles. Swirls up my legs, about my hips. Flutters my lashes. Fondles the petals of Willadeene's garden crown.

With her mossy finger, Willadeene gives the memory a flick. Leaves of creeping vine flutter crimson, beckoning the memory to hasten. Everywhere is vine. Poking through the mortar. Peeping keyholes. Papering Morningstar's rough-hewn walls.

The memory of Rushworth L. Wintergarden rises. Travels the curve of the stairs. Snags in the constellation of sparkles adorning the train of Rebecca's ancient ball gown. The memory rises further still, whispering in Salome's horsehair bow making its way to the Cupola.

"He was mine," Avery weeps, raising his hand, fluttering his fingers.

From a tangle of vines way above Rebecca comes a rustle. A flurry of *trills*. A *chirr*. Then a cloudburst of saltmarsh sparrow from ncsts knitted against the walls.

The commotion of wings scatter *Rushworth L. Wintergarden*, shred him through sharp-tailfeathers to drift melancholy over the place. Rushworth L. Wintergarden clings to Rebecca's lashes. Catches and melts on Avery's tongue.

"No, he was mine," my Blue Heron says. "Mine...."

I gaze woozy into the Up-Up There, from the place I fell two years back. In a *whoosh* of Siberian current, blows more of a memory that niggled from before. *What does any of it matter, Rebecca? We are all dead here on Good Hope.*

Candles weep their last bit of flame, the Kerosene lamp dimming from above, churning the last of its hoochie-coo dance. Abandoning us to the light of the Forever Moon. Painting us silvery in wide strokes of beautiful gloom.

Morningstar
The In-Between

Chapter 4

Willadeene and I watch my Blue Heron whisper to Fiddler Crab. How I envy them their secrets, the language spoken sometimes between them without the use of a single word, reading the dark river's current running cool and fast in the other's eyes.

Rebecca has managed to soothe Avery. He still might be weeping atop the Pyramid of Giza had she not come to her senses and seen clear to coax her brother down. I reckon it was the Undine's yowling that done it, the boat's calliope rousing Rebecca from her vengeful mood, reminding her that her daddy and the Singing Prophetess will be here soon.

"Rushworth L. Wintergarden is never coming back," Willadeene whispers, opening and closing Pocket Watch, her one and only prize possession.

"Shh," I say. "Would you?" For the life of me, I cannot imagine why anyone with sense enough to leave would find their way back around here to Good Hope again.

Plunk. A tiny cluster of shiny red berries dangling fancy as an earbob drops from the dainty lobe of Willadeene's other ear. Tatters and bits fall from her when she feels a hurt. When another has been unkind. I must have just been careless of her feelings. Insensitive to the fact she never could come back because she never can leave. It is the fate of all haints, even one special as Willadeene. The poor things are shipwrecked. Marooned. Unable to make their way back across the water again. Willadeene is terrified she will one day be left here alone.

"I beg your pardon," Willadeene says, looking down at the berries, her cheeks blushing a deeper shade of evergreen. She seems embarrassed pieces of herself have fallen to the floor. Before she can cover them with her foot, a starling swoops from a nest high upon the crumbling brick wall. Grabs her earbob berries. And that is that.

"I cannot imagine Mr. Wintergarden ever dare come back," I whisper.

Willadeene knows little of Rebecca and Avery's Mr. Rushworth L. Wintergarden. He was gone before Willadeene hatched herself loose from Damascus Tree two years back. Willadeene and I know only what Avery and Rebecca share when dark moods prevail. That once he was their tutor, a worldly man then of near abouts eighteen. That he taught Rebecca the violin. Acquainted Avery with the great poets: Lord Bryon, Mr. Shelley, and Keats. That it was their beast of a daddy who sent Mr. Rushworth L. Wintergarden away.

Avery takes the blue velvet ribbon from around Darkly.

"That is my hair ribbon," Rebecca says.

"Then Darkly is a thief." Avery sets my white rabbit down on the wide-planked floor.

"Darkly is no such thing," I say. "You take that back, Avery Longwood."

"I have been in such a fret looking for it everywhere," Rebecca says, cutting her eyes at Darkly scurrying ribbonless back across the floor to me.

"Do not fret," Avery says. "We have found it. Besides, it is only a ribbon." Avery fiddles his fingers through the waves cresting Rebecca's shoulders. The look upon his face is clear. He envies his sister's hair, wishes he had it for his very own.

"It is not just any ribbon, Avery. You know this good and well," Rebecca says. "It is a keepsake. A prize." She looks down at Salome.

Avery bites at his bottom lip. "I recollect a faint something or another."

For the life of me, I cannot recollect any business of a blue velvet ribbon. I have lost all but a few memories. But I know this for sure, Fiddler Crab claims things belonging to others for himself. Rebecca says he could not rest until Miss Constance Rose Longwood loved Avery best. Even now, he wears his dead mama's dress and forbids Rebecca her right to do the same.

"It was a time ago," Rebecca says. "Still, it means the world. It was the last gift he gave to me."

Rebecca's fingers tense about the neck of her violin, a sure sign she struggles to keep the truce, to keep Avery calm to coax him from his mama's dress before McKinley Longwood returns. Their daddy looks for reasons to send Avery off with Hushabye Byrd, the Singing Prophetess.

Avery fiddles again in Rebecca's hair, gathering the black sea into what looks like a pony's tail. He hums his waltz, tying the ribbon—a shimmer of tear blooming his eyes. Fiddler Crab makes a loop, then another.

The velvet's nap *rasps*. The sound scrapes my neck, scratching up to my ear. Clawing away at a scab of recollection until memory seeps, and I am standing with both my hands on the stairs with Darkly spying down upon Mr. Rushworth L. Wintergarden sometime back.

Whish and rasp slides the blue velvet ribbon.

Rushworth L. Wintergarden fashions a headband.

Pulls Rebecca's hair careful from her face.

Loops the fine ribbon into a bow with his long-fingered hands.

Green as Willadeene with envy I am—that he is so close to my Blue Heron.

"John the Baptist's head on a plate." I say, bringing me back around from the memory. Mirabelle *ticks* in her can, as if she remembers well as I do that day on the stairs.

"Pardon?" Rebecca asks. The dark river current slows in her eyes. "What did you say?"

"That is what Mr.... that is what the tutor said when he give you that ribbon, after he heard you play that nocturne he taught you on Salome. I think I remember you telling me about it a time before.

You played it so well he said he would chop off John the Baptist's head. That he would present it to you on a fancy shined-up silver plate. All you had to do was ask."

"Then it is Salome's ribbon," Avery says. "Not my sister's."

"We are one in the same," Rebecca says. "Salome and me. And this ribbon was never yours, Avery. Or Darkly's. Or Leontyne's."

Rebecca told me Avery could hardly bear not having Mr. Wintergarden's full attention. His every breath. His every stare. Those long-fingered, pale Wintergarden hands swimming the dark waters of his own hair with blue velvet ribbons.

Avery pulls the ribbon harder than he should. Rebecca gives her head a yank the other way. *Push and pull.* Best I can tell, this is the way it always has been between Fiddler Crab and Blue Heron.

"Avery, you must change from that dress now. Father will be here soon," Rebecca says.

"You are not the boss of me. I will do as I please." Avery unties the bow. Whips it back into an ugly knot. Yanks the ends one last time.

"Be gentle, Avery," Willadeene says, as if she is frightened of what Rebecca might do.

"What do you know about anything, you haint?" Avery walks away from his sister, his train sweeping the floor behind. "You do not even know your true name, who you were before. You could be a pirate queen for all we know. A murderess come around to slit our throats while we sleep."

Plink. One of Willadeene's red berry earbobs falls to the floor. Darkly races the flurry of hungry starlings, steals the berries. Prowls off around the corner to hide.

Avery pulls a blue leather-bound book from the bodice of his gown. "You have your ribbon, but he gave me this." Avery waves his *Book of Jubilation and Woe* in the air, a blank journal given to him by Mr. Rushworth L. Wintergarden. Avery tantalizes us. Makes it known he has filled it with stanzas of favored verse. Of secrets shared between Rushworth L. Wintergarden and him. Awful things he claims Rebecca has done. Really, it is nothing more than a book of lovelorn spells, but dangerous just the same, a Rushworth L. Wintergarden trophy his sister did not win. Blue Heron wears her own victory, the blue velvet ribbon, and she holds Salome triumphant, Mr. Wintergarden's prize violin.

Rushworth L. Wintergarden. He is everywhere. In the nap of Rebecca's ribbon. Upon the pages Fiddler Crab holds to his chest. I am miserable remembering him swimming his hands in my Blue Heron's hair.

"To Princess Odette," Avery reads from Mr. Wintergarden's inscription. "May true love one day break the spell." Avery's voice catches. He pauses, pressing a hand to his cheek. "Until then, you must dance eternal in the moonlight by a lake." Fiddler Crab closes his *Book of Jubilation and Woe.* Finishes the rest from memory. "Forever and always, Prince Siegfried."

Swan Lake. Avery says Rushworth L. Wintergarden told him this story some years back. Avery recites it to us time and time again. Avery fancies himself Odette, a princess turned to a swan by a wicked spell. Only at night can Odette transform back into a human to dance on the bank of a place called Swan Lake.

"Avery, we must go and take off these dresses," Rebecca says, tapping her hip with Salome's bow.

"I am the Swan Queen, Sister. You may call me Odette."

Willadeene steps forward picking at a pink azalea blossom blooming the nape of her neck with one hand while holding Mirabelle in the other. "Please, Odette. Do as Rebecca says." She drops the flower to the floor. Steps on it with the high arch of her pretty, naked foot.

Willadeene is frightened of McKinley Longwood as I am, both of us acquainted with the back of his calloused hand. When Rebecca will not allow him access to Avery, it is the two of us he comes angry for. There are matters McKinley Longwood will not suffer. Fiddler

Crab pretty in dresses. Memories of his dead wife. Haints. And tow-head gals traveling with their hands sealed up in cans.

A panic rises in me. "The Prophetess," I say. "She is coming, too, Avery." I think of Eulalee—hope she has managed to squeeze some piddlin' drops of Redemption for that awful woman to peddle.

"I will play it, Odette. I will play *Swan Lake* for you. But you must do what I ask," Rebecca says. "You must go and change."

"The finale," Avery says. "Begin where it ends."

The finale. Fiddler Crab's favorite part. It seems we are poor of beginnings here on Good Hope, and how I ache for something new. Rebecca lifts her bow. Plays Avery's *Swan Lake* tune.

Fiddler Crab collects the wrist loop sewn to his ball gown's train and takes a slow first spin. "Odette," Willadeene cries out, the sound of awe burbling from her haint-girl throat. Avery spins shimmery again and again. He slows, staring up into the Up-Up There, the Forever Moon abundant in his eyes.

Salome sings urgent, and I feel a little sick. I do not want to face who is coming. Do not want to face Eulalee coming aloose in the Marsh. This sense of dread might ease if only Rebecca will look up. If I can see the Forever Moon riding the current in her dark-river eyes.

"Dance with me, swan maidens," Avery says.

Willadeene takes off with my Mirabelle toward Avery, the golden tassel of her leash dragging the floor. Salome sings louder. I fiddle my hand in my apron pocket. Plunder a forgotten piece of *The Last of the Mohicans'* snow. *Every trail has its end, and every calamity brings its lesson.*

We are Avery's swan maidens, a wicked spell cast over the whole sorry lot of us. *Look up, Rebecca. Please.* I grab Darkly, put him in my pocket. Give us both a spin. There are others in the room, only I am too dizzy to see them clear. *Anna Karenina.* I think she dances in the far corner alone. I sense Constance Rose Longwood spinning-spinning nearby in shadows. *Look, up, Rebecca. Look up.*

The Undine sings faint in the distance, joining Salome. I tell myself a lie. It is not so very bad to dance here eternal. On the bank of a moonlit lake.

"Save us, Siegfried," Willadeene calls out.

Avery turns loose his wrist loop, his train sweeping-sweeping, and scratching the floor.

The sound resembles Rushworth L. Wintergarden's fingers looping Rebecca's blue velvet prize into a bow. Only this time, there is another thing I hear. An echo. A memory. The sound of Constance Rose and Baby Girl Longwood hitting the gallery floor. Skulls cracking. The flutter of cream silk baby blanket. I want to turn loose this dreadful sound, this memory of falling. I spin. Spin until I cannot spin another time more.

Avery twirls stars onto the dull floor and vine covered walls. Presses his hand to the book in the bodice of his gown. "The Sun," he says. "Go away. Go away. Do not ever-ever come here again."

We all cry out with the saltmarsh sparrows and starlings bursting from their nests, our prayers scattered by the flap of wings and slice of Salome's bow.

Save us, Siegfried.

Save us.

Please….

Morningstar
The In-Between

Chapter 5

Hushabye Byrd sings, her voice sweeping along the Forest path in gusts of stormy breath blown foul from the Sea, slithering invisible through the warped sashes and sills.

Willadeene arranges herself into a niche, only she is anything but discreet. She has come down with a case of the fidgets, petals tumbling from her head to the floor. I search for my own place to hide should I need it.

“Everything about this place is derelict. How is it the Undine is not riddled with holes?” Rebecca asks, fussing over Salome, polishing her gentle with a rag. “Is it unkind to wish that old boat would spring a leak? And off to the bottom of the River the Undine and Hushabye Byrd go.”

Across the room, Mirabelle flutters inside her can. Rebecca’s eyes roam over to the spot Mirabelle sits on a sawhorse that props up the Pyramid of Giza. "Have you captured some critter inside that can?” she asks.

I lie. “Just a cricket. A friend for Mirabelle to pass the time.” How might I break the stunning news? *Miracle of miracles. Behold, my sweet Rebecca. Mirabelle has come alive.*

I wish I had left Mirabelle back at the Chapel of Abundance to comfort my Ewell Day Higgs. Blue Heron holds little regard for my pitiful orphaned hand. I reckon it is on account of the fact Rebecca already got rid of it once. You should know, Rebecca was the one to save me in the wake of Tribulation Day. Sawing away my hand to keep the gangrene from toting me off to Beulah Land. All the while, Fiddler Crab came unlaced. He was nothing but a useless, wailing heap of satin spilling across the floor.

But it was Avery who sneaked my right hand back to me when his sister's head was turned. "I named her, Mirabelle," he said, weeping and pressing his cheek to mine. "She is frightened and all alone." Mirabelle is the name he hoped his parents might give his baby sister back before she fell down from the Cupola in her mama's arms, both of them landing dead on the floor. There is a tender streak within Avery cutting wide alongside the selfish one smothering the room.

"She is getting close," Willadeene says, chewing the nail of her pale green thumb.

Indeed, they are much closer now, the Prophetess's melody congealing to a gloomy procession of words. We all go quiet. Even the creeping vine stops its sneaking to give the night a listen.

Are you washed in the blood

In the soul-cleansing blood of the lamb?

From the bottom stair, without looking up into the Cupola, Rebecca calls to Avery. "Best finish dressing," she says. "Or there will be the devil to pay." Blue Heron already shed her mama's ballgown, pulling her lustrous hair from her face with Mr. Wintergarden's blue velvet ribbon tied perfect into a bow.

"Horror of horrors," Willadeene says. She covers her ears, hibiscus trumpets flourishing behind each cockle pressing flat to her head. "That song is a fright."

The prophetess does not suffer disappointment with gentle wits. If I had the sense God give a turnip green, I would not have run off from Eulalee. No, I would have stayed until at least that Sarah Fig was mashed up and traveling corkscrews through a stretch of pipe on Eulalee's still. There is never a time I know when there was not Redemption on the ready for Miss Hushabye Byrd to tote off and peddle.

Rebecca runs her bow through Salome's strings. *Cluck.* Rebecca winces. Even that temptress violin seems to have turned skittish. Rebecca lowers her bow. Untucks Salome from her chin.

From outside there is a horsey *clomp* on the steps, voices humming out of tempo with the Prophetess's ghoulish serenade. I take my turn, calling up into the gaping throat of the Gallery to the Cupola. To the Up-Up There. "Avery, they are near abouts here," I say. "Lazarus and Josiah, too." *The nephews.* Avery will not be able to temper his curiosity. As great is my dread to greet the Prophetess and McKinley Longwood, I cannot quell my urge to catch a gander at the boys.

The clatter of hoof echoes against Morningstar. Willadeene bolts from her niche to hide behind the stairs, her tasseled leash trailing behind. The doorknobs rattle. Doors scrape the floor—bang the walls. *Swoosh* and frenzy, Willadeene rips loose a scream. A tempest follows, plundering the place, ravishing our hems. Rocking the chandelier. Plucking petals from Willadeene, sucking them into the Up-Up There.

Oh, be washed in the blood of the lamb!

Quick as that, the winds go hush, and McKinley Longwood stands within the great frame of the doors, his eyes hidden behind sun goggles, the In-Between reflected in the dark lenses. Wafts of Redemption swirl sweet-stinking from his breath and clothes. He spreads his arms wide. Leans back. "Winter is past," he says. "The rain is over and gone, my dear children."

Rebecca stands, and I hurry over to her at the foot of the stairs. "Winter has not yet begun, Father," Rebecca says. "But it is on the way. It is bound to come."

Clomp. Hushabye Byrd makes her way up the stairs, the teardrop crystals from the chandelier swaying and *clinking*. Forever Moon catches in the weepy prisms, playing like moonlight upon nighttime waters on the vine covered walls and floor. *Is this what it is like to live beneath the sea?*

"There is news, my children. Just wait until you hear." McKinley Longwood says. Redemption has harvested most of his hair, the remaining strands floating like flotsam about his head.

"Go on then," Rebecca says. "What is this good news?"

"Where is your brother?" McKinley Longwood asks.

"Waltzing on a storm cloud," Rebeccas says, cutting her eyes at me.

"The Prophetess," McKinley Longwood says, paying no further mind Avery is not here to listen. "She has agreed to be my wife."

Willadeene gasps from behind the stairs. My Blue Heron, she makes not a sound, and I drown here beneath the Morningstar Sea.

"What day has been set?" Rebecca asks.

Beneath the great frame of doors, a billow of dark veil appears. Miss Hushabye Byrd speaks faint and from such a distance, her words melt to gibberish. *Ssss.... Ssss.... Ssss....*

"Begging you pardon, ma'am," Rebecca says. "I could not make clear what you said."

Miss Hushabye Byrd teeters two dainty steps across the threshold on her wood block shoes. The trim cut of her long skirt surrenders above her ankles confounding her movement further still. It is any wonder she can move at all.

Covered to the ankles in a veil, the Prophetess sings her words. *It is done. Has been written. And proclaimed.* She is unable to speak a hair above a whisper, a malady, we have been told she has long suffered from way back to when she was a child.

"Betrothed and hitched," McKinley Longwood says. "On the bank of Abraham's bluff an hour ago. Miss Hushabye Byrd is your mother now," he says. "Come over here, Rebecca. Give her a hug." He hollers up into the Cupola a hopeful tone, but the echo fades bleak. "Avery...."

Ssss.... Ssss.... Whatever Miss Hushabye Byrd says, there is no way of telling. She takes a few steps, one wood block shoe *clicking* the floor and then the other. McKinley Longwood offers his hand, but she shuffles right on by. *Ssss.... Ssss....* She is closer now, the coppery-penny smell of her upsetting my nose.

From beneath a deep purple veil, she sings. *Honor your father and mother so your days may be long in the land.* Her voice starts up deeper than expected, climbing a ladder to a near unbearable shrill. She holds so long and fierce to the last note it vibrates in Salome's strings.

"Amen," McKinley Longwood says. "May your days be long in the land."

Without near abouts any effort at all, the Prophetess wriggles her veil up and over her head, the purple tide whispering down her back. *Shh...* Miss Hushabye Byrd shocks powerful at first glance. She resembles a watercolor picture from Avery's book, *Wonderous Mysteries and Oddities of Japan*. Her face is powdered pale. Her raven's wing hair, starched stiff as Longwood napkins, is folded in pieces and fashioned into a bow. Only she is not from far away as Japan. Best we know, she has not one drop of Japanese blood flowing through her sing-song veins.

Lazarus, Miss Hushabye Byrd trills. *Come you. Come you. And brother, Josiah, too.*

Another rouse of wind pushes through the doors spinning and hissing through Morningstar. The nephews enter humming side-by-side, lanterns swaying on their wrists. *Are you washed? In the blood?* McKinley Longwood hurries to wrestle each door against the bluster.

Lazarus is on the left. Like always, Josiah is on the right. I marvel at how different the nephews are from the ones that last come around. This Lazarus, he is in possession of a wave of hair so thick a pomade cannot tame. This Josiah, he is shorter than the one come before. The Prophetess does not let on the nephews are always changing. McKinely Longwood, he is too busy sweet-stinking the place to notice. Never have I left Good Hope, but I am not so easily fooled. Something is happening to the nephews. Miss Hushabye Byrd seems always to be switching them out as if they are shoes worn through to the stitches. I cannot help but wonder where the old nephews go.

I turn to get a gander at Rebecca, the astonishment brightening her eyes every time a new crop of fine-looking nephews enters the place. Willadeene cannot resist, peeking her moonlit eyes from behind the stairs. Even Darkly is curious, rising from my pocket to give himself a look. We all ache for lovely things to admire here upon Good Hope. For anybody other than Sinners and singing prophetesses to happen into the room.

A door cracks the frame. Then the other. And we are left again beneath the frantic chandelier. The nephews' faces are alive with shock and wonderment. Their eyes snag the walls. Dart into the Up-Up There tracking the scatter of starlings and marsh sparrows. Though each new set of nephews is different from the set come before, their reaction is always the same. I hanker to know what the boys are thinking. If they should turn tail from Morningstar and run to the River and swim back across, or stay put and do whatever it is Lazaruses and Josiahs do. *Miss Hushabye Byrd is mistress of Morningstar now. It is done. Has been written. And proclaimed.* We should all run for the River and try our best not to sink.

Here comes a shower of Willadeene, the petals from blooms sucked up into the Cupola earlier by the wind. A drift of hydrangea, azalea, and Easter lily scatter gentle from above, lighting upon Miss Hushabye Byrd's veil, licking the nephew's cheeks and lapels of their suits, prying the boys' eyes even wider. From behind the stairs, I hear Willadeene stir and fret. I hardly can blame her. Of all the times for it to come up a scandalous flurry, it has the mind to come now. With Miss Hushabye Byrd just having *clomped* into the room.

"Abomination," McKinley Longwood says. "Willadeene," he screams. "Come out from wherever it is you lurk." He licks at the dogwood petal pasted to his lip, then peels it away with his forefinger and thumb.

McKinley Longwood pretends not to care much for our Willadeene, but other times I have seen him with her petals stuck to his cheeks, caught between his fingers—fluttering from the bottom of his shoes when he thought no one was about to look.

"Come stand next to me, Willadeene," I whisper. The nephews seem to have taken notice of Blue Heron and me, their staring eyes glossy from lantern light. I hide my no-hand arm behind my back. There is already plenty strange here to be seen. I wonder what they make of this towheaded gal and my beautiful Blue Heron.

Willadeene edges from behind the stairs. She bows her head. Nibbles her thumb. Try hard as she might, it is an impossibility she go unnoticed. From Lazarus's and Josiah's first sight of her, Rebecca and I are cast to oblivion. Who can blame the nephews? Who would not be stupefied by the sight of a haint turned evergreen and bright as spring.

Be assured, there is no other person or thing in the room when our Willadeene enters, her long velvet robe clinging, revealing the torrid secrets of her curves and swells. It is a great scandal this very evening she has forgotten her shoes. As enticing as her landscape, there is a quality equally shocking about the high-high arch of her mossy green feet. Something unseemly in the glare of her sand dollar toenails polished high-high to the lacquer of a moon snail shell.

Miss Hushabye Byrd sings deep. Urgent. *Lazarus and Josiah. Look away. Look away from this sinful, sorry sight.* The nephews seem hungry-eyed as the rest of us. As if they, too, long for lovely things to look upon.

Ssss.... Ssss.... Miss Hushabye Byrd wobbles as if undone by the whole Willadeene affair. McKinley Longwood hurries over to offer his new wife an arm to steady herself while she titters and swoons. The Prophetess is not what she seems. She is a parlor trick. Mark my words. Should a reward worth her while gleam precious at an opposite end, she would walk a burning circus tightrope *clickety-click* over a gator pit in her pair of wood block shoes.

Before the nephews can turn to face the doors, their eyes flit above our heads to the stairs, and I know without turning back it is Avery who has come.

"In the name of all that is decent and good," McKinley Longwood hollers. "What have you gone and done?" He stumbles. The last drop of Redemption he sneaked a moment back is just now kicking in.

Lord help, me. Lord, help Avery. Around I spin, knowing right off what our Avery went and done.

Morningstar
The In-Between

Chapter 6

"What a disgrace," McKinley Longwood yells. "To greet your new mother in this sorry state."

At the curve of the stairs, Avery dazzles, the Forever Moon shimmery in his dress's paillettes and beads. His hair is assembled high upon his head, adorned with a peacock feather, two tendrils of hair alongside each ear.

"I heard the news from up here in our dead mother's Cupola," Avery says, ignoring his daddy, his voice gossamer and frail. "That there is a new mother come to Morningstar."

A joy it is, Hushabye Byrd sings. *To have you for a son.*

"Did you bring me the things I asked?" Avery says.

"The things you asked?" McKinley Longwood takes a step forward pulling at the buckle of his belt. "The only thing you are bound to get is beat."

Miss Hushabye Byrd grabs hold of McKinley Longwood's arm. *Leave the boy be*, she sings. Of all of us, Miss Hushabye Byrd loves Avery best.

Avery addresses the Prophetess, though it is the new batch of nephews he studies. "Did you bring me more John Keats?" he asks.

She nods.

"And the book by Dickens?"

She nods again.

"*Great Expectations*? Just like I asked?"

Yes, she sings, pointing to the knapsack across Lazarus's shoulder.

Our Avery is not without kindness. The book by Dickens is for me. If the Prophetess knew, she would rip loose the pages and set them on fire.

"Vivaldi's *Four Seasons*?" There is no pretending the sheet music is for anyone else but Rebecca. Mr. Rushworth L. Wintergarden is said to have spoken often of these four violin concertos, and Avery is desperate to hear them all played. All we know here is *Winter*.

Avery has taken so much from my Rebecca. Their mama's affection. Now he tries to take all of Mr. Rushworth L. Wintergarden. Why should our Rebecca not have all the seasons? It is the least Fiddler Crab can do.

To God be the glory, the Prophetess tweets, pointing to the knapsack across the other nephew's shoulder.

"And the malted milk balls?" Do not tell, but it is Willadeene who possesses the tooth for chocolate candy treats.

The Prophetess lowers her chin slow. *Ssss....*

"Your generosity is wasted on an ungrateful, foolish boy the likes of this," McKinley Longwood says, pointing his finger up at Avery. "He can either come down and take his own whoopin', or pick who will take it for him." He pulls his belt from the last loop of his trousers. "Will it be this no count, haint?" McKinley Longwood licks at the place on his lip Willadeene's petal sat lurid. "Or will it be this Leontyne with rabbit shit stinking in her pocket and on her boots. Either one is bound to deserve it."

If I were not so nervous, I might find humor in McKinley Longwoods accusations. Afterall, he is the only one of us in the room with his eyes hidden—ruined by Redemption. His eyes glow gold, have turned to slits like those of a goat's. Lazarus and Josiah look down at the floor, and I think it is an act of tender-heartedness that they do not wish to see us beat.

Willadeene frets, holding tight to my waist. "Do not fret," I whisper. I already have decided to take the whoopin' McKinley Longwood promises. Willadeene is much too fragile of spirit. Her emotional wounds seep and linger weeks longer than my own. Besides, I prefer the belt to his hand. I cannot bear to have his clammy hands touch me, even when I pretend it belongs to Rebecca.

"I have a gift for you, Miss Hushabye," Avery says. "If you will see to it that Father leaves us all alone."

The Prophetess gestures for McKinley to give the belt over, extending her purple gloved hand. *Ssss....* This is not an act of succor. If it were not for the promise of Avery's gift, it might be Miss Hushabye Byrd doling the lashes herself. She is disgusted by haints, and I am told by Avery she has not cared a snail's trail for me since I lost my hand. Tolerating me even less than before.

Let all things be done with charity, the Prophetess warbles to Avery. Her mouth appears to barely move—her lips painted up red to fool you into thinking they are two tiny half-hearts. She *clicks* a couple steps forward, the buckle of the belt dragging the floor.

From his *Book of Jubilation and Woe*, Avery reads—his voice more delicate, more winsome—the quality of a mewling calf calling you to coddle and hold.

And the sunlight clasps the earth
And the moonbeams kiss the sea:
What is all this sweet work worth
If thou kiss not me?

Percy Bysshe Shelley. Avery has not tried this poem of his before. Miss Hushabye Byrd is anything but a fool. And somehow, Avery has tricked her into thinking this poem is for her. That all the poems are for her. It is meant to be a love spell, a charm cast over the nephews.

Upon any Lazarus or Josiah, Avery has conjured not so much as a twitch or grin, certainly not a pledge or hint of affection. But something has come alive in Josiah, and he looks up to Avery shimmering on the stairs. Josiah moistens his lips with his tongue. Turns them dewy. For a moment, I think Joshiah might call out to Avery, but he appears to think better of it, closing his mouth back shut. I consider the buckle Miss Hushabye Byrd drags on the floor, and I am glad Josiah has himself a bit of sense. The Prophetess forbids us to speak one word to the nephews, and the nephews are certainly not allowed to speak to us. Avery turns a page. Turns another as if trying to find the perfect verse to finish off his incantation.

"It is getting late," McKinley Longwood says, touching his wife's shoulder causing her to wince. "We must rest. If we are to be heading back out … come early morning." His words have begun to slur, his Redemption kicking in.

"You are leaving with her?" Rebecca asks.

"For a short time."

Never has McKinley Longwood traveled along with Miss Hushabye Byrd with her traveling tent revival show, and I am thrilled to have him soon gone. From the Pyramid of Giza, Mirabelle celebrates with me, *tick-tocking* inside her can. Miss Hushabye Byrd turns her gaze to me, and I remember what I was happy forgetting. The Prophetess has come for Redemption.

The Singing Prophetess whispers into her husband's ear. He leans to kiss her cheek. She pulls away. "Miss Hushabye has business with Leontyne," McKinley Longwood says. "Rebecca and Avery, it is off to bed with the both of you."

"I am not sleepy," Avery says. "Not with all this … wonderful news."

Avery hardly sleeps—pining for Mr. Rushworth L. Wintergarden, carrying on about his dead mama, Miss Constance Rose. It is any wonder he has not worn holes in the floor with all his worry. Holes big enough for us all to fall through.

"Boy, I do not give a damn what you do. Just get on away from here," McKinley Longwood says.

I am not allowed down in the bottom of Morningstar, the place called the Down-Below, the bottom floor where the Longwoods live and sleep. Skye women have never been welcome there, but Rebecca and Avery break the rules, sneaking me through their windows when bored or at the other's throat.

"Willadeene, you come here to me." Avery says. I am astonished Avery wants Willadeene to step foot into the Up-Up There. She and I are not allowed anywhere close to his precious Celestial Hall of Books, the place off the Cupola where he keeps his collection.

"Off to the barn with that haint before you turn in," McKinley Longwood says. "She is liable to suck the wind from our lungs. Kill us all while we sleep."

In the pecking order of things, Willadeene is not considered any better than me. McKinley Longwood would snap in two if he knew Avery has her sleep on the floor next to his bed. Willadeene turns me loose. Hurries to Avery. Fiddler Crab is smart enough not to follow his daddy into the Down-Below where the Longwoods dwell. But plenty nosey enough to listen in from the Cupola on the Prophetess and me.

Miss Hushabye Byrd sings, *Are you washed?*

The nephews hum along, marching away slow. Josiah gives a glance over his shoulder to Avery as he guides Willadeene by her leash behind him up the stairs.

Rebecca presses her shoulder into mine, whispering the thing she tells Fiddler Crab and me to soothe us before we might come undone. "Pianissimo," she says, following her daddy, playing the hymn on Salome. *Are your garments spotless, are they white as snow?*

Quick as that, I am near alone with the Prophetess, except for the nephews looking away facing the doors. She pulls the purple veil from her back. Lets it *swish* over her face and down to her ankles. *Shh....* And I cannot see her pale powdered face and her half-heart lips. I am more frightened now as I was when I could see her.

One wood block shoe glides in front of the other, skimming the floor, and she is not anywhere close to a teeter or topple. The belt buckle scrapes as she comes close. So close I can hear her whisper. So close there is no need for her to sing. Her coppery breath pushes at her veil. "Put that nub away when I am talking to you, gal. The sight of it turns me sick."

"Yes, ma'am," I say, putting my no-hand arm behind my back.

"It has been a long while since I lay eyes upon the Great Redeemer," she hisses. "Why is it you are the one of late to bring me my Redemption? Has something run amuck down at that ungodly place?"

If it were not for that ungodly place, there would be no Redemption, I want to say. But Miss Hushabye Byrd has only a sense of how Redemption is made. Best I can reckon, she does not know it is cooked from Sarah Figs soaked through with haints, though she does suspect Damascus plays a part.

"She is plenty good. Just busy is all." I will not tell her Eulalee is falling apart. That the chances are high there will be no Redemption, especially with her so close and dragging McKinley Longwood's buckle on the floor.

"Not busy enough," she says, taking hold of my good arm with her purple glove. "She was eleven bottles short last time. And eight the time before."

"She begs your pardon, ma'am."

The Prophetess gives my arm a squeeze. *Despair. Upon the land*, she sings.

Of all her divinations, Miss Hushabye Byrd's Prophecies of Despair are her specialty. The Great Depression. Influenza. A hailstorm with ice the size of watermelons. Her voice is soft and weepy, and if I did not know the reach of her whip or slice of her blow, the sound of her sadness might hook me by the gills. The Prophetess's breath crawls my nostrils. Slinks down. Tickles my throat. Quick as a split, the Prophetess pulls Darkly from my pocket. I freeze, my mouth stuck wide open and aiming to scream.

"*Shh. . . .*" she whispers, holding Darkly in one hand. The belt in the other. "Do not startle me. Sure would hate to drop your precious

Darkly. A low-down awful shame it would be if I mistook him for a rat and stomped him under my shoe."

I hold my breath, imagining those magic trick lips hardly moving beneath her veil. "Please give him back." My voice cracks. If I do not hold myself together, I might shatter all the way through.

"Calamity is no stranger to this place," she whispers, squeezing Darkly so tight he squeals. Though I cannot see her eyes, her head tilts as if looking into the Up-Up There. "Of all people, you should know. Such a pretty girl you were. Just look at you now." From below, Rebecca plays Salome. Miss Hushabye Byrd sings along, tapping her wood block shoe slow. *Lay aside your garments that are stained with sin.*

"Darkly," I say, reaching out my trembling hand. "Pretty please, ma'am. Give him back to me."

"Worse things can happen," she whispers, giving Darkly another squeeze. She hands the poor thing back. My Darkly trembles. "Think about that. If you do not bring me what I need. If you do not do what I say."

I kiss and hug my rabbit. Put him back quick in my pocket, trying to settle my sick stomach from splatting sick on the floor. "Forever grateful," I whisper.

"Forever mine," she swishes, turning away upon her wood block heels. She slides and *clicks* slow toward the door to the Down-Below, the belt buckle scratching the floor. I listen until I can hear the *click* and slide no more, until it is just Darkly, Mirabelle, and me. And the nephews standing guard facing the doors.

Avery calls down quiet from the Up-Up There. "For Josiah. What is all this sweet work worth?"

Something catches in the moonlight. I watch it float, wondering if it is the last of Willadeene's flowery snow. Only it is not. It is Avery's peacock feather plucked fresh from his hair. End-over-end it tumbles. Rockabyes lazy. I pretend to watch myself drifting, trying to remember how it happened the day I fell. *Was it quiet? Quick?*

Miss Hushabye Byrd's breath lingers in my mouth. The taste of copper pennies, of blood, grows stronger still, and I remember the awful sound when I hit the floor. The *crunch* of a carrot when I near about bit my tongue in two.

Avery calls down once more. "For Josiah," he says.

What was the thing the Prophetess just said? I reach for the feather. Whisper to the room.

Forever mine.... Forever mine....

The Marsh

Chapter 7

Trouble smarts in the nub of my no-hand arm, the tang of pennies still strong on my tongue. *Something is wrong.* Mirabelle feels it too, scraping the inside of her rusted coffee can.

From a distance, I spy Eulalee shucked naked as an oyster, dancing indecent on the Marsh's wetland walk. Only, it is not Mama. It is a figment. A Forever Moon trick turning the windblown cordgrass a silvery ill repute.

Darkly whimpers in my pocket, nervous and recovering from the good bruising Miss Hushabye Byrd give him. Be warned, that woman is a might stronger than she looks, and my poor Darkly could be easily dead if the Prophetess took it into her starch-haired head to do it.

"Quiet now, Darkly," I say. "Everything is going to turn out alright." How am I going to tell the Singing Prophetess that Eulalee has not made her a single, miserable drop of Redemption? Lord help Eulalee and me. Just what variety of meanness might Miss Hushabye Byrd inflict upon the two of us? Will she stomp us to mush beneath the tall heel of her wood block shoe? I get to moving, hurrying down the path to Damascus.

More.... More.... More.... The three sorry haints who crossed the River a few hours back yammer from inside Sarah Figs, their fishtails poking out and on the way to being swallowed.

"Serves you right," I say, looking up at the three pregnant fig bellies dangling shameless from the haint-trap-tree. "Quit with that infernal crying. What is done is done."

The brackish wind blows, sweeping my hair from my face and over my shoulders. I think of Miss Hushabye Byrd's veil whispering down her back. *Shh....* A chill shoots down my arms. I call out across the way to the Hornet's Nest, the name of our live oak cottage on stilts.

Beyond the cottage, smoke eddies in spectral blooms from the tabby chimney of Sepulcher, the small dependency from within which Redemption is made. Eulalee is most likely there. Toasting her failing carcass against the flame.

"Eulalee, the Singing Prophetess is here," I say.

The wind lifts Damascus's branches. Fondles her leaves. The tree makes not a single peep. She plays possum—holds her breath. She cannot fool me. *She never sleeps.* The whole of the place is too-too quiet, except for the haints, and rustle of something tumbling from the Marsh. I am ready to flee in case it is a boar set out running with tusks sharpened and aiming for me, but it is only Eulalee's cornhusk hat.

"Eulalee?" I ask, hoping she might be close behind, but she is nowhere to be seen. I pick up her hat. Darkly pokes his head from my pocket to give it a sniff. I smell it, too, taking in the musk of pluff. Sweat, and Sarah Fig treacle.

I head off to Sepulcher, but she is not there. Only the dirt floor and embers, and a velvety fig hide stretched raw and fresh on the table next to Eulalee's butcher knife. On the top porch step of the Hornet's Nest I find a tooth, and just outside the door, two more. I gather the three rotten pearls and drop them in my pocket with Darkly.

"Eulalee? It is me," I whisper, opening the door. "Your Sister Girl."

The Hornet's Nest is dim but for the moonlight stealing through open shutters. My boot catches on something strewn upon the floor. It is Rivière, Eulalee's necklace made from the ancient oyster shell bark that grows upon Damascus Tree. Eulalee says this necklace and something she calls Heirloom are both one day meant for me. She avoids the details of what this Heirloom is every time I make mention.

It is queer Eulalee has left Rivière on the floor. Even when she has forgotten herself, even when she is buck-naked and without a speck of shame or sense, Mama wears this necklace give to her by her mama, the very one give to her by her mama's mama. So on and so forth—as far back to when came the first woman called Skye. Eulalee says the story of the world is hardened and etched it its shells. All that has happened. All that is yet to come. To see these goings-on, Eulalee licks the inside of the shells, her tongue sliding slick inside the bowls, the same shells Skye tongues ravished years and years before. Why did these women stay? Why did they not leave if they could see tomorrow?

All the good these oyster shells have done you, Mama. I throw the necklace across the room. It skitters the floor. Disappears beneath my bed. In the looking glass above the dresser, I think I have found Eulalee, but it is my own reflection I see. I take in the pale glow I cast alongside the Moon, the shock of white curly hair blown wild, panic spinning madness in my faded blue eyes. I am every bit my Mama from just a few years back. Before the Worsening sank its teeth.

I hurry onto the porch, desperate enough to yell into the rambling murk for Eulalee. To wake the Marsh and all the trouble that lay beyond. I do not want to think what I am thinking. That what has always been coming has come. *The end.*

From somewhere comes a *thump.* Then another. It is not my Darkly or my Mirabelle. Both of them have turned hopeless and still. *Thump.* It is that harlot deer, Babylon, tapping a hoof beneath Damascus Tree.

Before I can holler to the hussy to get on away from here, I see it is Eulalee's basket and not the ground Babylon knocks. With Mirabelle under my no-hand arm and Mama's cornhusk hat in the other, I am down from the porch quick. Ready to see what is the matter. Babylon backs away keeping herself a cool distance.

Within the belly of the cordgrass basket, upon a bed of *The Last of the Mohicans* snow, rests a passel of tincture bottles gleaming and stoppered with cork. *Redemption.* A pharaoh's ransom of the stuff. How Eulalee has managed the feat in such a paltry *tick* of time is a wonder of wonders, but she has saved us from Hushabye Byrd for now.

Damascus takes a breath at long last. There is only so long she can hold it. I look out into the moonlit gloom, my eyes tracing her roots sprawling humpbacked. Mile upon mile into the Marsh. Clear out to the Doldrums, the wasteland she has made from suckling the place dry, where the Skye women venture themselves wasted to tend the final fall away of their gristle from bone.

Haints weep from inside their Sarah Figs. *More.... More.... More....*

In the far off, comes a rumble. Damascus drinks, and soon the hungry roots beneath my feet will quiver. I look down at the basket. *More.... More.... More....* There will never be enough. When this batch is through, the Prophetess will come back for me, sliding high upon her wood block shoes.

On the wind, rides the truth. It is coming, a thing I cannot quite yet fathom.

Through the cordgrass, it sizzles, trilling through the gaps in oyster shell bark. I brace myself. Stand still. Wait for it to knock against me. It is here. Has come. The Doldrums have called for Mama.

My Eulalee is dead and gone.

The Forest

Chapter 8

Beneath the forest's canopy, critters come *rat-a-tat-tat* for my feet, issuing warnings against my boots. I ponder if I should let the varmints have their way. If they do not bore holes clean through me, it will be Damascus. Or worse yet, the Prophetess.

Tincture bottles *clink* in the basket. I pretend the sound is something festive, the jingle bells Avery ties on the laces of his Christmastime shoes. My ears have turned scurrilous, hearing only the commotion of Eulalee's teeth stoppered in a bottle in my pocket rattling alongside poor Darkly.

My mind paints ghastly pictures of Eulalee lonesome in the Doldrums, worn and rickety as a scarecrow. Her skeleton plays a dreadful game of forget-me-not, one bone collapsing in on the next. *Clack. My Sister Girl forgets me. Clank. Sister Girl forgets-me-not.* How I wish our last together had been kind.

"Maybe she is coming back," I say to Darkly and Mirabelle. "Maybe she is not." Poor Eulalee. Poor me standing here pitiful beneath the crooked limbs of trees.

Babylon saunters by at a distance. She has trailed and taunted us the entire path. She stops. Looks to the bald spot in the low hanging branches to the Chapel of Abundance across the way. If a body has a mind to hurry from the Marsh to Morningstar, the Forest path yonder will lead you there quick.

Babylon looks back my way, her sultry eyes giving me the once over. She turns again. Starts back up her slow, hypnotic sway. I am in no hurry to follow, to come anywhere near my Ewell Day Higgs lying dead in the pit beneath the Moon. To hand over the last of Eulalee's Redemption to Miss Hushabye Byrd.

"I am not following you," I say, but something rubs away inside me I should.

I have stood still too long, and my boots will not budge. Quick-growing weeds gnaw their prickly teeth into my heels. Virginia creeper sneaks down from a tree weaving its gummy tendrils about a bundle of hair. "Get gone," I say, kicking the weeds. I wrestle my head from the vine, leaving towhead threads of myself with the creeper, a consolation prize. Leaving my eyes smarting from the pain.

Babylon keeps moving, and I follow. Resurrection fern rustles upon the Chapel's walls shimmery and alive still from the drizzle. If I were a stranger upon the place, I might kneel in awe of its splendor, but that deer knows what I know. Babylon vamps over to the edge of the pit looking down at my dead Ewell Day Higgs. The nerve that hussy has of being disrespectful.

"Leave the dead to sleep," I say, hurrying through the space a door once held onto with hinges. The bottles wiggle restless in my basket. I step across the threshold. Next to the wall, I set down Eulalee's batch of Redemption. Take Mirabelle from beneath my arm. Put her down soft.

A voice claws decrepit from below. I picture the voice sprouting fingers, its nails—dirty and bleeding. Scratching and tearing to the surface. Tumbling backward. Falling. *The long-long ways.*

"Starshine?" Wonder of wonders, my Ewell Day Higgs lives. From the rasp of his voice, I know he is in a terrible way. I go stiff. Hold my breath. Near impossible it is to quell my sobs. There is no pretending I am not here.

"This is Starshine," I say. "I come to see about you." It is a lie. There is not a lick of *star* or *shine* about me. And I did not want to come. I pretend to be everywhere and anywhere but here. With one hand, I row Blue Heron and me in a boat crossing the Indian Ocean heading off to an archipelago.

The voice scrapes back up the pit. "I hoped you would come back here. To see after me."

"It is the least I can do." I will not tell him it is to Babylon's credit I am here. "What might I do to make it better?" The last of my words are a sputtering mess of tears. There is nothing to be done. No making this better.

"Why do you cry, Starshine?"

Mama has fallen to pieces in the Doldrums, her skin peeling away easy as steamed cabbage leaves. I might tell him the truth she is dead, if I had not already lied. Told him she was gone. *And I cry Ewell Day Higgs, because I cannot bear to hear you suffer.* "I did not mean for this to happen," I say.

"This is no fault of yours, Starshine. It is mine."

"Can you bear the pain?"

"Since you have come," he says. "I am a might better."

"Is there any saving you, Ewell Day Higgs? If so, I will go quick for help." There is no one or nothing to run for but the mercy McKinley Longwood's shotgun brings.

"Before I come to Good Hope. To see the Moon. And call upon The Great Redeemer. I was done for. There is nothing to be done but to leave me here. There is no saving me."

"Why do you say you were done for before you even come? What is your burden?" I ask.

Time withers, not a speck of word he speaks. Nothing more do I want to know this instant than why from the beginning he was doomed. "Alsace-Lorraine." At last he speaks, his voice climbing the sides of the pit. He speaks gibberish now. This happens sometimes when the end comes near.

"Begging your pardon, Ewell Day Higgs, but I cannot make clear what you say."

"That was her name. The only one to ever love me. And now she is gone."

"Who, Ewell Day Higgs? Who is this Miss Alsace-Lorraine? And how come she run off?" For the life of me, I cannot conjecture a reason a body might take into her head to leave him. A fella with a fine crop of hair, with every last one of his teeth straight and gleaming.

"She is my wife," he says.

"Your wife?" My stomach flops to hear he promised himself to another. He is not mine, this Ewell Day Higgs. I have no right to claim him. We have just this very night become acquainted.

"My Alsace-Lorraine. She is dead."

Dead. I am ashamed to be joyous of the news—a smidge guilty my heart betrays Blue Heron. "My condolences," I say, smoothing Darkly's nap. "What was it, sir. That done it. If you do not mind me asking?"

There is a wicked streak inside me angling for every particular of this tragedy. Was it a sinister end? Did a murderous somebody drag Alsace-Lorraine to her death like Constance Rose done me and her Baby Girl Longwood?

Ewell Day Higgs goes quiet.

"Begging your pardon, sir. I hope I did not upset you."

At last, Ewell Day Higgs speaks. "Consumption was the thing that done it. That stole my beautiful Alsace-Lorraine from me. And took away our poor unborn child with her."

I reach in my pocket and rattle Eulalee's teeth. *Consumption and poor dead babies.* "When?"

"Two years ago," he says.

Tribulation Day. Two years back. I would like to know what day it was they died, if it was the same as mine. Would that not be something? That we are kindred in our misery. But I have asked too many questions.

Babylon taps Constance Rose's grave next to the one belonging to poor Baby Girl Longwood. Overcome I am by this place full up with dead mama's and their never-had-a-chance babies, the tiny things poked like carrot seeds lonesome into the sad-dark earth. Overtaken I am by how cold the wind has blown. Realizing now, with certainty, if I do not leave Good Hope, I will have no choice but to inherit the work of my mama. Of the Great Redeemer.

"I need to be going soon," I say. I have heard enough. I am scared.

A moan works its way from the pit. "Starshine, do not leave me here alone." His breathing is anything but easy. It is loud. It wheezes.

"I will not leave you lonesome," I say. "I will not leave you in pain." I run back to Mirabelle. Pick her up. Stow her in the small hollow of the wall. "I am leaving Mirabelle here to keep you company."

"Who is Mirabelle?" he asks. "I thought you were here all alone."

"She is my friend, but she is not one for small talk, though she is the best listener I know." For now, I feel it best not tell him Mirabelle is my hand sealed up in a can.

"It hurts," he says. "It will only get worse once you leave me."

I sit down next to the basket and pull off a boot and a grey wool sock. Careful inside it, I place a bottle of Redemption, folding the sock upon itself to cushion soft as a quilt.

"I am tossing something down to you, Ewell Day Higgs." Briary weeds sprout up nibbling my toes.

"Do not come too close. Do not look down."

"Here it comes," I holler. I possess a strong-handed aim, making up for the deficit of losing the other. My sock drops into the center of the pit.

"A sock," he says. "How come you give me only one?"

Would that not be a sorry affair? Me with only one hand, and my Ewell Day Higgs with but one foot. "Look inside it," I say.

"Starshine. It is too late for Redemption."

"It is to ease your pain," I say. "Until the end comes your way. But just one drop. A single drop beneath your tongue."

If he is smart, he will guzzle it down all at once—a bona fide way to end himself quick. But I do not want him gone yet. There are more things I feel he wants to share. More things I might like to say.

"Much obliged," he says, his voice turning weepy.

"Tell me a happy thing. A picture-pretty something of your sweet Alsace-Lorraine."

Ewell Day Higgs is quiet a long while until he speaks this next thing. "Fresh as rain," he says. "Is the way her skin smelled sometimes to me." His voice is dreamy, and I am grateful Redemption takes hold. "Rosewater and green tea leaves was the scent of her shiny chestnut hair."

I resign myself to stay here until he falls off to sleep. Or until he is dead. "Think more of them good-feeling thoughts," I say. "And look up, Ewell Day Higgs. Look up to the Forever Moon while you do it."

From down below, my Ewell Day Higgs sings a song.

Fresh as rain was the smell,
Of my one true love.
Rosewater. Rosewater,
And green tea leaves.
Alsace-Lorraine,
My sweet, summertime-summertime rain.

Eulalee's teeth come alive, buzzing from inside the bottle as if woke by Ewell Day Higgs's song. They clack against the glass. Go quiet. Then thrum up again singing the Great Redeemer's haint-dying song.

On across the River,
To where you ought go,
Way off beyond Zion,
Fields plentiful with gold.

This is all that is left of Eulalee, all that one day will be left of me. Rotten teeth singing to anyone foolish enough to fall themselves down-down a hole.

Fresh as rain was the smell,
Of my one true love.
Rosewater. Rosewater,
And green tea leaves....

Morningstar
The Down-Below

Chapter 9

The Undine wails. It is a comfort, the sound of the old steamboat retreating across the Acheron back to Abraham's Bluff. On matters of the Prophetess's travels—we all agree—her going is far joyous an occasion than her coming.

"I thought they were not leaving out until morning," I say, thinking of Ewell Day Higgs. Hoping that drop of Redemption lasts until I sneak off to see him again.

Rebecca fusses with one of Salome's tuning pegs. "Hushabye Byrd says idle hands are busy in Satan's workshop. Have we ever even seen that woman's hands without gloves? Maybe she keeps them covered because hooves sprout in place of her fingers."

"Hooves or hands," Willadeene says. "At least she is gone."

Rebecca's room is usually a comfort, the place lit soft with three cut glass oil lamps, a fire in the hearth when there is a chill. There is no peace to be found in Rebecca's room tonight here in the Down-Below, the only floor at Morningstar to be finished before all the Longwood money ran out. There are only a few windows. Remnants of Sun. Hardly any Forever Moon here.

I shiver at the thought of the Up-Up There, the eight-sided skeleton of a great house that never was. A carcass picked clean as Eulalee's. My eyes follow the vines poking through the fractures in my Blue Heron's bedroom walls. I pretend they are lines on a map. Longitudes. Latitudes. Meridians. *Which path will get us from here quick and far?*

Avery steps from the ball gown spilling stars at his ankles, puddling in twinkling pools upon the floor. "Are you sure he did not say more, Leontyne? When you gave my Josiah the feather?"

"Do not change the subject, Avery." Rebecca says. "It is rude."

"It is rude to tell another he is rude, Sister. Have you lost all your manners? Have you turned barbarian," Avery says. "Go on, Leontyne. What did Josiah say? Surely something was shared. Perhaps a remark about my hair? The sound of my voice when I recite poetry?"

"Good grief, Avery. Why you have taken it into your head that this Josiah is for your very own is beyond my comprehension," Rebecca says. "You have always been partial to Lazaruses. What makes this Josiah so unique you would toss him down your favorite feather?" Rebecca pays no mind to Avery standing resplendent in pantalets and laced in their mama's old whale bone corset. She fusses over Salome, giving the violin's purfling a nighttime kiss.

"He is the most special of all the Josiahs that have come around before," Avery says. "Have you gone blind as Sampson? Could you not see?"

"You mean he is the only Josiah to pay you a scintilla of attention." Rebecca lowers Salome into the polished mahogany cradle meant for her dead baby sister. "And how you can think of yourself at a time such as this is deplorable. Do you not care that Leontyne's Eulalee is likely dead in the Doldrums. That Hushabye Byrd is mistress of Morningstar, and now our new mother?"

"Of course, I care. I am only trying my best not to think about any of it. Am I meant to languish for all eternity from unpleasantness?"

Willadeene begins the chore of unlacing Avery's corset, loosening the yellowy cotton laces. Avery is never without a corset, even beneath his clothes meant for boys. It is poor Willadeene who is charged with tying him into and tugging him out of the thing. If any of us are to languish for eternity, it will be our beautiful Willadeene.

"For the love of Moses, Avery. How will ignoring this conundrum do a single one of us any good?" Rebecca gives the cradle a tender rock.

"A tonic for my nerves. That is what it will do, Miss Rebecca High-and-Mighty Longwood. The Prophetess, she will do her best to pirate me away. I just know it." Willadeene tugs the corset's bottom laces, then the top, while Avery pulls hairpins from his coiffure, tossing them to the floor.

Snap. A corset lace breaks.

"You brute," Avery screams.

A gardenia bloom falls from Willadeene.

"Dry rot, Avery. You cannot blame Willadeene for that," I say.

"I will blame Willadeene if I please." The corset slips beneath Avery's pale pink nipples. "Perhaps dry rot leaks from her fingers. She is a haint after all. There could be any manner of diseases she carries." Avery pushes the corset below his knees. He steps out one willowy leg at a time, his narrow feet delicate in a pair of snagged stockings.

Avery's unkindness is often quick receding. This time is no different. His voice turns gentle. "I managed you a bag of malted balls from the Prophetess, and this is how you repay me, Willadeene? Well now, go on and help yourself to them," he says. "Before I feed them to Darkly."

Willadeene is upset. Who can blame her? Avery has been careless of her feelings. With jittery hands, Willadeene pulls a cluster of blueberries growing from her right ear. She looks about as if searching a place to discard them.

"Give them here," Avery says. One after another, he pops a berry in his mouth until they are gone. Willadeene turns away so as not to witness his cruelty. "And you, Leontyne. You have not thanked me for the book." He points over to Rebecca's bed at *Great Expectations* lying next to his *Book of Jubilation and Woe.*

"I am grateful for it," I say, wondering how I will explain to Avery *The Last of the Mohicans* snow. He is particular of his things.

"I know what you are doing, Avery. You are distracting us. From figuring out what to do about Hushabye Byrd," Rebecca says. She looks down at Salome. Gives the cradle another nudge.

From the puddle of his gown, Avery steps, kicking his corset to sail across the room. I think of my sock filled with Redemption flying the sky to land safe with my Ewell Day Higgs. I hope he is not dead yet. I want to hear more of this Alsace-Lorraine. There is something more I need to know. What it is—I cannot remember.

"The business at hand is that you learn to play Vivaldi," Avery says. "You promised. Remember?" He points at the sheet music on the bed.

He longs for his sister to conjure the memory of their Rushworth L. Wintergarden. To play the man alive in the room with the very violin their tutor gave his sister. Only a Jezebel like Avery would muster the indecency to court two men in the same room at the same time: Josiah, and Mr. Rushworth L. Wintergarden.

"Salome is sleeping," Rebecca says. "And that is that."

Avery lifts his hands over his head. Wiggles his long Fiddler Crab fingers. "You are the most ungrateful of them all, Rebecca. More ungrateful than Miss Dry Rot Willadeene, and our Miss One-Handed Leontyne over there." Avery pulls the last three hair pins, tumbling a sky fall of midnight to his shoulders.

Willadeene hurries over to organize Constance Rose Longwood's wedding peignoir, a nightgown of ivory ruffles and lace to drift down over Avery.

"You will do well to remember that if it were not for me, Hushabye Byrd would drown you harpies in the Sea," Avery says.

Woosh. The nightgown fans Longwood smells across the place. *Black licorice drops and peel of Christmastime orange.* And with it, the certainty the Prophetess will never drown me. Not because she favors me. No, I turn her stomach sick. For now, I am safe. Long as she needs me to keep her bottles filled to their corks with Redemption. I am slave to Damascus just as I am a slave to her.

Rare it is my Blue Heron raises her voice, but this time she yells. "If not for you?"

Willadeene jumps. Knocking into the bed. Her malted balls bounce and scatter across the floor. Avery appears stunned as well, squeezing the neckline of his nightgown.

"I am not blind as Sampson, Avery McKinley Longwood," Rebecca says. "I know what you are up to. You mean to play games. To threaten us with Hushabye Buzzard's affection for you. Use it against us."

"Rebecca Rose Longwood, I will not stand accused of treason by the likes of you," Avery says, pointing his finger. He takes a step in his sister's direction.

"There is much worse I could accuse you of than treason," Rebecca says.

"I am guilty of nothing but falling victim to your hateful lies."

"Oh, you are quite guilty, Brother. Mother would be here if not for you."

"I did nothing to Mother," Avery says, looking over at me. "Do not believe her. She lies. She is not who you think she is, Leontyne."

"I am the very person I was yesterday. I will be her tomorrow. And the day after that. And just what might you be?"

"Then you were a liar yesterday, and you will remain one tomorrow. And all the days beyond that." Avery hollers. "Take back what you said about Mother. Take it back."

Avery is the liar of the two, though I think he means no harm. Like me, he imagines things different than they are. The sky blue when it is grey.

Rebecca turns away. Gives the cradle a rock. "You did what you did. There is no undoing it."

"And you did what you did, Sister. We have an agreement between us. I will keep your secret if you keep mine." Avery moves closer to Rebecca. "You are eat through to the center with jealousy. Resentful Mother loved me more than she loved you."

"You saw to that, Brother. That she would love no one more than you."

"And what of Mr. Rushworth L. Wintergarden?" Avery asks. "You have always been jealous of that."

Fiddler Crab has done it now.

Avery pokes his sister in the back. "Look at me when I am talking to you. Or I will tell Leontyne. I will tell her what it is you have done."

Blue Heron turns slow from the cradle, the fireplace flame burning up her eyes. She speaks soft and slow. "Mother is dead. It is much your fault as if you shoved her. Shoved Leontyne and Baby Girl Longwood from the Cupola with your own selfish hands."

Agamemnon! Rebecca's words smash us flat. Choking the air and good Longwood smells from the room.

Avery covers his ears with his hands. "Shut up," he screams.

"It is because you are jealous and selfish that you did it," Rebecca yells. "There is no one more jealous than you."

"I am warning you. Shut up."

"I am warning you," Rebecca hollers.

Tremors work their way from Avery's stocking toes. He is quick. A single swoop. And Salome is snatched from her crib. Avery takes off from the room through the adjoining door into his own.

Chasing the trail of his nightgown, all of us scream holy murder and hell behind him. Avery holds Salome above his head. His pale nipples heave, peeking scandalous and angry beneath the sheer lace of his dead mama's gown.

"Do not do it," Willadeene pleads, tugging at her tasseled leash.

Do it, Avery. Smash her to splinters. Let us get Rushworth L. Wintergarden gone from this place. Rebecca says nothing, standing still as a mollusk, her eyes staring up at Salome.

"If I am a murderer, then I aim to be good at it," Avery yells. "This is the time and place to practice."

"Be gentle with Salome," I say. "Rebecca did not mean the things she said. You are not a murderer." *Perhaps I am the villain wanting Salome dead.*

"There are no murderers here." Willadeene's voice catches in her throat.

Except for me. "Salome has been guilty of nothing but sad and pretty songs," I say, catching glimpse of Darkly at the door, a shock of white fur with one of Willadeene's malted balls in his tiny mouth.

"I would not have done it. I would have kept it to myself had I known what Mother would do." Tears swell the River current sweeping Avery's eyes until spilling their lovely almond banks. I think there is no beauty queer and wondrous as Avery in despair.

What was it Avery said to his mama? What was it Rebecca thinks made their mama do the thing she done?

Rebecca speaks at last. "You did not mean to do it, Avery. I cannot imagine you cruel as that. Remember this, Brother. Your actions do bear consequences. Look at Leontyne. She is your victim—not fully what she was before. None of us are."

"Leontyne is not my fault." Avery's eyes have gone wide. "It is your doing she is without a hand."

"Rebecca did what she had to do," I say. "To save me."

Blue Heron pulls the velvet ribbon from her hair. "A truce," she says, holding it out to Avery.

A present from Mr. Wintergarden in exchange for another gift from him. I am happy she is giving the ribbon away. There is plenty of Mr. Wintergarden remaining. With luck, time will whittle him slow away. When ribbons rot and violin strings break.

"If we are to survive the Prophetess, we must keep our heads about us," Rebecca says. "We must work together. Or else we are doomed."

Avery weeps. "I am sorry. Forgive me," he says. "I would not hurt Salome. I would not hurt you. Or Leontyne." Nice and easy, Avery lowers Salome. His eyes glitter, admiring the ribbon offered in his sister's hand. Blue Heron takes hold of her violin, and Fiddler Crab takes possession of his prize.

Rebecca leans into Avery, confides something into his ear, but I am not close enough to hear. Never am I allowed near when Long-wood secrets spill.

All I can hear are Eulalee's teeth churning and hissing from inside the bottle.

Psss. . . .

Willadeene ... Willadeene. . . .

Psss. . . . Psss. . . .

She is not what you think.

Morningstar
The Down-Below

Chapter 10

Damascus beckons for me through her hump-backed roots, rattling the floorboards, gyrating up the crumbling walls to Avery's bedroom ceiling, to his Eylsium. To where the heavens hang precarious from string: paper stars, half-moons, planets with watercolor rings. Bits of verse and stanza scrawled upon Fiddler Crab's tiny universe.

I extinguish one lamp, then the other, leaving only the flicker from the live oak logs in Avery's fireplace. We are accustom here upon Good Hope with wanton calls from Damascus in the dark, so I am not undone by the sound, nor is Fiddler Crab. Beneath the papery heaven, he sleeps nestled with his *Book of Jubilation and Woe*, Mr. Wintergarden's blue velvet ribbon tied about his neck into a bow.

Willadeene also seems not to be troubled one little bit. She sleeps by Avery's bed upon a pallet on the floor, her gold leash bound tight about his hand. Avery lies there appearing more angel than demon. Rebecca says Avery is selfish and a liar, and I do not disagree. Though he is not all bad, and none of us here are every bit good.

Blue Heron blames Avery for their mama, their sister, and my nub. She is wrong, it was Constance Rose Longwood who went and did this thing she done, and I shall hate her through all the days beyond tomorrow. Much obliged I am to Avery. Without him, Mirabelle might be tossed away by Rebecca to feed the hogs. My Blue Heron is many things wonderful, but she lacks a sentimental streak. Except when it comes to Salome and the tutor her daddy sent away.

Willadeene's toes peek brazen from beneath the blanket. Just what is this business about our Willadeene that Eulalee's teeth were carrying on about? How is Willadeene not what I think? I look down on the pallet at Willadeene sleeping and give her a good study. Where did you come from, friend? Who were you from way back when?

Little do we know of Willadeene. Far as we can reckon, there is not another like her. Scant are my memories after Tribulation Day when she first come our way. Quiet as a rutabaga I lay then, knocked clean from my senses. Busy learning again to walk and talk. Rebecca looked after me right here in Avery's room while sharing her own room unselfishly with her brother.

How Eulalee loved Willadeene, recalling her to be the teensiest of haints, the daintiest of puffer fish swimming the sky she ever did see. There is a ditty Eulalee would sing. The memory pulls at me. Taunts me.

Good glory, glory,

Quick did she grow.

Yes, that is the start of it. Now, how does the rest of it go?

Turning green and womanly,

Queer and seductive,

With them sand dollar toes.

Was Willadeene Eulalee's last thought as she peeled apart in the Doldrums? Did Eulalee love her haint better than she loved me? Or did Eulalee still hold a grudge? Willadeene chose the Longwoods, though it was Eulalee who raised her up from a haintling—suckling, mothering, and cooing her. I cannot fault Willadeene for leaving. Who does not want better? Who would not flee Mama, Damascus, the Marsh, and me, even if it meant being tethered to and held captive by Fiddler Crab for an eternity?

As for Mama loving Willadeene better than me, this is a ripe spot festering still. Sometimes I cannot stomach Willadeene. Sometimes there is no getting enough. Willadeene's face twitches. Her fingers jerk. Toes wiggle unseemly. I suspect she is dreaming. Of what a haint might dream, is a mystery to me, but I hope this. I hope she is not so very lonesome there as she is here. That in her haintly dreams, she escapes her leash. Crosses rivers and seas. Conquers a kingdom in Mesopotamia and crowned Queen Willadeene.

Ewell Day Higgs's song about Alsace-Lorraine riles, echoing sonorous from the rotten cavities of Eulalee's black pearl teeth in my apron's pocket.

Fresh as rain was the smell,
Of my one true love.
Rosewater. Rosewater,
And green tea leaves.

I wrap my hand around the bottle to muffle the sound. Willadeene mumbles in her sleep. "Are you awake, Willadeene?" Her eyes stay shut. Her face twitches. I go to my knees to give a listen.

Deep from her throat comes music. The lap of sea upon a shore. *Pop* and *fizz* of ancient oyster beds. The lonesome call of a shorebird. So close now I am to hear, it would be easy to lean down to kiss her.

Rosewater. Rosewater.... And green tea leaves.... The smell of Willadeene. I inhale the blossoms perfuming and parading as hair. Her malted ball breath—them sweet smelling strawberries tantalizing the lobes of her ears. I am a terrible kind of hungry. I sneak down shameful and nibble one. Willadeene does not stir. Does not wake. Does not indicate she feels a bit of pain. There is only the muttering in her sleep. *He kissed the boy ... kissed the boy ... beneath the moon....*

"What are you doing?" Rebecca asks from the door.

Rebecca has given me a start. I chew, swallowing the last bit of berry, hoping Blue Heron will not make clear what I have done. "Wishing them all good night," I say.

"Come away from there," she says, motioning me into her room.

I nod. She turns away. I pluck the other berry. Drop it into my pocket next to Eulalee's serenading teeth. Another berry already grows from the place I have eaten. I am almost out the door of Avery's room when Willadeene stirs. I turn. Her eyes flutter. In her sleep, she sings, *Alsace-Lorraine*. The name sounds peculiar spoke from her rose petal lips. Thrust red from her mouth by that hibiscus tongue. The name renders to nonsense the way a word is prone when spoken again and again.

Willadeene falls quiet—remains sleeping. I follow my Blue Heron from Avery's room into hers. Rebecca's hair, brushed to high luster, falls halcyon in jet waves to her hips. I must look a fright. My nest of frizzy towhead hair. Strawberry seeds wedged between my teeth. With my fingernail, I work to pry them loose while Blue Heron is not looking.

Rebecca smooths her pale cotton nightgown. Far modest than Avery's, the gown rises high up on her long, slender neck. She pats the bed with her willowy-fingered hand next to the copy of *Great Expectations*.

"Take your boots off and have a seat here," she says. "It is a heavenly wonder you are still able to stand."

Sweet mercy. A first of firsts. Blue Heron is particular of her bedchamber. Before she might change her mind, I plunk down on the floor and tug at a boot with my one, good hand.

"Let me help," Rebecca says, coming over, lowering herself to her knees. The first one slides easy. The second is a bit more of a chore.

"Your sock," she says. "It has gone missing."

Ewell Day Higgs. She would be full-up with disgust to know I give it to the likes of him, rolling up a bottle of Redemption and tossing it down a Sinner's hole. "For the sweet life of me, I cannot imagine where it got off to," I say.

"Are you sure your mother is gone?" Rebecca asks.

Eulalee. Dead in the Doldrums. I do not want to think about it, but there is no way around it. I imagine my words threading the eye of a needle, pulling taut through my gizzard, up my throat. "Mama is gone," I say. I poke my finger in my mouth. Run it over my tongue. Only now does it feel true. Final. And I do a thing I work hard to never do, cry in front of my Rebecca.

While others might wilt from tears, Rebecca, she goes stiff. Please know she is not without the means to comfort. Her heart brims with love, only it is a great chore for her to show it. I do not blame her. She had to be the strong one on account of her mama and brother. Both of them—near abouts worthless and frail, delicate as Avery's corset laces—always one good pull from a *snap*.

"Forgive me," I say. Wiping one eye with the hem of my apron and then the other.

Rebecca speaks softly. "Whatever for?"

"For all this carrying on," I say.

We face each other. Rebecca is on her knees, and I am sitting on the floor. Two lamps sputter and dim. The third burns low. And Damascus moans up through the floor. *Leontyne … Leontyne…. Come back here to me.*

Rebecca looks over to the cradle. I crave her to look upon me the way she studies her violin. "We are both without our mothers," Rebecca says at long last. "But I lost mine before she was even dead."

Blue Heron. Blue Heron. Sleek and tall. I will not contradict Rebecca, but my Eulalee, my own mama, also was lost to me before she tore apart dead.

"Tell me again, Leontyne. What was it that ailed the Great Redeemer these last few years?" Rebecca leans forward. Crawls graceful as a bobcat. Sits next to me on the floor.

Ashamed I am, of being ashamed of my own mama, her tending Damascus. Catching good-for-nothing haints in that gluttonous tree. I have been careful of keeping covered the life I share with Eulalee on the Marsh. "Took leave of her senses," I say. "I suppose there is only so much living a body is meant to do. So much remembering a head can bear until it falls into ruins."

No, I will not burden Rebecca with the particulars of tending the tree. That what happened to Eulalee is bound to happen to me. If ever I carved a warning sign to nail to a post, it would be this. *Beware. Tending the dead kills the living*. But what good are signs if no one pays them one bit of mind? Eulalee and her mama—and way back to the first of us Skyes—they all knew the crux of it. Still, they did what they did. *Responsibility* is what Eulalee said. *Tradition. And legacy.* To heck and hell with that, I say. I want to live.

Tingles and bliss. Rebecca's leg touches mine, and I suspect this is a gesture she musters to comfort me. I am grateful for whatever she gives. *Please Blue Heron, do it again.*

"She will be coming back around soon. That Hushabye Byrd," Rebecca says. "In those *clompety-clomp* shoes."

"I reckon she will," I say. Envious I am of Avery's gift for not bothering himself with matters he thinks inconvenient. How I wish I could sweep this business of Miss Hushabye Byrd to the trash heap. Live here forever in the Down-Below on the wide-planked floor with my Rebecca.

"Will you be ready?"

Will I be ready? I am abandoned, lonesome and shivering here at the end of Rebecca's question, her leg flush against mine. How this can be my sole burden is lost to me. "What do you mean?"

"Redemption," she says. "Are you able to make it? Do you know the way?"

If only she knew what she asks of me, would she? "We should all be ready for what is to come," I say.

"Leontyne, I am worried for you. For all of us, if you do not know how to make it."

Eulalee's teeth carry on in my apron pocket. Rebecca seems not to notice. *Psst.... Psst.... Selfishhh.... Girrlll....*

"I am not selfish," I say.

"Of course not. That is not what I mean. I could never think you selfish. Not you, Leontyne."

"Forgive me," I say, "I am not myself." How would I even know if I was or was not myself? There is so much from before I cannot recall.

"I can help you," Rebecca says. "You do not have to do it alone. Just tell me what to do. And I will do it."

How I can love my Blue Heron more, right here and right now, is unthinkable. If only she would allow me to wrap my arms about her. I would squeeze and squeeze. Love her up until the Forever Moon tuckered and cracked apart into the Marsh and Sea.

"It is beneath you," I say. "I would not let you do it."

"Then you know how Redemption is made? You can do it? The recipe is written down?"

"I am afraid so. I do know how the stuff is made. But the way is not written. It is kept right here," I say, tapping my temple with my nub.

Rebecca looks up to the ceiling, her dark-river eyes staring into the vines forking across the cracked plaster. She lays her pretty head back onto the floor.

"There is another way out of this mess," I say, inspecting the vines. "Without bottling up a sorry drop of Redemption."

"What way is that?"

I arrange myself on the floor with my head next to Blue Heron's. "We can run away from this place. Miles and miles from Good Hope."

"Where on earth would we go?"

"Anywhere and everywhere," I say, pointing up to the map of vines. "See there? That is the Great Wall of China. We could skip along the top of it until we run clean out of stone. Then—we take off for cooler weather to Iceland. Ride the backs of beluga whales beneath other midnight suns. Would that not be nice? Imagine. Just imagine the Aurora Borealis, Rebecca. Gleaming above us while we sleep."

"I would love to go all those places with you," Rebecca says. "But what would we do? We have no money. And how can we be sure what is out there? We have never been anywhere but here?"

"You could play your violin in every orchestra in every land. Folks would come from all around to hear you make Salome sing."

"And Avery? Is there another place in this world other than Good Hope meant for him?"

Of all the boys I have read in books. Of all the Sinners, Lazaruses, and Josiahs who have come this way, never have I heard of or met another boy like Avery. "He will be safe here with our Willadeene."

"Only if Hushabye Byrd is dead. And Father is lying alongside her. You know he would not survive the two of them. Nor Willadeene."

Eulalee's teeth *rattle* and *clack. Psst.... Psst.... Selfishhh.... Girlll.* I work my tongue at my teeth managing to poke a seed loose. "You are right. What could I be thinking?" I am being selfish. Eulalee's teeth are rotten with the truth. I do not wish harm upon Willadeene or Fiddler Crab, though I imagine there is no killing Willadeene, but she would most certain be cast deeper to misery if left here alone. That is not so different from dying. In the end, I reckon I love them both. Avery and Willadeene.

"Redemption for now. And I will help you," Rebecca says. "Until we figure a plan."

I stare at the ceiling, following the rivers and paths of the map above. "Point to a place," I say. "When you think we are ready, that is where we ought go. Any place. Any place at all. You, Salome, Darkly, and me." *And Mirabelle stowed away in her can.*

Blue Heron points a willowy finger. "There," she says. "To the right of Camelot. Beyond Shangri-La. Right there off the coast of the Indian Ocean. Do you see? That is the place I want to be."

"That is not right, dear Sister." Avery says from the door. "That is not the Indian Ocean. It is the Ephesians Sea. Just there, that is the island of Cherubim. Look how beautiful it is. Leontyne-Leontyne, listen here." Avery places his finger to his lips. *"Shh....* And this is a secret you can never tell. Though it is not on any map ordinary folk can see, right in the middle of Cherubim is the once great place called Seraphim House. Have mercy, it is held up by marble columns looking every bit like angel wings."

Seraphim House. Avery makes mention of it time and time again. The birthplace and family home of Mr. Rushworth L. Wintergarden. It is the very place Avery most wants to go. I imagine he has sketched renderings. Penned poems of it within his *Book of Jubilation and Woe.*

"Leontyne, you must promise not to tell," Avery says. "Swear it."

"I swear," I say. "Cross my heart, I will not die. Haunt the sky with lonesome eyes."

Avery has conjured Rushworth L. Wintergarden into the room. I see the waves reflected in Fiddler Crab and Rebecca's eyes. They are both swimming the Ephesians Sea while I am marooned here on land.

"Willadeene is dreaming," Avery says, tossing three petit point pillows from the bed onto the floor. "How can anyone sleep with that infernal commotion?"

Eulalee's teeth rattle. *Kkkk ... isss ... tha ... bbboy....*

Avery takes *Great Expectations* from the bed. He wedges his slender, pale foot between Rebecca and me. "Scootch," he says. "Little piggies-little piggies, let me in. I want Leontyne to read to me."

"Avery, leave us be," Rebecca says. "There is hardly any light left but the fire. She will go blind reading in the dim."

"There is plenty of light," Avery says. "Please, Leontyne. Pretty-pretty please. I will never ask again. If you do it just this once."

Again and again is all there is, and he has never and will never stop asking. "Okay," I say. "But you will have to help me hold it."

"It is the least I can do."

I take one side of the book. Avery takes the other. For pages, Fiddler Crab is quiet as I read from Dickens, Rebecca's naked foot against Avery's, and his—against mine.

"Seraphim House," Avery says. "It is not such an easy place to get to."

"Hush up, Avery. Let Leontyne read," Rebecca says.

Avery is quiet for a teensy bit more. I continue reading. "The marshes were just a long, black horizontal line then, as I stopped to look after him; and the River was just another horizontal line, not nearly so broad or yet so black…."

"The Ephesians Sea is wrought with pirates. But that is not nearly the most frightful part," Avery says, interrupting again. "There are piranhas the size of dolphins hungry enough to gobble a grown man whole. Can you imagine the horror of such a beast jumping into your boat? But Cherubim is so lush and green if you make it across. And Seraphim house, even in decline, is sublime."

From Avery's room, Willadeene's murmurs grow louder.

He kissed the boy … kissed the boy….

Beneath the moon….

Damascus drinks from the Marsh, trembling the ceiling. Down come bits of plaster. Down-down upon us.

A Seraphim House snow….

Morningstar

The Down-Below and The Up-Up There

Chapter 11

Calamity.

My heart gallops, rattling me awake.

"Calamity," Avery shrieks, stepping over me, the train of his mama's wedding night peignoir tickling my face.

I blink frantic at the ceiling until I make clear the Ephesians Sea.

"For the love of Moses, Avery. What is wrong with you?" Rebecca hollers.

"The Up-Up There," Avery says, his narrow feet slapping the boards. He grabs hold of his sister, yanks her from the floor. "I have just come from there. Follow me. Come see."

"It is the middle of the night," Rebecca says, wrestling herself free from Avery.

"Only it is not," Avery shrieks. He shovels his foot beneath my hip. "Get up, Leontyne. Come with me."

Willadeene holds Darkly wild-eyed at the threshold, her robe scared open, evergreen bosoms terrified and peeping out. "What has come? Who is here?" she asks, purple hydrangea petals tumbling from her head.

"Pianissimo," Rebecca says, her index finger pressing to her lips. There is no soothing Avery to quiet. No calming any of us to lay back down.

Avery grabs hold of his sister. Drags her barefooted from the room to the stairs. I take Willadeene by the hand, pulling her and Darkly behind me. A straight shot. A curve. Another few stairs, and we are in the gallery.

Fiddler Crab turns loose his sister. Hurries to the center of the place in a pool of Forever Moon's gleam. Up to the Cupola he raises both arms. "The Sun," he says. "Gone."

"You are talking out of your head," Rebecca says.

"I assure you I am not. I am right here. Right here in my very own head."

Willadeene's hand trembles in mine. "It is still night," I say. "That is all." Fiddler Crab is right. Something is wrong.

Avery's words roil wild in his throat. "Calamity," he screams.

"Take hold of yourself, Avery," Rebecca says. "You are fresh from dreams."

"It is well past cock's crow. I am certain of it. I feel it in my bones." With the airs of a grand lady stepping careful from a coach, Avery lifts his hem. He paces, his naked feet thumping heartbeats on the floor. "Calamity."

"Stand still, Avery. This is easy enough of a mystery to solve." Rebecca turns, pushing her hair over her shoulders and holds out her hand. "Willadeene. Hand me Pocket Watch."

Willadeene's hand is sodden from nerves, the smell of fresh rain and earth leaking from her haintly pores. She unravels her jittery hand from mine, pulls the watch from her robe's pocket. Out comes the watch and riot of flittery moths. Rebecca flicks the watch open with her nail. Her eyes blink. She nibbles her bottom lip. She waits a moment. Pulls the watch closer to see.

"What time is it?" Avery screeches, standing still, dropping the hem of his peignoir to the floor.

Eulalee refuses to be quiet. Refuses to be still. *Ssss.... Sssummer-time ... rain....*

Rebecca places the watch to her ear. "It *ticks* and *tocks*," she says. "Only something must be a matter."

"I have told you what is the matter," Avery says. "The Sun is gone."

"Silly talk," Rebecca says. "There is a reason it is still dark."

"What time is it?" Willadeene asks, a smatter of rose petals drifting from her head. "What does the clock say?" A sorry shame it is Willadeene has not been allowed to learn numbers and words.

"8:15. But it is hardly morning," Rebecca says.

"8:15 in the evening was hours ago," Avery says. "I know what I know. We are most assuredly beyond dawn."

"Then a storm is brewing," Rebecca says. "The clouds so heavy and dark … we cannot see the Sun. Maybe an eclipse. Or this watch has gone kaput.

"An eclipse?" Avery asks. "When have we known such a thing?"

"A storm, then," Willadeene says, squeezing Darkly to her chin.

Eulalee sputters. *Greeeen … tttea … leavesss….*

"Something is wrong," I say, careful with my words. Not wanting to stir Avery's hysteria. *Morning has come. Still, it is dark out.* And this is not the only thing that sits crooked. Willadeene, she is off-putting, only I cannot figure out why. She shivers, and I shiver with her. She pulls at her blossom hair, and I resist yanking my own.

There is a rumble, the sound coming way down deep from inside Willadeene. How can it be that I feel what Willadeene feels? Avery's lips flutter. Rebecca's lips seethe, and I cannot hear a thing either of them says. Willadeene is all there is, has taken hold of my senses. Turned me topsy-turvy.

Fiddler Crab scurries in circles. Points to the Cupola where the sun ought shine, the tail of his nightgown skimming moon puddles.

"Calamity," Willadeene hollers.

Faster and faster Fiddler Crab churns the floor, his fingers worrying the blue velvet ribbon tied about his throat in a bow. Down from Willadeene's lungs comes distant thunder, and off spinning with Fiddler Crab she goes.

I turn dizzy chasing the haint's leash with my eyes. Willadeene's worry takes up alongside mine like swarms of honeybees jailed in two jars *clacking* against the other. Flashes of the room come to me from yonder place Willadeene twirls, as if her haint eyes are now my windows, my view of the Gallery captured in panicked blinks of her butterfly lashes. *Where do I begin? Where does Willadeene end?*

Bam.

There is banging from outside against the two great doors. *Bam.... Blam....* Sparrows startle in their nests. Willadeene and Avery go still, grabbing hold of the other, my poor Darkly squished and squirming between them. Then there is quiet. Then there is not.

"Perhaps it is Josiah come back to see about me. To bring back my feather," Avery whispers.

Rebecca places a finger to her lips. "Don't be a fool, Avery."

"Jane Austen?" *Rebecca's pistol.* "Where is she?" I whisper.

Rebecca points to the Down-Below and whispers back. "With Salome."

"Agamemnon," Avery hisses. "What good is she down there, if it is not Josiah but a murderer at the door?"

Rose petals flee Willadeene's scalp and sprinkle the floor. I smell our haint from here. *Petrichor.* I feel the honeybee buzz and sting of her nerves.

Eulalee's teeth taunt from my pocket. *Ssss ... sss ... ummertime ... ummertime ... rrrr ... ainnn....*

Blam.... Blam....

"Who is there?" Rebecca asks lackadaisical, tapping Pocket Watch to her chest. As if every day there are knocks upon the great, carved doors of Morningstar. "Leontyne," she whispers, stretching each word slow, her dark eyes aflicker. "Go ... fetch ... Jane ... Austen...."

Bam.... Bam.... Bam....

"Knock all you like. We are not in the habit here of ushering wayfaring strangers through the doors," Rebecca says. "Introduce yourself."

How Rebecca is not terrified is miles beyond me. *My Blue Heron, sleek and tall. I love you best of all.*

We wait. And wait. Avery and Willadeene's eyes flit wild. Eulalee's teeth thrum inside her bottle. Now comes scratching. Clawing. A fury of beasts shredding the doors, a commotion so great Avery and Willadeene open their mouths to tear loose screams.

Agamemnon!

Rip.

Tear.

Slash.

Eternities come and go. Waves smash the shore.

Now quiet.... More infernal quiet, and I am near abouts turned mad from the hush. So unstitched by my own uprising terror, I no longer feel the stinging frenzy of Willadeene's honeybee buzz. A melancholy laughter stirs the quiet, the noise echoing hollow up one side of the eight-sided house, stealing through the crumbling mortar joints. Eerie whistles. Desolate moans. Cackles.

"Make it stop," Avery screams.

Rebecca glides to me. Grips firm my arm. "Jane Austen," she says, shifting her eyes to the stairs leading to the Down-Below. She hollers above the gruesome din toward the door. "State your business. I will not ask you again."

Halfway across the room, on my way to fetch Jane Austen, a beastly voice speaks.

"The Great Redeemer," it says. The dreadful voice strangles with croup, echoing gurgles against the bricks. It hollers out grisly, "Idumea. Idumea." Slow and decrepit it sings, turning my stomach sick.

Am I born to die?
To lay this body down!
And must my trembling spirit fly
Into a world unknown?

Idumea. I know now. Clear as clear. It is a Sinner that comes knocking the doors. This one must be a Hushabye Byrd Sinner, has heard the Prophetess warble *Idumea*, the hymn I hear tell she sings before unraveling her Prophecy of Gloom. The caterwaul ebbs. There is but a moment of hush. Pandemonium comes next. Scratches. Howling. Squealing hinges.

"Make it stop," Avery screams.

With a thundercrack, the doors shoot open.

Idumea … Idumea.…

Morningstar
The In-Between

Chapter 12

Wind sweeps the place, invisible whirly winds spinning putrid, as if all the rats in all the world lay dead beneath the house. Sparrows flee the walls. Willadeene, Avery, and I scream, pressing the backs of our hands to our noses. I open my mouth to holler for us all to run. I freeze, unable to believe I see what I see, the silhouette of a full-grow'd Sinner and child holding hands.

Next to the Pyramid of Giza, my Blue Heron stands. How easy she breathes in all this stink. If anything might undo her, it will be this Sinner child seen through her dark-river eyes. Sinners come old. They come young. Never are they younglings yanked so fresh from the teat.

In the shadowy distance, the Sinners' eyes glow eerie and golden, a sign these two have hunted and caught Redemption a long while now. The stench billows, boiling tears in my own eyes, slithering poisoned rivers down my cheeks.

"You are not welcome here," Rebecca says.

Hand-in-hand, the Sinners emerge from the chilly murk. Their feet, hard as horse hooves, drum lamentations upon the floor, an alternating hollow and heavy knock. *I-du-mea. I-du-mea.*

Avery and Willadeene ease back, Darkly squeezed between them.

"Can you not hear me?" Rebecca asks. "I am speaking to you."

The Sinners stop, letting go the other's filthy hand. *Creak* and *pop*, they throw back their heads, sniffing the air like coyotes. Wonderment confounds their sunken faces, both of them stupefied by the vine covered bricks, the *chirruping* sparrows, and vast, empty space between us all and the great Up-Up There.

The Sinners lock gaze upon me, no doubt detecting the faint smell of Sarah Fig stowed away in dried drippings on my hem. Leaking from Eulalee's teeth through her bottle's cork.

The boy comes first, loping towards me, fidgeting with something beneath his coverall bib. "Great Redeemer?" he asks.

Eulalee's teeth thrum in my pocket "I am Leontyne," I say. *The Great Redeemer is dead.*

The boy looks upon my tumble of wild, towhead hair. "Angel?" He stretches the word, the dimple on his cheek peeking sweet through the grime. He smiles, raw lips pulling back across two rows of rotting teeth.

I want to yank the tincture bottle of Eulalee's own teeth from my pocket and show her this thing she has done. *Look, Mama. Look. Is this the Heirloom of which you speak? My dowry? My legacy?*

The boy has come close enough now I behold the queer spell Redemption has cast upon the poor child's eyes. Like a goat's, his pupils have gone from circles to rectangles, turning the odd look of him stranger. Through moon puddles, the full-grow'd Sinner follows, his off-kilter stride thumping, *I-du-mea. I-du-mea.* Redemption has carved this Sinner's back crooked. But still he is dangerous. A good head taller than the rest of us in the room.

"Where is she," he asks, nose twitching the air. "If you ain't her, then where is the good and great, goddamned Redeemer?" His eyes, like the Sinner-child's, have turned goat. Still, there is something not all together unpleasant. I might be sure in better light that they were lovely once.

"The Great Redeemer is indisposed," Rebecca says. "Know this. She will not take kindly to you corrupting your son."

The Sinner's head turns and creaks over to my Blue Heron, his goat eyes affixed to me. After his wobbling head is done turning, his goat eyes creep slow and tricky to where she stands over by the Pyramid of Giza.

"Don't matter what Miss Almighty thinks," he says. "Her job ain't judging. It's saving." He rakes his long, greasy nails through the Sinner-child's thinning hair, curly strands coming loose between his fingers.

"Saving a soul is not cheap," Rebecca says. "It is a simple matter of commerce. This for that." She opens and closes the face of Willadeene's Pocket Watch. "From the look of things, you have neither a this nor a that."

The Sinner smiles a mile of glistening, cankerous gums. Nary a rotten tooth pokes about in his head, not even a chip of one dangles lonesome by a thread. "Got me that boy," he says. "And got me this." He thrusts his long, milky tongue from his mouth, wiggling it unseemly. "If the Great Redeemer makes me feel good. Then I'm obliged to make her feel right good, too. Or you. Or any somebody that needs tending." He smiles gruesome beyond Rebecca, his head turning on his rickety neck over to Avery and Willadeene.

The full-grow'd Sinner takes off toward Fiddler Crab and Willadeene, his face twitching. Gums grinding. A fit of wind birls across the threshold, past the open doors, stirring the reek of spoiling Sinner. The smell of decaying rats grows stronger, so fierce my tongue bloats—the vile taste leaking uncontrollable into drool.

"Leave them be," Rebecca says. "Not another step more."

Gentle, the Sinner-child reaches up, lacing his clammy fingers through mine. I flinch, almost pull away. Until I see his dimple, that tiny shallow of nothing near about sawing my heart clean through. With his other dirty hand, the boy strokes tender at his coverall bib. His mouth moving as if sucking a sourball candy.

He keeps moving, the full-grow'd Sinner making a wide berth from Rebecca, his humpback and jutted jaw tracing grotesque shadows on the floor. Wild-eyed, Avery and Willadeene retreat backward, both clutching Darkly until there is not another step of floor to tread, until they are trapped between two niches in the wall.

The full-grow'd Sinner beholds Willadeene. He ratchets his head one way, his goat eyes creeping the other. "In the name of sweet creation. What the hell is you?"

Rebecca leaves the Pyramid of Giza, her pale, bare feet quick on the floor. "Away from there," she says, from the first step of stairs, opening and closing Pocket Watch's lid.

"I asked you a question," the full-grow'd Sinner says. "What is you?"

"Her name is Willadeene," Rebecca says, her voice raising short of a holler. "Now, you go on. Leave her be."

To the rhythm of *Iduema*, the full-grow'd Sinner sings Willadeene's name off-key again and again.

"Willa," the child says, smiling and squeezing my hand. "Willa... Willa...."

Redemption must still run the full-grow'd Sinner's blood, for a desirous look burns wicked upon his sunken face. He ogles Willadeene's haintly pleasures, kneading his sore-riddled hands below his waist.

"Away," Rebecca yells, but the Sinner pays no mind.

The Sinner squats. From Willadeene's sand dollar toes, he begins to sniff, moving his way up to her knees.

"Get away," I yell, stepping forward, dragging the child a few feet along with me across the floor.

The child, oddly strong, holds tight my hand. "Play time," he says, shaking his balding head, jerking my arm for me to stay put.

The full-grow'd Sinner reaches up and yanks Willadeene's robe open. She stays still as a terrified creature can stay. Avery turns his head away, tucking Darkly beneath his chin. If we were not all in peril, I would turn my own eyes to the floor. Instead, I unravel my fingers from the boy's and cover his eyes to keep him from seeing.

Magnolia and peach rose petals fluster from Willadeene's scalp onto the Sinner's shoulders, accumulating in fragrant springtime heaps on the floor. Up between Willadeene's legs, the Sinner runs foul his hand to the place the velvet daylily blooms. *Lord, help me.* I feel it, too, his scabby hand between my thighs as he has his way with Willadeene. How is it I can feel what Willadeene feels?

"Enough," Rebecca screams. "Do you aim to revile the Great Redeemer?"

The Sinner stops. Pulls his hand away. He turns toward Rebecca, those goat eyes lollygagging behind. Slow, he eases from the floor, his earthworm tongue wriggling from his dreadful mouth laying a slimy trail upon Willadeene's cheek.

"Take me to her," the Sinner says, face twitching. Sniffing his fingers. "And I will ask forgiveness."

Rebecca turns, climbs a few stairs. Stops. "Follow me," she says. "To the Up-Up There."

My Blue Heron does not look up to the Moon. Only points to the Cupola. What dangerous game she plays, I cannot be sure. I want to call out to her. Tell her to stop. But there is no telling Rebecca what to do and when.

The Sinner licks the air with his tongue. Takes off toward the stairs, Willadeene-flowers scattering from his shoulders to the floor.

The boy runs for the man. "Papa," he hollers.

I am quicker, grabbing hold of the boy by his dirty collar. "Stay here," I say.

"Listen to that Angel gal. She's a pretty bird. I'll come see about her next." The man points down to the boy. "I need you to keep watch down yonder. Do what I done taught you if they run stray." He flinches and twitches. Squirms his vile tongue in the air. "Mind the boy," he says. "He's a might more dangerous than he looks."

Across the way, Avery stirs from the niche. Comforts Willadeene. Closes her robe. Wipes away the daisy petal tears stuck to her cheeks.

The boy stares up at me. Smiles his ruined smile. That dimple nudges at my heart. And I reckon he might be as fine of a boy that ever was if things were different. If he did not bear the woe of a daddy rambling the stairs warbling *Iduema* on his foolhardy way to see the Great Redeemer. I look down. Imagine the boy is mine for keeping. His pupils turned back to circles. His irises bragging a dazzle of cornflower blue.

"What is your name?" I ask. First thing I must do is trim the boy's long, filthy nails. File them down to a less murderous length.

The boy shrugs, twiddling again at something beneath his bib. Right then. Right there. I decide to call the boy Theodore Laurence after a character from a book called *Little Women*. That is a good, sensible name for a boy.

"What you got there?" I ask, glancing up to see about Rebecca.

"Sugar," he says. From beneath his coverall bib, he pulls a chick. A tiny thing so grimy, I have no way of knowing what color the poor babe might be. The piteous thing blinks those teensie watermelon seed eyes back at me.

"You call the chick, Sugar?"

The boy nods.

"Suits him," I say. From just a gander, it does not. The chick is more shades of mudpuddle than sugar, and our acquaintance is so early on, I have no way of knowing if Theodore Laurence's chick is the gentle sort. Theodore Laurence smiles proud. With my heart of hearts, I wish the boy could see clear a way to smile without showing every last one of his rotten teeth. It is a chore imagining them anything less dreadful than they are.

"Leontyne?" Avery whispers from across the way. "What is Rebecca doing?" Avery takes Willadeene by the hand. The two of them creep a little closer, Darkly tucked in the crook of Avery's arm. "Does she mean to get herself killed?"

I cannot imagine a thing worse than my Blue Heron gone. "Hush with that crazy talk," I say. "She knows what she is doing."

"And she always means what she does," Avery says.

Willadeene whispers. "Cover the boy's ears."

"His name is Theodore Laurence." With my hand and nub, I cover his squalid ears. *After his nails are trimmed, I will go to work cleaning these ears.*

Willadeene wipes a petal from her cheek. Scrubs at the place the Sinner licked. "I wager she means to lock him in the Celestial Hall of Books."

Avery gasps. "How dare she," he says. "Not with my books. That shrew."

The Celestial Hall of Books. Right off, I am jealous that Sinner is allowed a place I am not. "Be quiet, Avery. And just where do you propose she put him?" I ask.

"I do not care where she locks that stinking Sinner. Long as it is far from my things. This is every bit your fault, Miss Leontyne Skye."

Willadeene looks down at the boy covering her nose with her hand. "What shall we do with Theodore Laurence?"

Never before have Sinners made it this far. Never before have they walked through the doors. As for the matter of Theodore Laurence, I guess he will live down by the Marsh with my Darkly and me. I imagine Rebecca might love him in time.

The boy grins. "Willa-Willa."

From the stairs, the full-grow'd Sinner sets off singing louder than before.

Am I born to die?

To lay this body down!

Rebecca is farther ahead on the winding stairs from the Sinner. A starling flies from a nest. The Sinner is quick. Snatches the bird from the air.

"Pretty bird," the Sinner says, snapping the starling's neck. He tosses the bird down-down. Through invisible clouds of stink and moon beam. The sad thing tumbles, the sinner sniffing and licking his fingers.

Plunk. Pretty Bird lands atop the Pyramid of Giza.

"Uh-oh," Theodore Laurence says, tucking Sugar back beneath his coverall bib. The boy is probably seven or eight, and still, he pokes his thumb into his simple mouth to suck.

On the tread of the stairs, the Sinner's hardened feet knock in time with his singing.

Rebecca steps the last step into the Up-Up There. "We do not have all night," she says. "Best get along and hurry. The Great Redeemer hardly has time for the likes of you. And the starlings—they are not yours to kill." Rebecca steps beyond the landing. Dissolves from view.

The Sinner plods up the last of the stairs. Across the landing he lopes along where there is no rail, his footfall drumming. *I-du-mea.... I-du-mea....*

Rebecca calls from the shadows, her words tumbling down the beams and bricks. "Stay where you are," she says. "And sing for the Great Redeemer. Then I shall take you to where she dwells."

Near abouts undone am I with worry. I sort my nerves, petting Theodore Laurence's head, his greasy curls coming loose.

"If that Sinner does not kill Rebecca. I will," Avery says. "If she lets him lay but one vile finger upon a single book of mine. I will write it down. I will. I will." he says. "Inside *Jubilation and Woe.*"

The Sinner sings.

Soon as from earth I go
What will become of me?

From the Up-Up There comes a stampede upon the floor. "Pianissimo," Rebecca screams.

Thud. Here comes the Sinner howling down, a steaming, stinking rain. Theodore Laurence snatches away. Looks up. Snorts the air. The long-long way the Sinner falls, bare heels ripping vines. Brushing wings of sparrows. Skimming the side of the chandelier.

"Pretty Bird," the boy hollers, clapping his hands.

Thunk and *thwack.*

The boy keeps clapping until he realizes it is not Pretty Bird but his daddy cracked open like an egg—the full-grow'd Sinner's goat-eye popped from its socket and flirting with the floor.

Theodore Laurence sets out howling for Willadeene. He leaps. Knocks her to the floor. Latches on with his rotten teeth and filthy nails.

Rip.

Tear.

Slash.

"Theodore Laurence," I scream. Bits and bobs of Willadeene scatter the boards. I try to pull him off, but he is ferocious. "Avery, help me. Please...." I grab hold of Willadeene's leash. Manage to wrap it about his neck with my hand and pull. "He is killing her."

From my pocket, Eulalee's teeth roll in her bottle across the floor. *Pretty bird. Pretty bird,* they sing. Avery takes hold of the leash with both hands. Pulls along with me. Forever and ever we tug. Until the rope goes slack. Until my Theodore Laurence is dead.

Pretty bird. Pretty bird...

"Look what you did," Avery says, turning loose the curtain tie. "Look." Willadeene lay ravaged, bleeding lovely pine tar rivers onto the floor, petrichor and rosewater seeping from her evergreen pores.

Over and over, Eulalee's teeth stutter, *Ssss.... Sssummertime ... Rain....* Until at last I know the thing she wants me to know. *Dear God.* Mama's rotten teeth have been trying to tell me all along. Why did I not listen? *Summertime.... Summertime.... Rain.* Our Willadeene once belonged to my Ewell Day Higgs. She is his Alsace-Lorraine.

Fresh as rain was the smell,

Of my one true love.

Blue Heron looks down upon us here assembled in a heap, drowned in the ocean of Forever Moon gleam. My poor, sweet, murdering Theodore Laurence and his golden goat-eyes. His Sugar squashed flat and dead.

Avery weeps. Willadeene cries her daisy-petal tears. And there is nothing left for me to do but join them.

From the Up-Up There, Blue Heron opens and closes Pocket Watch. "Pianissimo," she calls down-down sweet and tender.

Pianissimo....

The Forest

Chapter 13

There is no closing Theodore Laurence's eyes. Not with nickels, or prayers, or dallops of candle wax dripped and pressed gentle with my thumb. Them queer looking eyes keep staring mesmerized into the salt-pruned branches of the passing live oak trees, as if compelled in the grip of some dark magic spell.

Alsace-Lorraine.... Alsace-Lorraine.... Over and over, I sing it silent to keep my mind from this business of murder and death while I watch Willadeene carrying the lantern, her leash arranged tidy by Avery so it does not drag the leaves. She walks ahead of the wheelbarrow Avery has nicknamed Sweet Chariot. She stumbles. The rusted wheel Rebecca and I steer knocks a stump. The handle slips from my aching hand, and there goes Pretty Bird bouncing from Sweet Chariot onto a carpet of live oak leaves. *Uh-oh. Pretty Bird,* I half expect Theodore Laurence to call out from where he lay cozy in his daddy's no-count lap. But it is Avery who speaks out in place of the dead.

"Look what you did, Leontyne" he says. "We shall never get to the River at this pace. With Willadeene's lollygagging and you turning loose the wheel. I suppose we shall have to take up here like monkeys. Make the Forest our home. Spend our days swinging and screeching in the trees."

It is a chore living here any day on Good Hope with Avery Longwood, and I sure do not want to endure it dangling by a monkey's tail high up in a crookedy-branched tree. "I am sorry," I say. "These Sinners may be nothing but burden and bone. But they are a fright heavier than they look." *The dead always are.* Write that down in your precious *Book of Jubilation and Woe*, Avery McKinley Longwood. "And let me be," I say, pulling away the string of my apron Avery holds.

Rebecca puts down her side of Sweet Chariot, turns to look back at Avery following behind. "You are welcome to take Leontyne's place or mine," she says from beneath the wide brim of her spiteful straw hat, the one keeping Forever Moon and me from her pretty face.

I think of Eulalee and her cornhusk hat. *Poor Eulalee. Poor Pretty Bird. Poor Sugar. Poor Theodore Laurence there in his dead daddy's lap.* I wish now I had not left my Darkly back at Morningstar tucked deep-deep down in the Pyramid of Giza for safe keeping.

"I have plenty more than I can manage, thank you very much." Avery says. Through the black netted veil fastened in place with sparkling hairpins of shell and paste, Avery looks down at his *Book of Jubilation and Woe.* Presses it like a sleeping baby to his chest. "I am undecided as to the particulars of which elegy I shall speak."

There is no question he will read "On Death" by Keats. From this ritual, Fiddler Crab does not stray.

"I just assume leave these Sinners here," Rebecca says. "Until there is nothing left of them but filthy toenails and coverall scraps."

Avery lifts his wrist loop higher, shaking the leaves from the train of his black beaded gown. "You are a heartless rogue, Rebecca Longwood."

"Better heartless than a fool."

My Blue Heron, like her daddy, does not take kind to suffering inconveniences toppled upon her by Sinners, unless they drop so close and dead to the house we might smell them. She only indulges Avery because it is easier than not. We all do. Please do not think my Rebecca cruel. She is practical, and I find no fault in that. Where would we be without her?

I still cannot work that one darn Willadeene seed free from my teeth. My stomach gurgles. How I can be so hungry with murder on my hands and Eulalee's teeth singing in my apron is a quandary. *One bite of Willadeene is never enough.*

Willadeene turns around, wobbling as if she might tumble over. She is unaccustomed to cavorting about in high-buttoned shoes. Though they sit cruel upon her exquisite feet, Avery insists she wear a pair of his mama's hand-me-downs for this solemn procession. Puny room there is for her to spread and wiggle her sand dollar toes. By Fiddler Crab's account, Constance Rose Longwood's feet were a might smaller. I cannot help myself but ponder what sort of shoe it was our Willadeene wore back before—if she wore any shoes at all when she was Alsace-Lorraine. *Summertime.... Summertime.... Rain....* On all accounts, it is a miracle Willadeene manages a single step, fresh from the latch of Theodore Laurence's rabid teeth.

"Look at me," Willadeene says, weeping. She sits the lantern down, her hands trembling. Like a parlor trick, she pulls a handkerchief from her sleeve. Already she has mended. Her head, snatched bald by Theodore Laurence, is now a field of blooms. Reindeer-moss skin ripped to ribbons—stitched back anew. I give Willadeene a curious look from her silly shoes to the collar of Avery's dead mama's everyday dress choking high on her neck. Does any part of our Willadeene resemble the Alsace-Lorraine she was before?

"Pull yourself together, Willadeene," Rebecca says. "You are good as new." She feels around the corners of Sweet Chariot for Jane Austen, positioning the pearl handle of her pistol on the ready should she need her.

Good as new. This is the root of Willadeene's conundrum. That in death, she is in right good health. One day she will be the last of us monkeys in the forest swinging by her tail in these gnarled-branched trees.

"Right as rain. Right as rain, is our Willadeene." Down upon himself Avery gazes, admiring the fit of gown on his teensy waist. "Why the brightness of her cheeks would shame those stars as daylight doth a lamp."

Avery quotes Mr. William Shakespeare, I believe. *Romeo and Juliet.* There is no knowing if Avery speaks of himself or Willadeene, but he is right on both counts.

Willadeene unwraps her prized Pocket Watch folded in the handkerchief. She slides the emptied linen back into her sleeve. *Click-clack.* She opens the face of Pocket Watch and closes it fast. "Good as new," she says. *Click-clack.*

"The Sun should be up by now," Avery says.

The fear in Avery's voice from earlier has withered, blossoming to an upbeat rhythm of glee. Seems now he does not give so much as a chicken bone he up and run the Sun off with a wish. With nothing left hanging in the sky but the Moon, and his daddy gone, I suspect Avery aims to take full advantage and be whoever it is he longs to be. He will insist we call him Odette. *Just wait and see.*

"Yes, Brother. Look what you have gone and done," Rebecca says. "Cheated the world of the Sun."

More my Blue Heron might say, but she is smarter than smart, stopping her tongue from tallying the ledger of things Avery has done wrong. *Their dead mama. Baby Girl Longwood. Mirabelle tangled in wedding lace and living her days in a rusted coffee can. And Rushworth* L. *Wintergarden gone....* As I have confessed before, Fiddler Crab is not all bad. And not a single one of us—every bit good.

"Willadeene does not mind it. Do you?" Avery asks. "That the Sun has gone missing?"

Willadeene rubs Pocket Watch beneath the steep bone of her cheek. If there is a thing our Willadeene cannot bear, it is the sky turned full bright and blue, the dizzying sensation of being sucked away and left orphaned on the Moon. I look down into Sweet Chariot, at the full-grow'd Sinner's eyeball hanging by a thread. I rub at my bottle of teeth. There are far worse and loathsome ways to perish than enduring an eternity there in the sky on Forever Moon.

Rebecca snaps her fingers at Willadeene. Points to Sweet Chariot. "Shall we get this chore over and done?" She snaps her fingers again. "Fetch Pretty Bird and toss her back in."

Odd as it sounds, our Willadeene is scared of dead things. So, I do her a mercy. I scoop up Pretty Bird and tuck her next to Sugar beneath Theodore Laurence's dirty coverall bib. I wrap the Sinner's arms about his boy, but they pay no mind, sneaking and drifting slow away from him. Not even in death can Theodore Laurence's daddy love on and keep his child safe.

Rebecca looks over to me. "Ready?"

"As I ever will be," I say. She takes hold of her handle. I take hold of mine, and Avery takes possession of my apron string. These last two years I have gained the strength of two hands in just this one, but Sweet Chariot grows heavier still. I will not disappoint my Blue Heron. I will not let go. I will while away the pain and stench staring ahead at Willadeene, at Salome swaddled in the sling Rebecca has draped wary across our haint's back. Avery insists there be music at River's side.

Right this very minute, I have decided to keep the secret of Willadeene to myself. That she once had herself a husband, a baby dead with Consumption. What good would grow from telling the tale? Soon—our Ewell Day Higgs will be dead. And there is no place our Willadeene can go but here.

Time stretches, Sweet Chariot's wheel moaning a dirge. Rebecca looks over to me, her face hidden by her hat. "You okay?"

"I have been better, Sister. But you know I am not one to complain." Avery says, as if he had been asked the question.

"You are a pillar, Avery Longwood. A martyr. A saint." In the husk of Rebecca's words, I mark the sweet ripening of a smile.

"Misery," Avery screams. "I am ruined."

Rebecca sets down her handle. I put mine down quick.

"For the love of Moses, Avery. What is wrong with you?" Rebecca asks.

"I am ruined."

"We are all ruined, Avery. This is hardly news."

Avery lets go of my apron string, lifts his hem and sticks out his shoe. "I have stepped in it, Sister." Already it reeks. *A Sinner's manure.* Sinners, they lose all propriety in the end, Redemption eating up their insides. The stink fattens now that Avery has pranced the monstrosity open with his black satin heel. Worms glow gangrenous squirming about on the ground in the dung and dangling from his shoe.

"You most certainly have," Rebecca says, covering her nose and mouth with her hand.

"Help me, Willadeene," Avery screams. "Misery and ruin."

"Your shoe is lost," Rebecca says. "And your foot will follow. Hurry. Take it off."

Avery screams louder. Willadeene and I hurry over to Fiddler Crab.

"Be careful of Salome, Willadeene," Rebecca says.

I balance Avery as he leans against my shoulder. Willadeene pulls the slipper from his narrow foot. "Willadeene, mind your fingers," I say. Already the shoe is steaming, holes burning clean through. Willadeene hurls the smoldering, stinking slipper willy-nilly to land in a sparkleberry bush.

"I should never manage with just one foot," Avery says, chest heaving, his naked foot positioned tippy-toed in the leaves. "You have saved me, Willadeene. You saved me from ruin. I would be a pariah with only five toes."

"It would not be bad as all that, Fiddler Crab. I would fetch your pretty foot back to you in a dented coffee can. And just what might we call her? Clytemnestra? Adelaide? How about Delilah? Or Penelope-Ann?" I do not know what has come over me talking to Avery like this.

Avery stumbles back. Gasps. Willadeene pulls Pocket Watch in that handkerchief from her sleeve. Back and forth, Fiddler Crab runs his fingers across the nap of the blue velvet ribbon adorning his throat. *Scratch* and *swoosh.*

I know this sound, Rushworth L. Wintergarden's handsome fingers looping the ribbon in my Blue Heron's hair, arranging it neat and pretty. The sound of the ribbon is so vivid now, I swear the tutor's handsome fingers ramble the jungle of my own towhead hair. Avery's mouth moves, but I do not hear him. Sparks toss, a dazzlement from his hairpins, embers burning me to the back when. *Tribulation Day. Two years back....* I remember now it was those same hairpins Constance Rose Longwood wore when she dragged us down. When she killed me. Now Avery wears them haughty as a French baroness.

"You are an ungrateful dragon, Leontyne Skye," Avery sobs. "How quick it is you forget it was I who saved you from being carted to the River there in Sweet Chariot. You are more hateful than Rebecca. You are a beast."

From beneath the shadows of her hat, Rebecca speaks. "Settle yourself, Avery. Be kind."

Avery pays no mind to Rebecca. "I am not the one who sawed off Mirabelle. Thank your precious Rebecca for that. Let that be a lesson. Never cross my sister." He lifts his wrist loop, shakes back his head. "Yes, I am guilty of bringing Mirabelle back to you in a can. I suppose I should have flung her to the gators. Yes, that is what I should have done. Would you have preferred that?"

"Enough," says my Blue Heron. "Pianissimo."

"Agamemnon," Avery screams.

Willadeene covers her ears. "You will wake the dead. Be quiet. Oh, please be quiet."

Avery's hairpins twinkle and flare. *Swoosh* and *scrape*. And I remember a whisper. *Pianissimo. There-there now....* Were these Constance Rose Longwood's last words she ever spoke as she lay dying on Morningstar's floor? Before her brains squished out like mayhaw jelly from a dropped mason jar.

Hairpins. Constance Rose Longwood wore the very hairpins our Avery wears now. *I am Leontyne Skye, and I am sixteen years old.* Why can I not remember more?

Behind Avery's spidery web of mourning veil, tears swell lush in the almond shell of his eyes. Why should he be the only one allowed to cry? Fiddler Crab cannot bear the look of me when I cry. He is lucky I am able to close my spigot and keep such weeping luxury to myself when no one watches.

"All this carrying on over nothing, Avery McKinley Longwood," I say. "You should be ashamed. Fever come to fury—five toes would be better than none. You are ungrateful. Just look at you. You still have ten."

Avery weeps louder. "You will not be happy until I am maimed. Disfigured. Or worse. Dead!"

I want to despise Avery, but there is no hating him for always. "Willadeene," I say, holding out my hand. "Your handkerchief, please."

Willadeene passes the handkerchief to me. Right off, I spy a thing I did not see before. Avery and Rebecca notice it, too. There is no pretending it has not been seen. That Willadeene did not pull the handkerchief from Constance Rose Longwood's abandoned sleeve, from the dress our Willadeene wears.

"What is wrong?" Willadeene asks. "Looks as you might have seen a ghost."

I trace my index finger over the monogram stitched at the corner with pale blue thread. RLW for Rushworth L. Wintergarden.

"Where did you get that?" Rebecca asks.

"It was already here in the sleeve of this dreadful dress."

"That is mine," Avery says, reaching to snatch it from me.

"Did it come from your own sleeve?" Rebecca asks.

"It has come from Mother's sleeve, so it is mine. We both know she would want me to have it."

From Mother's sleeve. Right off, I wonder how it got there. And just how Constance Rose Longwood could love Avery best. Better than my Blue Heron. I jerk the handkerchief out of Fiddler Crab's reach.

"What do they mean?" Willadeene asks. "The markings just there?"

"You should blame Rebecca for keeping you stupid, Willadeene. For you not knowing how to read," Avery says. "Give it here. Give it here."

I cannot resist the urge to press the handkerchief to my nose. To detect any memory of how handsome Rushworth L. Wintergarden smells. To understand why they all love him so. All I remember is a glimpse here and there. I press the handkerchief to my face. All that lingers is petrichor. The smell of Willadeene. And the faint smell of Longwood.

On one foot, Avery reaches for the handkerchief. "Do not ruin it."

"Pianissimo, Brother," Rebecca says.

"You will wake the dead, Avery." Willadeene whispers, opening and closing the face of Pocket Watch. *Click-clack.*

Avery gazes sad upon the bodies of Theodore Laurence and his daddy growing stiff in Sweet Chariot. "Look, Leontyne. Look what you have done."

This is not my fault, I want to say. *I have done nothing wrong.* This is Eulalee's and Redemption's doing. *None of mine.* I look to Rebecca for reassurance, but her face still hides from me in the cave of her hat.

Click-clack. Click-clack.

Avery grows quiet, balancing part of his weight on the tip of his big toe. A great hush lay eerie upon the Forest until Damascus sings, chiming seductive through Forest's canopy, lulling Siberian breezes to descend from the River and Sea wrapping us thick in cold. *My Leontyne.... My Leontyne.... Come back here to me....*

Eulalee's black pearls moan unseemly in my pocket. Oh, how the Great Redeemer pines for Damascus. I fight the urge to break Eulalee's tincture bottle. Flick her teeth to the sparkleberry to melt with Avery's slipper, yelling out Damascus is no longer hers. *She is mine, Eulalee. Mine.*

This is nonsense. What in the sweet heavens has come over me? I want no part of Damascus and her Sara Figs dangling wanton from the salty limbs of her tree. *Something is different. Something has changed.* And I feel a tether to Willadeene, as if I can feel what she feels this very moment, the shame of the memory of this dead Sinner scraping his filthy hands up her evergreen legs, of Theodore Laurence ripping her apart.

Willadeene hurries to help Avery. She strips off her shoes. Fastens them onto Avery best she can without a button hook. Soon, we are our way from the mouth of the Forest, Rebecca on one side of Sweet Chariot, and me on the other—Avery pulling my apron strings trudging across the understory in Willadeene's shoes.

Ahead, the River roils. The sky cracks open. Constellations startle, and Forever Moon floods Good Hope and Theordore Laurence's eyes in pale-blue glory.

Something is different. Something has changed.

The River

Chapter 14

A curtain of cloud billows across the River between Good Hope and Abraham's Bluff. So thick it is impossible to see clear beyond. In places, the vapor wears thin, revealing glimmers and hints of the Sun shining life on the other side.

"I told you it was morning time," Avery says. "There is your proof."

I look down at Theodore Laurence, the Moon alive and astonishing his dead eyes. Everything is beguiling here beneath the Forever Moon. Avery in his beaded gown, his hairpins twinkling.

Willadeene sets down the lantern. She takes all the steps she can take, Salome swaddled on her back. There is only so close to the River Willadeene can go before her head aches. Before she withers bald, her skin infested with boll weevils nibbling our haint to bits. Like all haints, Willadeene cannot travel back across water. She is shipwrecked. Marooned.

Alsace-Lorraine.... Alsace-Lorraine.... "Go no further, Willadeene," I say. "That is far enough."

Beyond the curtain, haints pulse purplish-red, appearing like flashes of lightning lurking beyond thundery clouds. I feel the haints' longing. Sense them in a way not known to me before: a flitter in my chest, a tumble of sorrow. Desire. Secrets and lies. How these haints beckon, calling me by my name. *Leontyne.... Leontyne.... More.... More.... More....*

Haints never have said my name before, and I cannot help but think it is because my Eulalee is dead, that I might only be able to hear and feel them because she is gone. A feeling rises portentous. If Rebecca and I are to escape Good Hope, we should go now. Float ourselves down the River on our backs with Theodore Laurence and his stinking daddy, abandoning poor Willadeene and Avery to squall like orphans on the bank.

I grab hold of Sweet Chariot. "Hurry, Blue Heron, hurry. The time is now." *Look up.* I am up to my knees in the River, the current running cold and fierce. Rebecca tips the wheelbarrow. The whole sorry lot comes tumbling and sliding to me down the bank. A star flees the firmament, traveling—I hope, to anywhere but here.

"Scheherazade," Avery says, then he quotes Keats. "Bright star, would I were steadfast as thou art." He laughs out to us. "Too late for the rest of you. I have already made a wish. That star is mine."

Another star tumbles. Willadeene calls out to it greedy there in the sky. "This one is mine," she says. Then more Keats. "Of snow upon the mountains and the moors." How she cannot remember she once was Alsace-Lorraine but can recite a line of Keats is a muddle of muddles to me.

I try to hold onto the full grow'd Sinner so I might hook his son to the strap of his coveralls. Too late. His daddy lets loose, drifting off good-for-nothing down the River in death as he was when he was living, his eyeball bobbing by a thread, staring up for wish-making stars.

"The next wish is for you," I whisper down to Theodore Laurence. *Look up, Rebecca. Look up.*

"Play *Swan Lake*," Avery says, opening his *Book of Jubilation and Woe*.

Blue Heron cradles and kisses her Salome, playing Mr. Vivaldi's *Winter* instead.

A third star flees the heavens. "Make a wish, Theodore Laurence," I say. *Make a wish.* I vow to stay here in the River until the waters wash the boy clean. Until the fishes nibble the sharp edges from his nails. I will stay until he is mine. *Come down to the River, Rebecca. Come down.*

Avery spouts Keats while Salome sings *Winter*. "Can death be sleep, when life is but a dream."

There is a stir beneath Theodore Laurence's bib—movement. *A heartbeat?* I press my hand to his chest, then my ear to listen. No, it is not Theodore Laurence come alive. It is Sugar shivering. I pull the poor thing *cheeping* and *chirping* from beneath the bib, holding him above my head for everyone to see. Theodore Laurence and Pretty Bird take off down the River. I am sad, and joyous, and covetous all at once he is leaving. I holler out to the boy. To his golden goat eyes to pay me some mind.

"Look up, my Theodore Laurence."

Look up....

The Chapel of Abundance

Chapter 15

I ought feel ashamed of myself for leaving Rebecca and the others down by the River, for telling them a lie. Telling them I have come to my senses and need to get myself down to the Marsh to mix a batch of Redemption before Miss Hushabye Byrd comes *clomping* back around.

Rebecca and the others would not take too kindly knowing I abandoned them to chase after this batch of fresh-hatched haints swimming the sky across the River, through the Forest. Heading toward the Chapel of Abundance on their way to the Marsh.

A confession: never has a sky filled with haints made me feel such a way as this. Wickedness and tenderness both wrestling around together inside me. Coupling my good parts with the bad. I stop. Look up through the branches and count to make sure I have not lost sight of a single, lowly haint.

One haint. Two haint. Three haint. Yesterday there were three haints. Today there are four. This fourth one straggles. He seems less enchanted by Damascus, not so desperate as the rest to prick and wheedle his way into the warm, pulpy-middle of a Sarah Fig. He is trouble, his eyes flickering a brighter yellow than the rest, a bird's feather stuck to his cheek, his earthworm tongue wriggling unseemly, licking across his catfish lips.

I want to stop and recline brazen upon the Forest floor to watch these haints. Enjoy this thing I feel. *Desire.* How they beguile, puffing up handsome shades of purple and red. I pull Sugar from my pocket to make sure he has not turned back dead, to give him a gander of the no-count haints glowing brighter than I have ever seen.

"Look up, Sugar," I say. Those watermelon seeds-for-eyes blink, beholding the glorious sight above, the pulse of haint-light washing the chick and me vermilion. Each flash of light—fingers courting soft that needful place at my neck craving kisses.

The four haints are closer now to the Chapel of Abundance. This very minute, I want no part of my Ewell Day Higgs dead or dying in a Sinner's pit, but there is nothing could keep me from tracking these haints no matter which course they go.

A flash of memory comes—a word tantalizing feathery as a whisper, spoken from another's lips, poking it into my ear with a slippery tongue. *Idolatry....* "Idolatry." I speak the word aloud, wondering who it was that once said this thing to me.

More. More. More.... The haints croon in unison, turning around to look down at me lurid, as if they like this unseemly word I have spoken.

One haint bumps into another. That one rubs against the next. Before I know it, they puff and croak, amorous moans and whimpers spilling from the dead. Cutting the fool like tree frogs in the throes of a mating dance. *Lord, help me.* I feel their pleasure. Their suffering. Vibrations and glimpses of the good and bad these haints done when they were living. One done murder. Another—pure eat-up with greed. In chorus, they wriggle my name vulgar from their tongues. *Leontyne.... Leontyne....* I savor the shameful way it makes me feel.

The lollygagging haint, the one with the feather stuck to his cheek, smarts up a bright glory of red. He drifts down close, flicking his fishtail vulgar my way. My wits leave me. I should shoo the scamp away, but I resist. He smells every bit good as a Longwood, only different. Salty Sea and River smells. *Has ever a haint smelled this good before?* He comes close and closer until he is whimpering in my ear. He groans a vile thing a God-fearing gal should never repeat. It creeps from my ear, wraps about my waist, fondling and taunting all the way down to my toes. All I ever have heard from a haint is *more, more, more.*

"Idolatry," I murmur back. "What is your name?"

He moans, licking his lips with that earthworm tongue. *Uncle Daddy,* he says.

I am unraveled this haint has a name, that he can speak it. "Uncle Daddy? That is a queer sort of name."

The deep-deep of Uncle Daddy's voice does something to me, and I ache to lay myself upon the leaves beneath a redbay tree, my hair fanning the Forest floor while he calls out my name. *Leontyne.... Leontyne....* Behind me comes a rustle in the hollies. *Babylon, that hussy deer.* She has caught me in a scandal with this haint, tapping her hoof in the brush.

Off in the direction of the Chapel of Abundance come ripples of laughter, an odd sound wrapped in suffering and glee. The haints turn away, abandoning me wanton, drifting the direction of Damascus towards where I left my Ewell Day Higgs and Mirabelle.

The resurrection fern sprouts lusher from the crumbling tabby, the Forever Moon appearing a might more swoled up than when I visited before. Above the pit where Ewell Day Higgs lay, the haints circle cunning as buzzards, dipping low on occasion to give him a look.

"Shoo away from there," I say. "Shoo!" The haints pay me no mind.

Ewell Day Higgs's voice rises, a mist of wonderment and rasp. "Is that you, Starshine?"

"Yes, sir. It is me." I am full-up with happy he is not yet dead. So happy I could cry. If there was room in my pocket, I would scrape and scoop him from the pit.

"You sound different, Starshine. Are you okay?"

"I am right as rain," I say. *Summertime.... Summertime.... Rain....* "How are you?"

"A might better since you left me with Redemption, and Miss Mirabelle up there to keep me company. She is a comfort," he says. "Starshine ... I do not say this to upset you, but there is no way around it. I reckon I am on the decline. My insides are doing something they ought not do. They have come spilling out."

"Just a drop," I say. "A drop every now and again. There is no more Redemption than what you have down there with you. Make it last best you can, Ewell Day Higgs." *Make it last.*

I will be damned if I make an iota of Redemption. I would rather slice off my other hand than fool with a Sarah Fig.

"I do not mean to be a burden, Starshine, but I like it here with you and Mirabelle. And the queer call of that wind chime song," he says. "I do not even mind so much those haints circling above looking down upon me like I might be their dinner."

Moments pass. Damascus chimes. The haints trace quiet circles.

Ewell Day Higgs speaks again. "And I must confess, Starshine. I am partial to looking up into the Moon."

What Ewell Day Higgs says is true. It is beautiful here.... "Was that you I heard laughing?"

"I reckon it was," he says. "Miss Mirabelle is not near quiet as you mentioned."

I look over to where I left Mirabelle, her can stowed in the opening of the crumbling wall. "I had no idea she possessed a good sense of humor."

Tick-tack. Mirabelle stirs in her can.

Ewell Day Higgs laughs.

"What is so funny?"

"Did you not hear her?" he asks. "She said you should pay her more mind."

He has taken leave of his senses. He imagines he hears my Mirabelle speak. "I pay her plenty of attention," I say. "I reckon she has taken to you better than she has to me." *It is the truth.* Now that I think of it, Mirabelle never made a peep until we met Ewell Day Higgs.

Clickety-clack.

"See now. She says she likes you plenty fine."

How he can decipher any sense from the racket is a marvel. "You can hear her clear?" I ask.

"I am not dead yet, Starshine. Of course, I can hear her speak."

If my Ewell Day Higgs thinks he hears Mirabelle talking, I will play along. "What did you chat about while I was gone?"

"At first, the weather, as strangers are prone to do. Then we carried on about them wishing stars that fell lonesome from the heavens," he says. "Did you see them, Starshine?"

"Sure did," I say. "Did you make yourself a wish?"

"Saw no harm in it. So I did," he says.

"I hope it comes true, Ewell Day Higgs. I really do."

I wonder if it was Alsace-Lorraine and his dead girl he made his wish for. I will not bear him the sorry news Avery and Willadeene already squeezed the wishes clean from them stars. That I believe my dead Theodore Laurence made himself a wish, too. Ewell Day Higgs might think it wasteful to wish a dead chicken be brought back around to the living.

"Mirabelle made a wish."

"Did she now?" I ask.

"She wished something for you."

"Telling makes them not come true," I say. I cannot help but smile and ponder if anyone ever—long as I have been alive and kicking—has cast a single wish for me.

"She did not tell me the thing she wished for. Did you, Mirabelle? Her wish is safe as they come."

Click-click.

"See. She said she did not spill the beans. I would never lie to you, Starshine." He is quiet a spell, until his next words rise so vaporous, I hardly can hear. "Not like some...."

Not like some.... A cool breeze lay across me like a shawl. My teeth give a little chatter. "Pardon me, Ewell Day Higgs," I say. "What do you mean by that?"

Babylon stands on dead Baby Girl Longwood's grave tapping her hoof. Mirabelle clicks back from her can, like the two of them are longtime bosom friends. As if they are in cahoots.

"Ewell Day Higgs, you up to par?" I ask, hoping he has not gathered the gumption to die before telling me this thing I want to know.

Ewell Day Higgs speaks slow, the sound of pain cutting deeper into his words. "Mirabelle told me someone hurt you." His voice trails. "Two years back...."

I nearly topple, awestruck Ewell Day Higgs truly hears Mirabelle speak—that my own hand only *clacks* for me—that he now knows the awful thing that happened.

Eulalee's teeth crackle. *Tttt.... Twooo.... Yearzzz.... Backkk....*

"That is not her business to tell," I say, looking over at Mirabelle, my hand trembling.

"She means no harm."

She means to embarrass me. Dull the shine my Ewell Day Higgs sees in me. "That one is prone to exaggeration," I say. "Pay her no mind."

Mirabelle does not seem to like this thing I said, *clickety-clacking* uppity in her can. I step a wee bit closer to her should I need to toss her from the Chapel beyond a gathering of rusty staggerbrush trees.

Ewell Day Higgs' voice melts weary. "My sweet Starshine. Is it true what Mirabelle just said?"

I wrestle the urge to runoff. To avoid what I ask next. I reach down. Caress Sugar with my pinky. "Is what true, Ewell Day Higgs?" Eulalee's teeth turn quiet. The haints slow, bobbing like cork in the Sea.

Ewell Day Higgs's voice is sorrowful and tender when it speaks this next thing to me. "That you was dead once. That you fell. The long-long ways...."

Swish and *scrape*. A memory tumbles. Words folding back into my ear. *You are no better than that whore down by the Marsh.*

Push and shove. And I am falling. *Falling* ... I holler out to right myself. To push away what was. "I am not dead now." I soothe myself with visions of stomping Mirabelle flat in her can. Cracking and smashing my personal affairs from her gossiping fingertips.

"There now, Starshine," says Ewell Day Higgs. "Of course, you are not dead."

I am crying big gloppy tears. "Was and is," I say. "They are worlds apart. Far apart as Good Hope from the Island of Crete. I am going there one of these here days to wander the ruins of Greece." *Rebecca and me.*

"We did not mean to make you cry, Starshine. Cross my heart and hope to...."

Die....

Ewell Day Higgs will be dead soon, and here I am carrying on like a fool. "I know you meant no harm," I say. I am suspicious of Mirabelle. She is up to something. Perhaps she covets my Ewell Day Higgs for herself. Maybe she has turned hussy like Babylon, that harlot of a deer.

"Leontyne?"

Fiddler Crab!

"Who are you talking to?" he asks.

My heart flops into my rubber boot. I twirl about to face Avery, hoping he does not look beyond me to the hole where Ewell Day Higgs lay. "What are you doing here?" I ask, astonished he wanders alone in the dark alone without Willadeene to hold a lantern to light his way.

"I asked you a question," Avery says. "Who are you talking to?" He presses *Jubilation and Woe* to his chest. Nurses it like a baby.

"Not a single soul," I say. "Except Mirabelle there in her can."

"Liar-liar," he says. Avery takes a few steps forward, noticing the glare of Moon upon the tabby walls, the bald spots the ferns fail to cover. He lifts his netted-veil from his chin. Peels it back from his face. Gazes the Forever Moon and star-drunk sky. Constellations reflect, orbiting the dark universe aswirl in his eyes. I know this look. *Dazzlement.* The way Avery is overcome when faced with magnificence. The shortness of breath. Heave of bodice. The manner he wobbles on the cusp of a swoon. I pray for it. That he will collapse so I might drag him from here into the Forest away from Ewell Day Higgs.

"Scheherazade," Avery whispers.

The haints—they pay Avery mind, riling up again. Slinking seductive in circles to grab hold his attention. *More.... More.... More....*

Avery is revived from his trance by the haints' caterwauling. He shakes his head. Presses his hand to his brow. His voice is dreamy when he speaks. "Who is here, Leontyne?"

"Only Sugar, and Mirabelle, and me. Them haints up there. And Babylon, that hussy deer prancing yonder on your mama's grave."

Mama's grave is what seems to fetch Fidder Crab's attention, jostling him fully awake. "Mother?" he asks.

A long while it has been since Avery last visited the Chapel of Abundance. Seems this very minute he realizes where it is he has traipsed. Before he unravels, I grab hold of the good sense to try and get him gone. "Come on," I say. "Come away from here with me. Back to Morningstar." I hurry to Avery. Nudge at his pale elbow. He closes the gap. Before I know it, he cloaks himself about me, pressing *Jubilation and Woe* hard against my back, refusing to turn loose.

"Leontyne-Leontyne," he sing-songs. "Run away with me from Good Hope."

"Where shall we go?" I ask, pretending Avery is his sister, his hip bones loving against my hip bones. My *Blue Heron. Sleek and tall.* There is no place in this world fit for Fidder Crab. *No place I can think of but here.* Damascus sings louder, stirring the haints, kindling love sounds and whimpers, setting off sparks inside me.

More.... The haints confess scandalous things. Of wandering mouths. Debauchery. Conceit. I try to pull free from Avery's Longwood smells. Distract myself from the salacious odor of haints. The fragrance conspires. Bewitches alongside Damascus. Calling to the devil inside me.

"Across the Ephesians Sea," Avery whispers. "That is where we shall go. To Seraphim House."

Seraphim House. I jerk away from Avery. His hand steals about in my apron pocket knocking against Sugar and Eulalee's teeth. Lickety-split, he pulls the handkerchief free. With a sorcerer's flair, he has conjured Rushworth L. Wintergarden. Resurrected him in blue monogram stitching.

"That was a low down, dirty trick," I say, grabbing for the handkerchief, but I am too slow to snatch it back. "Is that why you wandered all this way? To steal from me?"

"Preposterous," he says. "It was no trick. Of course I want you to run off with me away from my hateful sister. But this handkerchief is mine. It is not stealing." With great flourish, he waves the handkerchief about as a queen might signal a duel.

"Give it back," I say. I cannot imagine why I want the thing.

"Absurd. It is perfectly safe with me." He presses the handkerchief to his nose. Breathes in deep.

I only recall shadowy fragments of Rushworth L. Wintergarden. The reddish-brown wave of his hair. His teeth assembled gallant as soldiers marching bright in two straight lines. The smell of Longwood mixes with the intimate smell of haints, and I am near abouts beside myself thinking of grey frogs in trees. Right now, more than anything, I want to remember how Mr. Rushworth L. Wintergarden smelled.

More.... More....

I gnaw the inside of my cheek. Push my tongue at the strawberry seed stuck between my teeth. "What is so horrible you would run off and leave your only sister and poor Willadeene?"

Avery's eyes drift to Babylon circling his mama's grave. "Rebecca's mood has turned dark since leaving the River," he says. "She is up in the Cupola with that she-devil, Salome, playing Chopin."

The Nocturne. The one Avery cannot bear. How is it Fiddler Crab can wear Wintergarden's ribbon? Sniff deep into his handkerchief. But cannot listen to a song? "What is it about that Nocturne?" I ask. "That sends you running?"

'Round and 'round, Avery watches Babylon trace Constance Rose Longwood's grave, her brown eyes staring back. "It is what Rebecca was playing when I saw the thing I saw. The thing I told my Mother. Do not ask me what it was," he says. He pulls the veil down over his face. Tucks it beneath his chin and whispers. "It is also what Rebecca was humming when she sawed off your poor-poor Mirabelle."

Much as I long to know the things them haints done—to feel their unspeakable pleasures spill over me, I want to know this thing Avery saw. What he told his mama.

Ewell Day Higgs calls up weary from the pit. "Starshine.... You alright up there?"

Avery's eyes go wide beneath his spider-webbed veil. *Jubilation and Woe* falls from his arms. "Agamemnon," he shrieks. "You have trapped a Sinner there. Why is it you did not tell?" He runs willy-nilly, his gown sparkling Moon and dragging leaves. "I will fetch Jane Austen," he screams, flashing Rushworth L. Wintergarden's handkerchief all about.

Avery is slippery as a greased-up pig, and I cannot grab hold. "He is not a Sinner," I yell.

"Agamemnon!"

"Be still," I say, running close behind. I leap onto the train of his gown with my rubber boots. *Rip* and *tear*. Fiddler Crab whips backward. *Thud.* I follow, both of us sprawled on the ground beneath the Moon.

"How dare you," he screams. "You beast." Avery rights himself onto his knees, dark ringlets escaping his mama's hairpins, spilling plentiful and glorious about his face.

"He is not a Sinner. Listen to what I am telling you," I say. "His eyes have not turned goat. He does not stink. He is not anything like the others. He has every last one of his teeth."

"You know the rules. It is either Miss Jane Austin or Father's rifle," Avery says, his flat chest heaving beneath his gown. Avery is right. We have rules here on Good Hope on how to wrangle Sinners. But my Ewell Day Higgs is no Sinner.

"Starshine?" Ewell Day Higgs calls up from the pit to me again.

"I am fine," I say, on my knees facing Avery. "Right as rain."

Avery whispers, his eyebrows arching with questions. "Starshine?"

"Shh," I whisper, pressing my finger to my lips, shaking my head. Begging silently Avery does not call me, Leontyne. "That is the name he give me."

I am close enough to Avery to see the waters run dark, flooding mischievous in his lovely eyes. "How long has this been going on?" he whispers back. A smile curls from his cupid's bow lips on the ready to launch attack.

"Please, Avery."

"Nothing is free, Starshine," he says. "You are beholden to me now."

"Who is that there with you?" asks Ewell Day Higgs.

Avery is back on his feet. He does not so much as wobble, as if he was birthed with high heeled boots buttoned to his feet. "Odette," Avery says, brushing back curls seeming longer than before. He sniffs the handkerchief. Dabs it to his neck. His temples. "Odette Wintergarden," he says, grinning sideways at me. "And who are you, sir? Leontyne says you are not just any ole run-of-the mill Sinner."

He come to see me. Would that not turn Odette Wintergarden green as a pole bean? "To see the Moon," I say. "Never has anyone come just for that."

"The Moon?" Avery asks, his voice singing a lullaby. Quiet he goes. Teeters. For a moment, I think this sweet-sweet thought might tip Avery into a swoon. "I shall write this down," Avery says. "I shall take it down in my *Book of Jubilation and Woe.* Memorialize this man traveling here to Good Hope to see only the Moon." Avery looks back behind him to the ground, the book opened upon the leaves, the breeze from the Ocean rifling through its pages.

I wonder if Avery has written down all the things good and bad he has done. Or only makes mention of others' deeds. Perhaps all the things I cannot remember are scribbled down alongside bits and pieces of poems by Keats. Avery takes up the loop from the train of his ballgown, puts it about his wrist. He moves closer to the pit.

"Come back from there, Odette," I say. "Come on back."

"We should pull this sweet man free," Avery says. "Pull him out best we can if he is not dangerous."

"Keep away from here, Odette Wintergarden," says my Ewell Day Higgs. "I am not fit to be seen. It is hopeless. Do not look down at me."

Avery is close, so close I fear he might tumble in. "Listen," I say. "Do not look down."

He looks anyway, his mama's hairpins shimmering. He gasps, pressing the handkerchief to his nose, stumbling back. He regards the sky beyond the glow of haints to the Moon as if saying a prayer. "I am so sorry," Avery says, weeping. "For what has happened to you down in that hole." He turns around to face me, a look of beautiful hysteria on the rise. "Look what you have done, Leontyne," he says.

"What I have done? This is not my doing." I point over at Babylon on top of dead Baby Girl Longwood's grave. I hold up my no-hand arm. "Look what you have done," I scream. "To me. To your mama. Your dead baby sister!"

Damascus goes quiet. So quiet we hear Rebecca's Salome sing through the Forest from Morningstar way. Winds rise from all directions. The River. The Marsh. And the Sea. Higgledy-piggledy flap the pages of *Jubilation and Woe.*

"Siegfried, save me," Avery weeps, waving Rushworth L. Wintergarden's handkerchief toward the Moon.

The haints drift off talking filth, and I am desperate to follow them to Damascus, to enjoy the dreadful things they say. Whispering the thing to them somebody once whispered sinful to me.

Idolatry....

Idolatry....

Morningstar
The In-Between

Chapter 16

Avery tends my hair here on the splintering staircase, a chore to settle his nerves, his shaking hands. He sits behind me on a tread—his gown, a midnight waterfall spilling all around. He pretends to have forgotten about my Ewell Day Higgs, of Theodore Laurence floating the River to Nairobi then off to the Sea of Galilee. Pretends to have forgotten the awful thing I said back at the Chapel of Abundance. About his mama, baby sister, and me. Forgotten Hushabye Byrd is coming back for Redemption.

From the Up-Up There, Salome sings, tumbling Vivaldi's *Winter* upon us here in the Gallery. She slows the tempo. Turns it drunk and slurry. Willadeene, free from her corset, spins slow to Rebecca's violin, her evergreen bosom peeking from her robe. I poke my hand into my apron pocket, comforted to be reunited with my Darkly.

"I hate Salome," Avery says, looking up, running those Longwood fingers through my hair, fiddling the tangles loose. "I would like to see her wooden neck broken. Smashed into a thousand pieces and dead."

"We are knee-high in dead," I say. "Leave your sister and Salome be." I watch Willadeene dance her harem dance, her leash ambling behind her. Did this Winter dance thaw the summer loose from her husband, my Ewell Day Higgs? I can feel it, the need churning in Willadeene's hips. Scandalous words chewed into her lips.

I shut my eyes, let *Winter* transport me icy to the dizzy-high peak of Kilimanjaro. I pretend I am standing next to Blue Heron at the tippy-tipsy top, both of us wrapped in ermine, pointing down over here to Good Hope. *Look yonder, Blue Heron*, I would say. *That there is the onion dome of Morningstar. That there is the place we once lived.* I suppose I might feel an inkling of guilt speculating about poor Willadeene and Fiddler Crab marooned here without the Sun. Ambling together melancholy beneath the Moon.

I am undecided if I will pack up Mirabelle when time comes to go. Serves her right it would, if I orphaned her to the Forest *clacking* and spilling my business from the hollow of her can, with no one to gossip with but Babylon and dead Longwoods, their worm-worn ears pressed nosey to their coffins hearkening deep from the well of their graves.

Air … air…. Eulalee hisses from my pocket.

Avery pulls up a section of my long, curly mop. Fastens it into place with a hairpin he pulls from his own lustrous hair. "One day, my hair will grow twice as long as this."

Over McKinley Longwood's dead body. "That will be nice," I say. "Rebecca's hair already is longer and certainly more beautiful than mine."

Avery jabs one of his mama's hairpins into place. "Always it is Rebecca with you," he says. "My Blue Heron this. My Blue Heron that."

"I love you both the same." Avery is right. *I love Blue Heron more.*

"You would never know it. The way you carry on, you would think she fell straight from Elysium and landed here Saint Rebecca of Good Hope." Avery drops a hairpin. It plops shimmery in the scoop of my aproned lap. A chill runs my shoulder blades. A memory runs colder, of Constance Rose Longwood lying dead next to me where Willadeene sways her harem dance. *Poor Baby Girl Longwood.* Her tiny head split open like an oyster shell. *Gone quick as she come.*

Avery whispers. "It was not always like this with you, Starshine. Rebecca has not always offered you kindness."

Avery is forever stirring trouble. Always angling a wedge. I whisper back. "Do not call me, Starshine. Not here. You promised."

"Afraid your precious Rebecca might hear?" Avery sings hush-hush in my ear.

Leontyne has a boyfriend.
Leontyne has a beau.
Left the poor fella dying,
In the deep-dark, Down-Below.

"I hate you," I say.

"I despise you more." He kisses the back of my head. "Remember this. I am Odette Wintergarden by the light of that Forever Moon."

Eulalee's teeth call from my pocket. *Looommm ... Looommm....*

"What do you mean?" I ask. "That Rebecca was not always kind?" I do not know why I bother to ask him. Nothing he says will be true. My Blue Heron warns me he cannot be trusted. Always pitting one person against the next.

"I will tell you something, but not here," he whispers. "Hand me that hairpin."

"Say, 'pretty please.'" I lean back against him.

"Pretty please. Now give it here, you towhead beast."

I reach into my lap, pass back his mama's hairpin to him. I do not have the strength to let on I want no part of his mama or her pins hanging around in my hair. He is careful this time, working it gentle against my scalp. I watch Willadeene sway provocative. *Lord, forgive me.* I feel the slow rise of what burns in Willadeene. I yearn to know if it might feel heaps better if I inch closer to that shameless haint. If I move my hips in time to her *thump* and *whoosh*.

Tick and *clack*. Willadeene opens and closes Pocket Watch, pressing it to the good and plenty of her chest. She thinks of someone. *A fine smelling man.* Pine needles and vanilla. How is it I can think what Willadeene is thinking? How can I know the scent of her memory of this smell?

My Eulalee's teeth hiss. *Airrr.... Ooom.... Airrr.... Ooom....*

I try my best to decipher the particulars of this gentleman caller our Willadeene lusts after, only there is the ungodly distraction of Eulaee's rotten, smacking teeth. One thing runs clear from this feeling, from this vision. The man is not Willadeene's husband. He is not my Ewell Day Higgs. Can Willadeene remember a little bit of something from back before?

"Let me look at you," Avery says. "Stand up. Turn around."

I want to stay propped here against Avery and savor our Willadeene. Enjoy the entanglement of her petrichor with the woodsy pleasures of pine tree and vanilla bean. "A moment more, Avery," I say. *An eternity will do.*

Looomm ... Looomm....

"On up with you." He nudges my back with his finger.

I make my way lightheaded down the few stairs and turn around.

Avery gasps. "Scheherazade," he says, pulling himself up by the rail.

"Do not make a mockery of me."

"I do no such thing."

Fiddler Crab stares at me, his dark eyes turning glossy. He wobbles as if on the cusp of a fainting spell. All at once I am self-conscious. "Stop," I say. "You are embarrassing me."

He takes hold of himself. Shakes away his enchantment and curtseys. "You are the spitting image of Marie Antoinette." He rubs at the blue velvet ribbon tied at his neck. Presses his cheek to mine. "We should not let Rebecca see. She might get ideas. Then it will be your neck she chops next. She already has taken care of your hand. We will never be able to fit your head and all that hair into a coffee can," he whispers, pulling at my apron string. "Come with me."

"Blue Heron would never hurt me," I say.

"Where are you going?" Willadeene whispers.

“Not so very far,” Avery says. “Across the Mediterranean to the Red Sea. Then parade ourselves into Egypt.”

“Can I come?”

“Do not be a fool, Willadeene. You know your sort cannot travel across water.”

You are marooned here on land.

Morningstar
The In-Between

Chapter 17

Avery slides himself down into the Great Pyramid of Giza, *Jubilation and Woe* pressed against his chest. "Remember yourself, Leontyne," Avery calls up. "And take off those awful shoes. We are Queens of Egypt. Not fish mongers."

I oblige Avery and pull off my boots. "Keep watch over Sugar and Darkly," I say to Willadeene. "We will be back soon." I forgot I am wearing just one sock, its mate tossed down to my Ewell Day Higgs. I peel off the sock. Toss it down into the hot-hot dessert sands.

"Mind your hair, Antoinette," Avery says. "And hurry up. I am lonesome down here."

It is as lonesome where I am, I want to say. I give Willadeene a wave and slide myself below to Queen Odette Wintergarden. *Swoosh* and *scrape.* I hear those words again. *You are no better than that whore down by the Marsh.* Who is this hussy? *My Eulalee? Or Babylon, the deer?*

"About time," Avery says.

"Begging your pardon, your Highness. A sandstorm is brewing. I lost my way."

"Good thing you made it. We will be safe down here."

It is tranquil and dusky tucked pleasant in this Egyptian tomb, slivers of Forever Moon thieving through the rifts, currents of Vivaldi's *Winter* drifting above. Right off, I turn sleepy, lulled by the dark and Avery's good smells. Comforted in the soft nest of his mama's old ball gown he wears.

"Treachery," Avery whispers.

Across the Red Sea, Willadeene opens and closes Pocket Watch. *Clack-clack.* One moment withers to the next. And still, Avery says nothing.

"Heavens above, Avery. What are you going on about."

"Starshine, I thought you would never ask," he says. "And please do not make me remind you again." He leans his shoulder against mine. "I am Odette Wintergarden now. We will not tell Rebecca until the time is ripe. Of course, I will make no mention of the handsome man you have trapped in the Forest. Or that he calls you Starshine."

Treachery. "That man is not a Sinner, Avery. I did not break the rule. I would have come for the gun if I had caught one." When we catch Sinners here on Good Hope, it is a rule we shoot them dead.

"Then let us go and tell your Blue Heron. I am sure she and Miss Jane Austen will understand."

I am not at all certain Blue Heron would forgive my indiscretion. She remains firm on matters such as this: sinners and interlopers. She is sensible. Someone must be, or else we all might turn up dead. She could never be wooed by the notion of a gentleman caller come across the River to lay eye upon the Moon.

"No need to bother," I say. "He will be dead soon."

"Dead soon," Avery says. His breath catches. His body tenses. "Poor-poor handsome man with every last one his good-looking teeth."

If I am not quick, Avery will unravel, and there is no luxury of space here in this piano crate for Odette Wintergarden to carry-on and swoon. "What is it you wanted to say, Odette?"

"I am not afraid of her," Avery says, retrieving Mr. Rushworth L. Wintergarden's handkerchief from his bodice.

"Afraid of who?"

"Rebecca, of course," he whispers.

"Of course you are not scared of your very own sister." My Blue Heron says Avery is the one we should be frightened of, but I will keep this to myself.

Clack-clack. Across the Red Sea Willadeene broods, stoking lustful thoughts of that someone who is not my Ewell Day Higgs. The scandal flirts my bones. I want *more* of this thing that haint is feeling. A queen's ransom I would pay to keep it going.

Eulalee chatters over and over, knocking against the bottle. *Airrr.... Ooom.... Airrr.... Ooom.... Airrr.... Ooom....*

Lord, help. I know. I know. *Airrr.... Ooom.... Airrr.... Ooom....* I know what Eulalee's teeth have been trying to tell me. *Heirloom.* Is this what Eulalee's mama give to her? What Eulalee bequeathed to me? To know a haint's bliss? The pleasure of their every last sin?

"Are you listening to me, Starshine?" Avery pinches me on the arm.

"Forgive me. I am not quite myself." *None of us are.* Avery is Odette. Rushworth L. Wintergarden is a blue velvet ribbon and monogram stitches. My Eulalee, she is teeth rolling around rotten in my pocket. Even Willadeene is not Willadeene. She is Alsace-Lorraine. *And just who am I?* Where does Leontyne Skye end and Starshine begin?

"You are always thinking of yourself," Avery says. "Lucky for you I possess the good nature to look out for others. How you would manage without me is a terror of terrors."

"I am a lucky girl," I say, squeezing Eulalee's bottle. "Now, go on with it. What is this treachery you are going on and on about?"

"Leontyne, I am not so sure you are ready to hear."

"Then why did you bother bringing it up? I am as ready to hear anything unpleasant as I ever was. Perhaps you are not brave enough to say it."

"You take that back. I am plenty brave. Only, I am not rip-roaring glad to say something horrid against my own sister. I am not a monster." He leans against me. "But I think it is something you must know. I am not afraid of Rebecca. Not anymore…." He drags a breath into his corseted lungs. Eases it out. "I can make things happen, remember? I am the one who sent away the Sun."

"Then on with it, Queen Killer of Suns. Tell me what you think I should know." Now I am not so sure anymore I want to know what Avery aims to tell me.

Avery squeezes my nub. "Mirabelle," he whispers. "Treachery. Every shred of it is a lie."

For the life of me, I cannot decipher what Avery means. "What about my Mirabelle is treachery?" *Winter* drifts arctic and maudlin from Salome's strings, and I have the feeling something is missing other than my hand.

"Let me in," Willadeene says, banging from outside the Great Pyramid of Giza, giving Avery and me a start. "Something is a matter. I can feel it."

"The nerve of you," Avery says, his chest heaving. "Crossing the Red Sea here to Egypt. Serves you right and good if the boll weevil eats you up alive."

Willadeene hurries in nervous rings around our tomb, the tassel of her leash knocking the floor, her shadows haunting the place. *Thump- thump.* "Please let me in." She stops traipsing her lunatic circles, poking those evergreen fingers into the cracks. "I am feeling a strange sort of way." The smell of petrichor and her gardenia breath drifts through the moonlight and dust mote snow.

"Pianissimo," Rebecca hisses from the Up-Up There. "Listen."

Avery and I go still, his hand squeezing harder at my nub.

"The music?" Rebecca calls down. "Do you hear?" Through the door, across the Red Sea and dessert sands. Down into the murk of our Egyptian tomb. Another violin sings.

"Tchaikovsky," Avery says. "*Swan Lake*. Do you hear?"

Rebecca wakes Salome. Another burst of *Winter* beckons, serenading the other violin that is outside crooning *Swan Lake.* Back and forth, the violins court, teasing the other.

"Let me out," Avery says. "Let me out." He jumps for the opening. Scratching and reaching his way to be free, *Jubilation and Woe* tucked beneath his arm. "Willadeene," he hollers, reaching for the Moon. "Help me."

I push at Avery's backside, tangled and drowning in black satin until he dangles at the top, his high-heeled boots flailing and knocking me in the head. Willadeene peeks down, forget-me-not petals sleeting from her head.

"Me next," I say. I do not want to be left here for eternity all alone. I wedge myself between the two walls of boards, pushing up with my bare feet, reaching for Avery.

The air is a wrath of starlings. Beneath the Forever Moon, my Blue Heron haunts the Up-Up There, her hair storming dark about her face, her bow slicing wild across Salome. And I remember the sound. The *crunch* and *rip* of Blue Heron sawing my arm. And I remember moaning. Fiddler Crab weeping that poem by Keats.

"Who is here, Avery?" I ask, struggling to pull myself from the tomb. "Who has come?"

My sleeve slips from Willadeene's grasp. My fingers unwind from Avery's. It is Avery's whisper—a thing I already know that pushes me. And I am falling. *Falling the long-long ways.* Into the Pyramid of Giza. Through purple eddies of forget-me-nots. Through moonlight and dust mote snow.

Avery whispers again, his voice dark and hollow down here deep in the tomb. "Wintergarden...." he says to me.

Wintergarden....

Morningstar
The Entrance

Chapter 18

"This is a trick," Willadeene says. "Could be a Sinner. Or Avery's pirates. Or a ghost."

Avery yanks at Willadeene's leash. "Stop with such foolishness. It is Rushworth L. Wintergarden, my Prince Siegfried," he says, hugging *Jubilation and Woe*. "I made it happen. Cast a spell. Sailed it across the Sea."

"Do not open the doors, Blue Heron," I say. "Keep them closed."

"Too late for that," my Blue Heron says, drowning me with those moonless, river eyes. She reaches for the knob. We shiver, all of us on tenterhooks, the violin's chords beckoning this queer beginning, the moment before Rebecca swings open the doors. Leaves scrape. Forget-me-nots whorl. Moonlight pours in torrents across the threshold. The chore is done.

Rebecca steps onto the veranda, nestling Salome, wading waist-deep and barefoot through the rising Moon's tide. Avery hurries behind, dragging Willadeene with him. I chase the train of Avery's gown flickering and sopped in Moon.

My eyes are slow to focus. It is more vivid outside Morningstar than in.

"Where is he?" Avery asks.

"Yonder," Willadeene points. "Just there. See? Beneath the trees."

Under a canopy of gnarled live oak branches, a man stirs shadows. He starts up playing *Swan Lake* on his violin again. The music turns me nervous. For the life of me, I cannot remember the conclusion of Avery's fairytale story, but I recall things turn right bleak at the end.

Rebecca resurrects Salome at her chin. Runs her bow tender across her strings playing *Winter*. Willadeene riles beneath her evergreen skin at the playing of this duet. I feel what she feels. Prickles. I know what she knows—the scandal of frogs carrying-on carnal in trees, and I am ashamed the Sky and Moon can see me. That Eulalee passed down this godawful thing to me. *Heirloom.*

The man makes his way down the dead boxwood path. Avery looks to my Blue Heron, then to the caller. He opens *Jubilation and Woe*, flipping pages without giving nary one a look. He sucks breath into his whale-boned cage, casts out into the murk his courting spell, a tatter of poem by Shelley. The one he used to woo Josiah.

And the sunlight clasps the earth
And the moonbeams kiss the sea

Poetry steals rapturous from Avery's velvet tongue into the music sung by Salome and that other violin. He takes to the stairs, the train of his ball gown racing. *There is no stopping a comet in the heavens when it sets its mind to flee.* "Fiddler Crab," I yell. "Come back here to me."

Willadeene bolts, but I am quick, grabbing hold her hand. A dazzle of midnight stars, Avery keeps running, keeps casting his spell. Rebecca wields her bow.

Rip and *crunch*. And I remember….

Tribulation Day, two years back.

Avery weeps. Recites Keats.

Rebecca plays Salome.

Leontyne … Leontyne ... come back here to me.

I am dead. I am dead….

Constance Rose Longwood's mahaw-jellied brains stain the floor.

Idolatry…. Idolatry….

I remember now.

The Up-Up There....

You are no better than that whore down by the Marsh.

Willadeene squeezes my hand, and I am back here barefoot on the veranda, the trail of Avery's Comet dragging brittle boxwood leaves. *Swoosh.... Scrape.... Swish....*

Eulalee thrums, urging her haint-dying song from my pocket. I join her, singing out to Rebecca. To the stranger, to Willadeene. And to Avery.

On across the River,

To where you ought go,

In the gloom, I cannot see the man traveling the path. Cannot see the tail of Avery's Comet, but I can hear Avery cast more spell.

What is all this sweet work worth

If thou kiss not me?

Clouds knit, *slip knot, purl,* darning holes torn in the gloom until the Moon is gone. Until nothing can be seen, not so much as a hand before a face or spectral breath blown here in the chill. Only is there the perfume of Willadeene's garden. The ambrosia of my Longwood twins. Here, deep in the good smelling dark, the two violins croon star-crossed.

Willadeene's hand trembles in mine, squeezing flashes and spasms of good-feels she felt when she was Alsace-Lorraine. *Summertime.... Summertime rain....* Back before she was evergreen. When she was alive.

My legs quiver, coveting the dead. Desperate I am to howl out to the River, the Marsh, and Sea. To Rebecca and Salome. To the man antagonizing me merciless with his tempter violin.

Clouds unravel. Lo and behold, the blind can see. *Oh, look how Avery's Comet glitters. How my Blue Heron stares.* And there is the man lowering his violin a few steps away.

And the moonbeams kiss the sea....

Morningstar
The Entrance and The Boxwood Path

Chapter 19

"You have come back, Rushworth L. Wintergarden. I knew you would," Avery says, pulling the handkerchief from the bodice of his gown. "How I have wished and wished for this day."

I strain to see the man's eyes, to know if they are on their way to turning goat, only they hide beneath the shadows cast by the brim of his hat.

Rebecca calls down. "Pardon my brother, sir, but you are so very much like someone we once knew," she says. "Take no offense, but regrettably, I can tell from here you are not him."

With violin and bow gathered in one hand, the man pulls his hat from his head with the other. *Look up. Look up.* I need to know if any part of him might be no-good. If his eyes are on the verge of change. Willadeene loosens her fingers from mine, stepping forward to take a gander.

"Who are you then?" Avery asks, pressing the handkerchief to his cheek. "If you are not him?" The man is quiet, his eyes speaking the wonder of this eight-sided ruin, rambling wide all the way to the onion dome, up to the tippy-top of the spire.

Willadeene flutters. I suspect she sees what I see. Clear eyes. No creeping hint of goat. Not every bit of him might be good, but here with his eyes bright and spilling the heavens, I gamble not every bit of him is bad.

"Avery asked you a question, sir. Who are you?" I step forward, tucking my nub behind my back. "If you are not him?"

His eyes, moist with Moon, flicker to Avery, then to the rest of us ambling precarious at the edge of Morningstar's steps. We are not near majestic as this place, or decrepit, but I imagine we are as peculiar a sight all the same.

Pink chrysanthemums unfurl from Willadeene's temples, honeybees buzzing around to sniff. "Who are you, please?" she asks, more forward than I have ever known her to be with a stranger.

"Pardon me," he speaks at last, shaking off what must be the shock of beholding us gathered on the veranda to greet him, the shock of our Willadeene. "If I have disappointed you, then I shall aim to be whoever you desire me to be. I am an obliging sort of fella." He smiles, the Moon dazzling his teeth. "It is my specialty."

Right off, I am taken aback his voice sounds younger than he seems. He is a good piece taller than Avery. I guess him to be a might taller even than our Willadeene.

"This is not the time for games," Rebecca says. She runs her hand down her hip. I wonder if somewhere in that pocket of her dressing gown lurks Miss Jane Austen.

"Forgive me. I have come a very long way. I am not quite myself." He lowers his head.

"On a good day, who might you be then?" Rebecca asks.

"I might be Journey, ma'am," he says. "Journey Wintergarden on a fine sort of day. I believe you know my brother. Rushworth L. Wintergarden."

Avery gasps. "His brother." He reaches out to touch Rushworth L. Wintergarden's brother on the arm. "Did he come with you?"

"I only wish. I have not seen my brother for a long while now. I hoped you might know where to find him."

Avery resurrects Lord Byron again. "When we two parted in silence and tears."

"We did not know Mr. Rushworth L. Wintergarden had himself a brother." Rebecca runs her fingers down the side of Salome. "I admit, the resemblance is uncanny."

"I am his younger brother. His only brother. Tell me, if we are so much alike, what tipped you off that I am not him?"

"Now that I think about it, it is the way you are dressed. He was never without a tie. And here you are, with a sweater and collar opened to the breeze. And the way you play the violin." Rebecca bites at her lip. "Is different."

"How so?"

"Not better or worse. Different." Rebecca taps her leg quick with the bow.

"Rushworth is much more talented than me. And you, Rebecca Longwood, are every bit good as he said. My brother may have made no mention of me to you. But I know you all quite well."

"Did he write of me in letters?" Avery asks.

"Indeed, he did. He made mention of all of you."

"Tell me what he said." Avery presses the handkerchief to the ribbon at his throat. "About me."

Rebecca slows the tap of Salome's bow against her leg. "Yes, Mr. Journey Wintergarden. Do not leave us in suspense. What did he say? Unless it was unkind."

"Rushworth is many things. Though, I have never known him to be unkind. Not on his own volition."

"Of course," Avery says. "Please excuse my sister's insinuation. She really does belong alongside cows in a barn."

"I did not mean to offend, Mr. Wintergarden. I hold your brother in highest regard." Rebecca says, rubbing her hand across Salome's neck.

"Be assured, Miss Rebecca Longwood, he held you in similar regard." Mr. Journey Wintergarden looks up at me. "Miss Leontyne," he says. "I would know you anywhere, though I have never laid eye upon you a single time before." His eyes wander from my bare feet to the top of my Marie Antoinette hair.

"And what did your brother mention of our Leontyne?" Avery asks, corkscrewing about to look up at his sister, then me, that pretend look of innocence forever wreaking havoc on the place.

Rebecca taps her leg harder with the bow. "Be kind, Brother." She turns to me, hair pulled from her pretty face. "No one can be everyone's taste."

Be kind? My Blue Heron aims to spare me some truth. I am wriggling nerves now, wondering how a man I remember in only tatters and frays regards me. If Mr. Rushworth L. Wintergarden cared little for me when I was a two-handed gal, what might he think of me now?

"It is a miracle of miracles, Mr. Journey Wintergarden, that you arrived here safe," I say, shooing the subject from me to one even more bleak. "The path from the River to Morningstar is unkind to strangers not knowing the way."

"Miracle of miracles," Avery repeats. "This place is wrought with treachery just as our poor Leontyne says. Toils and snares. Toils and snares...."

And treachery....

"Was it your brother who directed you how best to find your way here?" Rebecca asks.

Mr. Journey Wintergarden laughs, and I have heard this laugh before. A morsel of Mr. Rushworth L. Wintergarden creeping back from before Tribulation Day.

"My brother never has been good at giving or taking directions. I owe my good fortune to that white-tailed deer." Journey Wintergarden points to the edge of the Forest to a congregation of rusty staggerbush trees. "I owe her a debt of gratitude for obliging to show me the way."

Babylon. That hussy stands pompous, gloating in silvery sheen, tippy-tapping her good-for-nothing hoof.

"I am so very glad you are here," Avery says, reaching for Mr. Journey Wintergarden's arm.

Willadeene blushes. Sheds pink chrysanthemums upon the veranda floor. "So very happy you are here," she says, glancing down at the impropriety of her sand dollar toes.

Mr. Journey Wintergarden has tried the longest while not to gawk at our Willadeene. At the very least he has himself some manners and a fine laugh. He can play Tchaikovsky on his shined-up violin. He possesses all his teeth. His eyes are not anywhere near turning goat.

"You there, ma'am. Standing next to Miss Leontyne?" Mr. Journey Wintergarden asks. "My brother has kept you a secret it seems. I can discern everyone here but you."

Avery speaks up. "She is Willadeene. She is mine."

Rebecca reaches over, taps Willadeene on the shoulder with her bow. "Your brother made no mention of her because she was not here before." Rebecca bites at her pretty lip. "Mr. Journey Wintergarden, you are looking a bit wild about the eye. Have you never had the occasion to meet yourself a haint?"

Willadeene flinches.

"Many things I have beheld, Miss Rebecca Longwood, but never a wonder such as she," he says.

Chrysanthemums flutter and fall from Willadeene, rouging her bosom, drifting onto the pale tops of Blue Heron's and my naked feet. Blue Heron shakes her foot free of petals. "You flatter Willadeene. At this inconsiderate rate, we soon might all be up to our throats and perish in her blizzard of blooms."

"Blizzard of blooms.... Blizzard of blooms...." Avery says, appearing enchanted by the spectacle of Willadeene molting. If Avery could weep and spill gardens, know this: *he would.*

"I do not mean to flatter," Mr. Journey Wintergarden says. "Only to tell the truth."

Avery recites more of his Lord Byron spell. "Half broken-hearted to sever for years."

"My manners have gone to seed," Rebecca says. "There are only ever Sinners here on Good Hope to entertain. It has turned off cool, and you have traveled a considerable way."

"Across the Ephesians Sea," Avery says, as if he just swam it himself. Landing salty and breathless on the beach.

"Do us the honor, Mr. Journey Wintergarden," Rebecca says. "Do please come in. You are welcome here at Morningstar."

Mr. Journey Wintergarden puts back on his hat. "I should protest. Apologize for coming all this way without an invitation. I should make some effort to turn. Pretend I might walk away. But I am afraid I am much too tired for all of that." He extends his arm to Avery. "By all means, show me the way."

Avery slithers his slim, naked arm through Mr. Wintergarden's. He flourishes more of his Lord Byron spell. "A shudder comes o'er me. Why wert thou so dear?"

If Mr. Journey Wintergarden is put off by Avery's poetic ramblings, he does not let on.

"Pale grew thy cheek and cold," Mr. Journey Wintergarden says, matter of fact. As if any ole' day the fella escorts and spouts incantations to peculiar, beautiful boys draped in yards of black satin.

Willadeene, Rebecca, and I step aside for this grand procession of Avery and Journey Wintergarden spinning whirlpools of chrysanthemums with their shoes.

"Ladies," Mr. Journey Wintergarden says, dipping his head, smiling as he passes.

There it glints, Mr. Rushworth L. Wintergarden's smile, same as his brother's. This smile is one of the few things I can now recall of the man, his two perfect rows of teeth. By the silver hue of the Moon, Mr. Journey Wintergarden's eyes might be pale grey. Or they might be blue. He is more youthful and handsome up close than he seems from afar. Wide shoulders. Small waist. Narrow hips.

Willadeene takes off behind Avery and Journey Wintergarden. Rebecca is nimble. She stomps the leash's tassel, bears her naked foot down hard. Rebecca hands Salome and her bow to me. Grabs hold of Willadeene by the arm. Yanks her backward and whispers.

"Your robe has come open. Look at you." She digs her nails into Willadeene's hand. "Indecent," she says.

Willadeene whimpers. I feel it, too, the slice of Blue Heron's fingernails one after the other, though she is not laying a single nail into me.

"You are no better than…." Rebecca says.

That whore down by the Marsh. The recollection of these words knocks the wind from me, that it was Rebecca who might have said these awful things to someone way back when.

"You are no better than a trollop, Willadeene," Rebecca says. "Vamping sailors by the sea." Rebecca digs her nails deep-deep into Willadeene. Deep-deep into me.

Blue Heron, Blue Heron, sleek and tall….

Morningstar
The Down-Below

Chapter 20

Sharks and pirates shimmer the dark currents racing Avery's eyes. "Were the waters very cold and treacherous when you crossed the Ephesians Sea?" Avery scoots a tufted stool closer to Mr. Journey Wintergarden's high-back chair, *Jubilation and Woe* parading on top.

Across from him here on the settee, by the light of the hearth's flame, I cannot yet figure if Mr. Journey Wintergarden's eyes are dusky blue or dreary grey.

Fiddler Crab launches more words quick. "What of the World, Mr. Journey Wintergarden? What news do you bring? Tell us the wonder of wonders you have seen," Avery says, sitting regal as a dowager queen. Weeping buckets of black satin on the floor.

Rebecca enters the parlor with Salome. Stops. Stands within the doorway's frame. "For the love of Moses, Avery, give our guest a moment's breath to speak."

The room goes quiet. All of us take in the look of Rebecca's curious clothes: close-fitting knee breeches, high black boots, and waist coat cut trim. A dashing figure. *My Count Vronsky.*

Where Mr. Journey Wintergarden's eyes once held Avery, they brim and drip my Blue Heron. Avery looks to Mr. Wintergarden. To Rebecca. "On your way to the stable, Sister?" Avery smiles. "Have you forgotten? There are no horses left here on Good Hope."

"Have you lost track, too, Brother?" Rebecca bows gallant. "Gone are cotillions and fancy-dress balls. Seems we are both well suited for things long since flung."

Avery sings out a lullaby to Blue Heron, the one his sister sings at night to Salome. Tilting dead Baby Girl Longwood's cradle this away. And that.

All the pretty little horses.
Blacks and bays,
dapples and greys....

This cradle song does not rest well with me. A clammy sweat breaks out across my neck. Have I always hated hearing this song sung?

Mr. Wintergarden speaks at last, pushing back a nuisance of coppery curls falling across his long-lashed eye—breaking Avery's spell, casting his own. "Where have all the pretty horses gone?" he asks.

"Those that did not fall dead from sickness a few years back, Sinners gobbled alive." One at a time, Rebecca kisses the tips of her fingers as if done dining upon a scrumptious meal. I am surely bound to be sick if Avery keeps singing that lullaby. If Rebecca keeps up more talk of eating horses alive.

Avery hugs *Jubilation and Woe,* terror and glee clashing in his eyes. "Do not be vulgar, Rebecca. Not here with our guest."

"The truth is often vulgar," Blue Heron says. "And inconvenient. This is why folks hardly speak it."

Mr. Journey Wintergarden laughs again. "I like you, Rebecca Longwood."

"Give it time, Mr. Journey Wintergarden." Avery says. "Give it time."

If anyone is *treacherous*, it is Avery, speaking ill of his sister in front of our guest.

Black moonstone and diamond earbobs shimmer, dropping like stalactites from Fiddler Crab's ears. *His dead mama's earbobs.* I do not think Rebecca has taken notice yet. That he has looted her jewel box. Has taken for himself one of the few things she possesses belonging to their mama.

"What of you, Miss Leontyne Skye?" Journey Wintergarden asks. "Do you share Miss Longwood's philosophy? Do you think the truth is inconvenient?"

I press my foot at the vine poking beneath the rug. I search my apron pocket, my fingers knocking against Eulalee, fingering a flake of *The Last of the Mohicans'* snow. "Every trail has its end," I say. "Every calamity brings its lesson."

"Is that not sublime? I will need to mull that sentiment over. Give it some thought." Mr. Wintergarden's eyes stroll to the top of my Marie Antoinette hair. I follow his gaze to the vines tangling and crisscrossing the ceiling. "Every trail has its end.... Sublime," he says.

I am the one now glimmering in Journey Wintergarden's eyes, and I do not mean to do it. *His eyes. Are they not more blue than dreary grey?*

"You would have to remember the truth to think anything of it," Avery says. "Poor- poor Leontyne. She hardly knew her name not so long back." Fiddler Crab turns the screw. "She was dead once." Avery is relentless. He will not be happy until he is all Mr. Wintergarden's faded eyes see.

"Leontyne suffered an accident two years back. There are things she cannot remember," Rebecca says.

"I am sorry to hear that," Mr. Journey Wintergarden says. "Though you appear to be on the mend now."

I put my nub in my lap. Hide it with my hand. Avery sings again.

Blacks and bays,

dapples and greys....

I reach up and pull out one hairpin, slipping it into my pocket hoping no one can see.

"You have a melodious voice, Avery Longwood," Journey Wintergarden says.

"Miss Hushabye Byrd says there is magic threaded in the words I speak." Avery smiles, looking to his sister. To me. Then back to Mr. Wintergarden.

"Do you mean *the* Miss Hushabye Byrd? The Singing Prophetess?"

"You have heard of her?" Avery reaches over touching Mr. Wintergarden on the knee.

"In this time of trouble, there are few, I would imagine, who have not heard of her."

Time of trouble....

"She is our new mother," Avery says.

"Is that a fact?"

"I am afraid it is," Rebecca says.

"Pardon me for intruding, but if the Singing Prophetess is your new mother, then what of Mrs. Constance Rose Longwood?"

Avery folds his hands into his lap over *Jubilation and Woe*. Looks over at Blue Heron.

"She took ill," Rebecca says, choosing not to say the *vulgar thing*. The truth. To suffer *inconvenience.*

You are no better than that whore down by the Marsh. Why did Rebecca say it? When?

"Tribulation Day," Avery says. "Two years back."

Mr. Wintergarden lowers his head. "My every sympathy."

"What of your own mother, Mrs. Wintergarden?" Rebecca asks.

"I am afraid she is as well as your own mother. She passed on from Consumption a short while back. That—and from what I suspect to have been worry. Not knowing what has become of my brother."

Dead mamas. We are knee high in this room with dead mamas, rotten teeth in my pocket, and Constance Rose Longwood's hairpins nipping my scalp.

Avery gasps. "Our Mr. Rushworth L. Wintergarden. When was he last seen?"

“We woke up one morning a year back, and he was gone. Not so much as a note. Or a good-bye carved in a tree. I would have come sooner looking if I had not been left alone to care for Mother.”

Mr. Wintergarden’s eyes. If I were pressed to decide a color, I would now call them *dreary grey.*

“Horrors of horrors.” Avery’s eyes glisten. “Do you think our Mr. Rushworth L. Wintergarden has been abducted? Held for ransom as we speak?”

Mr. Journey Wintergarden looks to each of us in the room. “I hoped Rushworth had made his way back here.”

Avery also hopes for Rushworth L. Wintergarden to come back around. Watch how his fingers rub across the ribbon at his neck. *Swish. . . . Swish. . . .* Blue Heron hopes for it. Look at her in the doorway in horse-riding boots coddling Salome. Does she dream of pretty horses? Of galloping away with Rushworth L. Wintergarden to far off lands? Here on this moldering settee, close to his brother—near his pale wandering eyes, I am nagged by a feeling. A feeling I miss Rushworth L. Wintergarden, too.

“I am afraid we have seen neither hide nor hair,” Rebecca says. “Of Mr. Rushworth L. Wintergarden.”

“Kidnappers and fiends!” Panic burbles Avery’s throat. “There is no other explanation. Why would he leave Seraphim House except to come here to visit me?”

Journey Wintergarden reaches over. Touches Avery’s hand. He sets eyes upon me, dusky blue and grey. Upon Rebecca. “The world is wide and deep with wonders, my friends. And there is so very little time.”

Time. I hardly can breathe, as if Avery has caged me in an ancient Longwood corset. Snatched the ribbons tight. *Bushels and bushels we have of midnights. A sinking treasure ship of time.* And I feel empty. *Something is missing. Something is gone.*

“Wide and deep with wonders,” Avery repeats back quiet. As if whispering a prayer.

Willadeene. I know she is near. I hear the honeybees. I feel her, the *tick* of Pocket Watch against her springtime skin. The haint is richer and poorer than we, her purse bursting its seams. Overflowing time, with no place to squander but here.

"Marrakesh," Rebecca says, stepping from the doorway. The word rolls from her tongue seductive. "Mr. Rushworth L. Wintergarden calls it a city of wonders." She runs her fingers down Salome. "He said once he would take me there."

"My brother sometimes speaks of Marrakesh. Of one day wandering the Medina and sipping mint tea."

Rebecca's eyes skim the room, skipping like dark pebbles tossed across a stagnant pond. *Marrakesh. I will run away with you to anywhere but there, my Blue Heron.*

Avery trails his fingers, loving across the top of *Jubilation and Woe*. "He told me he would one day sail me across the Ephesians Sea to Cherubim. Take me on a grand tour of Seraphim House." He lifts the book, touches the edge of it to his lips. "He says Cherubim's moon is nervous. The silly thing never stays put in the sky. Always fiddling like me. Never knowing exactly what it wants to be. A half-moon. A crescent."

"Cherubim is as beautiful of a place as this." Journey Wintergarden turns a gold ring engraved scrolly with initials about his pinky finger. "I sprouted there from a cotton seed and hardly ever have left. It saved me. Only now things are different. More lonesome since Mother is dead. And Rushworth is gone."

"Saved you?" Rebecca takes a few more steps into the room, her boots come-hither with all their *creaking* and carrying-on. "How did a place save you?"

"I am being silly," Journey Wintergarden says. "Pay no mind to me." He reaches down to check that his violin remains propped safe against his chair.

Marrakesh and Cherubim. This jibber-jabber of hightailing off from here without me has turned me nervous. Turned Willadeene nervous, too. I feel her lurking there outside the door.

Avery's earbobs catch and toss firelight with the tilt of his head. "Please, Mr. Journey Wintergarden, say anything you want. Talk and talk. Stack words to ceiling. We never have anyone to visit with other than the folks you see here in this room. Except for Lazarus and Josiah. And Miss Hushabye Byrd never allows us to speak a single word to them." Avery leans forward. Presses *Jubilation and Woe* to his chest. "Have you had the occasion to meet them? Lazarus and Josiah?"

"I cannot say that I have."

"The last ones Miss Hushabye Byrd brought around were better than the rest," Avery says. "You would surely remember them if you saw them. Both are handsome. But Josiah was the best. Perhaps you saw a young fella in passing? A fella toting a peacock feather held close to his chest?"

"The last ones?" Journey Wintergarden fidgets with the ring on his finger.

I pay mind to Journey Wintergarden's trailing, neat fingers. Clean and tidy fingernails. I have seen these fingers before. Only they were not his. Memory creeps, and I am certain those fingers were much like his brother's. *Rushworth L. Wintergarden. Swish* and *swoosh.*

"The Singing Prophetess thinks we are too stupid to notice her nephews are never the same," Avery says. "But they always are changing."

I trace the path of Avery's eyes. Take in the veins wriggling lurid from beneath the skin of Journey Wintergarden's wide pale hands. The thatch of coppery hair creeping his thick wrist, sneaking out from the cuff of his sweater. I cannot help but wonder if his feet are near nice as his hands.

"Never the same? That is certainly strange," says Journey Wintergarden. "Who is this Lazarus? This Josiah?"

"Miss Hushabye Byrd's nephews. They have no last names." Rebecca takes a few more steps across the room, boots creaking. "I must agree with Avery. This nephew business is all very queer."

Avery sings soft. Watches me watch Journey Wintergarden. Paying careful attention to our visitor's hands.

Blacks and bays,

dapples and greys....

My stomach aches. Churns and sours. A vine jabs at my other foot from beneath the rug. I pull another hairpin quick. Into my pocket it goes.

"Willadeene," Rebecca calls across the room to the doorway.

Lord help. Rebecca has spotted Willadeene. That haint is not so good at hiding. The tips of her sand dollar toes poke out beyond the doorframe. If she has herself a bit of sense in that pretty head, she will stay out of here. Run the other way. She has defied Rebecca. Refused to button on shoes to cover her scandalous feet.

"Unless your biscuits with ham are to sprout wings and fly into Mr. Journey Wintergarden's mouth, you will need to deliver them into the room." Rebecca taps her nails against Salome, growing less and less patient with Willadeene.

Rebecca watches Willadeene hurry into the parlor, Darkly and Sugar following behind her dragging leash. Rebecca glimpses Willadeene's feet, the flash of knee escaping her robe. "Put them down there, Willadeene," Rebecca says, pointing to the half-moon table, the one with a base shaped like a harp.

Willadeene pays no mind. She keeps walking a wide berth so Rebecca cannot stomp her leash, until she stands between Avery and Journey Wintergarden, the tarnished tray of good smelling ham biscuits quivering in her hands.

"Much obliged," Journey Wintergarden says, turning his ring. His eyes come alive. Flood with Willadeene. "They look delicious."

Willadeene's stomach spins circles, setting off palpitations in mine. I am not sure I will ever grow accustom to feeling what Willadeene feels. What haints feel. *More.... More.... More....*

Journey Wintergarden reaches for a biscuit.

"No. Not that one. The one on the top is yours," Willadeene says, a honeybee fussing over the lavender buzzing her head in extravagant streaks. "Yes. Right there. That is the one I made special for you." She lowers her head. Looks up coy through her feathery lashes.

Journey Wintergarden takes a bite. Closes his eyes. Up his throat, a murmur works its way, his Adam's apple bobbing immodest when he starts to chew. But this is not the moan that unsettles me most. There is another coming from somewhere outside a fair distance away.

Mmmm....

Journey Wintergarden's eyes open. Bright and wide. Dreamy. Not dusky or dreary. *Sapphire blue.*

"What on earth is it that makes this ham biscuit so delicious and good?"

"Strawberry mashed up in molasses," she says. "Spread across the ham."

Willadeene, you have gone and done it now, girl! Know this. There is nary a strawberry to be found anywhere here on Good Hope, only the ones growing and dangling comely from Willadeene's ears. She went and churned herself up creamy as butter. Slathered herself across Journey Wintergarden's ham.

Avery wobbles on his stool. "Agamemnon," he whispers, keeping balanced leaning forward against *Jubilation and Woe.*

A crumb of biscuit dangles in the pinkish dallop of Willadeene-jam, glistening the corner of Journey Wintergarden's mouth. He parts those lips. Steals the crumb, the last sticky bit of Willadeene with his Wintergarden tongue. "Hallelujah and amen," he says, kissing and licking the shoreline of his finger.

Mmmm.... Another moan comes from outside. This one is closer.

I think of half-eat alive horses. Of Constance Rose Longwood's mayhaw-jelly brains. *Dead Baby Girl Longwood gone quick as she come.* Of these damned hairpins drilling my skull.

"Come here, Willadeene," Rebecca says. "Bring those biscuits on over here to me." Rebecca steps forward, the boot leather threatening something awful if Willadeene does not comply.

Sugar toddles up across Journey Wintergarden's foot. Darkly sniffs the soles of his shoes, the crumbs of biscuit scattered on the floor. Journey Wintergarden leans down, his head nearly careening Willadeene's tray. "Who do we have here?" He scoops up my marsh rabbit in one hand. My chick in the other.

"That there is Darkly in your right. And Sugar in your left," I say.

"Pleased to make your acquaintance." Journey Wintergarden hugs at Darkly. Gives Sugar a peck on the head. "This rabbit is no bigger than a Lilliputian," Journey Wintergarden says. "Where did you come from, ole Darkly? The Isle of Lilliput?"

"It was a spectacle of spectacles," Avery says. "The way Darkly arrived here at Morningstar."

"Is that so?" Journey Wintergarden's eyes are wide with question and delight.

"Indeed, it was, sir." Avery points and squints off into the distance beyond Rebecca as if seeing it all unfurl again. "That Darkly. He came riding in from the Marsh on the back of an alligator." He whispers this last bit of impropriety. "Peeking out from inside a rusty, dented coffee can."

"What a sight that must have been." Journey Wintergarden gives Darkly a nod.

"Never have I seen anything like it." Avery says. "Probably never will again." There is a catch in Fiddler Crab's throat, waters rising to spill his eyes' almond banks. "Poor-poor Leontyne lay wounded, calling out for her Mirabelle." His voice trails. "Tribulation Day.... Two years back...."

"Avery McKinely Longwood. Stop telling tales," Rebecca says. "Stitch yourself back together. Quit this ridiculous carrying-on. Mr. Journey Wintergarden will think he has wandered into a lunatic asylum."

"That is how it happened, dear Sister. It is hardly a tall tale." Avery holds out *The Book of Jubilation and Woe*. "I have written it all down here. Every scream. Every whimper." Avery's earbobs glimmer. "How you can forget such a thing, Rebecca, is a mystery of mysteries to me."

Avery has weaved this story of Darkly time and time again since I have recovered, since coming back around to my senses. *An ancient alligator. A dented, rusty coffee can.* I must concede. I find it a comfort. Even though I doubt it is the truth. No truer than Avery was the one who brought me back alive with recitation of a few stanzas of a poem by Mr. John Keats.

"You are lucky, Miss Leontyne, that Darkly found you. And Darkly, I hope you know you are equal in luck." Journey Wintergarden smiles at me. He puts Sugar in his lap and gives my Darkly a kiss on the head. "What of this Miss Mirabelle? Did she ever make her way back around? Did you find her?"

Rebecca has taken hold of Leontyne. Holds her boot firm on Willadeene's leash. Slices her fingernails into the haint's back. I would not know this *treachery* if I could not feel Willadeene's pain, the never-ending want bleeding from her wounds, smelling up the room like *summertime... summertime rain.* What in this woeful world has come over my Blue Heron?

Mmmm.... Ahhh.... Another bellow comes from outside. So much closer, it well might have been uttered into my ear.

Clack. A knock against the window. Sugar's eyes blink over my shoulder at the gold velvet drapes. *Mmmm...* comes a sound from outside.

Journey Wintergarden cuddles my Darkly beneath his chin. Exploring my rabbit's wiry fur with those lank fingers. Willadeene pays attention, I feel her roaring alive with tingles at the thought of his Wintergarden hands prowling her skin, that same finger that scratches Darkly flicking away her honeybees.

"Rushworth said he was sent away from here." Journey Wintergarden's eyes fade to *dreary grey*. His tongue searches for remnants of biscuit, for Willadeene. But his mouth has been licked clean.

Clack. Something is definitely outside the window.

Rebecca's fingernails ease from the small of Willadeene's back. "What did your brother tell you?" Rebecca asks, both hands now around her Salome.

"He spoke of it. And I will tell you this, the very thought of not being able to come back here again troubled him."

"Avery is a fountain of stories this evening," Rebecca says. Her eyes catch the moonstone earbobs on her brother's ears. "Perhaps Avery might tell you more of why your brother was sent away."

"How would I know?" Avery asks. The River takes up rushing his eyes again. "Father is the one who did it." McKinely Longwood tells Avery plenty. That he is his vexation. An atrocity set forth upon him from God, but hardly anything ever useful.

"Perhaps you have written it down there in *Jubilation and Woe*. With all the rest of your *spectacular* of *spectacular* stories so you would not forget. If you scribbled down the comings and goings of Darkly, surely you documented our Mr. Rushworth L. Wintergarden. Shall we open up your book and take a look?"

"How dare you," Avery says. "Lay one of your devilish fingers on *Jubilation and Woe*, and you will be sorry, Sister." He gives his head a shimmy, flicking his earbobs alive. "Be warned, there is nothing in here that would flatter you."

"Sounds like something worth reading," Rebecca says.

Crack. This time all of us hear the commotion at the window. *Crack*—goes the window again.

Journey Wintergarden stands, puts Darkly and Sugar side-by-side in the chair.

"Where are you going?" Avery says, reaching for the leg of Journey Wintergarden's britches.

Mmmm.... Ahhh.... Mmmm.... The moaning sends goose pimples up my legs. Down my back. Journey Wintergarden stands at the window, reaching to pull back the velvet drapes.

"Stop! What if it is marauders?" Avery asks. "Thieves! The ones who took your brother?"

"Be quiet with your nonsense, Avery." Rebecca takes two steps, her boots teasing me.

Mmmm....

Journey Wintergarden pulls at the drapes. The velvet relents, falling apart from its moorings in faded, golden heaps, conjuring apparitions of dust. Light pulses purplish-red through the window, across the parlor hypnotic. Obscene.

"Agamemnon," Avery shrieks, jumping up, *Jubilation and Woe* tumbling from his knees to the floor.

Journey Wintergarden steps back from the window through a magenta haze of curtain dust. "Great God almighty," he says.

"Uncle Daddy," I scream, at the sight of the haint drifting beyond the window. I would recognize them yellow eyes burning bright with trouble anywhere. That tongue licking the air. He has grown impressive, to the size and shape of a bobcat. A bobcat without any legs.

Mmmm.... Uncle Daddy bloats like a pufferfish, tines burgeoning from his skin. He presses himself against the window. *Starshine ... Starshine,* he groans. Only ever have I heard a haints beg alms. And this one. This one here has the gall to call out to all God's creation the name my Ewell Day Higgs give special to me. *Starshine ... Starshine....*

Uncle Daddy backs up a far piece. Turns loose a war-cry howl. Tooth and nail, he heads for the window. Avery screams *holy hell and murder* while Rebecca's nails carve Willadeene.

Glass shatters, glistening shades of plum.

Wind churns the room Siberian.

Forever Moon and Uncle Daddy come spilling-spilling.

Ahhh ... Uncle Daddy sails the ceiling vines. Spins slow circles, his head impaled with flickering shards of glass. He opens his catfish lips and out falls a bird's feather.

Mmmm ... I moan to myself. It feels good and awful to be Uncle Daddy. To be me. I pull a Constance Rose Longwood hairpin free. Then another. Pitch them to the floor to twinkle in shattered bits of wreckage. I feel better and worse than before. *And who am I again?*

Uncle Daddy throbs purplish red, uttering vile-vile things. Things he did. Things he aims to do. I long to hear and feel the *more, more, more* of it. *Starshine ... Starshine....* Uncle Daddy's fish-tail has transformed into a large cat's tail, and he carries-on vulgar with it, rubbing himself against the ceiling, sanding and shaving up a mix of plaster and creeping vine snow. He opens his eyes beautiful and alluring upon the room, burnished gold and every-bit goat, and I do not care now if I ever feel the chill of a real-life, Kilimanjaro snow.

Who could blame my Eulalee? If she offered herself over. If she lay herself down tender with a haint. If that haint was a low-down sort of sorry, and every-bit good at bad as this good-for-nothing haint.

Journey Wintergarden's long-long fingers lace through Avery's. Curl around my Rebecca's shoulder, his tongue searching for crumbs. I breathe the rotted curtain dust. The sweet and woodsy smell of my Longwood twins. I draw in Willadeene's petrichor, her strawberry jam. I feel the tick of Pocket Watch taunting Willadeene's thigh. The buzz of her honeybees.

Blue Heron shifts her weight, the sound of her boot leather turning me mad with desire. In the deep-deep of me, here in the Down-Below, I call out into the dark and wait for the echo to return back to me.

I am the no-good that comes from Skye women and no-count haints. Rotten teeth cackle. Vibrate in my pocket. *Lord, help me, Jesus.* My Rebecca is right. I am no better than Eulalee.

I am no better than that whore down by the Marsh....

The Forest

Chapter 21

Willadeene trails me to Forest's edge as I sneak off to see about my Ewell Day Higgs, leaving the others at Morningstar to contend with Uncle Daddy. Leaving my Darkly tucked safe in the covers next to Avery.

I do not let on I know Willadeene lurks the Moon's spun shadows behind me. I might have taken it into my head to send her back to Morningstar by now if I did not crave the distraction of her lustful heart. I slow down. Let Willadeene creep closer, let the perverse fantasies she is having about Mr. Journey Wintergarden slither through my mind.

Treachery. Willadeene is shameless pining for another man while her poor Ewell Day Higgs lay dying off in a pit. Look at me enjoying Willadeene enjoying Journey Wintergarden. *I am no better than that whore down by the Marsh.* "Do not think I cannot see you, Willadeene. That I cannot smell you. Come out from over yonder."

She whispers from behind a magnolia. "I cannot sleep. Not with that Uncle Daddy roaming and moaning around the house."

Willadeene is lying. The reason she cannot sleep is Journey Wintergarden, the thought of him burning her hip bones good and hot. Smoldering mine. I bend down. Pick up an acorn. Throw it at the tree. "Get on out from there. Git!" I say.

Willadeene steps from the tree's shadow, her sand dollar toes lustering moonlight. She looks back to Morningstar, magenta light glowing from the windows. "How long have you known Uncle Daddy?"

I do not care for Willadeene's tone, like I have been up to no good. "I only just run across him in the Forest," I say. "Met him just once. From the get-go, I knew he was trouble."

I push at my teeth with my tongue, checking to see if they are still there. *The Worsening*. Has it begun now that Eulalee is gone?

"How long do you reckon that awful Uncle Daddy aims to stay?" asks Willadeene.

"How in creation should I know?" Willadeene's insinuation, and the fact I can read this scoundrel's mind, rubs me raw. I will not let on I up and asked him already when none of them were around. I will tell you this, what it was Uncle Daddy had the nerve to say. He looked them pretty, golden goat-eyes down upon me, running that smooth tail across my cheek. *When I is good and damn ready. When I remember. When I know for sure what it is I come for.* "You best get on back before Avery finds you missing." I say.

"Avery sent me down to the kitchen house to get him more biscuits and ham," she says. "What he does not know is not likely to kill him."

"Best get to it then. You know he is a cramp in the foot when he gets hungry."

"He will get a biscuit when he gets a biscuit," she says. "And I will get going when I am good and ready."

Good and ready. Uncle Daddy and Willadeene are two uppity, dead peas in a pod. And I am in a conundrum as to what has come over Willadeene.

"Where are you going, Leontyne?" she asks.

To Kilimanjaro with my Rebecca. To build castles in the snow. "To see about Redemption. And just why did you come following after me, Willadeene?"

Willadeene looks back to Morningstar, pointing a finger at the place. "Avery says that is where Rushworth L. Wintergarden stayed when he lived here on Good Hope. In the Up-Up There. In the Celestial Hall of Books. Journey Wintergarden will sleep there now."

She is working herself up into a lather, blossoming a glory of blooms. Honeybees hover. More than before. *Buzzing*. Sniffing.

The Celestial Hall of Books. "A mighty fine state of affairs it is to call yourself a Wintergarden," I say. "If ever I stepped one pinky toe up yonder into that Hall of Books, I do not recall." Except I must have been up there at least once. *Tribulation Day.... Two years back....*

"Count your blessings, Leontyne. At least you can read," she says.

"What is the good of reading if Avery is stingy with his books?"

Willadeene closes the space between us, takes hold of me by the arm. "It is Rebecca's doing," she whispers. "Not Avery's."

"Rebecca's doing?"

"Avery is selfish. That much is true. But Rebecca is the one who keeps you from the Up-Up There. Keeps me miserable and stupid. Keeps me from learning to read."

Treachery.... "Set no store by what Fiddler Crab says. He always speaks ill of his sister."

"I might be dead, but I have a mind, Leontyne. I have eyes."

"I can see, too, Willadeene. That Fiddler Crab has you on a leash."

"And Rebecca has latched one about you. Only it does not drag the ground. She does not stomp it with her boot. You cannot see it," she says. "But it trails long and tricky."

She squeezes my arm hard. Digs her nails. "Let me loose," I say, wrestling to be free. "You are hurting me."

"You are a fool, Leontyne Skye. Believing everything that one says is true."

My resentment spills. Gushes through the cool-hot tear of my flesh. *You abandoned my Eulalee. And she cared more for you than me. Here you are bad-mouthing my Blue Heron....* "Get your ungodly hands off of me." I shove her hard and spiteful. "You wretched haint."

She stumbles. Her naked feet turn nimble, drop anchor to steady her to the ground.

And there is quiet. Quiet…. And more quiet. Row upon row, we plow and seed silence. Corn fields ripen—wither—the two of us staring dazed at the other through brittle stalks of gloom.

"I am a wretched haint." Willadeene says. "That is the gospel truth."

Journey Wintergarden … Journey Wintergarden…. I hardly can think here with the echoes running slipshod through Willadeene's mind. "Forgive me, Willadeene. I did not mean those hateful words." *I am not Eulalee. I am Leontyne Skye.*

"I am not quite anything I can remember," Willadeene says.

"How is it?" I ask. "That you cannot recall. Is there not a smidgen of anything seeming familiar?"

"I might ask the same of you," she says. "In the by and by, what does it matter? Is it not simpler keeping on forgetting the things you forgot?" She pulls at her leash, dragging magnolia leaves. "All there is, is now."

Willadeene lies. Beyond the now, there are the catacombs of all her lonesome tomorrows. Fever ravages this haint's hips with Journey Wintergarden. And I know this. I know what Willadeene knows. Always, it is desolate when there is no one to keep warm but you. And I feel the ache and tumble of Willadeene's days. The stretch from here and now—clear all the way to forever. Still, I cannot comprehend the immensity of eternity. Honeybee after honeybee. The always and always. Everlasting. Never ending. And I want no part of Kingdom Come. Falling the long-long ways, one-handed through Willadeene's great forever.

Willadeene pulls more of her leash. "It is not easy," she says, turning to look back at Morningstar.

Purplish light creeps across the ruined lawn toward the Forest. Uncle Daddy has found his way to the Up-Up There, stalking the Cupola. "What is not easy, Willadeene?"

"Being dead," she says. "And more alive than the living."

Ewell Day Higgs's song comes to me. I take it into my head to sing to Willadeene, aiming to scrape a few flecks loose of her memory from back when she was Alsace-Lorraine. "Summertime … summertime … rain."

Willadeene looks upon me queer. Nods her head in time. Catches quick to the rhythm. "Summertime … summertime."

If there is a glint of recognition of who she was before, so much as drift of cloud swirling feathery across the ether of this here haint's eyes, I decide I will hurry her off to be with her Ewell Day Higgs.

Willadeene reels more of her leash, the tassel lifting from the ground. 'Round and 'round, Uncle Daddy swims slow circles, beaming crimson, transforming the place into a lighthouse. A honeybee drops dead from Willadeene's garden. There is too-too much of Willadeene. Too much even for a ravenous honeybee, saddlebags bursting their seams. Uncle Daddy swims around the Cupola, pulsing like a plum-colored lighthouse across the withered lawn to the edge of the Forest. Across our feet.

"He is mine," Willadeene says. "He is not Avery's. He is not Rebecca's." Another honeybee drops dead from her garden. "Journey Wintergarden is mine."

"He is better off dead here with me," she whispers, pulling up the last of her leash. "I will love him better than Avery. Better than Rebecca." She reaches for me. "Help me, Leontyne."

Idumea…. Idumea…. I know what wickedness she is thinking. How is it she can ask this *treacherous* thing of me?

The last bee buzzes her final buzz, falls dead and bloated between Willadeene's beautiful toes. "Leontyne," she says, pressing her hand against her bosom. "Help keep Journey Wintergarden forever here with me."

Willadeene is an awful kind of right. Journey Wintergarden is better here and dead with her. Better here and dead than runoff to Marrakesh with my Blue Heron. I close my eyes to the fall of Willadeene's dead honeybee snow. To Uncle Daddy's light casting magenta out to the Good Hope Sea. 'Round and 'round.... *Always and always*.... More. And more.

And more....

The Chapel of Abundance

Chapter 22

"Ewell Day Higgs. Ewell Day Higgs," I call out, wondering what awful thing I up and done to give Willadeene the notion I am the murdering kind. That I would hatch a plot with her to kill Journey Wintergarden. *Was I a murderous sort of girl before?*

There is no path to a road of knowing if Journey Wintergarden might find himself back here a haint. And then Journey Wintergarden is just dead. And Willadeene is still alone. And I am standing here a murderess with blood on this one hand. I study Mirabelle, imagining her hunkered quiet in her can, no doubt daydreaming and plotting, wrapped warm in Constance Rose Longwood's wedding lace.

Ewell Day Higgs calls up from the pit. "Starshine…?"

"It's me," I say. *Your Starshine.*

"In case you were wondering," he says, trying to laugh. "I am not dead yet." He coughs and coughs, wet and phlegmy. "Did that Odette Wintergarden come back here with you?"

"She did not," I say. "And I am pleased. Pleased as a June peach to know you are not dead," It is true. I am grateful he is not gone, happy to have Ewell Day Higgs with every last one of his teeth all to my very own. "How much does it hurt?"

He coughs again. "I imagine there are folks worse off than me," he says.

I comfort myself making believe Ewell Day Higgs is half-alive instead of half-dead. "I like the way you set your eyes on the bright side of things," I say. I wonder how bright he might think this here world if he knew his Alsace-Lorraine cavorts Good Hope scheming murder so she can love up shameless on Journey Wintergarden. *To have him all to herself.*

"I set no store by complaining, Starshine."

There is an itch I got needs scratching, a quandary needing to be known—whether it was or was not the case his Alsace-Lorraine ran wild, barefoot, and half-naked same here as Willadeene. Are haints near abouts good at being bad when they were living? Are they better or worse off when they turn dead? "Ewell Day Higgs," I say. "Do you miss Alsace-Lorraine? Do you pine for her a powerful sort of awful?" *Will I suffer misery wanting Blue Heron more when my flesh falls tender from the bone?*

Not a scrap of word comes from my Ewell Day Higgs. Not so much as a cough barking up wretched from his throat. The thought crosses my mind I might have killed him, stirring memories bitter-sweet of his Alsace-Lorraine.

From Mirabelle's can comes a *tick-tick-tick.*

Ewell Day Higgs calls back deep from the pit with his tongue. *Clickety-click-click.*

I do not care for the sound of this. Mirabelle *ticking*. My Ewell Day Higgs *clickety-clicking*, the two of them in cahoots. "I asked you a question, Ewell Day Higgs."

"I know you did, Starshine, but I hope you do not mind that I would rather know me a thing or two about you," he says. "I sure would appreciate a few new nice things to think on other than my life from before."

He is sweet to think I have anything nice at all to share, and I wonder how not remembering Alsace-Lorraine makes him feel better. He sounds every bit like Willadeene. *Is it not simpler keeping on forgetting the things you already forgot?* "What do you want to know?"

"Everything, Starshine," he says. "Then tell me heaps and heaps more."

"There is not a very lot to tell." When you hardly remember anything at all.

Tick-tick goes Mirabelle.

Clack-clack goes my Ewell Day Higgs. "Mirabelle says you aim to travel away from here one day. Just where is it you plan on going, Starshine?"

Before I can give Mirabelle a piece of my mind for meddling in my business, Ewell Day Higgs lets loose on a coughing jag. "You sound a fright, Ewell Day Higgs," I say. "How much Redemption do you have left down there with you?"

"Near abouts a drop or two," he says.

"Make it last," I say. Soon my Ewell Day Higgs will be gone, only two drops of Redemption left of living to be done. If it will ease his suffering to know where I am going, I will tell him. "I promise not to leave while you are still here."

"When I am gone, Starshine, where are you thinking you might go?"

I want to tell him to ask Mirabelle, since she knows every bit of my business. "The Great Wall of China," I say. "I plan on skipping along the top 'til I run clean out of stone."

Wonder lay upon wonder in Ewell Day Higgs's voice. "Is that so, Starshine?"

"I reckon I will then head off for cooler weather. Far-far off to Iceland. Where I might take the notion to ride the backs of beluga whales. Beneath other midnight suns."

"Mighty fine. Mighty fine," my Ewell Day Higgs says to me.

"Of all the places I want to go," I say. "The thing I want most to know. The thing I want to feel is a real-life Kilimanjaro snow." I shut my eyes. Pretend I am tippy-toed at the tippy-top, squinting through a blizzard, counting mongooses and the African buffalo roaming way-way down below.

Tick-tick.

Mirabelle is at it again. I refuse to let her *tack* her way to the better of me. I keep my eyes shut here in this Tanzanian storm. "What does she want now?" I ask, my teeth turned cold and chattering.

"She is worried is all," Ewell Day Higgs says.

"Worried? About what?"

"About who you might keep company with. When you venture far-far off from here."

"No need to worry, Ewell Day Higgs. I can look after myself," I say.

Ewell Day Higgs calls up from the deep of his pit. "That Blue Heron." he says. "Listen careful to me, Starshine. Mirabelle says she is not the gal for you."

How dare she. "Mirabelle is a good-for-nothing, five-fingered liar," I say. "She is eat pure down to the knuckles with envy." *Mirabelle likes Avery best. Trusts him more.* She listens to his lies about my Blue Heron, presses herself nosey against the tin of her dented coffee can.

"Starshine?" Ewell Day Higgs asks.

"I am listening."

He coughs a spell. When he speaks, his voice is worn through at the edges. "I want you to go all them places you dream of going. I want you to see yourself an honest-to-God, real-life, Kilimanjaro snow. Mirabelle wants that for you, too."

Mirabelle *tack-tacks.*

Ewell Day Higgs *click-clacks* back. "I do not think this is the time, Mirabelle," he says.

I search at my feet for a piece of tabby. For something to throw at Mirabelle. "What is not the time, Ewell Day Higgs? What is Mirabelle saying?"

Tickety-tack. Tack.

"Swish and swoosh," he says. "Swish and swoosh. There is a thing Mirabelle thinks you ought know."

"Tell me," I say.

"The blue velvet ribbon is not Avery's. Or Blue Heron's."

Swish.... Swoosh....

Tick-tick.

“Look up, Leontyne,” Ewell Day Higgs says. “Look up.”

Like a lighthouse beam, Uncle Daddy’s beacon passes magenta over the tops of the trees. ‘Round and ‘round. *Forever and always. The blue velvet ribbon is not Avery’s or my Blue Heron’s. Swish.... Swoosh....* I remember. “It is mine,” I say to the Island. To the Forever Moon. To the Marsh. The River and the Sea. Mirabelle does not lie.

The blue ribbon is mine.

The Marsh

Chapter 23

For the life of me I do not know what compelled me to come down here to the Marsh to fetch Eulalee's oyster shell necklace. Perhaps it was some sort of intuition, a feeling I should have it, a memento from Eulalee. Something other than her rotten teeth to keep.

I fiddle with the necklace, wondering if I ought fling it to the pluff for the periwinkle snails to wear, or if I ought put it around my own neck and lick the insides of every shell to taste and see what all the Skye women have known before. To see if one thing they might know now is why my Blue Heron lied about the blue ribbon. Why she says it is hers and not mine.

I drop the oyster shells into my apron's pocket and head back up the path to the Forest to make my way back to Morningstar. The necklace *clinks* against Eulalee's bottle. Eulalee's teeth do not make even a little fuss or show any recognition of her precious Rivière. Seems to me, Mama's teeth have been quiet awhile now. When was it she last made a peep? I pull out the bottle. Rattle it around. "What is wrong with you, Mama?" I ask.

"Who are you talking to?"

I near abouts turn loose a scream. "Journey Wintergarden, you scared the daylights out of me."

"Forgive me," he says, walking toward me from the Forest. "I should have called out to you to let you know I was coming."

"What on earth are you doing out here?" If it is not Avery or Willadeene, it is Journey Wintergarden following after me.

"I came to see about you?" he says. "Avery was in a panic when he could not find you. He mentioned something or another about you maybe being kidnapped by pirates."

"You should not have come here alone." *You should not have come here at all.* "It is dangerous in the dark."

Uncle Daddy's magenta light streaks across us. "It was not so very dark. I passed a congregation of haints lighting up the Forest on their way to Morningstar. And then there is the light Uncle Daddy is casting out here into the Forest. Besides, I am not at all alone," he says. "I have you. And look, I brought Treachery." He turns around and shows me the violin he has strapped across his back. "Avery has seen fit to give my violin a name."

Treachery. "Avery is good at that. Naming things belonging to others."

"I have a spot already softening for your Fiddler Crab," Journey Wintergarden says, smiling.

"The feeling is mutual. Avery already has turned fond of you." Aside from Sinners, Avery is fond of any man with two legs worked into pants. *Pirates. Josiahs and Lazaruses. My Ewell Day Higgs.* A thing Journey Wintergarden just said comes tinkling back to me. *A passel of haints on the way to Morningstar.* Haints ought not be heading to Morningstar. They ought be heading to Damascus. And another thing I realize is that Damascus has gone quiet. It has been a good piece back since I have heard her sing.

The wind shifts. Comes west from the Doldrums, prowling fetid through the groundsel trees. Blithering. *Blither-blither.* Trying to rile Damascus. The wind is worthless, only stirring the stink of fallen Sarah Figs, swelling the air intimate. Damascus keeps herself quiet. Holds her breath.

Journey Wintergarden sniffs the air. "Pardon me, Miss Leontyne. What is that awful smell?"

"It is the Marsh," I say. Sullied Sarah Figs. The Doldrums. The stink of frogs making love in trees. The smell of his burning shoe leather. *Burning shoe leather!* "You have stepped in it," I scream. I grab hold of Journey Wintergarden. "Your shoes. Take off your shoes."

From Journey Wintergarden's soles rise tentacles of steam. "Holy hell," he hollers.

"Hold onto me. Pull off them shoes. Hurry."

Toe to heel. Toe to heel, he works his feet free, the large palm of his hand pressed into my shoulder, the weight of him weakening my knees until he has pulled off his shoes. His socks. Until both of his long, pale feet are naked.

"What was that?" he asks, letting go of me. "On the bottom of my shoes?"

I look down upon his naked feet, every bit glorious as his hands. I study the high-high arches. Take note that his second toes are longer than the first. I admire the creep of coppery hair sneaking to his ankle. *Have I ever seen a man's naked foot before? One not rotting at the root of a Sinner's leg.* "Manure. A Sinner's," I say. "From the look and slow burn of things, it is old. Thank your lucky stars it is not fresh."

"I owe you a debt of gratitude, Miss Leontyne Skye," he says.

"I told you it was dangerous coming out here alone."

"But I am not alone. Remember?"

"That is right," I say. "You brought Treachery." I keep staring away. Trying my best to not look down at them handsome feet.

"I might have been left with nothing but ankles," he says.

Those ankles. "It is dangerous here. Remember?" *It is beautiful here.* "I bet things are safer out there across the Ephesians Sea, out yonder on Cherubim. You might should have stayed home."

"Cherubim...." he says, dangling the word. "Miss Leontyne. May I tell you something? Something true?"

Tell me truth. Tell me lies. "Say whatever you have a mind to say, Journey Wintergarden." *Just cover those toes.*

This is the thing he says that pries my eyes from the Moon, spinning me 'round to look at him. "There is no place I know of ever called Cherubim. No such place ever drawn on a map."

"Cherubim is not a place?"

"Only in our imaginations," he says. "Rushworth's and mine. Rushworth was the architect."

The magenta light passes again, burning across us both. Hoot howls hoot. Squirrels claw trees. Warblers warble.

"Where did you come from, then? If there is not such a place?"

"A sickly mother," he says. "Never was she right in the head. No father to speak of. Only Rushworth and me, and this daydream of a fine place he built for us called Seraphim House. Seems we are all orphans here on Good Hope. You and me."

"You appear well looked after," I say. "For someone living in the figment of a dream." I regard his immaculate hands. His Don Juan feet. "Your brother was a tutor. An educated man. You both play the violin. I reckon being an orphan does not get much better than that."

He laughs. "All is not what it seems. Little ever is, my sweet Leontyne. This is the short of it. The story of me. Pay attention, now." He lifts my chin with his wide-acre hand. "There was a woman. Tales of woe are carved always at the dark heart of them by women. Of unscrupulous means."

Women of unscrupulous means. I know a thing or two about that. As we speak, Willadeene whittles and whittles. Carves and carves.

"This particular woman of whom I speak, took us in," he says. "Saw about our clothing. Our schooling. Turns out she came at us with motives." He caresses a finger beneath my chin. "The world is filled with nothing more than that, my friend. Motives. She did what she did. Now—Rushworth is gone. Mother is dead. And I am here. That is that. Amen-amen. The end."

Motives. He turns loose my chin. Looks to the sky. It is hard to see color beneath Forever Moon, everything pale and silvery except for Uncle Daddy's magenta light. *What color is Journey Wintergarden's eyes?* "I am sorry," I say. "About your mama. Your brother. That unscrupulous woman." I trace the curve of the high-arch of his good-looking foot. "Please do me a favor."

"Anything. Just ask."

"Do not tell Fiddler Crab about Cherubim. About Seraphim House."

"I can oblige you that," he says. "Afterall, you saved my life. My ankles. My feet."

Those ankles and feet. Those teeth. "It is just.... Well, Avery dreams of going there one day. To Cherubim."

"Me, too," he says, flexing his foot like he might set out hiking a trail to make-believe. "You are kind, Leontyne Skye. Rushworth was right about that."

"What else did your brother have to say about me?" If there is something not fit for telling, Journey Wintergarden might as well tell me now. With Rebecca and Avery not around.

"I am sorry you cannot recall him, Leontyne. He is worth the bother of remembering. He is nothing like me."

I remember the smell of him. His voice. His long-long fingers. The blue-blue ribbon he gave me. *Swish and swoosh.* I remember I must be like Eulalee. *No better than that whore down by the Marsh.* "Maybe he will come back to me," I say. "In bits and bobs." In good-looking, sweet-smelling pieces.

Journey Wintergarden shimmies his arms from the straps holding Treachery. He pulls the bow and violin from her swaddling. "He said you learned fast as anyone he had ever seen."

"Learned what, sir?"

"How to play the violin, of course."

The violin. The magenta light comes sweeping back again. Knocks me off kilter. "That is a lie," I say. "I never played the violin."

"Of course you did, Leontyne. Rushworth said you played better than Rebecca." He looks those eyes of uncertain colors at me, runs them across my nub. "Avery told me about your accident. Tribulation Day. That you fell the long-long ways."

Avery McKinely Longwood is a sneaking snake. "How can it be? I would remember such a thing." It is Blue Heron who would have played the violin best. *My legs.* I feel my legs collapsing right out under from me. I wobble.

"Hold on there now," Journey Wintergarden says, grabbing hold of my elbow. "I did not mean to upset you. Steady now. Steady."

"I am fine, Journey Wintergarden. It is a frightful shock is all. A shock I could play the violin." That I could be fit for something beyond the gathering and gutting of them Sarah Figs.

"Why do you think Rushworth named your violin, Salome?" He smiles. "To hear you play her, to hear her sing, a body might grant you a world of anything. Anything." he says. "A head chopped special. Laid out gruesome on a tray."

Salome… Salome…. I cannot breathe. *She was never mine.* "I know nothing of it," I say. *Nothing is better than anything. Shut up, Journey Wintergarden. Be gone. Stay.*

A tremor rumbles beneath our feet. A monstrous gasp. A dreadful wheeze. Damascus can no longer hold her breath. She drinks.

"Leontyne," he whispers. "What in heaven's creation is that?"

Desire. Motive. Obligation. A liar. A thief. "Eulalee's haint-trap tree." *She belongs to Eulalee. Not to me.*

Journey Wintergarden takes off ahead for the Marsh on the wetland walk, his feet plodding sonorous, a mating call against the boards to Damascus.

I follow. Watch his feet. *Anyone would follow you anywhere, Journey Wintergarden.* Heel to toe. Heel to toe, I listen to them handsome feet thump. *Come with me…. Come with me….* He stops. Gazes at Damascus's hourglass trunk. Admires the peculiar bark of her tree—oyster shells opening and closing come-hither. He works his eyes up. Gapes at the rise and curves. Her crystalline branches. The up-and-up. Her forever and always. Out he looks across the horizon, coveting the shadowy humps of her banyan roots. Out to the Doldrums. Out to eternity.

Journey Wintergarden turns back to me, Moon filling his eyes, both of us in Damascus's eclipse. My own eyes have grown strong in the dark, in this Forever Night. My senses turned keener. *Rebecca will love Journey Wintergarden. She will leave me here all alone.*

Here comes again the lighthouse beam, Uncle Daddy swimming faster, laving us purplish with light, coloring the silvery Marsh magenta. Damascus drinks and drinks.

Willadeene … Willadeene…. I know what must be done.

Dark heart. Dark heart.

Deep carved and cruel….

Journey Wintergarden … Journey Wintergarden….

You are as good as dead …

and gone….

Morningstar
The Boxwood Path and The In-Between

Chapter 24

Uncle Daddy slows his swim at the top of Cupola, his light spilling afterglow across the dead boxwood path. How will Willadeene and I do it? How will we kill Journey Wintergarden dead? *With poison? A spikey pit? A snare's rope pulling him from the ground by his neck?* What are the chances he might escape a Sarah Fig and come back here like Willadeene? *Dead is not really dead.* I might be doing Journey Wintergarden a favor. What was it Willadeene said? *She is dead and more alive than the living.*

Uncle Daddy … Uncle Daddy…. A dozen haints drift down the boxwood path ahead of Journey Wintergarden and me, calling up to the Cupola. The haints ought not be here. They ought be heading to the Marsh, only Damascus is not singing. And Eulalee's teeth are not keening.

From Morningstar comes a scream. "Will-laaa-deeene…."

Fiddler Crab. He is the one screaming bloody murder and hell. He is the one always screaming. The commotion gives the haints a fright, their tines rising like hackles. Journey Wintergarden grabs my hand, and down the dead boxwood path we go, his bare feet and my rubber boots wailing against the ground. Journey Wintergarden's knapsack scrapes and plucks at Treachery, the chords shrieking along with Avery. In the racket, I try to recollect Salome being mine, wondering if Mirabelle recalls which notes go with which fingers.

Journey Wintergarden fidgets the knob with his glorious hands. *Clackety-clack.* We both stumble into the gallery. Into the In-Between. In a puddle of purplish moonbeams, Avery sways, grabbing at his neck. At the blue ribbon. *My blue ribbon.* Over and over he screams. "Will-laaa-deeene … Will-laaa-deeene…."

At the foot of the staircase stands my Blue Heron. *Look.* There is Willadeene—halfway up the stairs. *And yonder.* Uncle Daddy gloats in the great Up-Up There peering down lascivious and moaning.

"Do not do it," Avery shrieks.

Willadeene rips a page slow from *Jubilation and Woe*. Rebecca reaches for the rail.

"Do not come any closer, Rebecca," she says. Willadeene takes another step up, ripping a little more of the page. "Do not make me do it."

Avery howls. "What did I ever do to you, Willadeene, but love you?"

"What in God's name are you doing, Willadeene?" I say.

"This is your fault, Brother," Rebecca says. "You are the one to blame. I told you nothing good could come from it."

"What is the matter?" Journey Wintergarden asks, walking up behind Avery, taking hold of Fiddler Crab's bare shoulders, running his long Wintergarden fingers down to the short, puffed sleeves of his black satin gown.

Rebecca squeezes the rail. Looks up at Willadeene. "I will tell you the matter," she says, "Avery has taught this haint to read."

To read. Willadeene can read? Willadeene has lied. Fooled me all along. Making me think she cannot read one lickety-lick. Uncle Daddy moans and groans. Laughs.

"I caught her with *Jubilation and Woe* while Avery was sleeping. Turning page after page," Rebecca says.

"Will-laaa-deeene...." Avery screams. "You have betrayed me."

I am regretful I did not think of it first, getting a gander inside Avery's *Book of Jubilation and Woe*. Better Willadeene get caught at it than me. *What was it she saw?*

"I do not see a harm in that," Journey Wintergarden says. "Willadeene learning to read."

"That is not the betrayal, Journey Wintergarden," Avery says. "She has plundered my private thoughts. My longings. My poems. My prayers. She looked without asking."

"You are right, Avery," Willadeene says. "I am wrong to do what I did. But I am not sorry I did it. I am only sorry you have yourself such a hateful sister as this."

"Take that back, Willadeene," I say. "She is a good sister to Avery. A good friend to me. To you."

Rebecca steps onto the stairs.

Rip. "Not another," Willadeene says.

Uncle Daddy whimpers, as if the sound of misery gives him pleasure. I love the feel of his despicable yearnings. They flutter nervous at first like moth wings, dithering at my knees, working their way up devilish, caressing slow across my chest.

"Look at her, Avery," Rebecca says. "How she tries to find her way to the Up-Up There. A place she has no business going."

Rip. "Avery did not lie when he said there was nothing to flatter you here in this book," Willadeene says.

"Remember yourself, Willadeene," I say. "Do not say something you will regret." *Say it. An awful thing. Any 'ole lie will do. Make Uncle Daddy feel good. Make me feel bad.*

"You would not take up for her if you knew the thing she done." Willadeene *rips* a little more.

"Writing words does not make words true," Rebecca says. "It only makes them words." Rebecca turns back around again. "You should know this, Journey Wintergarden. My brother is prone to fits of whimsy. And delusion. This haint will believe anything he says."

"How dare you, Rebecca. I am in my right head almost all the time," Avery says.

"Hardly any of the time," Rebecca says. "Just like Mother. You deserve one another. God, look at you now. No wonder Father cannot bear the burdensome business of you being his son."

Avery gasps. Another moan works its way through Uncle Daddy.

"It is a shame, Rebecca, your poor, lunatic of a mother killed Baby Girl Longwood instead of killing you," Willadeene says.

Uncle Daddy grumbles. Low and deep. *Mmmm....* I bite my lip hard. Hard as I need to bite to keep a vulgar good-feeling commotion from spilling out.

Rebecca takes off up the stairs, her riding boots a gallop. *Murder and hell.... Murder and hell....*

Journey Wintergarden turns loose of Avery, heads for the staircase. Snatches hold of Blue Heron before she snatches hold of Willadeene, Treachery's strings *pluck-plucking.* Backward, he pulls Blue Heron, the heels of her riding boots dragging the treads back down again. *Murder and hell.... Murder and hell....*

Rebecca whispers over and over. Leans back against Journey Wintergarden. "Pianissimo."

Willadeene ruins the last bit of the page. *Rip....*

"Agamemnon," Avery screams.

Willadeene tosses the pieces to the whim of salt marsh sparrow wings.

On cruel currents, pieces of page lift and lower. Flit and flutter. Then comes down upon us a dusting of snow. *Jubilation and Woe.* We watch it come down. *Down and down.* We are all too spent to speak. To weep. Or scream. All of us catching our breath. All but Uncle Daddy. He wants more. *And more.... And more....* And I cannot take *more* of maelstroms swirling good and bad. Cannot bite my lip *more* until it bleeds.

The last piece lands gentle and quiet atop Journey Wintergarden's naked foot. And I want him and all the others gone from the room so I can sweep up the pieces. Puzzle them back together. To know what Avery knows. What Willadeene knows.

Journey Wintergarden speaks. "There now," he says, hugging his arms about Rebecca. His cheek against her cheek. "All is well. All is well."

Avery lowers himself to the floor in a swoon. "I never told the buried gold. Upon the hill—that lies…."

"That is Emily Dickinson, I believe," Journey Wintergarden says, his lips close to my Blue Heron's cheek. "How about a little more? I am such a fan."

Avery murmurs. "I saw the sun—his plunder done. Crouch low to win his prize…."

From the destitute look of Avery there on the floor, Emily Dickinson's words might well be his last.

"Settle down, everyone," Journey Wintergarden says. "We can sort this trouble out. Dear Avery, now get a hold of yourself." He calls up to Willadeene. "Come on down from there. You and Avery, and I will make our way downstairs."

"I will come away from here," Willadeene says. "But you must promise to keep Rebecca at bay."

"I promise to hold her here until you pass, Willadeene. Remember now, we are all friends here," he says. "Storms come. Storms go. It is with whom we weather them that matters most." Rebecca does not wiggle or squirm. I suspect she likes it there in the vice of Journey Wintergarden's arms.

"Pay no mind to me," Avery says. "I shall die here. Right here on this very floor. Ripped apart like poor *Jubilation and Woe*."

It occurs to me that upon the very spot Avery wallows is the dismal spot his mama and baby sister perished, the heap of Fiddler Crab's black satin hiding mayhaw jelly stains on the floor. Where Journey Wintergarden and my Blue Heron stand is the very place on Tribulation Day I lay gasping. Where I am told I died.

Listen. This is something I remember….

Avery weeps.

A poem by Keats.

Salome sings beneath the Moon.
Look. Look what you have done!
A Chopin nocturn.
My blue ribbon in my Blue Heron's hair.
Pianissimo.... Pianissimo....
Where is my Mirabelle?

"I am coming down," Willadeene says. "Hold her there. Like you promised, or I cannot be held responsible."

"Responsible for what?" Rebecca says.

"For what I might do."

"Enough of that, you two," Journey Wintergarden says. "Willadeene, come down."

Willadeene sets *Jubilation and Woe* on a step, tilts it back. Sends it sledding atop pieces of freshly ripped snow. There is a thrill set free in Willadeene, and I wish I could feel more of what she is feeling, but Uncle Daddy's ardor overpowers the place. The Up-Up There. The In-Between.

A wave of change seems to have washed over Willadeene. Baptized her anew. Her blossoms do not weep. Do not drop dreary to the floor. Her earbob berries do not bruise easy. *Look.* Another dang-fool honeybee *buzzes*. Willadeene will be too much for the bee to take. Mark my words, that honeybee will be dead soon. And so will Journey Wintergarden.

Willadeene pulls Pocket Watch from her robe. Opens and closes it. *Click-clack.* Down the stairs toward us she comes, all ten of her lovely sand dollar toes. Her leash drags, the tassel knocking behind her. *Click-clack.... Clack-clack....* She picks up *Jubilation and Woe*. Hands it to Avery. "Forgive me," she says. "It was your sister who made me do it. She is filled up all the way to her Longwood tongue with spite."

My Blue Heron does not speak or stir. She only cuts her eyes to Willadeene, opening the dam holding back the dangerous current of her dark-river eyes.

"I will join you soon," Journey Wintergarden says. "We are friends here, remember. Storms come. Storms go."

Willadeene folds an evergreen arm around Avery. With thumb and forefinger, she flicks open Pocket Watch and closes it. *Click-clack.* Willadeene's tassel dawdles at the Pyramid of Giza. Stops. Starts up again. Slithers the dessert sand. Then they are gone.

"You can let me go now," Rebecca says. "Unless you aim to succumb to my Longwood spite."

Yes, let her go now, Journey Wintergarden. Turn my Blue Heron loose.

"I hope I did not hurt you," he says.

"I am afraid, much to Willadeene's fury, I will survive."

"Good to know it," he says, smiling long enough I count eight of his teeth on top and four on the bottom. "I hope you will oblige me and stay up here a spell while I tend to the emotions below."

"Storms come. Storms go, like you said. I will wait here with Leontyne until this one passes. We are good at riding together through storms."

Together. Rebecca and me. I relish the sound of that.

With those wide-acre hands, Journey Wintergarden touches Rebecca's shoulder gentle. He does the same to me, then makes his way across the floor past the Pyramid of Giza.

Rebecca is stock-still, her finger pressed to her lips, until Journey Wintergarden has crossed the Mediterranean Sea, until she hears the door shut to the Down-Below. She looks to the Up-Up There. At Uncle Daddy leering down-down at us.

"A storm is brewing, alright. A tempest," Rebecca says, taking hold of my arm. "One I fear will never pass. Listen to me, Leontyne. We have to leave this place. You and me."

You and me…. You and me…. "What on earth has happened?"

"There is a thing I have not told you. Something that needs telling."

Salome? My blue ribbon? "Tell me," I say. "It cannot be so very bad."

"We have to lay a plan. We have to do it quick."

"Tell me, Rebecca, what you mean. You are scaring me."

"You will not want to hear this, but it is our only hope. Listen, I promise you do not have to do it alone. I am here to help you. Show me how. But you must make Redemption. Enough bottles to sell to pay our way."

"I do not understand." *Redemption.* Only are there two drops left here on Good Hope. *Two drops.* Two drops of living for Ewell Day Higgs to get done. I will not leave until then. Until every last drop is gone.

Uncle Daddy takes to turning slow circles again. *Leave Leontyne … when you is good and damn ready. Not a damn moment before. Admit it, girl. Mmmm…. You like it here.*

"The Great Wall of China," Rebecca says, leaning in, pressing her lips against my cheek. "Then off to cooler places. Just like you said. Do you not want to see all the wonder-of- wonders with me?"

"Of course, I do." Uncle Daddy is wrong. I hate it here.

"Do not be angry. Promise?"

"Angry for what?"

"I only kept it from you and Avery because there seemed more harm in telling you than not. Now, we are in peril it seems." Rebecca looks down at the floor, at the mayhaw jelly stain blooming beneath our feet. The cruel dusting of a *Jubilation and Woe* snow. "I am fearful more for you than me." She steers me from the spot. Strong arms me over to the enormous window flanking the door, out of reach of moon puddles and moonbeams spoiled and turned magenta. "She has unfinished business with you, Leontyne. She is not what she was before. She is worse?"

Uncle Daddy makes vulgar sounds. *Mmmm…. Mmmm….*

Uncle Daddy… Uncle Daddy…. The passel of haints knock themselves against the window.

"Who?" I holler, wiggling away, trying to pull loose from Rebecca.

"Willadeene is not Willadeene. She is even less Willadeene today. More dangerous than she was before. You heard her with your own ears. She cannot be responsible for what she might do."

Riddles and more riddles.

Rebecca grabs back hold of me. "Willadeene is not Willadeene," she says. "She is Constance Rose Longwood. She is … my mother."

Starlings burst from their nests in the walls.

Them honeybees will be dead soon.

And I am falling….

And falling….

The long …

long …

ways….

Morningstar
The Down-Below

Chapter 25

The sound of hammering and Salome singing *Winter* play upon me like smelling salts. Up into Avery's paper heaven I stare, wondering if for a second time I have died and Rebecca has cast a hoodoo spell with the violin to save me. *Our violin. My violin.*

"What has happened? How long have I been here?" I ask. Was Willadeene really once Constance Rose Longwood? What is the God's honest truth?

Rebecca lowers Salome from her chin. "Not so very long, I suppose," she says. "It is hard to know nowadays. Every second is a day. Every hour—a year."

Blue Heron is right. There is no inkling of time since Avery wished the Sun away. "My head hurts," I say. It dawns on me I ought check my other hand and both my feet. To make sure there is as much of me now as there was before. *10 toes. Five fingers. 32 teeth in all.*

"You knocked it hard on the floor when you fell." Rebecca says, laying Salome and bow next to me on Fiddler Crab's bed.

Blam ... blam ... blam....

"What is that infernal racket?" I ask, reaching my no-hand arm for Salome, giving her a chance to sniff. To see if she remembers me. If I might feel a tingle of something from back before.

"Journey Wintergarden is covering the window Uncle Daddy broke." Rebecca leans in, rubbing my arm. "I did not mean to shock you." She leans in closer. "We must keep this business of Willadeene, of Mother, between you and me. Make no mention of it to Avery. I trust him as little as I trust her. The two of them always were plotting revolutions against me. They are always whispering still."

Why would Eulalee let me go on thinking Willadeene is Alsace-Lorraine? Did she believe it? Or do cruel intentions burrow rotten in the caverns of her teeth? "How can it be? Are you sure Willadeene is your mama?" I flick my finger against the tincture bottle in my pocket. Eulalee gives me not much as a rattle.

"I did not suspect at first when she ran away from Eulalee, toddling her way stark naked and evergreen up here from the Marsh. When she was just a babe and stinking sweet of Sarah Fig. When you were sung back alive and broken, lying right here in this very bed." Upon the coverlet, she pats her hand gentle. "Now that I look back on it, from the onset, the signs were clear. That she was plotting trouble. Pulling berry earbobs from her lobes to feed the birds. Endearing herself. Gathering bouquets of daisies from her garden hair to give to you. To Avery. To me. And Father. To come back here and finish the business between the two of you."

"What business between her and me?"

Rebecca passes through my question as if it were vapor. "Knowing for certain was a slow creep," she says. "Willadeene grew up quick. Fast as a kitten grows to a cat. One day she was a bitty thing, nothing more than a sprout, pulling off her booties. Wiggling her sand dollar toes at Sinners. A week later she is heads taller and has turned out to be a flibbertigibbet of a silly girl, blowing kisses to haints snagged in trees. Up-up she went on growing. Lithe as a pole bean. Turning to high cheekbones and curves. Mother was beautiful when she was of the living. She is even lovelier now that she is dead. More wanton now than she was then."

Wanton. There is more of that godforsaken hammering. *Blam-blam.* My head hurts worse than before. "I still do not understand how you can be sure, Rebecca. That Constance Rose Longwood is Willadeene. And what is this business you speak? Between Miss Constance Rose and me?"

"Have you not been listening?" she says. "Willadeene is every bit like Mother. Mercurial. Nervous one moment. Throwing tantrums the next. Mother and Avery share this unfortunate temperament." Rebecca squeezes my arm. "In a way, I have always felt sorry for Mother. Father hardly ever paid her any mind, his good-for-nothing eyes turning goat. Whatever he is looking for in a companion, in a wife, he never found it in Mother. She was and still is searching for another to give her attention. Desperate for someone to be kind. On this account, she and Avery are very much the same. And there were other clues."

"What other clues?"

"What Willadeene says in her sleep. What Avery told her, the thing he thinks turned her crazy and made her jump with Baby Girl Longwood. The thing he thinks he said killed you."

I want to know what it is. This secret they keep. The thing Avery told his mama. I think back on what I last heard Willadeene speak in her sleep. *He kissed the boy ... kissed the boy.... Beneath the Moon.* "Does your daddy know Willadeene is your mama?"

"Oblivious," Rebecca says. "He cannot be bothered with anything else but Redemption and that Hushabye Byrd. He doles as much piddling attention to Mother dead as when she was living." Rebecca puffs breath into the air as if scattering invisible dandelion seeds. "Nothing," she whispers.

Blam-blam.

"Please, Blue Heron. Tell me what business your mama had with me."

Rebecca's eyes look up to Avery's paper stars looming in the shadows cast upon the ceiling by the fire burning in the hearth. "On second thought, I think it better that you do not know. Not knowing is as good as never happening."

"It is too late to turn back now. You cannot hint at such a thing. Then ignore it."

"I harbor no ill will, Leontyne. I do not blame you," she says. "It is not your fault."

'Round and 'round Blue Heron spins me in circles. "Sweet loving, God, Rebecca. What is not my fault?"

"What Avery said he saw. What he told Mother. The thing I promised him I would never tell."

Blam … blam….

I can take no more of this: the noise, Rebecca, my head splitting. "Agamemnon," I scream. "Bloody hell and murder."

Rebecca's eyes widen angry, as if I possess some gall to speak to her such a way as this. She pulls back. Whispers. "Suit yourself, Leontyne. If you insist, then I will tell you. But remember…." She stares at me, pulling miles of her dark pony's tail over her shoulder, letting it spill down her front. "You were warned."

My Blue Heron, sleek and tall. I love you best of all. If she does not think I should know, I should pay heed. Only, I cannot form the words to stop her. She comes close again. The Longwood smell of her overwhelms me, the touch of her hand on my arm. For a moment, I think I might persist, that I can survive whatever thing she tells me. Then my Rebecca speaks.

"Off King's Bottom Trail beyond the Forest. In a clearing. Avery said he saw you."

Blam….

I pull myself up on my elbows. Drop anchor against the pillows.

"You beneath the Forever Moon. You lying there … corrupted."

Blam … blam….

"Wriggling and writhing beneath Father. Haints staring down and moaning from the trees."

Blam….

Corrupted…. "That is a disgusting lie, Rebecca."

"It is the thing Avery told Mother."

"It is a lie," I say. "A terrible lie."

"If it is a lie, it is not the worst of them."

Corrupted....

"Shall I continue? Or should I leave this be?"

Blam....

Not knowing is as good as never happening. "Go on," I say.

Rebecca runs her hands down the thick rope of her hair, as if she needs a thing to hold onto. "I was there. Tribulation Day. Two years back."

"Standing below," I say. "Looking up from the In-Between. That is where you said you were on Tribulation Day."

"That is the first of the lies, Leontyne, I told to protect you." she says. "I was in the Up-Up There. In the Celestial Hall of Books, eavesdropping. And there you were, in the place Mother and Avery forbade you."

"Protect me from what, Rebecca?" I place my hand in my pocket, searching. My knuckles scraping and slicing against Eulalee's oyster shell necklace.

"Mother confronted you about what Avery told her. About Father. And there was more that Avery said. That you were promiscuous with haints."

"More lies," I say, pressing my feet into the mattress, pushing myself harder against the pillows. "Why would he say such a thing?"

Blam ... blam....

"Mother was hardly a saint. The nerve of her judging you for the very things she herself has done."

"You do not believe it, do you?"

Rebecca closes her eyes. "Then there is the matter of poor, Baby Girl Longwood."

Gone quick as she come. "What matter is that?"

"The simple matter the child was not Father's. That she was a bastard." Rebecca goes quiet for a moment, as if her words have stunned her. "Born into this world a disgrace. Half-haint. Purplish tines poking shameful from her little back." She opens her almond eyes. "There is no hiding an abomination such as that."

"My head hurts," I whisper. "You are right. It is better not knowing." *You warned me.*

"It is almost over. I am nearly done."

Blam. . . .

"She said terrible things to you. That you are every crumb like Eulalee. That you are no better than that whore down by the Marsh." Rebecca grabs hold of my arm. "That you have no more business here. She swore to banish you from me."

Something comes to me now. A flash. Of Constance Rose Longwood holding the baby close to the edge where there is no rail. She sings. *Dapples and greys, pintos and bays. . . .*

"You said you would make Mother sorry if she ever said such a thing as that again. If she said she would keep you from me."

Blam . . . Blam. . . .

"Again and again, she said it. You went running. And running. Pushing. But she grabbed hold of you. Then you were falling. Falling...." Rebecca looks up to the ceiling, to Avery's Elysium. Up into the stars. "And I told the others Mother is the one who did it. That she jumped." Rebecca's eyes trail back here to me to Good Hope. "I told them you tried to stop her."

Running.

Running.

Pushing.

Falling.

How could I have done such a thing? "I do not remember," I say. "For the love of God, Rebecca. Why would Fiddler Crab tell such lies?"

"Because you love me more than you love Avery."

"Why did you lie, Blue Heron." Rebecca looks back up into the ceiling. "Why did you lie for me?" I want Rebecca to look up so I might see that hand cut moon reflected in her eyes.

“Because I love you more than I love all of them,” she says. “We will go. Off to cooler places. You and me.”

You and me. Blue Heron keeps looking at the stars instead of the paper moon, and I do not care. The stars are plenty pretty enough of a glory mirrored in the dark current running her eyes. Who needs that hand cut moon when she loves me better than she loves any other?

Running.

Running.

Pushing.

Falling….

Morningstar
The Down-Below

Chapter 26

I have counted the hand cut stars again and again. Traced each and every one with my eyes trying to find a path clear to understanding why Fiddler Crab done the thing he done.

Wriggling and writhing. If ever I was McKinley Longwood's paramour, I do not recall so much as a *swish-swoosh*, or nary a glimpse of a haint moaning down at us from a tree.

The vile thought of McKinley Longwood loving up on me turns my stomach sick. The nerve of Avery Longwood, accusing me of carrying on promiscuous with haints and his goat-eyed daddy. Fiddler Crab is a liar.

In the deep-deep, between you and me and this paper moon, I feel it is only as of late I might pay a haint any bit of mind. Before Eulalee was gone, I never did. And know this, if I am a murderer, Fiddler Crab is one, too. And my Rebecca is a liar with the sweetest of sweet intentions to keep me safe from harm.

Saturn's rings. I count them. Wondering if I ought make Redemption, the littlest batch to get my Blue Heron and me off to where we are going. *Off to cool-cool places....*

"You are alive," Avery says from the door.

"I am of the living," I say. *No thanks to you.* "And just a little bit dead."

Avery stands stately at the bedside holding my Darkly in one hand. Sugar roosting and riding grand as a warrior queen on his pale, bare shoulder. *Jubilation and Woe* is tucked beneath Avery's spindle of arm.

"I am glad. Very glad, indeed." Avery turns back to the door. "*Shh* ... Rebecca told me to leave you be. That you need rest." Avery kisses Darkly on his head. Puts him down on the bed. "I thought you might care for company." Avery whispers, "Miss High-and-Mighty is not the boss of me. Besides, this is my room. I will do as I please." Avery scoops Sugar from his shoulder. Kisses him on the head. Places him on the coverlet to waddle behind Darkly over to me.

"Would you like me to leave? I can head back down home to Hornet's Nest." *Would you like me to strangle you slow to death with the ribbon you stole from me?*

"Do not be a silly 'ole cuckoo bird," he says. "You are welcome here long as you please."

Darkly prowls up into my lap, nudges his nose cool against my wrist. Sugar burrows against my leg. It feels good to be touched. To be loved. Needed. A rise of tears makes its way up inside me along with the inkling something is amiss. A part of me gone. *Poor-poor Mirabelle. Nothing left of Eulalee but these here silent teeth.* I poke and scratch at the nape of my neck. I try my best to tamp down this feeling. These tears. This feeling more of me is gone than just this hand.

"What is the matter?" Avery asks.

It is too late. He spots the sadness abloom inside me. Never is there a tear Fiddler Crab does not match with three of his own. "Nothing," I say. "My head aches is all." *Great God-a-mighty. Look!* Down-down comes a glory of Fiddler Crab rain. Tear after beautiful tear. And I am done for.

Fiddler Crab weeps. "You are an orphan now, Leontyne. I know what it is like to grieve a mother."

"Eulalee is dead. This is true. But I am fine, Avery. She has not been herself since a great while ago. Of all the piddlin' things I remember, I recall she once was kind. And young. And pretty. Way back before. I reckon it is best she is gone."

Down comes a rapturous more pouring of Fiddler Crab rain. "I miss my mother," he says, pulling Rushworth L. Wintergarden's handkerchief from his bodice.

"There now," I say. "Enough of that." *I have had my fill of you.*

Tides turn quick here on Good Hope, especially when Avery is dropped in the mix. A twinge of sorrow for Avery comes over me that Rebecca has allowed him to think it was what he said that killed his mama—though it serves him right. I reckon it was his fault as much as mine. It was the thing he said. *The lie.* And me that did the final pushing that killed her. And that poor half-breed of a baby. *Gone quick as she come.* I wonder if it would be any comfort for him to know his dead mama come back here a haint. That it is a good thing he has gone and tied her up with curtain strings, because she is here baking biscuits and plotting murder.

Into the hand-hewn sky I stare, to stop myself from looking upon Avery. For feeling any bit more sorry for him than I do now. I endure him best I can while he cries and carries on a spell, lying himself prostrate onto the bed. *Jubilation and Woe*—his pillow. His hand reaching-reaching for mine.

Avery's Comet. I follow the sprawl of its celestial tail. Spy it sweep vaporous between planets and stars. Watch it ride a close danger to the Sun *whooshing* back a memory of a time I was here in this very bed before.

Blue Heron seethes.

Sawing … sawing….

Mirabelle…. My Mirabelle….

Blood-wept droplets pimpling the floor.

Avery reaching … reaching …

Weeping….

Avery sputters tears and phlegm. "What are you looking at?" he asks, squeezing my arm. He cannot tolerate me studying the ceiling instead of admiring him.

"Avery's comet," I say, pressing Darkly beneath my chin.

Avery sniffles. "Avery's Comet," he says. The sound of his own name casts spells. Enchants him. He turns onto his back. Avery props himself against a pillow. "Every hundred years it comes back around. That is what Rushworth L. Wintergarden says. One hundred years."

"That is a very long time," I say. "Between coming and going."

"He says it is more magnificent than even Halley's."

"I imagine it would be. With a name grand as Avery's Comet."

Whimsy hums in Avery's throat. "From a sand dune on the beach of Cherubim, Rushworth L. Wintergarden saw Avery's Comet when he was a boy of six. Watched it glitter and sail the sky across the Ephesians Sea."

For a split-pea second, I think of telling Avery the Island of Cherubim is a fraud to wound and make him suffer. "Sounds like a glory of glories," I say. I itch to ask Fiddler Crab other things Rushworth L. Wintergarden might have seen and said. About me when I was a girl with two hands. *The way Salome sang when I held her.* There are other things I might ask Avery. If ever he saw Mr. Rushworth L. Wintergarden's naked feet. *Is his second toe longer than the first?* And why it is Rebecca never looks up to the Moon. And if he is swole the teensiest with regret he played a part in stealing my hand. My memory. If he even is a thimble full of sorry I am only a little bit dead.

"Would it not be wonderful, Leontyne, to live long enough to see Avery's Comet when it comes back around the world again?"

"We would be many years old. Or many years buried," I say. "But yes, I would very much like to behold Avery's Comet." I think of my Ewell Day Higgs and how much he loves the Moon. I ponder how many drops of Redemption would need dropping to keep him alive to see Avery's Comet just once.

"Willadeene is lucky," Avery says.

"How come?" *She is dead and more alive than the living.* I am propped here on this pillow trying my best to fathom her having any luck, at all.

"Oh Leontyne, think of all the times she might see it."

My head aches. My stomach curdles with much too guilt to bear contemplating Willadeene's great forever. Her great forlorn. "I imagine it might be sad watching a glory such as that all by your lonesome year after year when we are gone."

Avery blinks up at his comet. Only now does he seem to understand. The direction changes, and downriver go those ebon eyes. "All by her lonesome," he says. "Poor-poor Willadeene." He presses the handkerchief to his cheek. "Would it not be a marvel of marvels if Willadeene could find herself a beau?"

"Who might you have in mind, Fiddler Crab? The pickings here are skimpy."

Sugar toddles over chirping at Avery. Avery picks him up, kisses his noggin. Nestles the chick beneath his heart-drop chin. "There is that Uncle Daddy," he says. "But he is every bit a brute, and I cannot understand a gibberish thing he says. Can you?"

Yes indeed. I understand every bit of the trashy talk that Uncle Daddy speaks.

"On second thought. Take back what I said. Uncle Daddy is not nearly good enough for our Willadeene."

Not nearly good enough. This could be the time to confront Avery. To slice and serve him up a big piece of my mind for telling Rebecca and his mama I run wild and scandalous with haints. I reckon he thinks another haint is beneath Willadeene but plenty fine for me. This thing I am about to say next ought teach him.

"There is always Journey Wintergarden," I say. "Willadeene can make plenty due with him while he still is breathing. Woe is she. In the by-and-by, Willadeene will be alone again. Nothing left but Pocket Watch to hold close." I pick up Darkly and kiss him between the ears. "But for now, they might have themselves some fun." I take up singing a bridal chorus. *All that is bright, all that is fair....*

Avery cannot catch wind at first. Stammering and stuttering. "How dare you," he gasps. "Journey Wintergarden is mine," he whispers. "Mine."

"I beg your pardon," I say. "I had no idea you were intended."

"Did you not see how much he adores me?"

"*Hmm.* I could not quite tell if it was you or Rebecca he took a shine to more." *Put that in your little pipe and smoke it, Fiddler Crab.* I listen to his black satin kettle boil. I wait for it to howl.

"Well now, Starshine," he says. "I reckon it best for all concerned if Journey Wintergarden likes me best."

Starshine.... He threatens me with secrets. Threatens me with my Ewell Day Higgs. "That is between the two of you," I say. "I would be careful of Willadeene if I were you. She seems smitten with your Journey Wintergarden," I settle Darkly in the crook of my arm like I might nurse a baby. Pretending he is Baby Girl Longwood with reddish-purple quills. "She might get in the way." *I might just help.*

"It would be best for you if no one gets in the way," Avery says, tucking Rushworth L. Wintergarden's handkerchief back into his bodice, leaving a peek of blue monogram poking out of the dress that once was his mama's.

Treachery.... Fiddler crab is extorting me. God help Rebecca and Willadeene if Journey Wintergarden does not care for Avery best. And God help me.

"What about the Sinner you have out there in the pit?" Avery asks. "For our Willadeene?"

Ewell Day Higgs is mine. "I already told you he is not a Sinner."

"I hope I am not interrupting anything," Journey Wintergarden says, standing at the door. "I am here to see about Miss Leontyne."

Avery straightens himself. Smooths his gown. Puts Sugar on his shoulder to perch. "This sweet-sweet angel is on the mend," he says. "I have been holding vigil here." Avery squeezes my hand. I work it loose. "As I did once before."

As he did before. After I come back around here from the dead. When I lay here knocked senseless. Nary a memory to call my own. What lies did he whisper? What schemes did he plot?

"You are a good friend, indeed, Avery Longwood," Journey Wintergarden says. "I brought you these, Leontyne." He holds a bouquet of begonias, such a deep shade of purple that here in the half-light they appear almost black. "A gift from Willadeene. Of Willadeene. Just plucked fresh." He hands them to Avery. Avery steals one for behind his ear and passes the rest over across the bed to me.

A smell of spice permeates the blooms, the faint aroma of Christmastime orange. Of black licorice drops. How is it I have not smelled this on Willadeene, these Longwood smells swirling heady in this haint's petrichor? Is Avery suspicious? How has he not noticed it before?

"I did not realize you were having a celebration," Rebecca says, from the doorway. "Do you mind if I join you?"

"We are only taking in the evening air, Sister. Marveling and remarking upon how Avery's Comet sets off the heavens." Avery looks to the ceiling. "It is the crown jewel of Elysium."

"Elysium...." Journey Wintergarden looks up, the hearth's light shimmering his eyes. He turns his neck this way—that. Shifts weight onto one hip and the other.

"What is the matter, Mr. Wintergarden? Have you never seen the heavens hung down from strings?" Rebecca asks. "If you are not careful. If you do not duck just there, you might knock your head against Mercury."

For a glint, I think the room—my heart—might be endanger of Rebecca smiling.

"That is exactly the matter," he says. "I have seen this very Elysium before."

"Surely you have never been," Avery says, astonished. "To the heavens." Here he comes back around again as a memory—the littlest Avery, his curly head daydreaming in my lap.

"No, but I have seen it, Avery. This very one. From the ceiling of my boyhood room. "It was my brother Rushworth's doing. A heaven of his very own." He rubs the bridge of his nose. "Seeing it here again. Well, it is like I have fallen back into that very room from these very stars. And here I am. Standing back in yesterday. Missing my brother."

"Seraphim House...." Avery says. "Across the Ephesians Sea...."

Click-clack.... Click-clack. There stands treacherous Willadeene. Opening and closing Pocket Watch.

"Pay attention, everyone," Journey Wintergarden says, pointing and squinting. "Not sure if you know this, but that is the constellation called Leontyne." He looks over at me. Tosses a wink.

Click-clack....

"That fine looking planet there. See it, Avery?"

"I surely do. I surely do."

Journey Wintergarden casts glance at Rebecca. "A maze of never-ending rivers. A mystery named Blue Heron."

For once, Rebecca does not bale her hair over her shoulders. She frolics. Finagles her fingers through her pony's tail. Swims her hands through their alluring depths.

Clack....

"*Woosh....* Trailing across all of Elysium is Avery's Comet." Journey Wintergarden flutters his fingers at his side, expanding his arms wide and spectacular. A coppery albatross is he.

"More magnificent than Halley's," Avery hollers. "*Woosh....*" He flourishes his lissome arms.

"One hundred years." I spread my own arms. "*Woosh....*"

"It comes. It goes," Avery says, laughing. "*Woosh....*"

Comes and goes.... Comes and goes....

"*Woosh….*" Rebecca says, spreading her Blue Heron wings.

"*Woosh….*" calls out Willadeene. "*Woosh….*" Out go her evergreen arms, Pocket Watch clutched in her hand. Hours. Days. Years.

Woosh….

All of us, we are anywhere and everywhere but here. Journey Wintergarden is in his boyhood room beneath Rushworth L. Wintergarden's make-believe sky. I am shivering, looking down-down from Kilimanjaro. Willadeene's arms reel loathsome back to her side, landing back here on Good Hope. Wherever that haint has got off to, she is sad to be flown back here again.

Click-clack…. Click-clack….

"Willadeene, leave that Pocket Watch be," Rebecca says.

"That is not the sound of my Pocket Watch," she says. "You are forever blaming everything on me."

"What is it then?" Avery asks.

"Shh…." Rebecca presses a finger to the cushion of her lip.

The sound goes again. A *clawing*. A *scraping* from outside against the bricks. A *clatter* against the windowpanes. Journey Wintergarden motions along with Rebecca for us all to go quiet. Avery and I manage ourselves down from the bed to stand close to Rebecca.

Knock-knock.

Sccc… rrrr … aaa … pppe….

"Remember last time," Avery tells Journey Wintergarden. "Be careful."

Mr. Wintergarden's fingers reach for the drapes. *Woosh….* In sheets of magenta velum, Forever Moon spills the room, prehistoric curtain motes revived. Fleeing all directions.

Journey Wintergarden battles the quick rise of these Saharan dust storms. Swats the air. Covers his nose. Peers out through the long window.

"What is it?" Avery asks.

Journey Wintergarden moves closer. Turns back. Motions with one arm for us to follow. "You will want to see this," he says.

"What is out there?" Avery asks.

I grab hold of Avery. Rebecca follows. Journey Wintergarden spreads and lifts his albatross wings. We bow under. Gather close at the window.

"There are so many," Journey Wintergarden says.

A shiver works its way through Avery. He spreads his affliction, my teeth chattering cold. And there—an army of haints scrape against the windows, dozens more snagging stupid in branches. Others spinning circles. A herd rustles distant in the Forest, a queer dawning of purple through the trees. Down the lawn, a grotesque procession draws near. *Reprobates.* Bloated puffer-fish heads. Swollen tines and tongues. Maws agape. Two-by-two. Three-by-three. First, I cannot hear clear what they say. Their voices rise. A chorus. A chant. A plea.

Uncle Daddy....

Uncle Daddy....

There are so many. More haints than I have ever seen. More than Damascus and her Sarah Figs could ever devour. I listen for her ancient wind chime song. For her to call, begging me back to her. To take up where Eulalee left off. Damascus lurks. She drinks. She broods. Carves her silence deep-deep. Rooting into Good Hope, into the Doldrums, and—

me....

Morningstar
The In-Between

Chapter 27

The haints gather outside in belligerent swarms while Journey Wintergarden hammers and nails. Laying board upon board across the windows crackling against the weight of these Peeping Toms. He goes about the chore from inside rather than outside, keeping himself clear of the fiends. "192 windows so far here at Morningstar," Journey Wintergarden calls down. "I do not believe there were any more windows in all of ancient Rome."

Avery and I balance atop the sawhorses at the entrance to the Pyramid of Giza, gawking into the Up-Up There for a glimpse of those Wintergarden ankles. It is all I can do to be close to Fiddler Crab pretending to not know what he has done. To not murder him.

"What about the windows in the Cupola?" Rebecca asks, walking in from the Down-Below. "There are quite a few more there to cover."

192... 192 Windows.... How many things have you and Avery not told me, Rebecca? That I could play the violin well as you? That Rushworth L. Wintergarden thought I played it best. *Can you tally all the things on this one hand of mine?*

Avery leans into my ear. "Rebecca has no use for the Moon," he says. "She does not care that we will be smothered soon. All of us nailed tight here inside this Morningstar tomb."

Should I endeavor to massacre Avery on the sawhorses here in Egypt, I would only have to tell him his sister and I will be gone soon. Or that Journey Wintergarden has pledged his love to Willadeene. That I murdered his mama and his half-haint of a sister. *Bear good thoughts for me.* I have not yet told Rebecca I refuse to make Redemption.

"We are nearly out of boards," Journey Wintergarden yells. "There is hardly anything left of the barn but frame. Nothing left for me to take. I am going to have to start pulling up the floors. It seems Uncle Daddy draws the line with me boarding the Cupola's windows. He will not let me anywhere near them, and he seems to be growing larger by the minute. I reckon he likes to look out," he says. "These other haints seem to want to be close. For some reason, they steer clear of knocking themselves against these upper panes."

I will not let on I know the reason why they do not venture near Cupola's windows. Uncle Daddy has told them haints this. *Keep the damn hell away.* He has said little more, but I figure he is swimming circles in the Up-Up There to light the way. To keep other haints coming.

"Why will they not go away?" Avery asks.

"Damascus is not singing. That is why," Rebecca says, looking right up at me. "Before we know it, we will be stacked to the rafters with haints."

"Stacked to the rafters with haints," Avery repeats.

Avery pretends to be terrified, but he is exhilarated we are in the throes of a peculiar happening. I catch another of Avery's arctic shivers. *Rebecca blames this calamity of haints on me.* From the Pyramid of Giza, I watch. Watch Darkly prowl over to Blue Heron. He sniffs at her boots. Quickety-split, he runs.

"Why does Damascus not sing?" Avery asks. "Can we not make her?"

I am fed up to my eyeballs with all of this. Fed up with Damascus. With haints. With Eulalee not making a peep.

"Miss Hushabye Byrd," Avery murmurs. "She will know what to do."

Damascus does not sing because I do not tend her. That is why. *There is no one here that can help but me.* I call out to Morningstar. To Good Hope. To Journey Wintergarden and all the haints at bay who have a mind to listen. Mark these words down in *Jubilation and Woe*,

Fiddler Crab. *Pay attention, my sweet Rebecca.* "I am not Eulalee. I am not the Great Redeemer." *I will never be.*

Morningstar
The Down-Below

Chapter 28

Avery is the one, not Willadeene, dreaming fitful. Fiddling and fiddling. *Whimpers* and *bleats*. Does he dream of 192 windows? Of telling his mama lies? Of dragging her around on a leash?

Every second is a day. Every day, an hour. Little chance there is I might find my way to sleep. With each *tickety-tick* of Willadeene's Pocket Watch, I ruminate on Journey Wintergarden's hands, his feet. On Ewell Day Higgs with one drop of living left to do.

Visions of Uncle Daddy come lurking. He is changing from one minute to the next. His tail grows longer. Muscles: leaner. Teeth: sharper. I contemplate all the haints that keep coming across the River. Knocking-knocking the doors. The bricks. The boarded windows. Rising in gruesome chorus of carnal groans. Confessing felonies. Insurrections. Showing off. Trying their dead-best to seduce me. *Let me in, Leontyne. Let me in....* I am no fool. It is Uncle Daddy they aim to get at.

Eulalee's haint-dying song keeps my desires burning level, from me catching fire and losing control of myself. *I am no better than that whore down by the Marsh.* I am not sure how much more of this courting and caterwauling I can take. I sing inside my head, deciding I ought get up here from Avery's bed and make my way to the stairs to the In-Between to trace circles upon the floor. Until I am overcome with stupor. Until I tire myself out.

On across the River,
To where you ought go,
Way off beyond Zion,
Fields plentiful with gold.

I step over Willadeene sleeping next to Avery's bed.

Pssss.... Willadeene grabs my ankle. "Where do you think you are going?" she whispers, raising her head to check on Avery.

Avery fusses in his sleep. *Whimpers* and *bleats. Whimpers* and *bleats.*

"Off to think," I say, lowering myself to my knees. If Willadeene had breath in her lungs, I would smother here right here and right now with this horsehair pillow. But her grip has grown stronger these last hours. These last years. So ferocious, I fear she might snap my leg in two.

"Think about what?"

I lie. "About how I might help you," I say. "About Journey Wintergarden." *I killed you once when you were Constance Rose Longwood. I swear, I will do it again. I will drag you to the River. Flower by flower, feed you to the boll weevils.*

Willadeene loosens her grip. "I have something for you," she says, reaching beneath her pallet. From under the quilt, she pulls pieces of torn paper.

A snow of Jubilation and Woe.

"Something that might help you," she says, stuffing the ripped pieces into my apron pocket. She reaches with her evergreen hand. Grabs hold of my towhead hair. Pulls me down slow-slow.

"Let me go," I say. Down-down she pulls me more, so close, I turn dizzy from the ever-after scent of petrichor. From layer upon layer of Longwood. Down until we are eye-to-eye.

"Be careful of Rebecca," she says, enticing me the rest of the way to kiss me. "Be careful."

I tumble... tumble.... Falling and falling through Kingdom Come, thy will be done. Blue-blue passing through, the eyes of Willadeene's great forever.

Morningstar

The In-Between

Chapter 29

The Cupola glowers, the Forever Moon cascading through Uncle Daddy's magenta, spilling carmine puddles onto the cold, desert floor here of the In-Between. In the largest moon puddle, atop the mayhaw jelly stain, I lay out tatters of the page ripped from *Jubilation and Woe*, the gingery flavor of Willadeene still carousing the tip of my tongue.

I sort through the shreds. Assemble the border of the page. Crawl back from the scatter to take a look. I scrutinize the shapes of these pieces. I cantor more of Eulalee's haint-dying song, taking mama's teeth from my pocket. I agitate them good and plenty, wishing for her to forget she is not speaking to me. Hoping she might join in with her daughter and sing.

On across the River,

To where you ought go....

There. I see it. The beginnings of a word. Another right below. A picture. On my hand and knees, I lean forward. Shuffle more pieces. Shift and shuffle. Follow the thrall of elegant strokes from Avery's pen.

My eyes dart in the thicket of words, of the lullaby he wrote down, roaming higgledy-piggledy across the tattered page.

When you wake, you shall have

All the pretty little horses

Blacks and bays,

Dapples and greys....

My eyes spiral down-down to the bottom of the page, down-down to the bottom to Avery's sketch of my Mirabelle—my gone-away hand, wrapped like an infant in wedding lace in the gruesome belly of a rusted, dented coffee can.

Swoosh. Here comes a memory cold as the floor....

In the Up-Up There

Constance Rose Longwood swaddles sweet Baby Girl,

Sing-sings a lullaby.

Hairpins sparkle.

Moonstone earbobs bob black.

"Give her here," someone says.

"Mine."

And I am running.

Running....

Uncle Daddy laughs from the Up-Up There, interrupting my recollection until I am back here on my knees in the In-Between, wallowing upon this mayhaw jelly stain on the floor, staring down at this puzzle. And there is more. A smaller picture at the bottom of the corner of the page of Rebecca wearing a hair ribbon. Sawing at my arm with Salome's bow, an expression of a lunatic's glee stretched across her face. My mouth is drawn open, screaming. The name *Mirabelle* is written and slithering out of my mouth like a tongue. I cannot bear the sight of it, this gruesome puzzle from *Jubilation and Woe.*

Uncle Daddy laughs again. I cannot yet spot the haint, only the opaline glow of his hide. I am grateful I cannot see him. *Shh....* I yearn to see him. A glimpse would be plenty. *Heirloom.* I need to behold him much as I need to remember everything happening that day in the Up-Up There. *Tribulation Day. Two years back.*

Uncle Daddy sing-songs down. *Great Redeemer-Great Redeemer. Hair swinging low to the Marsh.*

Eulalee stirs in my pocket—a seed about ready to sprout. I stand up, gazing through the switchback of stairs at Uncle Daddy hovering high at the landing. "I am not the Great Redeemer," I say.

Uncle Daddy makes his way down the farthest floor of stairs, scraping his tines against the bricks. *Rrrr … eee … kkk.…* A flutter of starling wings. *Crunch.*

"What do you want with me?" I say.

Great Redeemer-Great Redeemer, he sings again. *Whatever I damn well please.* He flourishes, his purple-red light filtering through the chandelier's crystals eerie.

"Sir, I am not the Great Redeemer. I have every last one of my teeth. Every strand of hair. How can I be the Great Redeemer when I need me some saving myself?"

Uncle Daddy is closer, his bobcat muscles flexing down the final sweep of stairs. Shards of his windowpane crown glint and woo. He stops. Hovers. Casts his tail into a nest knitted in vines against the wall. *Fishing-fishing.* Out comes a warbler reeling and wrapped in the hangman's noose of Uncle Daddy's tail. Into the haint's maw, that warbler goes.

Crunch.…

A wing flitters.

Another *crunch.*

The bird is gone. A flurry of feathers. Drifting-drifting.

Uncle Daddy spits gristle. Bones of warbler and gore. *Idumea-Idumea. Come here, Great Redeemer. So I can do to you whatever I damn well please.*

I should go no closer, but I cannot help myself. I have to see. I step over the page of *Jubilation and Woe*, the lullaby and picture I stitched back together whole. It troubles me, the something here on the page I cannot see.

Uncle Daddy slanders and entices me with indecency. Each obscenity lusting him up more than the one before. *Sorceress … Conjurer… Harlot… Redeemer*, he says. This next one pulls him near abouts to the crumbling edge of bliss. *Nec-ro-man-cer.… Mmmm.…*

The closer I come up the stairs, the hungrier Uncle Daddy gets. "I am none of them things," I say. *Least not today.* "Whatever I might have been yesterday, I cannot tell for sure."

Mmmm.... You is what you is, girl. You will be what you will be.

"Who are you," I say.

The goddamned Sun, he says, licking his catfish lips with that swollen, purple tongue. *That is who the hell I am.*

Hungrier and hungrier Uncle Daddy gets, his goat eyes more golden and bright. I am hungry, too. *Starved.* The feeling when the last spoon of grits is over. The last oyster—gone.

Journey Wintergarden looks down upon me and Uncle Daddy from the Up-Up There, his Wintergarden toes lurking the edge, watching me hold Uncle Daddy's broad face in my only hand.

Uncle Daddy is close enough now I see my reflection in the shards of his windowpane crown. So close I whiff the intimate smell of River leaking from his hide. He carouses his tail again into a nest, pulling a sparrow. Bringing the bird to his thinly lips.

I am quicker. I pull the sparrow loose, set the bird free. Watch him swoop the desert floor, scattering the page of *Jubilation and Woe.* The lullaby. The drawing of Rebecca sawing.

"You are hungry," I say, pulling Uncle Daddy down-down by his catfish whiskers to kiss him on the cheek. I remember the dip of Salome's bow when I played her. Feel the tear of my flesh when Rebecca slices my wrist. I hear Avery weep. Listen to my Blue Heron whisper sweet and low.

Shh.... It will all be over soon.

Morningstar
The Down-Below

Chapter 30

Rebecca and I wait for the others, sitting unnerved here on Avery's bedroom floor in front of the fire burning the hearth beneath Elysium.

Rip and claw. Claw and rip. The haints tear at Morningstar, their upstart fingers sprouting foul from where once grew fins. Like Uncle Daddy, the haints are changing. Looking less like puffer fish and more like floating bobcats with front pairs of wriggling crocodile claws. These haints *scrape* and *scrape*, speaking exotic tongues of filth only I can hear, sweet-sweet nothings once meant for Eulalee and now served up special for me. This is Heirloom. This is Eulalee's gift to me.

"This is what comes from not tending the dead," Rebecca says.

Blue Heron accuses me. Blames me, though she tries to hide it with the slow blink of her eyes. I stop myself from pulling out Eulalee's teeth and shaking them in the air. To show her what comes from tending Damascus and the dead.

"Can you recollect a time haints acted up like this before?" I ask.

"If this ever happened before, we would all be dead and buried beneath that godforsaken Moon," she says. Rebecca sits with her legs crisscrossed, Salome sleeping across her lap. "We have to figure our way out of here, Leontyne."

"We could go now," I say, but I do not mean it. I cannot leave with Ewell Day Higgs in the Forest and still maybe breathing. How do we know it would be any bit different out there than here? This next part I am ashamed to confess. I am growing keen on the way these good-for-nothing haints make me feel. *Tingle and thrill. Tingle and thrill.*

"Leontyne," she says, reaching over touching my knee. "You have heard Hushabye Byrd and Father. Times are paved hard everywhere. The soles of people's shoes worn through. People pay pretty and plenty to forget. Even in times when money is hard to come by. Pay foolhardy for tincture bottles filled with affection. A temporary fix. A little of something is ours out there for the taking, if you and I make it happen together. Let me help you, Leontyne. Let me help you make Redemption."

"What is so wrong with remembering?" I ask. "I would pay fifty cents to have me a bottle of that. A drop of remembering."

"Remembering is not all it is cracked up to be," she says, pointing a finger like she is warning me. Threatening me.

"That is easy enough for you to say when your pockets are full-up and spilling memories." *Your memories. And mine.* Right off, I am sorry I said it. "Forgive me. I did not mean it."

Rebecca pulls her hand away. "Suit yourself," she says. "Stay here with that Singing Prophetess. Until she has used you up. Until you are dead. With no chance of ever knowing a Kilimanjaro snow."

"I want nothing more than to see a real-life Kilimanjaro snow, Rebecca." I say. "You know that." What I want right now is to pull the puzzle pieces from my pocket. Assemble them here on the floor. Ask Rebecca to tell me what it means. What it is I cannot see. This thing I am feeling.

"Have you seen the way Willadeene looks at Journey Wintergarden?" Rebecca asks. "Scandal of scandals."

"I have," I say. *I have seen the way you all look at Journey Wintergarden.* I cannot say I blame them.

"She looked the same way at his brother, Rushworth," Rebecca says. "Back when she was Constance Rose Longwood. It is disgusting. Was disgusting. They are both young enough to be her sons. The shame she has brought on this family. I am only glad there are no decent folk here on Good Hope to see it."

Constance Rose Longwood pined for Rushworth L. Wintergarden? This is a revelation to me. It never dawned on me this could be a reason. "Is that why your daddy sent him away?"

"Avery would have you believe it was because Rushworth L. Wintergarden loved him. That Father would never stand idly by and let Avery be happy," she says. "That is hardly the truth, though Avery and Mother did their conniving best to take Rushworth L. Wintergarden for themselves. The two of them are always taking everything for themselves."

"What is it then? The truth?"

Rebecca stares her dark-river eyes at me. Slows the current until it near abouts goes still. "Because Rushworth L. Wintergarden loved me," she whispers.

Claw and rip.

I float on the calm, cool current of Rebecca's eyes. Bob and dip. Sink. Then swim. *Because Rushworth L. Wintergarden loved me.* "I know you loved him," I say. She has never made a secret of that. I feel around in my apron pocket. Run my fingers through pieces of paper snow. I never imagined he loved her. "But I need to know, Blue Heron. Would you have run off with him? To our Great Wall of China? Would you have left me here alone?" I watch her eyes. Tread their waters. Feel the tow pulling me under-under.

"He is gone away," she says. "And I am here. What is done is done." She touches my knee again. "You and I," she says. "We have many a mile before us. Maybe you can be at least a little happy just remembering from this point on. I have told you all you need to know from before. Anything worth a nickel."

"Many a mile to where?" Willadeene asks from the door. "Are you going somewhere?" Willadeene covers me up with her blue-blue eyes.

"My comings and goings are none of your concern," Rebecca says. "Where is Avery? I told you to fetch him."

"Go fetch him yourself," Willadeene says.

Holy murder and hell.

"You forget yourself, Willadeene," Rebecca says, her eyes blinking slow.

"Where is Fiddler Crab?" I ask. "I thought he wanted me to read him more *Great Expectations*."

"Up yonder in the In-Between cozied up with Mr. Journey Wintergarden. With your Darkly and that Sugar." she says, staring holes. Wielding daggers. Opening and closing Pocket Watch. *Click-clack. Click-clack.*

"In your precious Pyramid of Giza."

Click....

Morningstar
The In-Between

Chapter 31

Forever Moon pours through the Cupola. Reflects in the mirrors. Floods the Pyramid of Giza with torrents of Uncle Daddy's magenta. I should make myself known to Fiddler Crab and Journey Wintergarden, only my curiosity shoos away the better of me. It stings like I imagine a Willadeene honeybee might sting, Avery taking another into our Pyramid of Giza. Worst yet, he has stolen away my Sugar and Darkly with them into the tomb.

I sneak until I am close, but not so close they can see me through the cracks. Close enough I can hear plenty well. I ease down. Lay myself on the floor. Right off, I am sure as sure they mock me. Certain Journey Wintergarden has told Avery what he has seen. *Me kissing Uncle Daddy over yonder on the stairs.* I imagine Avery, this very moment, writing down every word Journey Wintergarden speaks in *Jubilation and Woe.* Doodling another one of his gruesome Fiddler Crab portraits, like the one in my pocket of Rebecca carving off my Mirabelle with Salome's bow.

"Darkly likes you," Avery says. "Bushels better than he likes Rebecca."

"Give Darkly some time," Journey Wintergarden says. "Some folks are more an acquired taste than others."

"We have sifted through bushels of time. Heaps and heaps," Avery says. "Still—Darkly does not seem to like my sister."

"We will have to see what we can do on that account. To help things along."

Avery Longwood is up to no good. I hear it in the lilt of his words. The way he seems to tote them breathless up a hill. "Do you know who else did not care for my sister?" he asks.

"For the life of me, I cannot imagine who."

"Mother," Avery says.

"Avery," Journey Wintergarden scolds. "That cannot be true. A mother has to love her child. It would be unnatural to feel anything less."

"I did not say Mother did not love her. What I meant is that she did not like her very much. There is a difference. Between loving and liking. Just like Mother, I love Rebecca. But I do not like her." Rebecca is right. Avery is a saboteur. He and his mama always teaming up against Blue Heron just like she said.

"That is an unkind thing to say, Avery. That you do not like your sister."

"Is it? I would think it more unkind if I did not love her. To be both unloved and unliked, I could hardly bear it. If I had to pick between the two, I would rather be loved. What about you?"

"I suppose I would want to be loved," Journey Wintergarden says. "But I also want to be liked."

"I venture that is what most folks would say. Do you think you can like someone and not feel even a little bit of love for them?"

Journey Wintergarden laughs. "You are making my head spin, Avery Longwood."

"Just so you know, Journey Wintergarden. I like you."

"Thank you, Avery. That is kind," he says. "I like you, too."

A sweep of time passes, haints moaning and groaning dirty words, and I wonder what might be going on in my Pyramid of Giza. *Sweet mercy.* Journey Wintergarden speaks at last.

"What about Leontyne? How do you feel about her?"

I regret lying here listening like a dead rat on the floor, dreading what Avery might say. Serves me right, it will, to hear Fiddler Crab give Journey Wintergarden a piece of his treacherous mind. Me sneaking and snooping. To tell Journey Wintergarden all the lies he told his mama. Making out like I am a harlot.

"I always have liked Leontyne," he says. "Even now that she is missing a hand. And yes, I love her."

"That is generous of you."

"It is hardly her fault she is missing a hand. For that, you can thank Rebecca. I cannot remember if I told you. If it were not for me, Leontyne would be dead."

"You mentioned something of the sort when I first arrived. She is lucky to have you."

"Agamemnon ... Agamemnon...." Avery says teary, as if he might come unseamed. "The deed did not need doing. Cutting off a perfectly good hand. I begged Rebecca not to do it. To leave her be. Oh, you should have heard her, Journey Wintergarden. When Leontyne used to...."

"Used to what, Avery?"

"I have gone and done it now," Avery says. "You must promise. Promise to make no mention of it ever. Promise?"

"I promise, Avery. Now, go on with it."

"Rebecca cannot know I told you. Leontyne must never find out."

I know what is coming next. What Journey Wintergarden told me down by the Marsh. I should get up from here. *I should run.*

"You have my word."

"You should have heard Leontyne, Journey Wintergarden. Oh, how she once played the violin. How she could make Salome sing," he says. Fiddler Crab's words take off. *Rolling-rolling. Fiddling-fiddling.* "Leontyne does not remember. And now she never will play again. Do you not think, Journey Wintergarden, that it is best she not remember this beautiful thing she lost? I would die a thousand and one deaths. A thousand and one deaths I would die, if something so tragic ever happened to me. Do not tell Rebecca I told you. You promised. Remember?"

Remember.... I try my best to remember playing. I tickle at my lonesome, empty wrist. I wait for Journey Wintergarden to tell

Avery it is too late, that he already spilled the beans. That I know this thing I lost and it has not killed me. *A thousand and one deaths I would die....*

"A perfectly good hand?" Journey Wintergarden says. "I do not understand what you mean."

"The whole dreadful story is here, Journey Wintergarden. Every tragic, treacherous word of it, I have taken down here within these pages of *Jubilation and Woe*. I have accounted for the acres of awful things my sister has done."

Avery whispers. Journey Wintergarden whispers back. And I might go mad from all the whispering. From all the haints talking filth.

Crunch.

Twack.

A headless bird, a warbler, has fallen gruesome, writhing in my lap. I roll over. Send it sliding across the floor with my foot. I pull myself up onto my hand and knees and look up.

Uncle Daddy. He snatches another bird from a nest. *Crunch.* Uncle Daddy bites off the head. Throws down the body atop the Pyramid of Giza. Wings—a flitter.

"Great Queens of Egypt," Avery says. "What was that?"

One after another, headless birds tumble-tumble down. Mourning doves mourning. Screeching hymnals of terror.

Out across the desert and sea, I take in the wreckage, the flock of headless birds. *Dithering-dither. Writhing-writhing.* Avery poking his head from the Pyramid shrieking *holy hell and murder.*

My bare foot snags a nail. Across the floor, I trace the smear of blood, the red winged starlings falling down upon me hard. Little by little. Board by board. Drop by drop. Bird by bird. It comes to me....

Pretty Bird....

Pretty Bird....

I know who Uncle Daddy was.

Pretty Bird....
He was Theodore Laurence's daddy. That is who he was before.
Bright eyes burning yellow. Tongue licking the air.
Coo-ah, coo....
Down comes a warbling-warbler and mourning dove snow.
Coo-ah....
Coo-ah....
Coo....

Morningstar
The Down-Below

Chapter 32

In firelight flicker, we sit in a semi-circle on the floor of Avery's room passing the minutes. The hours. The years.

A good piece away, Willadeene is busy on her knees leaning over a silver tray on the rug cutting biscuits in two, sliding thick pieces of ham into their middles. Darkly is shameless, prowling the floor for crumbs.

From Willadeene's earlobes, clusters of red berries flourish in showy cascades. I admire their sway, watch them reach so low they near about dust her shoulders. Now and again, she looks over here at Journey Wintergarden seated between Rebecca and Avery. *Tingles and bliss.* And trouble is what I feel. Something is amiss with Willadeene. *Something is strange.*

"Darling birds … darling birds," Avery weeps from beneath his mama's old wedding veil, holding a parasol of yellowing white silk above his head. He is not so overcome by our recent Armageddon of birds he has lost the gumption to costume himself as Miss Havisham for my reading of *Great Expectations.* Not so distraught he could not manage to wrap himself about the shoulders in a white lace tablecloth to become the jilted bride.

"We have to get Uncle Daddy gone," Rebecca says. "Who does he think he is? That haint has no business here."

"Get him gone," Avery says sniffling. "Before Uncle Daddy gobbles every last bird from every last nest." He gives Sugar a kiss through his veil.

Revenge. That is who Uncle Daddy is. That is this haint's vocation, only he cannot remember yet the particulars of why he has come. Lucky for us, lucky for Rebecca, he does not seem to remember she killed him. I will not speak this conundrum aloud. It is in our best interest, especially my Blue Heron's, that Uncle Daddy should never know. What Uncle Daddy has gone and done to them birds is a thing I fear he might do to my Rebecca. For now, I will keep this business of Uncle Daddy to myself. That he was Theodore Laurence's father. No sense worrying the others.

I stare down at Sugar wobbling around sleepy atop *Jubilation and Woe,* remembering Rebecca leading Uncle Daddy to the Up-Up There. I retrace Avery's drawing of Rebecca sawing my hand off with Salome's bow. I rethink what Avery said to Journey Wintergarden. About thinking it a kindness not remembering I played the violin. A gift forgetting I can never do it again.

Rebecca. I imagine her strolling abandoned Morningstar fields. Sowing seeds of awful into acre-upon-acre of despicable rows, her black riding boots sinking into the soil. Avery follows behind, reaping all the trouble, inventorying it in his *Book of Jubilation and Woe.* One despicable thing she has done after another.

"Avery, take down that ridiculous parasol. You look a fool," Rebecca says. "Besides, you are bound to poke poor Mr. Journey Wintergarden in the eye."

"Tend your own business, Sister." Avery twirls his parasol. "You will be the sorry one when Uncle Daddy spits down a flock of headless birds. Flippety-flappety down from Elysium. To rain on your bossy. Hateful. Head."

"Flippety-flap," Rebecca says back, snapping her fingers.

Journey Wintergarden takes hold of Avery's parasol. "Fiddler Crab, let me help with that." He lifts it high above both their heads toward Avery's Comet. "We are ready now," he says. "Leontyne, Rebecca, Willadeene, you are all welcome to join us should it come down one of those flippety-flapping rains."

Flippety-flap. Flippety-flap. I watch the parasol spin and spin. Conjure a flash of a younger Rebecca. No hint of bosom yet. Baby fat. No cheekbones to speak of. Snapping-snapping her Longwood fingers. Singing a dreadful nursery rhyme to me.

Leontyne, Leontyne, pudding and pie,
Kissed the haints,
And made them die.

"Leontyne? Leontyne?" Avery snaps his fingers gentle. "Where have you got off to?" he whispers. "You seem oceans and continents away."

"I am not that far away," I say. "I am here beneath Elysium with you." *Beneath your parasol of doom.*

"Thank you, Mr. Journey Wintergarden," Rebecca says, touching Journey Wintergarden on the coppery hair at his wrist. If only Rebecca sat on the other side of me and away from Journey Wintergarden. Away from those handsome hands.

"For what, may I ask, do you need to thank me for?" Journey Wintergarden asks, his long legs crisscrossed. His naked toes stretching.

I root around in my scant bag of memories wondering what else I might remember of childhood with Rebecca, supposing if my mind plays tricks. If it was Avery who mocked me with that nursery rhyme song. *Leontyne, Leontyne, pudding and pie....*

"For taking care of the birds," Rebecca says.

"For saving us," Avery says. "For boarding up all the windows."

Haints wash and wash upon this shore. We are hardly saved yet, but I am most grateful to Mr. Journey Wintergarden for taking care of that mess with the birds. Or else Willadeene and I might have been the ones to sort out the gore. Journey Wintergarden has been kind, gathering up all the bird carcasses and heads. Stacking them outside in Avery's Sweet Chariot. *How many birds? How many birds are dead?* I wonder if Journey Wintergarden counted them as he counted all the windows. I wonder if I smile if he might try and count my teeth.

"I should be the one thanking you, Rebecca. All of you. For taking me in," Journey Wintergarden says. "For your kindness." He wraps an arm about my Blue Heron. Switches hands holding the parasol. Hugs Fiddler Crab next.

Across the way, Willadeene watches Journey Wintergarden embrace Rebecca and Avery, pulling the brother and sister into him. She snaps a bouquet of berries from her ears. She hums, mashing them in a small bowl with a pestle. *Shh.... Listen.* To what she sings low.

Stricken, smitten, and afflicted
See Him dying on the tree!
'Tis the Christ by man rejected
Yes, my soul, 'tis He, 'tis He!

Outside, the haints stir, rubbing and knocking themselves against the house. They seem to take a fancy to what Willadeene is up to. The haints tickle at the air with their crocodile arms reaching for my funny bone. To make me laugh along with them. Know this. I feel not one bit funny. *Tingles and bliss. And trouble.* Willadeene and them haints are up to no good.

"We should have a celebration," Avery says. "An evening of entertainments. In honor of Mr. Journey Wintergarden."

"Now is hardly the time for a cotillion, Brother," Rebecca says, staring up into Avery's parasol. "With that Uncle Daddy on the loose."

"Maybe we could invite him," Avery says. "Extend an olive branch."

Rebecca nearly topples backward. "Have you fallen on your head, Avery McKinley Longwood? I hardly think Uncle Daddy is the sort one invites to a party."

"I see no harm in asking," Avery says.

"You are considerate to think of it, Avery," Journey Wintergarden says.

"It seems we are back to where we started," Rebecca says. "With Uncle Daddy."

"We should have a party regardless," Avery says. "With or without Uncle Daddy."

Rebecca raises an eyebrow. "Perhaps you could have a word with Uncle Daddy, Willadeene," she says, a touch of accusation in her voice. The tone she took with me earlier. "Find out why he is here. What it might take for him to leave."

Just where Rebecca thinks Uncle Daddy might go is beyond me. For him, like Willadeene, there is no crossing the River or Sea. I might ought tell them what Uncle Daddy said to me. *I am the goddamned Sun.*

Willadeene leans back on the lush balls of her feet. "I cannot understand a single word that heathen speaks. We are hardly the same," she says. Willadeene drops a biscuit and knife on the tray. "How dare you put me in the same hamper with him." Willadeene drizzles molasses into the bowl of mashed berries. "Just what are you insinuating I ought offer him to leave?"

My face fevers up thinking of Journey Wintergarden watching me kiss Uncle Daddy on the cheek. *What on earth could have come over me?* I try to catch his eye. To see if there is any hint of change in his opinion of me.

"I am suggesting nothing sordid, Willadeene," Rebecca says.

Willadeene looks to Journey Wintergarden, trails her eyes down to his feet. It is a good thing Rebecca and the others cannot think what Willadeene is thinking. Feel what she feels when she looks Journey Wintergarden up and down. *Frogs carrying on carnal and cutting the fool in trees.* Scandal of scandals, I try my best to think of something else. To catch my breath and tamp down this good feeling. Swallow down a rising whimper.

"An evening of entertainments," Journey Wintergarden says, "I like the sound of that."

"I will give a recitation," Avery says, clapping his hands. "That is what I will do. Something that will make you weep and weep. And Journey Wintergarden, you and Rebecca can duel on your violins."

"A duel?" Journey Wintergarden asks, spinning the parasol. "That is perfect, Avery. Our Evening of Entertainments will be a contest. A friendly one, of course." He nods at Rebecca and Willadeene.

Willadeene pulls the tumble of earbob berries from her other ear. There is something different about these tiny berries. I have never seen them grow from her cockleshell ears before.

"And who will be the judge of this friendly contest?" Rebecca asks, taking a sneaky peek at Journey Wintergarden's toes.

"Willadeene!" Avery says.

"Then you are sure to win, Avery," Rebecca says.

"Consider this." Journey Wintergarden spins Avery's parasol slow. "I will play, but I will not compete. I will be the judge. I am fairer minded than most. Besides, Willadeene will be joining the fun."

Avery giggles. "Doing what? Juggling biscuits and ham?"

"If she did," Journey Wintergarden says. "No doubt it would be a glory."

Willadeene's eyes tumble back down to Journey Wintergarden's feet. She entices honeysuckle blooms from her temples. Sprinkles them in the bowl. Drizzles more molasses. Mashes and mashes her berries and blooms with the pestle.

And I recognize them berries now. *Holly berries.* Poisonous as they come. Them haints, they know these berries, too. They scratch and claw the bricks. Riled up. Chanting. Hankering for agony. For ecstasy. *The bitter end.*

Darkly sniffs around the biscuit tray. "Come away from there, Darkly," I say. "Come over here to me."

"Leontyne, I expect you to join us," says Journey Wintergarden. "In our Evening of Entertainments."

My heart drops straight to my ankles. I look to Rebecca and Avery. Study the both of them, waiting for Avery to mock me. I wait, trying to figure out if they lie to save me or hurt me. If it is Fiddler Crab or my Blue Heron filled with the truth. They sit quiet. And quiet. "If ever I was good at anything, you will have to tell me."

"Everyone is good at something. Is that not right, Avery?" Journey Wintergarden asks. "In time, Leontyne. I have no doubt you will remember." At long last, Journey Wintergarden looks at me. Looks at me no different than he has ever looked since we first met. If he ever cared a minute I loved up on a haint, it seems long forgotten now.

Avery stares at his sister. Fiddler Crab looks up blinking at Journey Wintergarden and nods. "Leontyne is good at reading," he says. "I taught her myself."

"How about that, Fiddler Crab. Then she must be very good at it." Journey Wintergarden wiggles his good-looking toes. "So, it is settled. Leontyne will read."

"I will be the one doing a recitation. Remember?" Avery asks, fiddling and fiddling. "Seems dull to have us both doing the very same thing."

"Yes, Avery," Journey Wintergarden says. "Remember, Blue Heron and I will both play the violin. But which one of us will do it best? And which one of you will be better?"

"I will of course," Avery says.

Willadeene cuts a biscuit. Slathers it with poisonous holly berry, honeysuckle jam. On top goes a hefty piece of ham. *Stop it, Willadeene.* I clear my throat, trying to get her attention.

Willadeene slathers-slathers. Sings soft. *Stricken, smitten, and afflicted....*

Avery scoops up Darkly from the floor. He stands. *Whoosh* comes a downpour of black satin. A tumble of wedding veil, and flourish of white tablecloth lace. Out from beneath the parasol he strolls, black earbobs bobbing. "I do not mean to hurt your feelings, Leontyne. Sadly for you, this is the truth. I am bound to win."

Tell me the truth, Avery. *Tell me, tell me.*

"Willadeene, I hope that biscuit is for me," Journey Wintergarden says, looking beyond Avery. "I am mighty hungry."

"Made it special," she says.

Rebecca calls out. "Bribing the judge, Willadeene?"

Killing him.... Killing him.... With haint-berry jam. Do I keep Journey Wintergarden from eating that biscuit and ham? Should I feed it to him myself? Poke it into his mouth with my thumb?

Avery hugs Darkly. Spins slow as the parasol goes 'round and 'round in Journey Wintergarden's hand. Spins until he is good and ready. Until he is Miss Havisham. Until his eyes are dark shadows beneath his veil.

I open the book. Find the page Fiddler Crab marked for me. Not sure if I ought read or scream out, *Willadeene is on the brink of murder. Look out!* I keep my eyes busy between Willadeene and *Great Expectations.* I decide it best to read, until I figure out what comes next.

I nod at Avery, reading best I can in this fireplace flicker. "I saw that the bride within the bridal dress had withered like the dress," I say. I pause and take a breath for Avery to spin slow. The way he told me.

"And like the dress, and like the flowers, and had no brightness left...." Willadeene says, stopping Avery from spinning. Making him turn loose a gasp. Willadeene has read the book before when none of us were looking. "But the brightness of her sunken eyes," she says. Willadeene stands up with the biscuit and ham, the one with haint-berry jam. The one she made up special for Journey Wintergarden.

Avery whispers. "Sit yourself down, Willadeene." She keeps on walking, the tassel at the end of her leash slinking the floor, her robe slipping down from her shoulder. Lower and lower. Exposing the swell of her deer moss breasts.

Pop and *crackle* goes the hearth. A downdraft follows, spooking the flame, bouncing shadows on the walls. Willadeene hums. Sings more of her eerie biscuit slicing song.

Tell me, ye who hear Him groaning,
Was there ever grief like His?

Avery is furious Willadeene has walked into his scene. Onto his stage. He speaks into Darkly's ear like he thinks my marsh rabbit is Pip Pirrip from the pages of *Great Expectations*, staring at Willadeene, reciting more Miss Havisham, his breath fluffing the veil. "Love her, love her, love her! If she favours you, love her. If she wounds you, love her. If she tears your heart to pieces—and as it gets older and stronger, it will tear deeper—love her, love her, love her!"

Willadeene comes closer, serenading with her biscuit and ham. *Tcll mc, yc who hcar Him groaning….*

"Love her, love her, love her," Journey Wintergarden says, smiling at Willadeene.

"If she wounds you, love her," Rebecca calls out.

The haints moan and groan. *Love her, love her, love her.*

I watch my Blue Heron watch Journey Wintergarden. "If she tears your heart to pieces," I say.

The haints rise up together. *Love her, love her, love her.*

Sccc-rrr-appe…. Down the chimney comes a sprinkle of soot and debris. *Whoosh* goes the hearth. Spook goes the flame. *Oooeee … oooeee* … oooeee…. A haint has dropped himself down the chimney. He rolls around, squealing and catching fire. *Uncle Daddy … Uncle Daddy….* the haint hollers, bolting from the hearth. Swooping the room.

Journey Wintergarden swings the parasol over his head at the burning haint. Knocks him into the curtains. *Swoosh….* The curtains catch fire. The haint streaks through Elysium, burning past

Avery's Comet, catching the planets and stars on fire, his crocodile fingers singeing the air. *Oooeee … oooeee …* oooeee….

Avery careens into Willadeene. "The world is on fire," he screams. Down-down goes the biscuit and ham. Down goes the heel of Rebecca's boot, down-down into the haint-berry jam.

If she wounds you, love her,
Love her,
Love her,
Leontyne, Leontyne,
Pudding and pie.
Kissed the haints,
And made them die….

Morningstar
The In-Between

Chapter 33

Twenty-six.... Twenty-six fireplaces there are here at Morningstar. Mr. Journey Wintergarden has counted every last crumbling one, boarding them up with floorboards pirated from what Avery calls *the Ballroom of One Thousand and One Nights*. Avery says the ballroom was to have had a night sky painted on the ceiling. Sphinxes. Fountains. And an enormous Bedouin canopy—if the great room ever had been finished. Like the rest of Morningstar, the ballroom is nothing but beams. And unfinished dreams.

"We must be careful of the ballroom. Coming and going," Journey Wintergarden says. "To not fall through the floor."

Falling down-down like Willadeene's biscuit and ham. If I am good at nothing else in this world, it is falling. This ought be the spectacle I perform tonight during our Evening of Entertainments. *Falling.... Falling.... Through the floor.*

"Great Queens of Egypt," Avery says, lifting his wedding veil from his face, up over his head to weep down his back. "Move that candelabra over there, Willadeene. That is not the place I told you it goes." *Snap-snap* goes his Longwood fingers.

Willadeene says nary a word to Avery. Murder still percolates her mind. She sits on the sixth stair from the bottom, holly berry clusters waterfalling sinister from her ears. She hums and sings what I heard her mutter in her dreams. *He kissed the boy ... kissed the boy ... beneath the moon.*

What in this sweet world I reckon Avery might think if he knew it was his dead mama he keeps tethered close on that leash? What havoc would it wreak if I told him? Good thing Fiddler Crab has the preparations for the Evening of Entertainments to keep him busy. Otherwise, he surely would be stricken with misery and grief from his bedroom near abouts burning down. From Elysium dangling charred at its edges, and the Galilean moons turned to ash.

"Are you sure this is safe?" Rebecca asks. "I think it best if we move our soiree to the Down-Below." She gazes part of the way into the Up-Up There, but not so far she can see the Moon.

"Avery will have it no other way," I say.

"It will be divinely perfect in this very spot. Here in the Rotunda. Beneath the Forever Moon and chandelier. The sound is much better here than in the Down-Below." Avery spreads his arms wide like he might take off spinning circles.

Fiddler Crab has instructed Journey Wintergarden to drag a Persian rug from the Down-Below. To unfurl it across the desert. Fiddler Crab is busy himself cordoning off an imaginary stage in front of the Pyramid of Giza with candles and kerosene lamps.

Rebecca arranges flowers Avery plucked from Willadeene into vases, watching Darkly and Sugar cuddling on the floor. "Should Uncle Daddy run out of birds, let us hope he does not have an appetite for rabbits or chickens."

"Perhaps he might be famished for Blue Herons," Avery says, standing back admiring his work.

We are safe best I can tell. At least for now. Uncle Daddy and I have come to an understanding. I have tricked him into thinking I have secrets to tell. Insinuated I might kiss him again there on the stairs under one condition: if he will leave us and them birds be, no more gnawing on warbling-warbler heads. Still, I do not trust him. I do not trust the goddamned Sun any more than I trust Damascus Tree, holly berry-honeysuckle jam. Or Willadeene.

I watch Uncle Daddy swim slow, mourning dove feathers wedged between his whetted teeth. I watch him watching us and all our goings-on. How queer we must seem from the Up-Up There. All of us assembled strange down here. Might it nudge a memory loose? That he once was here before?

Uncle Daddy. Please, Uncle Daddy. Mmmm.... The pitiful haint who came down through the chimney trails the goddamned Sun, begging and begging. This haint is a wretched sight. Burned up. Black and crunchy edges. I will say no more than this. What this haint wants from Uncle Daddy is a scandal of scandals.

The hell away from here, Uncle Daddy says. flicking away the trifling haint like a cow shoos flies with its tail. Best I can tell, Uncle Daddy will never have time for the likes of this namby-pamby haint. And time is all Uncle Daddy has along with a smattering of birds, and Morningstar pressed beneath his growing crocodile thumbs.

"Journey Wintergarden," Avery says. "Please put the chairs right here. In front of the stage. How dramatic it will be. Performing here in front of the Great Pyramid of Giza. On these hot-hot desert sands."

"Indeed it will, Fiddler Crab." Journey Wintergarden says.

"What prize will there be?" Willadeene says. "For the winner?" She strings a garland of her own magnolia, dogwood, and camelia blooms. Sews herself with needle and twine, parts of Willadeene Avery took without asking. Boughs of haint Avery plans to drape across our Pyramid in glorious festoons.

Willadeene looks so lonesome there on the stairs. I feel a burden of guilt swell up inside for what I done to Constance Rose Longwood. *To Willadeene.* To dead Baby Girl Longwood. *Gone quick as she come.*

For once, I hardly can muster looking yonder at my Blue Heron, watching her arrange stems of her mama in a fine crystal vase. How can someone so beautiful be so cruel? Lying to Avery. Letting him think the terrible thing he thinks. *Treachery.* Has Rebecca done something awful to me like Avery hinted? When was it I first loved Blue Heron? Wanted her for myself? How many rows of awful can a person sow until it is too bountiful a harvest for another to reap? How many pages of dreadful things did Avery mark down-down in *Jubilation and Woe*?

"Prize?" Avery asks. Willadeene has snagged Fiddler Crab's attention. Pulled him away from arranging his handmade paper lanterns about the place.

"Of course, there must be a prize," Journey Wintergarden says, flexing his toes careless in the desert sand.

"Well then. What will it be?" Avery asks.

Journey Wintergarden rubs a long finger across his lips. "Something of great value, I suppose." He looks about the place, at each and every one of us. "What about your blue ribbon, Fiddler Crab? The one about your neck. It would make an honest-to-God blue-ribbon prize."

Avery covers his neck with his hand and gasps. "How about my earbobs instead?" Avery points over at me. "Or something from Leontyne?"

I root around in my pocket. *Puzzle pieces. Eulalee's necklace and teeth.* "All I have is Darkly," I say. *And Mirabelle gossiping with Ewell Day Higgs from her can.*

"Tick-tock," Rebecca says. "How about Willadeene's Pocket Watch?"

"How about a look inside *Jubilation and Woe* instead?" Willadeene says, pulling her needle and twine, staring at Rebecca. "An abundance of riches awaits us there. Tick-tock."

"Leave *Jubilation and Woe* be, Willadeene," Avery shrieks. "Have you not learned your lesson?"

Journey Wintergarden waves his hands in the air. "Let us not go back to war for heaven's sake." He looks over at Willadeene. "May I take a look at Pocket Watch? If it is not any bother. On several occasions, it has caught hold of my attention," he says.

"Tick-tock," Rebecca clicks with her tongue.

Willadeene startles. Pricks her finger. I jerk, feeling it as if she jabs the needle into my very own hand. She places her finger in her mouth. Nurses the wound. "Very well," Willadeene says. She lays her garland of flowers in her lap and retrieves Pocket Watch. "Look here," she says. "Is this what you want to see?"

Journey Wintergarden squints at Willadeene from a good piece away. "A fine watch it is," he says. "I cannot recall. How was it you came by such a handsome thing?"

"We would all like to know that," Rebecca says. She leans down to the vase. Sniffs a hydrangea bloom.

Avery joins in. "It is mystery of mysteries how she came about Pocket Watch."

"There is not so very much harm in that," Journey Wintergarden says. "We should all be left to guard a few secrets. Imagine how dull the world would surely be if we carried our histories about scribbled on our sleeves."

"Or how very scandalous it might be," Rebecca says. "What of you, Mr. Journey Wintergarden? What prize might you have to give? It is mighty convenient asking the rest of us to search around in the coffers."

Avery giggles. "I agree with Sister," he says. "What do you have to give?"

"I am afraid my coffers are bare," he says. "Except for this gold ring on my pinky." He finagles his wide hands into his narrow pockets. Out comes one hand with nothing. The other holds something he seems surprised to see. He wraps his fingers around the thing hidden in his hand.

"What do you have there, Journey Wintergarden?" Fiddler Crab says.

"Something I found when I was down by the Marsh. With Leontyne."

"Let us see," Rebecca says, looking a little surprised Journey Wintergarden and I were together at the Marsh.

"Guess I put it in my pocket and forgot I had it."

"Go on then," Rebecca says.

"Yes," says Avery. "Let us see."

Into magenta moonbeams, Journey Wintergarden pinches something between his index finger and thumb. *A tincture bottle. Redemption.* Sparkle and gleam.

Uncle Daddy smells the Redemption from the Up-Up There. He calls out smacking and licking his catfish lips. *Great Redeemer … Great Redeemer....*

"I suppose some might think this a prize," Journey Wintergarden says. "A few drops of bliss."

"Best put that away," I say. "I have had my fill of that."

"We all need saving," says Willadeene. She bites at her lip, balancing the hurt of passing the needle through her stems. "One way or another. Which way will it be? A bottle of this? A bottle of that?"

Journey Wintergarden tucks the Redemption back into his pocket. "The blue ribbon it is," he says. "That will be the prize. Be a good sport Fiddler Crab. I have faith in you. In the end, you might win it back."

"It is my ribbon," Avery says. "Mine." His fingers streak frantic back and forth across the nap.

Swish.... Swoosh....

Swish.... Swoosh....

Rushworth L. Wintergarden's fingers tie the blue ribbon in my hair.

My hair....

Rushworth whispers.... Whispers....

What is it Rushworth L. Wintergarden is saying? I try to remember, running my tongue across my teeth. *Sixteen on bottom. Sixteen on top. Five fingers. Ten toes. Swish.... Swoosh....*

The blue ribbon is mine. *Mine.* And this is what Rushworth L. Wintergarden whispered. This is what he said to me.

Idolatry.... Idolatry....

Uncle Daddy leans back virile on his bobcat haunches. Presses the air with his crocodile thumbs. He cackles, feathers wriggling loose from his teeth. A flurry. A worry of—

mourning dove snow....

Morningstar
The In-Between

Chapter 34

Journey Wintergarden plays the finale of *Swan Lake*, accompanying Avery reciting a poem by Mr. John Keats. Haints gather outside the windows of the Cupola, defying Uncle Daddy to keep the hell away. The haints cannot help but look down through the windows from the Up-Up There to Avery here in the In-Between. Catching glimpses of the rhinestone tiara placed careful upon the tippy-top of his swan princess head. *Twinkle-twinkle. Sparkle and gleam.*

Avery has corseted himself into a gown of the palest pink satin, the palest of pale pink of a delphinium bloom. Silver beads. Crystal embroidery. In each of his Fiddler Crab hands, he flourishes a white feather fan.

Here I sit, trying my best to listen, pondering why Rushworth L. Wintergarden whispered *Idolatry* to me. Why Fiddler Crab and Blue Herron have not fessed up that the blue ribbon is mine. I will never be better than Avery this evening to win that ribbon back. Will never be better reading than Rebecca plays Salome. *How was it I once played the violin better than Blue Heron?* Would Mr. Journey Wintergarden tell me such a lie?

Avery lifts and lowers his white feather fans, his eyes skimming the place.

Who dances on bubbles where brooklets meet,
Hush, hush! soft tiptoe! hush, hush my dear!
For less than a nothing the jealous can hear.

Avery is wonderous. There is no competition, and I am so overcome by everything reeling all at once, I keep forgetting my passage from *Anna Karenina*. If only Avery would let me read from the book. He insists I do it from memory. He says this is the rule. How does it go again? *Sometimes she did not know what she feared, what she desired....*

I watch Avery look to the candles burning in the chandelier, the candelabras lit in the bricked niches. His eyes skim Willadeene's flowers scattered in vases, the hem of his dead mama's lovely House of Worth gown he wears. I am acquainted with this look welling in Fiddler Crab's eyes, the quickety-split rise and fall of his hoecake chest. He teeters the ledge of a powerful emotion in matching delphinium slippers, stupefied from the much-too-much beauty all around. The haints go quiet to give a listen.

The stock-dove shall hatch her soft brace and shall coo,
While I kiss to the melody, aching all through.

Avery slows his swan wings. *Flit-flit. Dither....*

Journey Wintergarden holds the final note while Fiddler Crab shimmers in the spotlight of Forever Moon in front of the Pyramid of Giza. Glimmering while he curtseys. While the rest of us clap. Until the haints rile again.

Clawing.

Scratching.

"Avery, that was a sensation," Journey Wintergarden says, the blue-ribbon prize tied about his wrist. "Well done. Well done. A stupendous beginning to our Evening of Entertainments." Fiddler Crab smiles, a trail of a tear spilling through the rouge on his cheek.

Journey Wintergarden announces Willadeene is next. We look around, but she is nowhere to be seen. What does she plan on doing? Might she up and do what Avery said? Juggle her biscuits and ham. I suspect Journey Wintergarden and Willadeene have a surprise tucked away into the coppery hairs curlicuing up Journey Wintergarden's sleeves. The two of them have been scheming when they thought no one was looking, murmuring off to the side. Sneaking off with one another. I have been keeping my eye on Willadeene, not sure if I am ready yet to help her do murder.

"Scandal of scandals," Avery says, arranged regal in a chair on the other side of Rebecca. He is the first of us to see Willadeene emerge barefoot from the wings covered in nothing but a cotton chemise. No leash. No tassel.

Haints at the Cupola's windows call down obscenities to the other haints, enticing them to claw their crocodile fingers up to take a look at Willadeene. Uncle Daddy hovers at the place where there is no rail. *Willadeene … Willadeene …* he calls out, licking those catfish lips with his mollusk-like tongue. *Mmmm….* The burned up haint lurks behind Uncle Daddy caring lesser than less about Willadeene.

Blue Heron is quiet. Utters not a sound. Avery is beside himself *dither-dithering* with his feather fans, watching Willadeene take the stage aside Journey Wintergarden. In the spotlight of Forever Moon, in the spill of Uncle Daddy's magenta, Willadeene's chemise casts a parlor trick. It turns translucent. Haints gather in droves outside the un-boarded windows of the Up-Up There, the purplish glow urging the Moon, undressing Willadeene further still. The haints pay Uncle Daddy heed. Not too close to the windows do they get. Just close enough to steal a look.

Journey Wintergarden pulls his bow across Treachery's strings, beckoning Willadeene's hips to sway. She dances a nomad woman's dance, an *I have been every place* dance. From the Hanging Gardens. To Persepolis. To nary single place left to go dance.

Haints assemble in greater numbers, the light growing brighter. Crocodile fingers wiggle for the windows. Reaching. Scraping. *Mmmm….* It is good and bad to be Willadeene. *To be dead and more alive than the living.* It is good to be her hips. Her thighs. The arch of her back. Her pretty head upon her long-long neck. Her honeybees. The hummingbirds whirring all around. No heaven or hell to fear. Only here. Her forever. Her always.

More… More… More…. The haints cry out. *Thighs. Hips. Bosom.*

Would the haints be covetous if they knew Willadeene pulled me down-down by my hair? Down-down to kiss me. *Shh ... I want another Willadeene kiss.* It is bad and good to be me. Bad and good to be Leontyne Skye. With five fingers. Ten toes. Tending the dead—knowing what they know. *Ecstasy. Sorrow. Pain.*

Bosom. Thighs. Hips. Feet.

More...

More...

More....

Up bow. Down bow. Misery of miseries, Willadeene's dance is done.

Journey Wintergarden's cheeks color rosy. His toes stretch and curl. Haints lament and whimper. Straight ahead, Rebecca stares. Avery *dithers.* My heartbeat turns beast. *Knocking. Knocking.* Off goes Willadeene from the stage. Her hips. Bosom. Her feet. No leash for Avery to grab. For Rebecca to stomp.

Journey Wintergarden speaks at long last, his cheeks a paler color. "Stupendous," he says. "Brava, Willadeene. Brava."

Avery's eyes glisten danger. "A gypsy's dance," he says. "All this time I thought you might be part pirate. Now the truth is revealed. You are Willadeene, Gypsy Queen. Teach me your dance, Willadeene. Promise? Promise?"

Rebecca sounds every bit like her daddy when she says this thing she says next. "An abomination. That is what that was, Brother. An abomination." She snaps her fingers. "Willadeene, go put yourself on some clothes."

Leontyne, Leontyne, pudding and pie,

"Who is next, Journey Wintergarden?" Avery asks. "Rebecca or Leontyne? Aside from me, Willadeene is second best so far. Do you not think?"

Lord, help me. Do not pick me next, Journey Wintergarden. I cannot remember my *Anna Karenina* passage. How does it go?

"Leontyne Skye," Journey Wintergarden says smiling, motioning me to the stage with his blue-ribbon hand.

"I am not ready," I say. "Please, pick Rebecca."

Avery chants, "Leontyne Skye ... Leontyne Skye...."

Kissed the haints and made them die. "I am not ready."

"You are as ready as you will ever be," Willadeene says, sitting behind us on the bottom stairs.

"There now. Do not be irksome, Leontyne." Rebecca looks down at Salome resting in her lap. She plucks a string. "Go on. It will all be over soon."

It will all be over soon. This is what my Blue Heron said. Two years back as I lay yonder on the floor. Avery weeping. Rebecca sawing. Humming-humming the nocturne by Chopin. I beg and beg. *The pain is too much. Please stop. You are killing me.*

Journey Wintergarden calls out. "Ladies and Gentlemen. Gypsy Queens. Swan Queens. Great Queens of Egypt. Darkly and Sugar." He squints into the Up-Up There into the magenta glare. "The not so nearly departed," he says. "Please, welcome Leontyne Skye. To our Evening of Entertainments."

I am a goner. At least I look less barbarian than I did before. Avery has conquered the gnarls in my hair, tamed them civilized into towhead curls down my back. He lent me slippers, keeping an account of his kindness in *Jubilation and Woe,* and to remember to get them back. There is nothing left for me to do but to make my way onto that stage. Make myself a fool. *It will all be over soon.*

Journey Wintergarden does not leave the stage. He stands close. So very close that Treachery, his violin, rubs against me. If he plans to play the violin while I forget the words to *Anna Karenina*, he has made no mention of it.

Quickety-split, Journey Wintergarden is behind me. Arms wrapped about me. The violin placed in my left hand, tucked beneath my chin. In Journey Wintergarden's right hand is the bow.

Avery gasps. Blue Heron sits still-still. Willadeene rises slow from the stairs.

Morningstar
The In-Between

Chapter 35

Journey Wintergarden moves the bow across the strings. Treachery shrieks. The haints groan, scratching the bricks, the glass. Avery covers his ears with his white feather fans.

"First position. Second. Third. Fourth position and beyond," Journey Wintergarden whispers. "Do what your fingers tell you. Fingers hold memory. They never forget."

I watch Blue Heron hold Salome, remembering her humming Chopin. The memory vibrates through my fingers. My wrist. My chin. Journey Wintergarden strokes Treachery with the bow. I listen to what my fingers tell me. Where they want to go. Into the catgut strings, I press my fingers. And we are playing, Journey Wintergarden and me. *Chopin's Nocturne Number 20,* Rebecca's hand-sawing song. The song playing when Avery saw what it was he saw. The thing he told his mama.

The room grows brighter, a sunrise of haints. *Up bow.... Down bow....*

I love the feel of Journey Wintergarden all about me. Warm breath against my cheek. Naked foot against my slipper. I like the way Willadeene looks at me jealous. The look of horror mounting on Fiddler Crab's face. What of Blue Heron? Does she hope *it will all be over soon*?

I lust for the sound of Uncle Daddy wanting more, the smackety-smack of his lips. The lickety-lick of his mollusk tongue. I love them haints watching from the Up-Up There. Looking down at Journey Wintergarden and me. I love Treachery singing sad between us. Making Avery weep. I listen to my fingers. Let them tell me where it is they ought go. Wishing they would tell themselves to grab hold of Journey Wintergarden and pull him close.

Is Rebecca ignorant of that fact that fingers hold memory? Did Fiddler Crab know fingers never forget when he sealed up my Mirabelle and all five of her fingers in her dented coffee can?

Acres and acres.

Row upon row.

Up bow....

Down bow....

Listen.... Journey Wintergarden and me are done playing. My fingers have finished their business telling me what to do. We are through playing Rebecca's hand-sawing song. *My blue-ribbon winning song.*

Avery caterwauls. "Rebecca told me not to tell you," he says. "That you once could play the violin."

Journey Wintergarden unwraps himself from around me. Rebecca stands up holding Salome, her hair slithering her back. *Ssss...* comes a recollection.

Blue Heron snatching Baby Girl Longwood away.

On Tribulation Day.

Mine. She is mine.

"Leontyne," Rebecca says, beckoning me back here to the In-Between. "I thought it best not to tell you out of kindness. We did not withhold it to be cruel."

"You confuse which is which, Rebecca. Cruelty and kindness," Willadeene says. "The lines are a blurry maze inside of you."

"Willadeene, you know nothing of me. And you have the gall to stand there half-naked as a savage talking down to me. If there are any lines blurred here. They are the ones running amuck and indecent inside you."

Journey Wintergarden sets down Treachery in a chair. "Rushworth said you were quick to learn the violin, Leontyne. One of the quickest he ever had seen. Look how swiftly it all came back to you."

"What else might come back to her?" Willadeene asks, staring down Rebecca. "If only someone with some knowing gives her a little nudge."

"Cruelty and kindness," Journey Wintergarden says, paying no mind to the commotion between Willadeene and Rebecca. "It would be a great cruelty to never know what has become of my brother."

"Or maybe it is a kindness," Rebecca says. "A kindness not knowing an awful thing?"

"Do you suspect something awful has been done?" Journey Wintergarden asks.

"I suspect a great deal of many awful things happen all the time. But I cannot speak to the particulars of what has happened to your brother."

Avery is up from his chair weeping. "Has something dreadful happened to my Mr. Rushworth L. Wintergarden? Do not withhold it from me. I cannot bear not knowing what has become of my Prince Siegfried."

"Forgive me, Fiddler Crab. I do not mean to upset you," Journey Wintergarden says. "Not on our Evening of Entertainments. I am certain my brother is alive and well." Journey Wintergarden smiles over at Willadeene. "What time is it?" he asks. "How very late has it gotten?"

"I am afraid I do not have Pocket Watch with me," she says.

"There is no place to keep it, her wearing nothing but that chemise. Unless she has swallowed it down. Tick-tock," Rebecca says. "To take the place of her peach pit heart."

"It is time for Rebecca to play," says Avery. "That is what time it is."

"Indeed. It is exactly that time," Journey Wintergarden says. "For Rebecca to play."

"There is no sense in me following Leontyne," Rebecca says. "Me playing with two hands could never compare to the spectacle of her playing with just one. As far as I am concerned, the evening is over. Leontyne has won."

"Do not be so sure of that," Avery says. "Journey Wintergarden is left to be the judge of that. Not you. So, who is it, Mr. Journey Wintergarden? Who has won?"

"There is only one blue ribbon," he says, showing it off, holding his large hand in the air. "You were all so very good."

"Then cut the ribbon into three sections and give us each a piece of our own," Willadeene says.

"Do not dare do it," Avery hollers. "Ignore Willadeene. Keep the ribbon in one piece."

"You are right, Fiddler Crab." Journey Wintergarden digs his hand deep-deep into his pocket. Pulls out the bottle of Redemption. "There is one easy solution."

"What are you doing?" I say.

"A drop of Redemption, Leontyne. I have always been curious about it. How it would make me feel. Tonight, I want to feel different. Be different. What about you?"

I want to be different. Not sure if I want to be the girl I was before. Or the one I am now. "Put that away."

"Have you never wondered?" Journey Wintergarden says. "I cannot imagine a more special way to celebrate our Evening of Entertainments than this. To share a thing together none of us have ever done." He pulls the tiny cork. "Who is with me?"

Willadeene is the first to speak. "We all need saving," she says, as she said before. Across the room, she walks upon the stage, into the light. She tilts back her head. Opens her mouth. Offers her tongue.

"One drop," Journey Wintergarden says. "Of saving coming up." He drops a drop beneath her tongue. Then beneath his own.

"I am next," Rebecca says.

"What are you doing, Blue Heron? Do not do it," I say.

"Me next.... Me next.... I want some," Fiddler Crab says.

Journey Wintergarden motions Rebecca to the stage with his blue-ribbon hand. "There is plenty to go around." He stands between Rebecca and me, not giving me space to shoo her away.

Rebecca tilts her pretty head. *Look up. Look up, to the Forever Moon.* But it is Uncle Daddy's sunrise reflecting in her eyes instead. Fiddler Crab is next. Head back like a baby bird. Mouth open. Tongue curling.

Now I am next. The last of us in line.

"We all need saving," Willadeene says. "A tiny-tiny drop."

Sparrows and warblers stir their nests. Eulalee's teeth vibrate. I look up. Look up through the chandelier. Through magenta moonbeams. I open my mouth watching Uncle Daddy open his mouth. Both our mouths opening wider and wider together.

"Just a drop," I say.

The namby-pamby bumed up haint draws close to Uncle Daddy. Works his way into his maw. Past his catfish lips. Beneath his mollusk tongue.

Anna Karenina. I recall it now. The line I could not remember fully before. *Sometimes she did not know what she feared, what she desired....* And I am tumbling through words. *Tumbling.*

Willadeene whispers-whispers. "We all need saving."

"Just a drop, Journey Wintergarden," I say.

Just a drop beneath my tongue....

Morningstar
The In-Between

Chapter 36

Pianissimo.... The word brushes warm and soft against my ear, and I am awake staring up into the chandelier, its candle flames extinguished. Unsure of how I got here. *Where was I before?*

"Leontyne," Willadeene whispers, kneeling at my side. "Come with me. I need your help, and there is something I must tell you." A hummingbird falls dead from Willadeene's shoulder. Bounces against my cheek and onto the carpet. She picks it up. Lays it careful behind her on the floor.

"What has happened?" I ask, sitting up, my heart *thumpity-thumping*. Head pounding. A threat of sick rising up and burning my throat. *Redemption*. What have I gone and done?

"Shh..." she says. "Do not wake them." She presses her finger to my lips, regarding Journey Wintergarden, Rebecca, and Avery sleeping.

They are near abouts too much to look at. *A glory-glory*. Journey Wintergarden's shirt is undone. His chest hair travels bronze in eddies to his naval. A Wintergarden, wide-acre hand drowns in the flood of Rebecca's hair spilling darkness across the gold Persian carpet. Fiddler Crab dreams, twitches and murmurs in his corset and pantalettes. Darkly and Sugar nestle in the wreckage of Avery's white feather fans. Treachery and Salome couple on the sawhorses leading to the Pyramid of Giza.

"How long have we been sleeping?" I ask.

"For centuries and centuries," she says. "Or maybe only a few hours. Tick-tock. Tick-tock. What does it matter?" she whispers.

Redemption. A drop beneath our tongues. The centuries, the hours before rush back to me in perfumed, purplish swirls. Black licorice. Christmastime orange. All of us waltzing. Spinning. Rebecca is Avery. Avery is Rebecca. It is hard to tell who is who. From one to the next, Journey Wintergarden's blue-ribbon hand presses at the small of my back. The small of Blue Heron's, Fiddler Crab's, and Willadeene's. Journey Wintergarden whispers-whispers *idolatry* in my ear.

Willadeene grabs me by the arm, pulls me from the floor. The smell of petrichor, jasmine, and rose billow so strong I might turn sick. It occurs to me I ought check if Journey Wintergarden still is breathing. Ensure Willadeene has not killed him yet with the poison red teardrop-berries cascading from the lobes of her lovely ears. I hold myself steady, wait until I see his chest rise and fall. *Up.... Down....* "Okay, okay," I say, turning myself over to Willadeene, letting her strong arm me from the stage across the desert.

Away from the others on the far side of Giza, Willadeene speaks. "He has it, Leontyne."

My vision is blurry. My lips are chapped. Slippers gone. My feet are bare. "Who has what?"

"Pocket Watch," Willadeene says, grabbing hold of something around my neck.

Rivière, Eulalee's oyster shell necklace. Why am I wearing it? When did I put the damn thing on? "What of Pocket Watch?" I ask. Do my eyes play tricks? Do Willadeene's honeybees sputter? Are they squirming around half dead in the scoop of her pink azalea blooms?

"Journey Wintergarden has it. He took it from me."

"Why in the sweet heavens would he do that?" *Up bow.... Down bow....* I watch Journey Wintergarden breathe, recall his arms about me, Salome beneath my chin. He is not a liar or a thief. I very well might scream this very next part out to the rafters. Scream it to Uncle Daddy. To the haints leering down from the windows. Hear me when I say. *I once could play the violin.*

"Journey Wintergarden knows," she says, "It did not dawn on me he would know it was his." She pulls Eulalee's necklace tighter, the oyster shells digging-digging into my neck.

"You are speaking gibberish," I say.

"I lied. Told him I found it," Willadeene says. "In the Forest."

I sway into Willadeene. So close my pale toes tussle with the high-high arch of her evergreen feet. "Lies.... The Forest.... What does this have to do with Pocket Watch?"

"Rushworth L. Wintergarden," she says, loosening the slack in Rivière, her chemise falling from her shoulder.

I step back. "What of him?"

Willadeene breathes in deep. Shakes her head. Honeybees fall from her azalea hair. Drop to the floor like gum drops. *Plop … plop….* "Pocket Watch was his."

"And you found it?"

"He gave it to me."

Across the desert, Avery mumbles in his sleep, lying alongside Journey Wintergarden and Blue Heron at the foot of the Pyramid of Giza assembled magnificent in a heap. I watch their chests. Make certain they are still amongst the living. *Breathing.*

"Rushworth L. Wintergarden came back here, then?" I stumble back onto a dead honeybee, its barbed stinger piercing the soft flesh of my big toe. *Mmmm….*

"There is more," she says, grabbing hold, stopping me before I can bend down to tend the stinger.

Uncle Daddy makes his way down the stairs to listen, spilling magenta across the treads, across the room atop the others sleeping. Outside, the haints scratch themselves slow against the bricks.

"What more is there to say, Willadeene?"

Across the desert, Rebecca stirs. "Do you hear that?" she asks, sitting up. Her hair—a tidal wave flooding her shoulders.

"The Undine," Avery says, awake now beside Blue Heron. "They are coming back."

McKinley Longwood. The Singing Prophetess. They are back. "Tell me, Willadeene. Tell me."

"Do not tell the others," Willadeene says, wrapping herself about me, the Undine's calliope sending shivers through us both. "Rushworth L. Wintergarden is dead," she whispers. "He is dead."

"How do you know?"

Uncle Daddy is so near I smell the burned-up haint on his breath: collard greens and cabbage. I can see Willadeene and me in the reflection of his windowpane crown. Charred bits of the eaten-up haint stuck to Uncle Daddy's whiskers.

"I killed him," Willadeene says.

Mmmm.... Killed him.... Uncle Daddy groans. Shakes himself like a dog shuddering off water. Bits of haint splatter my cheek. Splatter Willadeene.

"Rushworth L. Wintergarden," I whisper.

"They are back," Avery says. "They are back."

And Rushworth L. Wintergarden is dead....

Morningstar

The In-Between and The Boxwood Path

Chapter 37

Across the River, down the live oak path, through the Forest—the Undine's calliope sings, serenading its unnerving song to Good Hope in puffs of croaking steam.

Mine eyes have seen the glory of the coming of the Lord.

He is trampling out the vintage where the grapes of wrath are stored....

"The blue-ribbon prize," Avery says. "Leontyne has stolen my blue-ribbon prize."

"I did no such thing," I say, tending my throbbing, quick-swelling toe. "Watch out for the fallen honeybees. They are as dangerous dead as they are living." Willadeene works quick, fastening the back of Avery's gown. All I can think is that she has killed Rushworth L. Wintergarden. *Killed him dead.* How did she do it? *Poison him with haint-berry jam?*

"You are a sea wolf, Leontyne Skye," Avery says, straightening his tiara. "Lying about it in plain sight. Showing off. Bragging. With it wrapped around your thieving head."

Around my thieving head? I reach for my hair. Sure enough, the velvet blue-ribbon prize has been threaded beneath, pulled against the nape of my neck, collecting my hair from my face.

Journey Wintergarden buttons his shirt. Tucks the tail into his pants. "She won it fairly, Fiddler Crab. Do not be a spoilsport." Fiddler Crab opens his mouth like he might want to shatter us with a scream.

Rebecca gathers her hair. Ties it off with black ribbon. "That blue-ribbon prize is the least of any of our worries," she says. "The

Undine draws near. Or have you turned deaf. And just look at this place. Look at us. Look at you."

Just look at us. Fiddler Crab and Blue Heron's ebon eyes churn even darker. Journey Wintergarden's and Willadeene's eyes are filled with nighttime, too. Though I cannot see my own eyes, they feel different. Forever Moon's light seems too-too bright. *Poor Ewell Day Higgs.* Are his eyes pitch as ours? Does he think I never am coming back? Is he dead?

The Undine's calliope plays louder. *They have builded him an alter in the evening dews and damps....*

"What is wrong with me?" Avery asks. "I think I look nice for our new mother. As for this place, I have filled it for her with flowers."

And look what I have done. *Filled it with Uncle Daddy. Cluttered the place with haints.*

"Father is going to kill you when he sees you in Mother's clothes. Consider yourself warned. And bite your treacherous tongue, Brother. That Singing Prophetess will never be my mother."

Poor-poor, murdering Willadeene. She finishes fastening her son into the dress she once wore. Is there not even a thread, a stitch of the frock she finds familiar?

"Mr. Journey Wintergarden is here to protect me. Is that not right, sir?"

Journey Wintergarden is here to fetch his dead brother. I run my fingers *swoosh-swoosh* across by blue-ribbon prize. *Idolatry.... Idolatry....*

"I will do my best," Journey Wintergarden says, buttoning his pants with his long-fingered hands.

"And what of Mr. Journey Wintergarden?" Rebecca asks. "How should we explain him to Father? Do not be offended, sir, but Father is the one who sent away your brother. He is the one who said he would shoot him if he came back here. Along with any of his kin."

"This certainly is a conundrum," Journey Wintergarden says. "I suppose we should have considered this before now. Before I might get myself shot."

If Journey Wintergarden is the least bit frightened, he does not let on. He flashes a blinding blizzard of teeth, too bright for my eyes to linger.

"Father was keen on Mr. Rushworth L. Wintergarden, Sister. He will no doubt take a shine to his brother, too." *Swish.... Swish....* Avery smooths his hands down his tiny waist, staring into the deep-deep dark well of Blue Heron's eyes.

Keen on Rushworth L. Wintergarden.... Something passes between Avery and Rebecca. A stone pitched. I listen for a *thud* at the bottom of their inky wells. Wait for a blink. A *splash.*

"Then why do you think he would have sent my brother away?" Journey Wintergarden asks. "It is hardly a thing one does to someone they admire."

"What was it that your brother told you?" Rebecca asks. "Surely, he said something when he returned to Seraphim House."

Journey Wintergarden sets his eyes on me. "He was not himself when he returned."

The center of Journey Wintergarden's eyes are so swole-up black from Redemption, I see nary shade of blue or grey. Not dusky. Not dreary. I am so frightened I do not see Journey Wintergarden how I saw him before, I almost scream out to him. *Look up. Look up.* The Moon spilling through Uncle Daddy's magenta is better than no Moon at all.

Avery's eyes turn weepy. He dabs the almond border of his eye with Rushworth L. Wintergarden's handkerchief. "I think perhaps a person can like a person so very much he cannot bear to be too close to them. If he cannot possess them completely. That he would sooner have them leave than stay. I think that is why Father sent my Rushworth L. Wintergarden away."

Rushworth L. Wintergarden is dead. Dead. Willadeene has killed him. I almost say the thing out loud. But what good would it do? Morningstar tips this very moment toward pandemonium with Hushabye Byrd and McKinley Longwood coming. Surely, there is no harm in all the rest of them thinking Rushworth L. Wintergarden is alive.

Avery dabs and dabs his eye. Why did Constance Rose Longwood have Rushworth L. Wintergarden's handkerchief tucked in the bodice of her black satin gown? If what Avery says is true, I suspect McKinley Longwood is not the only one of his parents keen on Rushworth L. Wintergarden. Fiddler Crab and Blue Heron certainly took a shine to him to the point of obsession. I rub my finger across the ribbon hidden beneath my hair, at the nape of my neck, searching and scratching away at the meaning of this thing said to me. *Idolatry.... Idolatry....*

"Pianissimo," Rebecca says. "Shh.... The Undine's calliope has stopped."

"They are here," Avery says.

My toe. It aches. No longer is it red. It darkens to purple. Now it is turning black. Is this from Redemption? Or the sting of Willadeene's dead honeybee?

"I will go out to meet them." Rebecca says. "The rest of you stay here with Journey Wintergarden, and I will figure out a way to explain him." She looks back over her shoulder. "I will try and prepare them for Uncle Daddy. For this mess they have come back to."

"Treachery," Avery says. "Do not think for a moment I will allow you to go without me, Rebecca, that I trust you to greet our new mother without me. Have you forgotten I am the one she likes best?"

"Have you forgotten you are a coward and terrified of Sinners and haints?" Rebecca asks.

"I remember a great many things, Sister. Acres and acres. Between Sinners and haints, I reckon I am more afraid of you."

"By all means, come with me then, Avery. Leontyne, you might as well come along, too. To help me protect Avery from Father when he sees him in our dead mother's dress."

"Are you sure I should not go with you, Rebecca? In case you are bothered by the haints?" Journey Wintergarden asks.

Rebecca tidies her waistcoat. "Stay here with Willadeene. The sight of her tends to upset the Singing Prophetess. Besides, the haints will hardly pay us any mind. Like Leontyne said, it is Uncle Daddy they are trying to get at." Rebecca reaches down. Pulls Miss Jane Austen, her revolver, from her boot. "And there is this."

I do not know who is in greatest peril. Avery at the hands of his daddy, or Journey Wintergarden in the clutches of Willadeene. *Willadeene is sneaky.* All this time not letting on she can read, and now she has confessed to killing Rushworth L. Wintergarden. Willadeene hums again, even though the Undine's calliope has gone silent. *Glory, glory, hallelujah....*

"Put on your slippers, Leontyne," Rebecca says. "Father and that woman will be headed this way soon." I shimmy my foot fast in my slipper so no one can get a gander of my toe swelling and turning black.

"I wonder what this Josiah and Lazarus will look like," Avery says, grinning at Journey Wintergarden. "I hope they are handsome," he says. "I hope these nephews are the best ones yet."

"They are forever changing," Journey Wintergarden says. "Is that not what you said?"

"Forever changing," Avery says, "From last time to the next."

"Forever changing," Journey Wintergarden says, pushing his hand into his pocket. I can make it out clear, the outline of Willadeene's Pocket Watch. *Rushworth L. Wintergarden's watch.* He smiles at Willadeene. "Tick-tock."

"Watch out for Willadeene's dead honeybees," I say, one last time, staring down at Journey Wintergarden's handsome toes.

Tick-tock....

Watch out....

Morningstar
The Boxwood Path

Chapter 38

The haints cast eerie sunset across the grounds of Morningstar, robbing Forever Moon of her glory. The haints, like Uncle Daddy, are changing. Growing tails. Hatching crocodile arms. Most of them are right puny. None of them near abouts large as Uncle Daddy.

From the branches of live oak trees, haints dangle upside down by their tails. A smatter of these ne'er-do-wells carry on like Sodom and Gomorrah in the boxwood hedge. Grunting. Rolling topsy-turvy on their backs, soliciting us with the bulbous parts of their undersides. *Look at us. Mmmm.... Look at us....*

"Abomination," Rebecca says. "Look away, Avery. Look away...."

"Sheherazade." Avery clutches the bouquet of Willadeene's flowers he has collected fresh for his new mama, *Jubilation and Woe* beneath his arm.

Like me, Fiddler Crab cannot draw his dark eyes away from the thrill of this depravity. In droves, most haints gather along all eight sides of Morningstar, sharpening their crocodile claws on the bricks, calling obscenities out to Uncle Daddy. Feathering caresses tender across my intimate places, distracting me from the hurt throbbing in my shoe.

Eulalee feels what I feel. *Ecstasy.* She cannot help herself. Pleasure vibrates in the rotten roots of her teeth, but she will be good and goddamned to the Doldrums before she deigns to pay me any mind. I have figured Eulalee out. She intends to ignore me until I succumb to the Marsh and travel back to tend her precious Damascus.

"We will stop here and wait," Rebecca says, at the edge of the brittle boxwood hedge, a good piece from the end of Forest's path.

Back and forth my fingers go beneath my hair along the nap of my blue ribbon. I try recollecting what Journey Wintergarden whispered into my ear when we danced naked foot to naked foot, both of us out of our cotton-picking minds from a single drop of Redemption. What was it that he said? No, it was not Journey Wintergarden who said it. It was something his brother, Rushworth, once said. Something or another about idolatry. *Idolatry....*

"I hear her singing," Avery says. "Miss Hushabye Byrd is getting close."

"I hear her, too," I say. She is singing *The Battle Hymn of the Republic*, the song the Undine's calliope was caterwauling before.

Glory, glory, hallelujah....

"I hope she has brought me everything on my list," Avery says. "I forgot to write it all down for her before she left."

"What will you say, Leontyne?" Rebecca asks. "When she inquires about Redemption?"

"I reckon I will have to tell her the truth. That I have made nary a drop." *Tell her Damascus refuses to sing.* Rebecca and I should slip off from Good Hope when everyone is sleeping. Sail away on the Undine leaving the rest of them stranded before Good Hope is so mired with haints it breaks off and sinks into the Sea.

The Singing Prophetess starts up singing. *Mine eyes have seen the glory of the coming of the Lord....*

"She is here," Avery says.

The Singing Prophetess teeters in the distance, holding onto the handles of Sweet Chariot, her veil coming alive in the wind. Journey Wintergarden must have left the wheelbarrow at the River when he dumped the headless birds.

"She is alone," Rebecca says.

Avery calls out. "Where are the others?"

The Singing Prophetess is indeed alone, except for Babylon following behind her. Hushabye Byrd stops. Teeters and totters. Singing not a single word. Holding onto Sweet Chariot. Staring at

Morningstar. Her veil billowing. Until at last she sings out a terrible shriek.

For the love of God.

What have you done?

What have you done?

She is quicker than I have ever seen her on those wood block shoes, keeping her balance, holding onto Sweet Chariot's handles. Coming at us. Coming for us.

What have you done?

What have you done?

The haints stop their clawing, their perversions in the bushes. Some of them are so startled their tails let loose from tree branches, and they go falling in heaps on the ground.

Rebecca calls out the thing that stops Hushabye Byrd from coming, from plowing Sweet Chariot's wheel through the dirt. "Where is Father?" she asks.

Avery calls out behind Blue Heron. "Where is Josiah? Where is Lazarus?"

We wait and wait. I rub beneath my hair at the ribbon. *Idolatry.... Idolatry....* What was it Rushworth L. Wintergarden said?

Hushabye Byrd holds out her arms at long last, her veil flapping helter-skelter while she sings.

Your father,

Your father,

Drifted into peaceful slumber,

Slept himself away to Beulah Land....

"I do not understand," Avery says. "Where has he gone off to?"

Beulah Land,

Beulah Land,

Swish.... Swoosh.... I drag my fingers back and forth across the ribbon. It slippety-slides back to me. Rushworth L. Wintergarden's arms folding about me. His lips against my ear.

The Singing Prophetess sings another dreadful shriek.

Your father,

He is dead.

He is dead.

The haints start up. *Scratching. Clawing. Screeching. Groaning.* My big toe swells and swells. Aches and aches, hurting up a memory.

Rushworth L. Wintergarden's arms about me.

Whispering-whispering,

Leontyne … Leontyne …

Loving you,

Loving you is like idolatry.

Idolatry….

From somewhere beyond the blurry edge of this memory, Hushabye Byrd sings. Blue Heron, Fiddler Crab, and the haints join her squawking chorus.

McKinely Longwood is dead.

He is dead….

Morningstar
The In-Between

Chapter 39

Hushabye Byrd gazes into the Up-Up There at Uncle Daddy staring down-down. She gathers her red veil. Pulls it from the depths of her ankles from the desert. Pulls and lifts. Casts it down her back to lurk the floor listening for shivers, whimpers of sorrow now that McKinely Longwood is dead. Not a single one of us makes a sound except for Hushabye Byrd when she sings.

Peaceful.... Peaceful....
Asleep he went.
Come morning,
Woe morning.
Never did he wake.

Hushabye Byrd puts her arm around Fiddler Crab.

I am your mother,
Your Singing Prophetess,
Mistress of Good Hope.
I am your father now.

My head is a whirl, my big toe swelling, stretching the satin of the slippers Avery lent me. I care little McKinley Longwood is gone. Hushabye Byrd is here and in full charge. This is the thing for which we should most be worried. And Rushworth L. Wintergarden, while he was loving me, was I busy loving him back? I want to lay down. No, maybe I ought run. Grab hold of Blue Heron's hand and run before Hushabye Byrd can take a hold of me by my nub. Who knew Rushworth L. Wintergarden loved me? Did anyone? His brother? Rebecca or Avery?

Hushabye Byrd stops her singing. She studies Journey Wintergarden's naked feet. Pinches Avery's chin. Leans down measuring the darkness swoled up in his irises. Peering into the midnight lurking all our eyes. She whispers, "Praise be. I have come back it seems, on the precipice of you all turning heathen, the light gone from all your eyes. Depravity! Which one of you here is to blame? Who here can tell me what has happened to the Sun? No light left but the Forever Moon and that haint swimming circles in the Up-Up There. Who pockets the answer why my Good Hope is dripping and sinking with haints?"

"There is something wrong with Damascus," Avery says, cutting his eyes at Sugar resting on his shoulder. "Eons and eons have passed, and she has not so much as sung a single note of her wind chime song."

Treachery…. Fiddler Crab blames me. *Hushabye Byrd, your precious Avery is the one who killed the Sun.*

"All was well when McKinely Longwood and I left." Hushabye Byrd drifts her hand toward Journey Wintergarden. "Tell me, wayfaring stranger, what part of this calamity is yours?"

"If I have played any part in this mess, I am truly sorry, Prophetess. I only came here looking for my brother." Journey Wintergarden pulls out his brother's watch from the pocket of his pants.

Rushworth L. Wintergarden is dead. Should I go ahead and tell the room? Stop the searching, the misery. Willadeene rubs at her belly as if she might be unwell, but she is lovely as ever I have seen her. Three springtime's worth of blooms.

"Mr. Journey Wintergarden has been a savior," Avery says. "I do not know what we would have done had he not come. We might all have been ripped to tatters by these good-for-nothing haints." Avery's dark eyes glisten.

"Journey Wintergarden has kept the haints from taking over and coming in," Rebecca says.

Hushabye Byrd sings.

Thank you.

Thank you, wayfaring stranger.

For caring for my property,
Now that Morningstar is mine.

Blue Heron and Fiddler Crab glance at the other. "A terrible thing has happened, Miss Hushabye Byrd," Rebecca says.

Hushabye Byrd spins her head all about the place like she is curious what is the most terrible of all the things. "What thing is that? Tell me," she says. *Tell me,* she sings.

"Eulalee Skye. The Great Redeemer. She is dead."

What is Rebecca doing? Does she mean to do me in? "We are all dead here on Good Hope," I say, remembering that thing I once heard said. "If some of us are not completely, some have been for a blink. With the rest of us on the verge at the very least."

"It was bound to happen," Hushabye Byrd says. "It is a burden to tend Damasus. To look after the dead." *A burden,* she sings.

The Singing Prophetess is not wrong. I watch Willadeene rub her belly. *It is a burden being dead and more alive than the living.* A burden being the one doing the killing. A burden to have your bones *clank* against bones in the Doldrums. To have been loved. To not remember. "A burden," I say. *Not knowing who to trust.*

"You must keep on doing what it is your mother has done," she whispers. *You are the Great Redeemer now,* she sings. "Aside from God, you are the only one who can save us." She reaches her hands to the Up-Up There, her eyes steering clear of the Moon. *Save us, Leontyne,* she sings.

Hushabye Byrd's voice plants quick growing seeds, seeds taking off in prickly shoots under my skin. And it is hard not to be a believer when Hushabye Byrd sings. When the tears swell crocodilian in her hooded eyes. For a moment, the others seem to be believers, too. Believing I am the one to save them. I do not want to be the one to disappoint them. To tell them I am not the Great Redeemer. Confess the one true Great Redeemer is dead and pouting in my pocket.

"Save us, Leontyne," Avery cries out, pulling at his bodice. "Save us."

My Blue Heron whispers, "Save us."

"Save us." Willadeene rubs and rubs at her belly.

"Save us, Leontyne," Journey Wintergarden calls out when the others are done.

"Amen … Amen …" Hushabye Byrd whispers. *Amen … Amen …* she sings.

There would be quiet if not for the haints outside mauling the bricks and Avery sniffling, the sound of my toe swelling and stretching the seams of my slippers. Except for the sound of Uncle Daddy calling down to me. *Do what you please. Run off from here. No need for any goddamned Great Redeemer.*

Fiddler Crab is first to speak. "Miss Hushabye Byrd. What surprise did you bring for me?"

A dead daddy. That seems plenty enough surprise to me.

Hushabye Byrd says nothing.

"I almost forgot," Avery says. "These are for you." He offers the bouquet of Willadeene he picked special for Hushabye Byrd, his eyes catching hold of something on the bodice of her embroidered garment. Something beneath her pearl stick pin. *A peacock feather.*

"Abomination," Hushabye Byrd says, curling up her geisha lips, cutting her eyes at Willadeene running her evergreen hands over her belly. "Get that damnation away from me."

Damnation, Uncle Daddy says, as if the word arouses. *Mmmm….*

Avery drops the flowers to the floor. Stares at the feather. I recognize that feather, the one Fiddler Crab sneaked and gave to Josiah when Hushabye Byrd was gone from the room.

"Miss Hushabye Byrd, where are the nephews? Where are Lazarus and Josiah?" Avery asks.

Hushabye Byrd pretends to ignore Avery, pressing her gloved hand to Josiah's feather. Making sure he sees what she has done. That she has retrieved the thing. A threat. She has done God knows what with them ever-changing nephews. She turns her head this way and that. *Pssst.... Sssss.... Pssst....* "Leave us now. Leave me alone here with Leontyne. Our Great Redeemer."

Journey Wintergarden spreads his albatross arms. Collects Rebecca and Avery. Calls out to Willadeene. "Off we go," he says. "To the Down-Below. Shall we cut fresh stars? Hang ourselves a new Elysium."

I trouble after Journey Wintergarden's feet, take in the petals of Willadeene stuck to his high-high arches, spying a petal sucking tight as a leech to his neck. *Swish* and *swoosh.* I see whorls of Willadeene and Journey Wintergarden dancing through our Evening of Entertainments. Naked foot to naked foot. I watch Avery turning back putting two-and-two together about Josiah's feather. I watch Rebecca lean into Journey Wintergarden.

"Be on the lookout out for the honeybees," I say, as they trek the last of the desert. *Do not leave me alone here with Hushabye Byrd. Keep watch out for that Willadeene. Do not eat her biscuits and ham. Do not leave me.* They keep-on keeping leaving me. *Do not believe a thing Avery and Rebecca tell you, Journey Wintergarden. Go on then. Eat Willadeene's biscuits and ham. All of you. Slather them with haint-berry jam.* And now they are gone. *Gone.* From the In-Between. Out of sight and safe in the Down-Below. Several feet of space are all there is between Hushabye Byrd and me.

Pssst ... Pssst ... Sssss ... she mutters.

Around the corner comes Darkly sniffing, creeping like a cat. He takes off running to me. Hushabye Byrd is quickety-split. Raring back her wood block shoe. Raring and raring. Until she kicks him.

Holy terror.... Holy terror....

Darkly screams. Rolls and rolls. Over and over. Across the floor.

Rolling-rolling....

Morningstar

The Ballroom of One Thousand and One Nights

Chapter 40

Darkly rights himself. Runs squealing for the entrance to the ballroom. I chase after him, my toe *popping* and *cracking* in my shoe. Squashing-squashing dead honeybees. *Cracking.... Popping....*

"Do not go in there, Darkly," I holler. It is too late. Darkly wobbles across the ballroom's floor beams whimpering, getting far away from Hushabye Byrd as the poor thing can. A queer sort of beauty it is here, firelight and lamps lit with kerosene streaming through the holes and cracks in the plaster ceiling from the Down-Below, mushrooming up here to the In-Between. Shining like shooting stars up through the ruined ballroom's floor.

"Come back here, Darkly." I take one step with my aching foot onto a floor beam, the foot with the fast-swelling toe. Then I move my other foot, balancing myself like a circus lady from one of Fiddler Crab's picture books. Vines meander through the plaster. Wreak havoc. Strangling themselves about the beams. Making it hard to gain solid footing.

Sssss.... Sssss.... Pssst.... Hushabye Byrd has come up on me from behind. I balance myself. Turn around to face her. *Sssss.... Sssss....* "Be careful," she whispers. "It is a long ways down."

She takes a step toward me. I take a step back. "I have fallen the long-long ways before," I say.

"How many times can a girl fall the long-long ways? And get herself back up again?" she whispers.

"As many times as she needs, I reckon." She takes another step on them high, wood block shoes. I slide myself back a little farther, the vines unbalancing my feet.

"You are the Great Redeemer now," she says. "That is no small bit of business."

"Stop calling me that," I say, holding my arms out for balance. "I am not now. And I will never be the Great Redeemer."

Great Redeemer. Great Redeemer, she sings, mocking me. "Do not be a one-handed little fool. Folks rarely choose what they get to be," she whispers. "Life is what does the choosing. Not you. There is a price for not being what you are meant to be. For refusing to be the Great Redeemer. Look at me," she says. "I am what life has made me. What it has told me I must be. Who is to know? I might have set out to be what I am anyway, if I had been given a choice."

What has life made you? "What is it I must pay then? I will pay it."

"Look around," she says. She takes another step, sure footed through the shooting stars, trampling the heavens, as if her feet and shoes are the same. No teeter. No totter. "But there is more for you to pay than keeping this sorry world covered up in haints, and for keeping your rabbit from being kicked to smithereens. More to pay if you do not do what I tell you."

"Tell me then. How much do I owe?"

"More, I reckon, than you are willing to pay."

"Go on with it, Miss Hushabye Byrd. I want to know."

"Take not another step," she says. "You are more a treasure to me living than dead." She tamps the air with her gloved hand. *Stay there. Stay there. I will tell you.*

Mmmm.... Uncle Daddy hovers at the ballroom's entrance. This haint has floated himself lecherous down the stairs, steering reptilian with his claws. Paddling down with his ever-growing tail. *Do what you damn well please, Leontyne.*

"Look what you have done, Great Redeemer. Look what being sorry has got you. Not tending the dead like you should." She looks back over her shoulder at Uncle Daddy. *Damnation.... Damnation...* she sings.

Uncle Daddy likes the way Hushabye Byrd sings *damnation*. He touches all over himself with his mighty-fine-looking tail. He says vile things. *Sweet-sweet nothings.*

"What is it that fiend is saying?" Hushabye Byrd asks. "Like your dead mama, I know you know the way of haints. Understand the rotten tongues they speak."

Mmmm.... Rotten, Uncle Daddy says. *Tell that whore I can sniff the rotten smell of her from here. Tell her.... Mmmm....*

From the Down-Below, Rebecca plays Vivaldi's *Winter*, the notes drifting up mingling in the starshine, turning these precarious heavens chill, taunting my gone-away hand that once held Salome's bow. I peer down through the crisscrossing vines. Through cracks and holes in the plaster. *Would any of you below bother to catch me if I fall?* "How much?" I ask. "How much to not be the Great Redeemer? To not do what you say?"

Who cares? Uncle Daddy groans. *Do whatever the hell you damn well please. Leontyne ... Leontyne ... Starshine ... Starshine....*

"I am Rebecca and Avery's mother now," Hushabye Byrd says. "I hope they do not suffer from an infirmity such as their father. One from which I cannot keep them safe." *I hope ... I hope....* "They do not go off to sleep. And never wake."

Mmmm.... Never wake....

"I suppose I could take them off with me next when I travel across the River in the Undine. Off to faraway lands," she says. "Redemption and pretty-pretties. They sell for good prices out of the back flap of my revival tent." *Sssss....*

Pretty-pretties, Uncle Daddy says.

A vine urges the bottom of my feet. Knocks me off balance. I spread my arms. Steady myself. Another vine wraps cold around my aching foot.

Save them, Hushabye Byrd sings. *Save them.* She reaches behind her. She pulls a bit of her red veil. Pulls and pulls. Until it is over her head, tumbling back over her, covering her geisha lips. Covering her ankles. "Pretty-pretty," she says. "Listen to how lovely Rebecca plays the violin."

The vine wraps the vine tighter about my foot. *Crack* goes my toe.

Hushabye Byrd steps back. *Hisses.* Slides on her wood block shoes. "So pretty," she says. "One of these here days. One of these here days. Rebecca is liable to sing down the Moon with that violin."

Pretty-pretty.... Mmmm.... One of these days.... Do it Rebecca, Uncle Daddy moans. *I am the goddamned Sun. To hell with the Moon.*

Crack and *pop* goes my toe.

Hushabye Byrd stomps the heavens backward singing a Prophecy of Doom.

One of these days,
One of these Good Hope Days,
Blue Heron is going to do it.
She is going to sing down,
Down-down,
The Moon....

"Save the pretty-pretties, Great Redeemer," Hushabye Byrd mutters.

Save them....

Morningstar
The Great Pyramid of Giza

Chapter 41

"There now, sweet baby," I say, kissing and hugging on my Darkly, soothing his frittered nerves. "You are safe here with me." Except I cannot imagine there is anywhere or anyone safe on Good Hope with that Singing Prophetess *clompety-clomping* on her wood block shoes, kicking the living daylights out of my sweet angel. I reckon we are not even an iota of safe hidden away down here murky in this Great Pyramid of Giza.

Squish. Something is wrong in my shoe. The swelling in my toe surrenders, my slipper feeling less tight than before. I am too nervous to give it a look. Too full-up with worry figuring on if I ought tend Damascus to keep my Blue Heron and Fiddler Crab safe. Safe from not waking up like their dead daddy. Safe from being sold out of the back flap of Hushabye Byrd's revival tent.

How much might Rebecca and Avery cost? A king's ransom? Does she mean to sell them off for good? Does she aim to rent them by the hour? How much could she get for a one-handed girl like me? Is that what she went and done with Lazarus and Josiah? Sold them to the highest bidder?

Journey Wintergarden. I am sure he might help if I ask him nice. Explain to him we are slipping and sliding into doom, that his brother loved me. *Idolatry.... Idolatry....* I cannot be certain, but I might have loved him, too. "What do you think, Darkly? What ought I do?"

I sit Darkly in my lap, rubbing at the blue ribbon holding my hair back, deciding it might be better not knowing if I loved Rushworth L. Wintergarden now that he is dead. What would be the point? He is not ever coming back.

I fiddle with Eulalee's oyster shell necklace, contemplating what could happen if I give it a lick. Tallying how much of yesterday or tomorrow I might see. *Squish.* There goes my toe again and the inkling maybe I could muster the courage to wake up Damascus, to play nice. Tempt these haints to her Sarah Figs. Make one batch of Redemption. Run away with Journey Wintergarden, Rebecca, and Avery when Hushabye Byrd leaves out again to peddle her stolen wares. We will head off to far-far places. *The Great Wall of China, the Arctic, paddling the Tyrrhenian Sea to behold the limestone sea stacks rising from the water off the Island of Capri.*

"What do you think of Italy?" I ask Darkly. "I bet Sugar would think visiting there would be a treat." *Squish.* I do not much care for the sound of what is going on inside my shoe. I set down Darkly. I decide it best to go on and get it over with. To give my toe a look. I pull at the heel of the slipper. I pull the rest of my foot out of the shoe. What has happened? Something is wrong. *Agamemnon!* My big toe is gone.

I stop myself from screaming for someone to come help. A rise of sick comes up over me. My skin goes slickery, cool as a corpse. I shut my eyes. Breathe deep. Lean back. I settle myself. Breathe deep. Open my eyes slow. Rally the gumption to give my foot a look. *Sweet heavens above.* How queer it looks. Only four toes shivering lonesome without a fifth. I shake my slipper upside down. My toe *plops* into my lap looking like a dried up plum. Darkly paws up close to give my fallen-off toe a look. A sniff and farewell.

I take inventory of myself. *Five fingers. Nine toes. One hand. Two feet. Thirty-two teeth in all. Sixteen on bottom. Sixteen on top.* There is a larger thing missing. An artifact. A treasure to subtract. Another part of myself gone. But I cannot place it.

Clank... clank ... clank.... Knocks come from outside against the Pyramid of Giza.

"Leontyne? Are you in there?"

Willadeene. I look down at my toe. I reckon she has come back to finish me off with more honeybees. "Leave me be," I say. "I need me some time to think. To be alone." To figure out how I am going to make due with less than ten toes. *To sort through how I am going to leave you.*

"Can I come in?" She circles the Pyramid, stirring the light spilling through the cracks. "I need you. I need your help. Help me, Leontyne."

She sounds every bit like a Sinner singing out *Idumea*, as if I am the Great Redeemer here to save her. "Go away."

Willadeene knocks and knocks. Walks 'round and 'round. "I have something I need to show you."

"I thought you needed my help."

"I do," she says. "And I have this thing here you must see."

I have a dandy of a surprise here for you, too, Willadeene. I give my big toe a poke with my finger, but it just lays here, give-out and shriveled in my lap.

"Willadeene, you know Avery does not allow you down here." There is a powerful itch needing scratching where once sat my toe. I reach to tend it, but there is a happening so peculiar I do not know what to make of it. *Twigs.* Creeping and curling from the abandoned joint. It is hard to make it out clear here in the magenta-tinted gloom with Willadeene whisking the light while traipsing circles on the floor.

"*Book of Jubilation and Woe.* I have sneaked it away, Leontyne. You should see what I have seen. Avery's account of history. Of treacherous goings-on." *Treacherous....* This next thing Willadeene says is what stops me from fussing over the twigs growing in place of my toe. "I will show you, Leontyne. All the evils Rebecca has done. Page after lowly page. Acre after acre."

Acre after acre. "Words are just words. Speaking them aloud or writing them down fancy in a book does not make them so," I say, remembering what it was Blue Heron said before. I want Willadeene to go away, but more than I want her away from here, I want her to stay. To slide herself down here in this tomb and show me more of Fiddler Crab's lies.

"I might be dead, but I know a lie when I hear one. I know the truth just the same. Better than you, it seems."

Willadeene does not know everything. Not every truth. *You do not know I am the one who killed you.* "If you are coming, come on. But wait. Listen to me, Willadeene. Before you do, shake loose your dead honeybees," I say. "Flick away any bees still living." Not much more of me do I have left to spare. I drop my big toe into my apron pocket. Shimmy back on my shoe, not wanting her to see what I see. What my poor shivering Darkly knows. *Five fingers. Nine toes.*

"Pianissimo," Willadeene whispers, the same thing Rebecca sometimes whispers. The thing Rebecca said her mama whispered when she wanted us all to hush. Willadeene slides down, the high-high arch of her feet skimming beside me as she makes her way here to the bottom of the tomb, smelling up the place glorious and big with her blooms. Holding Jubilation and Woe to her bosom as though Avery's book were her baby. *Poor dead Baby Girl Longwood.* Does Willadeene remember her tiny-tiny thumbs?

"How on earth did you get your hands on it?" I ask.

"While he was busy fussing over the Singing Prophetess. And eating up his biscuit and ham."

I give her ears a look, appraising the state of holly berry earbobs, checking to see if they recently have been picked clean. Willadeene sees me gawking.

"I know what you are thinking, Leontyne. Put your mind to rest. There is no time for haint-berry jam. But do not think I have not given some thought to feeding it to the Singing Prophetess," she says. "Except that woman refuses to eat anything prepared by what she calls my *ungodly hands.*"

"Hushabye Byrd is no fool." I study *Jubilation and Woe* guessing to myself how long it will be before Fiddler Crab realizes it has gone missing. Picturing how pretty he has written down all things he claims his sister has done. "What help is it you are needing?"

"I have already told you. I want Journey Wintergarden for myself," Willadeene whispers. "Avery and Rebecca want him, too. Especially Rebecca. I have seen the stares she gives him." She fans her hand at a hummingbird whirring at a cluster of begonias falling against her neck.

Sccc… rrrr… aaa… pppeee… comes a sound from the Up-Up There.

Willadeene looks up to the mouth of the Pyramid of Giza like she is checking to make certain no one is looking down. "It is only the haints," I say impatient, feeling the panic Willadeene is feeling. A spell of sickness tumbling around in her stomach. "Get on with it." I pick up Darkly and put him in my lap.

"Rebecca and Journey Wintergarden have been whispering together. I have seen them. I tell you that girl is up to something. And I have a feeling, Leontyne. A feeling she aims to take Journey Wintergarden for herself. A feeling she aims to run off with him. Away from here. Away from me."

Maybe it is the tumble of sick come over Willadeene, the worry stirring around the tummy ache in her belly, but I feel it, too. The feeling Willadeene might be right. "I am listening," I say, wishing Willadeene was not so close to me. Wishing she was busy feeling lurid thoughts instead of feeling poorly.

Willadeene opens up *Jubilation and Woe*. Turns a few of the pages. "First, I wanted to have you help me kill Journey Wintergarden. Bring him back here a haint." She takes hold of me by the arm, pulls me into her. "I also thought it best if you take Rebecca away from here. I know now that would have been wrong."

Mmmm…. Kill… Uncle Daddy is outside the Pyramid of Giza listening in.

"I am glad you have thought better of it." I say.

"I have. There is no guarantee Journey Wintergarden will come back here a haint. You said it yourself. Besides, you are needed here to tend Damascus. To help keep Avery safe and from pouting when Journey Wintergarden is mine." Willadeene moves her face close. Her breath is fecund, heavy with damp soil and cool rain. "It is best for us to go on ahead and be done with it. To kill Rebecca."

"Kill Rebecca." I come close to screaming, but I tamp it down. "Willadeene, have you lost your mind?"

Kill.... Mmmm....

"And let nature do the rest," she says. "Journey Wintergarden is sure to love me. With Rebecca gone, it is easier done. I feel Journey Wintergarden is halfway there. There is no stopping Rebecca now that she has taken it into her head to have him."

"Halfway to where?"

She squeezes my arm harder. "To loving me."

I pull loose from Willadeene. Place Darkly again beside me. "How can you be sure Rebecca means to have him?"

"How can you be sure she does not?"

I pull *Jubilation and Woe* from Willadeene. Open it up in my lap. Turn a few of the pages to settle myself. To have something to do with my hand.

"She deserves it," Willadeene says. "Deserves herself a slow, horrific death. But I know you love her. So we will make it swift."

Swift. I cannot believe what I am hearing. "How easy you speak of murder, Willadeene." I think of poor Journey Wintergarden's brother. "How many others, aside from Rushworth L. Wintergarden have you killed?" *How many did you kill when you were Constance Rose Longwood?*

"I am not a fiend, Leontyne. I am hardly a monster. Murdering is not such an awful crime if the one doing it is dead. Rushworth L. Wintergarden is the only one, I promise. And it was mostly an accident. Partly on purpose, I suppose."

"Mostly? Partly? Either it was or it was not, Willadeene. Tell me what it was you have done. Before I climb myself out of here with Darkly and tell Rebecca what you are plotting." Maybe I ought tell Willadeene that Rebecca is hers. Surely to goodness she would feel a twinge of love. Obligation.

"I will tell you the truth, but you must promise to not hold it against me," she says, wrapping her arms about herself.

I look up from *Jubilation and Woe*. "What is there to hold against you?"

"Promise me you will hold no grudge. Promise."

"If you swear to not hold a single one of your own."

Willadeene looks upon me queer. "There are a great many grudges twisted up inside me. Lucky for whoever put them there that I cannot for the life of me remember them fully. Not yet, anyway. Only smells. Feelings. Glimpses here and there. I think I might possess the beginnings of glimmers of who I might have been before. When I was living."

"We share that in common, Willadeene. Remembering tatters and bits of ourselves. I think you might hold the turning end of a key to unlocking part of me, if it was you who last seen Rushworth L. Wintergarden. If it was you who killed him. Mostly. Or even partly."

Mostly…. Partly… Uncle Daddy mocks us from outside the Pyramid of Giza, breathing heavy, his magenta light pinched through the cracks, shooting across us in fits and streams. He circles around the Pyramid once and slow before Willadeene speaks, the purplish light weaving through the runnels.

"The Forever Moon. She saw everything, Leontyne. The night it happened. When Rushworth L. Wintergarden came back here. I had no idea it was him at first. At first, I thought he was a lowly Sinner, but he sang not a single verse of *Idumea*. And he was so handsome there beneath the Moon when I sneaked out to be alone. Wandering the path to the River. To be close, but not so close to the water I would be eaten alive by the boll weevil. Close enough to imagine crossing it."

"How long back was this?"

"Might have been yesterday. Could have been today. There is no way for me to be sure, but there is one thing I remember. You were on the mend back at Morningstar. After falling the long-long ways. And I was grown up into this haint I am now, a stretch of time after I up and escaped that Sarah Fig."

A stretch of time after I up and killed you. After we both fell the long-long ways. "What was it Rushworth L. Wintergarden was wanting?"

"He was looking for you," she says, still not looking at me. Shooing away the hummingbird.

I grab hold of Willadeene. I cannot understand what I am hearing. "For me?"

"To take you back with him. To take you away from here. That is how I came by Pocket Watch. He gave it to me so I would help him. A payment. To take him to you."

"Sweet loving God, Willadeene," I holler. "Why are you just telling me this now?"

Uncle Daddy speeds up. 'Round and 'round the Pyramid he goes. *Sweet loving God*, he groans.

Willadeene stares at me now, the tomb filling up with her huffs and puffs of petrichor breath, her sickly stomach turning me unwell. "I told him you were dead."

"Dead?"

Dead. Uncle Daddy is beside himself, clawing his crocodile claws against the wood.

"Why?" I ask, trying to keep myself from choking Willadeene. From ripping her apart like Theodore Laurence once tried before. I should have let him do it. Finger by finger. One sand dollar toe at a time.

"Because I wanted him," she says.

"And you killed him?"

"Mostly…. Partly…. It was an accident," she says. "I let him fall into a pit I thought was newly dug. One without spikes and spears. One not filled up with killing. One I could keep him trapped deep-down in until I could figure out what was to be done with him next. Only that pit was ready for killing." She takes hold of my arm. "Do not hold a grudge. Please. I would do it different. If I could do it all again."

"Leave me be," I say, snatching my arm away. If Rushworth L. Wintergarden had found me, would I have let him carry me away? I stare down into *Jubilation and Woe*. To the tip-top of a page. To this thing I read next.

> *Confessions of a Swan Princess, the beautiful Odette:*
> *Agamemnon! I am the one who killed Mother and poor Baby Girl Longwood, murdered the both of them with the truth. Never should I have told Mother I saw Father kissing my Prince Siegfried beneath the Forever Moon on the shore of Swan Lake. Save me, Prince Siegfried. Save me. Please.*

"Tell me you do not hold a grudge," Willadeene says. "Tell me."

My head reels. My nose burns from the smell of Willadeene's damp soil and summertime rain. From the springtime smell of her flower garden hair. From this thing Avery has written down. The thing he says he told Constance Rose Longwood. Is this what he thinks killed his mama? Half-killed me? Is this the cruel business Rebecca lets him keep thinking?

Uncle Daddy swims 'round and 'round, spinning magenta threads through our tomb. Avery has made no mention of me carrying on with his daddy in *Jubilation and Woe*. Or of carrying on promiscuous with haints. None of this is what Rebecca has told me, everyone loving Rushworth L. Wintergarden. Even Avery's daddy. *Who is lying? My Blue Heron? My Avery? All of them?*

“I need your help,” Willadeene says, taking hold of my hand, pressing it against the peculiar swell of her stomach.

Thump-thump.... A knock comes from inside Willadeene’s belly against my hand. “What is that?” I say. “What is wrong?”

Uncle Daddy claws our tomb. *Mmmm*.... *Kill*....

From the Down-Below roars a scream. And another.

“What is wrong with you?” I say.

Willadeene squeezes my hand. Tethers it to her evergreen belly. “I am with child, Leontyne,” she says.

Up comes another Fiddler Crab scream. A great commotion rumbling below.

“It is Journey Wintergarden’s baby....”

Morningstar
The In-Between

Chapter 42

Floors vibrate. Walls thrum. Frantic footfalls knock the stairs from the Down-Below to up here in the In-Between. Echoing to Willadeene and me down-down here in the Pyramid of Giza.

In the distance, Fiddler Crab screams. "Save us, please."

"Pull yourself up," I say to Willadeene, pushing her the last bit of the way from the Pyramid. *Princess Odette's confession. Willadeene with child. Rushworth L. Wintergarden coming back for me. The queer feeling I have lost more of me than a hand.* Everything Willadeene has told me—glimmers of memories of me from before have turned me so wretched dizzy I might tip over.

"What about Darkly?" Willadeene asks. *Jubilation and Woe* slips from beneath her arm, sliding-sliding down into the tomb.

"Leave Darkly be. He is safe down there. And leave that damn book be."

Avery is the first to come run screaming from the Down-Below, a delphinium pink comet scorching across the desert land. Rebecca comes a full gallop next in her riding boots. Hushabye Byrd wobbles frantic on her wood block shoes. Last is Journey Wintergarden, slamming the door behind him, pounding his broad shoulder against it.

"The haints have broken in," Avery shrieks, holding Sugar beneath his chin. "Clawed through the boards covering the windows. They have come for us."

More... More... More.... The haints screech from the Down-Below. Wail obscenities. Declare their perverse intentions for Uncle Daddy.

"They want him, Avery," I say, pointing at Uncle Daddy. "Not us."

Mmmm... Uncle Daddy floats backward up the stairs, making his way to the Up-Up There, looking down at us, his golden goat eyes clicking all about the In-Between. Like he is listening and seeing both at the same time with them good-looking eyes. He presses the air with his crocodile thumbs. Steers himself with his tail.

Hushabye Byrd sings out across Egypt, out across the dunes, Constance Rose Longwood's black moonstone earbobs bobbing on her rouged-up ears.

Leontyne Skye, Leontyne Skye,

Look what you have done....

Here comes a dreadful quiet, not so much as a Fiddler Crab screech. Stretch and stretch goes the silence so taut it rings my ears. Everyone stares at me. Accuses me here with the Forever Moon shining down. *I am not the Great Redeemer.* Stretch and stretch. The silence rings louder. Any more of it and I will go mad. *Pianissimo....* Here in this wretched hush, I remember.

My Blue Heron.

Sawing-sawing.

Me screaming.

Screaming.

"Bring me my Mirabelle."

Fiddler Crab weeps. Cradles my hand.

"Here she is, Leontyne."

"Look. She is not dead."

Journey Wintergarden hurries from the door across the desert, his naked feet tantalizing me back from yesterday, back here to today. I hear now what the rest of them here in the In-Between are hearing. A rustling. The sound of rats scampering about in the walls. Except the sound is coming from beneath us, vibrations buzzing the floor. As if thousands and thousands of Willadeene's honeybees are coming from beneath the Ballroom of One Thousand and One

Nights. But they are not honeybees. They are haints. Chewing the plaster. Gnawing the beams. Scratching and crocodile-clawing their way up here to Uncle Daddy.

"They are coming up through the floor," Avery screams.

Haints also gather outside the Cupola's windows, the In-Between growing brighter. Blue Heron and Fiddler Crab hurry close to Journey Wintergarden, abandoning Willadeene and me a far piece across the desert floor, wheedling their way beneath the stretch of his arms.

The ballroom floor cracks, a noise so terrible it sounds as if the whole world is one big breaking egg. Uncle Daddy backs up into the Up-Up There. Gazes down upon us at the place where there is no rail. He licks his catfish lips. *I am the goddamned Sun*, he says. *The goddamned Sun....*

Crack....

Splinter....

Avery turns loose a howl.

Then comes next this sound, the Tower of Babel reaching the heavens. Losing balance. Collapsing. Down-down. *Bloody hell. And murder.* Up-up through the ballroom wreckage cleave the haints, caterwauling in swarming hordes from the ballroom. Pummeling against us. Pitching us to the floor.

Journey Wintergarden hollers. "Cover your eyes.... Cover your eyes...."

Face down I lay next to Willadeene, covering my head. Frantic to roll over and watch the haints swim over the top of us. To count every sorry last one of them. *How many haints? How many?*

Swoop.

Rub and skim.

Fondle.

Diddle-diddle.

Swoop.

Their claws snag my hair. Rip my dress, magenta tails beating against us passing by on their way to the Up-Up There.

In monstrous chorus, the haints rise up. *Uncle Daddy … Uncle Daddy….*

So many. So many haints all at once I can hardly breathe, the weight of their want pressing heavy against my chest, so violent I fear my heart might stop. *A million years.* A million Good Hope years I will lay dying on this here floor to keep feeling this thing I am feeling. To feed my desire. Fill the empty places. *Hand. Fingers. Toe.* 'Til my heart is rolled thin as paper. 'Til I have accounted for all of me that is gone.

"Cover your eyes…. Cover your eyes…." Journey Wintergarden hollers.

Open your eyes…. Open your eyes…. I want to roll over and see. To speak vile in the tongue of haints—sing out indecencies with these ravenous fiends. *Uncle Daddy … Uncle Daddy….*

Willadeene calls for me, "Leontyne … Leontyne…." On her knees, she pulls at me by the hair, gawking into the Up-Up There.

The haints have passed us by on their way to Uncle Daddy. Up-up, we all stare, balancing on our knees. Clothes in tatters. Cheeks scratched fresh and weeping. Hard it is to fathom and detail what I see. A writhing knot of haints. Magenta gnarls of earthworms. Frogs carrying on carnal in trees. *Mmmm….*

They have overtaken Uncle Daddy.

Ripping.

Tearing.

Pulling him apart with their teeth.

Uncle Daddy groans and moans, and I know this is the last of the goddamned Sun we will ever see. From outside the Cupola, the haints are desperate. Clamoring to get in. They want themselves pieces of Uncle Daddy. They rare up. Buck. Thrust themselves against the glass. This world is an egg. *An egg. Cracking-cracking.* Breaking apart from the Up-Up There. *Spilling-spilling.*

Creak.... Crack.... Woosh.... The windows shatter. Flocks of haints smother the place, calling out, *More... More... More.*

I lean back on my knees. Open my mouth to catch gooey flesh, bits and bobs of Uncle Daddy torn apart by the mob. Tail and slimy slivers of mollusk tongue. Golden flecks scratched from his eyes.

Hushabye Byrd sings out one time more.

Leontyne... Leontyne....

Behold what you have done....

The Marsh

Chapter 43

One batch. One batch of Redemption is all the poison I will make. *Not a drop more will I squeeze.* And I will wake Damascus. Make her sing. Fool her into thinking I have come to stay. Mark my words. Write them down with haint-berry ink. I will escape that tree and leave here when Hushabye Byrd teeter-totters off peddling the last of my wares.

Poor Willadeene. No choice do I have but to leave her at Morningstar to tend her half-haint baby. If she is lucky, she will finish weaving her plan. She will make Journey Wintergarden love her more than halfway. *Mostly.... Partly....*

One batch. A few steps more until I am at the Marsh. I would be there already except I am unbalanced, traveling slower, my ears ringing from Hushabye Byrd proclaiming me the Great Redeemer. From Avery bellowing, *Save me. Save me, Leontyne.* For the life of me, I cannot imagine how a body could manage moving about missing every last one of her toes. It is so very hard losing one.

I flutter my hand in my apron pocket, pretending I do not see the magenta splatters of Uncle Daddy snow melted on my dress. I run my fingers across Sugar. How he got there in my pocket is a wonder of wonders to me. A wonder he was not torn to shreds by them haints. I suspect Sugar found his way over to me in the maelstrom, taking up alongside my fallen-off toe, cuddling next to Eulalee's teeth here in my pocket when we were toppled to the floor.

Please Lord, please keep Darkly safe down in the Pyramid of Giza. "Sweet, sweet, Sugar," I say, stopping to give myself a rest. To tend the itch in my slipper. I shut my eyes. Wiggle my foot out of the shoe. I count to three. Open my eyes. Look down to see it.

Have mercy! How my foot has changed since I last saw it. Twigs have taken up camp, weaving an osier skeleton, knitting me a brand new toe. "Look-a-there," I say. Something fuzzy grows from the withy. I bend down to touch it, the spongy tufts of reindeer moss the color of Willadeene. *Evergreen.* Whatever that honeybee drank from Willadeene is a dangerous brew.

I slide my foot back in my shoe. *One batch. One batch....*

Heading down the last of the path to the Marsh, I smell it. *Manure.* I spot the culprit glowing in greenish plops of wormy swirls. I cover my nose. From the fresh state of the droppings, the Sinner cannot be far. I should have listened to Journey Wintergarden. Allowed him down to the Marsh with me to make this last batch of Redemption. Like Rebecca, he seems most keen to learn how it is all done.

A sorrow comes upon me more than I would have expected. *This is the last time I will ever see the Marsh.* I grab hold of Eulalee's oyster shell necklace tempted to learn how this will all turn out, but I am frightened I might not care much for what I see.

Damascus. She looms bigger, her branches longer. More crystalline than I remember. When last was I here? How long has it been? *Every second—a day. Every hour—a week.* I reckon I have been gone long enough from here for haints to sprout tails. Cut teeth. Gone long enough to lose and sprout myself a toe. Play the violin. For paper heavens to burn. Plummet. To lose Rushworth L. Wintergarden. Long enough to not fully trust my Blue Heron. To think maybe I am brave enough to head off away from here. All by my lonesome.

Woosh ... comes a stir in the cordgrass.

"Who is there?" I ask. I listen. *Nothing.* Just a faint *ticking* in my apron pocket. *Eulalee's teeth.* They stir after being silent a long while now—a groundhog yawning from inside her winter's burrow. She is shameless, happy I am here to tend Damascus. Perhaps even proud. Regardless of her intentions, it is good to hear her. To have her here by my side.

I make my way closer to Damascus. Close enough and far enough back I behold the lion's share of her. Nearly the forever of her. Close enough I hear the faint whistle and huff of breath coming from her oyster shell bark.

I am not the Great Redeemer. "I am here, Damascus," I say, treading in the Moon's lace, gazing up through her branches, pretending not to see her glaring at me brackish through her miry eyeballs, thousands of eyeballs hiding and peeping from inside every glistening oyster bark shell. How is that I could never see these eyeballs before?

Damascus stays quiet. Plays hard to get. Her branches relent, releasing a faint *tink* and *twinkle.* She hankers to take hold of me. Aches to bamboozle me. Her Sarah Figs betray her, ravenous they are for haints. Scandal of scandals, the haints swell and pucker. They moan, *Hither... hither....*

"I have come to tend you, Damascus. Can you not hear me? Have you gone deaf?"

Way-way off across the Marsh comes a rumble. So far-far I know it comes from out Doldrums' way, the lurid sound of Damascus suckling. Mile upon mile, through her banyan roots, comes the Marsh racing greedy. *Rumble-rumble. Gurgle. Swish....*

"Go on Damascus. Go on and sing," I say. "Do you not know who I am? I am Leontyne Skye." I move closer. Lean myself against the tree. Wrap my arms far about her as they will go. "I am yours, and you are mine." *I will break your heart before you wither mine.*

Damascus breathes in through her oyster shell bark. Breathes out. Whirls a fetid breeze up through her salt-jeweled branches. Stares at me in all directions with all her rheumy eyes.

One branch knocks into the other. So on and so forth. Knocking-knocking all the way up, forever and always, to the tippy-top of the infernal tree. All of Damascus is swaying. She sounds her mating call. Makes love to me with her wind chime song.

Every second—a day. Every hour—a week. I will wait here 'til the haints come. I will stay until I make this last batch. *What will happen when I am gone?* What will become of the world when I am traipsing through China? Riding the slippery backs of whales? What will happen when the haints gather and gather? Shout obscenities. Fornicate. When the sky is full-up with goddamned suns and the Forever Moon is gone. When nary a Skye woman is left here on Good Hope to carry on.

I hold my Jezabel arms tight to Damascus. Enjoy the warm surge of Marsh flow up her trunk, trembling through her branches, titillating her Sarah Figs. *Pucker and swell.* Her breath blows over me in sweet caresses. Whispers-whispers. *Never leave me.*

I pay no mind to the rustle in the cordgrass. To the sorry so-and-so Sinner hiding and watching me make a fool of and ravish Damascus.

I could stay here a thousand and one years.
Dwell here in languor as long as my Eulalee.
I could stay here like a Skye woman should.
'Til I am whittled down-down to the bone.
One batch of Redemption is all....
And I must be gone. One batch.
One batch,
Is all....

The Chapel of Abundance

Chapter 44

Damascus sings, enticing the haints from Morningstar to the Marsh. Never before could I make out anything but the melody of Damascus's branches. Every lyric calls upon me now. Palpitating. Thrumming through me. Muscle and bone. Clear down to my evergreen toe.

Sweet, sweet, are my Sarah Figs.
Lay down. Lay down,
Amongst my bounty.

The haints are lathered up into an ungodly fervor by this lustful singing. They *screech* and *squawk.* Run the sky amuck, protruding their mollusk tongues. Rubbing their tails beneath their underbellies. I pray Morningstar is free of all the haints by now. And the others are safe, all but Hushabye Byrd.

Damascus sets me to hum and vibrate, rattling in the tincture bottles of Redemption in the basket dangling from the crook of my no-hand arm. *Heirloom.* If Eulalee felt anywhere near about good as this when she was living, I reckon this is why she never packed up and left. Why she still relishes Damascus from inside my pocket. I try to collect myself, hiding here behind the tabby wall. I eavesdrop on Mirabelle who is on the other side *click-clacking* mournful. I listen in to know if she might be turning Ewell Day Higgs against me. I listen for any peeps or groans coming from the pit, any signs my Ewell Day Higgs is not dead.

Tat-tu-tat-tu-tat-tat. Seems to me my Mirabelle is crying, thumping a sorrowful tempo from inside her can. I listen, hearing something familiar in her *clickety-clack.* I listen until the rhythm becomes words. Until I recognize it as the lullaby I remember Rebecca singing, the one coming around time to time to dance through my head.

All the pretty horses
Blacks and bays,
Dapple and greys. . . .

Ewell Day Higgs's voice rises weak from the pit, tamped down by the haints *hissing* the sky trail on their way to Damascus. "You are sweet to sing to me, Mirabelle. To comfort me my last few breaths."

Ewell Day Higgs is still living, and I do not know if I ought rejoice or if I ought wail. I listen a while longer running my eyes over my basket of bottles, deciding at last I will go and give Ewell Day Higgs a farewell, deciding I will not leave Mirabelle out here *tat-tu-tat-tatting* for all eternity turning the resurrection fern sad. I will take her with me, even if she does not want to go.

"Ewell Day Higgs. Ewell Day Higgs," I say, from the shadows, stepping into the spill of Forever Moon into the Chapel of Abundance.

Mirabelle quits her singing. Her weeping. The haints bellow and cavort above, the look and sound of birds escaping frantic from winter.

"Starshine, thank goodness you are here. I was worried you would not make it back here in time," Ewell Day Higgs says. "In time for me to say goodbye to you."

There is vigor in his voice, and I feel there might be an iota of hope. I am fast to think better of it. I should not fool myself. This is how it always is, a quick rise of living before the bitter, joyous end. "I could play the violin once," I say, to give my Ewell Day Higgs a lasting, good impression of me. "I could play it beautiful."

"That is exactly what Miss Mirabelle has said."

I give Mirabelle the side of my eye. "I reckon that is good to hear." Whatever gossip she has *clickety-clacked* with Ewell Day Higgs about me, at least he will not think me a lie.

From the Forest comes Babylon preening across the graveyard, stopping to stand atop Constance Rose Longwood's burial plot. I let my mind wander down-down below, imagining our Willadeene's earthly body rotting in the grave.

"There is something I have been meaning to tell. A truth. Something I did not know until after I fell into this here pit," Ewell Day Higgs says.

"It seems we have known each other a long while now, Ewell Day Higgs," I say. "Feel free to confess anything to me."

"A long while now..." he says dreamily. "How long do you reckon it has been, Starshine? That we have known one another."

"For an eternity, I think. For as long as Redemption lasts." I glance down at my basket of bottles.

"I wish I had known before now," he says.

"Known what?"

"Who you are. That you are here."

The bloom begins its wither from Ewell Day Higgs's voice sudden as I suspected it would. "I am Starshine," I say. "And I have lived not another place ever."

"And I am Ewell Day Higgs. Or at least I was, Starshine. Now I need to tell you a thing before I go. I need to confess to you I came here to Good Hope a time once before."

A time before? "Why in creation did you come?" I ask, taken aback by this revelation.

"I traveled here from across the River to see your mama, the Great Redeemer, a time far back when I was feeling low. When I was good-for-nothing. Less even than I am now."

Eulalee's teeth go still. Seem to settle down from the pleasure she is enjoying from Damascus, from the haints flapping debauchery overhead to listen to what Ewell Day Higgs is saying.

"You are plenty good," I say. "A mouth full of teeth. A handsome head of hair." *Eyes gleaming glorious when drowning in Moon.*

"I will admit I am better than I was returning to Abraham's Bluff after visiting your mama. After finding my Alsace-Lorraine. I have lived a good life since then," he says, the bloom withering still.

"You are every bit lovely as your mama was then. Pale blue eyes. Hair down to her waist. Mirabelle has told me your mama has fallen apart in the Doldrums. Please know I am very sorry to know it. So sad to think of you living here mostly alone. Me unable to help you in a single way except to tell you a truth I think you should know."

I move closer to the pit, but not so close I can see down. "Tell me, then, Ewell Day Higgs. What you want me to know."

"It was on the Marsh I met your mama." There is a bit of wonder in Ewell Day Higgs's fading voice, as if the Moon is keeping his eyes and spirits bright. "She was surprised. Surprised I made it that far, that I found my way to her. Flabbergasted she was I had not been snatched up in a snare. Left hanging in a tree. Run clean through with poisoned spears. I told her it must have been because I needed me a good killing some other way than death, the slow kind I could feel every rung of the way," he says. "Starshine, your mama smiled at me with a mouth full of teeth pretty as yours, and she told me this. 'Dying quick and easy is free. Doing it slow ain't cheap.' I asked her how much it would cost. Told her I had no money. Told her I wanted it slow. Not free. Great Redeemer, help me. Help me, please."

Idumea … Idumea… "How much was your bill? Did she give you what you come for?"

"She said she reckoned we could save one another, if…." Ewell Day Higgs stops speaking. Says no more. Mirabelle and Babylon go quiet. Eulalee's teeth make not even a stir.

"If what, Ewell Day Higgs? Finish what you are saying."

"Eulalee told me it made no matter I had no money. The cost of Redemption is ever changing, you see. Told me that night I was mighty lucky. One time only, saving a soul that very night was free. Free long as I agreed to love her gentle beneath Damascus Tree."

Poor Eulalee. My poor-poor mama. Never did it occur to me she was lonesome. Wanted to be loved. That she desired anything but tending the tree. "Did you? Did you love her for a while?"

"Long as I could. Long as she would let me before sending me away. She did not ask for much. Only asked me to love her and for me to tell her my name. That is a price near about free far as I can gather. This is what I need to tell you. The thing I told her when she asked me for my name."

"You are Ewell Day Higgs," I say. "That is who you are. Is that not what you said?"

"That is who I am, but it did not seem hardly good enough when I was there loving your mama with the Forever Moon so beautiful in her eyes. Her chin pointed up at me."

"What did you tell her then, Ewell Day Higgs?" I take a step back from the pit, my legs shaking so bad, I fear I might fall in. Afraid of what he is going to say.

"Before I leaned myself down to kiss your mama, I lied to her. Made myself out to be more special than I am," he says. "Listen careful, Starshine. To what I am about to say. Are you listening?"

"I am listening." *I am listening to you. To Damascus. The haints howling in the sky. To my heart thumpity-thumping fast.*

"At first, I thought you were your mama. Thought she somehow looked the same after all the years having passed. I realized soon after, you were her daughter. Then I went and asked about you about your daddy like I did. Do you remember?"

"Yes, sir. I remember. But what of my daddy? What does he have to do with what name you gave my mama?"

"It has to do with everything. About me telling her this. Calling out to her, Great Redeemer. Great Redeemer, I am the Forever Moon...."

The Forever Moon.... Here it comes, like the tide upon the Marsh. I imagine myself spinning. One time 'round I go.

"I am the Island...." Ewell Day Higgs says.

Second time 'round faster I go. *Stop, Ewell Day Higgs. Stop.*

"I am the River...." he says.

‘Round and ‘round, I am whirling out of control, feeling I know where this is going. Mirabelle *clack-clacks* a frenzy in her can.

“The Forest and the Sea....” he says.

I am of the Forest and Sea...

“I am your daddy, Starshine. Do you not see?”

“I see ... I see.” I am spinning dizzy in place, my vision blurred. The Chapel of Abundance—a whir. My bottles of Redemption and Eulalee’s teeth tremble. I shut my eyes. I wrestle the urge to lie down on the cool, damp earth. To claw myself deep-deep down where dead Longwoods lay. A quiet place to think.

“Forgive me for not knowing about you. Forgive me for not telling you until now. I know keeping it secret could have been less cruel. Easier to protect you from wandering the never ending highway called What-Might-Have-Been. Tell me. Tell me. Are you sad, Starshine? Sad I told you I am your daddy? Could you have gone living right as rain without ever knowing.” His words are a zephyr, spinning fast and fast as me. “Are you disappointed I am only this here Ewell Day Higgs?”

Are you sad I have gone and killed you? “Are you sad I am only Leontyne Skye? That I am your daughter and nothing near abouts close to a Miss Starshine?”

“I am sorrowful, indeed, my Leontyne Skye. So sad we have had ourselves only an eternity together. The wee bit of time Redemption lasts is not nearly enough time to be with you.”

“I have more bottles,” I say, trying to convince myself to stop shaking. From my teeth *clacking*. “I will send more down.” *Down-down.*

“Sweet girl,” he says. “I have done stepped over the line of saving.” The bloom in his voice is a full wither. Dried up. Scraping his throat like he is breathing autumn leaves. “A few more breaths is all that is left.”

All that is left. A few more breaths. I shut my eyes. Listen to my Ewell Day Higgs, to my daddy rattling leaves. I listen to Damascus sing.

Lay down. Lay down.

Amongst my bounty.

"Are you looking up?" Ewell Day Higgs asks. "At the haints and that there Moon?"

"I am," I say, best I can through tears. "I am looking." *Looking-looking.* I pull out Sugar from my pocket. Hold him up so he can see. A haint straggles, trailing the air magenta. I play-pretend the haint is a shooting star and make myself a wish.

"It is beautiful here, my sweet Leontyne Skye. My Starshine. Look up," he says.

"It is beautiful here," I whisper back.

Look up....

The Chapel of Abundance

Chapter 45

A fine mist comes upon us, the resurrection fern stretching all directions. Fronds unfurl, reaching-reaching out to the next. Joining our sad congregation in a circle of grief. Mourning that my Ewell Day Higgs is dead.

Tat-tu-tat. Mirabelle cries and I rest here on my knees listening. Daydreaming a life where my Ewell Day Higgs and Rushworth L. Wintergarden still are living. Traveling down that sad-sad highway Ewell Day Higgs spoke of, the one he called *What-Might-Have-Been*.

Tat-tu-tat. Mirabelle is near about inconsolable, and I am sorry for her loss as I am for my own. Poor Eulalee, she has gone quiet, just now realizing the truth of Ewell Day Higgs. That he loved on her once. Knowing now he is my daddy. That once, a time back, she was more than a lowly rattle of teeth.

"I reckon it is better that we knew him a spell than never knowing him at all," I say.

A rustling at the edge of the Forest and the feeling someone is watching wrenches me back around from my stupor. *Tat-tat …* Mirabelle feels it too, feels someone lurking. Babylon's hitches her hussy tail out straight. There goes the rustle again. I stand up, preparing myself to run.

The Singing Prophetess. I hear her crooning *Idumea*. Now I see her. Coming through the Forest, her raggedy mourning veil lifting like a red kite behind her. Quick and easy, she glides the way on her wood block shoes, and she is carrying something. Into the Chapel of Abundance, she makes her way across to the other side of the pit from me. Resurrection ferns retreat. *Sssss….* Slither-slithering back. Escaping being smashed beneath her feet.

Dear God. Hushabye Byrd is toting my Darkly. "What are you doing with him?" I ask, trying not to panic. To scream.

She takes Darkly by the ears. Dangles him out before her, his tiny legs *thump-thumping* the air. "He has come to see about you. Making sure you finished up your chore," she whispers, her words shucked away by the wind.

"I am done," I say, looking down at the basket beside my feet.

Hushabye Byrd sings.

Gone, you were,
A long-long time.
So long, I was growing
Worried....

"Glad you woke that whore of a tree back to her business of singing," she whispers. "Lucky for you, and the pretty-pretties, and this marsh rat here, that you had good sense to make me some Redemption."

The last I will ever make. "Be careful with my Darkly."

Hushabye Byrd walks closer to the pit. Draws Darkly to her chest. Looks down. Jerks her head away but not up into the Moon. "Rebecca said you caught yourself a Sinner here. Keeping him like a tiger moth inside a jar."

Fiddler Crab. Why would he tell Rebecca? Why would Rebecca betray me to the Singing Prophetess?

"Do not look so sad," Hushabye Byrd whispers. "This tiger moth was dead before he got here."

"He is not a Sinner," I say. "He is nothing like the others."

"Pitty sakes, then. What a most unfortunate end." She gives the pit another look down. "He was very handsome," she whispers. "I can see why you kept him." She wipes the back of her gloved hand below her eye, smearing a trickle of blood a haint scratched from her cheek back at Morningstar. *Look what you have done*, Hushabye Byrd sings, holding her blood smeared glove out before her, holding

Darkly reckless with the other wrapped about his neck. His legs *thumpity-thumping*.

Branches snap. Leaves bristle. A sound different from the wind footfalls through the Forest. Hushabye Byrd trills.

Josiah … Josiah …

Come forth

In this direction.

Damascus duets with Hushabye Byrd, singing of her sweet-sweet figs.

Come to me. Come to me.

My whoremongers,

And my thieves.

Branches snap.

Swish.

Swoosh.

Crack.

I hold my breath, pondering which Josiah will be here soon. *Avery's Josiah?* The one he gave the feather. A new Josiah? One better than the rest? *Was he the one spying on me down by the Marsh?*

Josiah … Josiah … Hushabye Byrd sings.

Crack….

Swish….

Journey Wintergarden. He treads barefoot through the leaves. "Be careful, Journey Wintergarden," I say. "A Josiah is out prowling no-good beyond them trees."

No-good…. No-good … Hushabye Byrd sings, throwing back her head and laughing. The wind sucking her tattered veil. Fluttering the shreds all about her. Giving the impression she is a sea anemone.

Journey Wintergarden appears spellbound by these chapel ruins, the resurrection fern lush on the crumbling tabby, the Moon near abouts touching the ground. He is dazzled the same as my Ewell Day Higgs before he fell into the pit. Journey Wintergarden stands on the other side of my daddy's grave. Away from the Singing Prophetess. Away from me. "I am sorry you had to find out this way, Leontyne."

"Find out what?" I ask, my ear sharp to the distant sound of thunder grumbling at the bottom of his throat.

Journey Wintergarden looks up to the Moon. "I was once Hushabye Byrd's Josiah," he says. "I am him. He is me. Least I used to be."

Josiah? "You are lying," I say. "I have never seen you here before. Do not play such tricks on me. This is not the time." Not the time while Hushabye Byrd is abusing my Darkly. When I am trying to run off from here forever.

Journey Wintergarden fiddles his long fingers through his coppery hair. "I was never a Josiah she brought around to Morningstar," he says. But you are right, I am a liar. I am sure of that. I am good at that, but little else. I am not sure of the name I was called before I became Hushabye Byrd's Josiah. That is a truth and not a lie. Another truth is that I have been this Journey Wintergarden a long while now. Long as my brother has been called Rushworth. Here I stand now, wondering who I might be next. What Hushabye Byrd will name me. What she will have me do after I am through with you."

After I am through with you. "Slow down. You are speaking in riddles," I say. "Slow down." I shift my weight. Knock my foot against the basket.

Be careful, child, Hushabye Byrd sings. "Do not break a single bottle," she whispers, squeezing Darkly. Making him squeal.

"Leave him be," I holler.

"Listen to the Singing Prophetess," Journey Wintergarden says. "She is liable to hurt your Darkly. He holds no value for her. We are nothing, none of us, if we cannot be sold."

Unscrupulous.... Unscrupulous woman.... The story Journey Wintergarden told me by the Marsh comes back to me. "Hushabye

Byrd. She is the unscrupulous woman who took you and your brother in?" I ask. "She is one with motives."

"She is, indeed," Journey Wintergarden says, flashing a bit of teeth. "You are a very good listener, Leontyne Skye. I admire this about you."

"Unscrupulous," Hushabye Byrd hisses, squeezing Darkly, making him howl. Making Sugar squawk in my pocket. "Great Redeemer, you speak the word as if it is filthy. When in fact, it only means survival. That is all any of us are trying to do. To survive," she whispers. "It is good to debate these things now she says. Since we are settled into business. You, Josiah, and me." She shuts her eyes and sings, holding Darkly by the throat.

To God be the glory.
To God be the glory.
Amen. Amen.

I imagine myself behind the Singing Prophetess on the other side of the pit. Grabbing back my Darkly. Pushing her in. "Redemption and pretty-pretties," I say, staring down at Journey Wintergarden's naked feet. "Hushabye Byrd says they sell for good prices out of the back flap of her revival tent." I keep staring down-down at his handsome toes, not sure I want to ask about this next thing my heart needs to know.

"Go on, Leontyne," Journey Wintergarden says. "Go on."

I run my tongue across the top of my teeth. Counting. Rubbing my fingers across Sugar. Until I have the nerve to ask. "Were you a pretty-pretty?" I keep my eyes down-down at his handsome toes. "Was Rushworth?"

Swoosh.... Swish.... More rustling. All of us blink out to the Forest's edge. Blink until we are convinced there is nothing out there. Until I am looking straight back across the pit into Journey Wintergarden's eyes. *What color are these eyes?* It is hard to know here beneath the Forever Moon. With everything polished and gleaming silver.

"I was a Josiah for a spell," Journey Wintergarden says. "And Rushworth was a Lazarus."

The wind stops to listen. Turns loose of Hushabye Byrd's veil. "You were better than any of the other nephews. You and your brother," she whispers with fondness. A pride. She loosens her grip about Darkly's neck. Pulls him to her bosom. "I saw that soon after the start."

Hushabye Byrd and Journey Wintergarden gaze upon the other queer, as if gentle words never have been spoke between them.

"I was better at it than my brother," Journey Wintergarden says. "Pretending to love when I hate. Pretending to feel good when I ache. Lying for so long now, I hardly know the difference."

"Lazarus, our Rushworth, was a disappointment in that regard," Hushabye Byrd says. "But he held great promise. He was more handsome than you. Unfortunately, he was kinder. Kindness is a hazard, but he certainly was well suited in most regards for the unseemly tastes of a better class of people."

I can hardly stomach what I am hearing. This awful business of Lazarus and Josiah. "How was it?" I ask. "That Rushworth L. Wintergarden came to be a tutor here on Good Hope? What business did he have here when he was no longer a Lazarus?"

"You are not a stupid girl," Hushabye Byrd hisses. "His business was the same as his brother's here." She winks down at my basket of bottles. She throws back her head and sings.

To Stir trouble,

Steal hearts.

Drive wedges....

"It is better, do you not think?" she asks. "For me to learn how it is you make Redemption. For me to do it myself. Rather than rely on Eulalee. On you. On any trifling harlot calling herself the Great Redeemer." The wind has heard enough. It riles back up. Lifting the ribbons of veil. Turns Hushabye Byrd back to a creature. A sea anemone.

Crackle. Swish … comes stirring from the Forest.

Agamemnon. Holy hell and murder. At the Forest's edge, a Sinner's eyes glow golden and goat. *Theodore Laurence.* He is alive. Alive as Sugar. Alive as my Ewell Day Higgs is dead. *Alive.*

Journey Wintergarden and Hushabye Byrd turn to see what I am looking at, the boy standing there half-dead.

Theodore Laurence squats.

Sniffs the air.

Howls and howls.

Leaps.

Takes off toward us.

Running-running.

Leaping.

Howling….

The Chapel of Abundance

Chapter 46

Theodore Laurence is alive! Barreling toward us. *Howling-howling* toward Hushabye Byrd.

The Singing Prophetess knows what is what. He is coming for her. She drops Darkly. Takes off running on her high, wood block shoes. *Running-running....*

Theodore Laurence takes to all fours. Jumps the air like a bobcat. *Leaping-leaping....*

Theodore Laurence grabs hold. Snatches her veil. Her geisha hair.

Snatching-snatching.... Ripping-ripping....

Dragging her backward.

Screaming-screaming.

Off come her wood block shoes.

Off comes her veil.

Dragging-dragging.

Into the Forest. Deep-deep.

Screaming-Screaming.

Singing one last terrible sing.

Singing-singing.

Help me, Lord.

Help me.

Idumea.

Idumea.

The Chapel of Abundance

Chapter 47

An eternity passes, a forever of Hushabye Byrd's screams. Journey Wintergarden and I wait, gaping out into the Forest. Until the sky has run low on haints. Until there is nothing but for the faint echo of *Idumea.*

Creak.... Crack.... Swoosh.... Comes a sound from the Forest.

Journey Wintergarden reaches into his pocket. Pulls out Miss Jane Austen, Rebecca's pearl handled gun. "Do not hurt Theodore Laurence," I say, holding tight to my shivering Darkly. "Unless he aims to hurt us first."

Theodore Laurence walks slow around the saw palmettos, into the full gleam of the Moon, his goat eyes swimming with as much wonder as Journey Wintergarden's. Full-up with as much glory as was my Ewell Day Higgs at the rapturous sight of this Chapel of Abundance.

"Theodore Laurence," I say. "I thought you were dead. I am so very glad you are not. I hope you do not hold a grudge on account of me setting you adrift down the River."

Theodore Laurence stops. Ogles up at the Forever Moon.

"How far down the River did you go?" I ask. "Did you spill out into the Indian Ocean? Did you get yourself a gander of Sri Lanka when floating by?"

Theodore Laurence sniffs the air careful. Not wild. Like he is catching a drift of a pleasant memory with his nose. What is it he is smelling? Uncle Daddy snow melted on my tongue? Smeared on my apron? My withered fallen-off toe?

"I am sorry about your daddy," I say. I think it best not tell him his dead daddy came back here a haint. Torn apart by the others and swallowed down. Would Theodore Laurence be a might proud if he knew his daddy was—for a spell—the goddamned Sun?

Theodore Laurence comes closer. Comes slow. The resurrection fern lays low. Does not move. Allows the boy to walk across it gentle with his ten filthy toes.

"I reckon you were the one keeping watch over me down by the Marsh," I say. "I am glad it was you, Theodore Laurence, and not some other so-and-so."

Journey Wintergarden keeps Miss Jane Austen on the ready. Babylon watches the boy stock still from atop Dead Baby Girl Longwood's grave. Theodore Laurence is close enough now, I smell the rot of Sarah Figs. Of River's water. So near I behold the splatter of Hushabye Byrd's gore across his coveralls. So close the flesh beneath his long fingernails shimmers dewy.

He sniffs the air. "Pretty bird," Theodore Laurence says. "Sugar?"

Sugar. "You remember Sugar?" I ask, astonished. "He is safe here in my pocket. Safe and warm right here."

Theodore Laurence blinks at me slow with them gold goat eyes. "Sugar," he says, holding out his hand. "Mine."

"He is yours, I reckon," I say. "I have kept watch after him though, while you were drifting down the River."

"Mine." An edge of agitation sharpens Theodore Laurence's voice.

"I have looked over him such a long while now, I sure would miss him. If you took him away from me."

"Sugar mine."

"Give the boy his Sugar," Journey Wintergarden says. "There is no way around it, Leontyne. Unless you want me to shoot him. Give me the word, and I will get it over quick. A single bullet between his eyes."

"No shooting," I say. I am slow putting down Darkly on the ground so I can get a hold of Sugar. I pull the chick chirping from my apron pocket.

“Pretty bird,” Theodore Laurence says smiling, blood smeared across his rotten teeth, a strand of geisha hair dangling from his bottom lip. The feather Avery give Josiah is stuck to the boy’s shoulder, the one Hushabye Byrd had pinned to her dress.

I take a step toward Theodore Laurence, giving Sugar one last kiss. “Darkly and I will miss you a terrible kind of awful, Sugar,” I say. “Be kind to him, Theodore Laurence.” My hand trembles passing the chick over to the boy. I peel the feather from the boy. Poke it down into my pocket.

Theodore Laurence takes hold of Sugar. Kisses him. Cuddles him in the crook of his neck. Holds him gentle in both his blood-stained hands. A powerful sorrow comes over me. A sorrow I might not ever make my way back from, the pitiful look of this boy with his Sugar. The hopelessness I feel knowing he can never be saved. That maybe none of us can ever be saved.

Theodore Laurence turns. Walks across the resurrection fern. Beyond the tabby walls. Away from the Chapel of Abundance, clear of the spill of Forever Moon. Into the Forest.

“I will miss you, Theodore Laurence,” I say, wondering if ever a person died from crying. From the sight of a little boy walking away.

The Chapel of Abundance

Chapter 48

Tatters of red veil tumble from the Forest across the dampened earth. Prowls no-good into the Chapel of Abundance, drifting woeful, sailing down into the pit where my Ewell Day Higgs lay dead. Gliding-gliding light as the peacock feather Fiddler Crab give Josiah. The feather I hold here in my hand.

I figure on what I should say to Journey Wintergarden, speculating if I can trust him. Trying to squeeze out of my head the thought of Constance Rose Longwood's black moonstone earbobs lost out yonder in the Forest on Hushabye Byrd's torn apart ears.

"You came here to Good Hope to trick me," I say, staring down at the feather, wishing I could climb into my apron pocket with Darkly and hide. "To learn how it is I make Redemption." *Ewell Day Higgs. Poor Theodore Laurence. My sweet-sweet Sugar.* I am so near about choked on grief and anger, all I want to do is hurt somebody. Hurt Journey Wintergarden. I stop myself from asking how much he cost back when he was Josiah. If any ole somebody with change in their pockets could have him.

"I came here looking for Rushworth," he says. "That was not a lie. And I did come here to stir trouble like Hushabye Byrd said. Never did I come here to hurt you."

"That is all well and good. But tell me this. What would have become of me if I gave you what you wanted? Showed you the way to Redemption. What need would Hushabye Byrd have had for me then?"

Journey Wintergarden is quiet. I stand here waiting for him to explain himself, listening to Damascus sing. "I would have never let her harm you," he says, at last. "I would have kept you safe the way Rushworth would have wanted. I promise I will keep you safe best I can now." I glance over at Journey Wintergarden a few steps away from me. Watch him run his hands up and down Miss Jane Austen.

"Rushworth? Keep me safe?" I am dumbfounded. "Seems to me your brother came poking around here up to no good just the same as you."

"My brother is not nearly the same as me, Leontyne," he says. "He is so much better. He was here because Hushabye Byrd had him over a barrel. The Longwoods ran him off in the end. And he was not sorry about leaving except for having to leave you. But he was coming back to get you."

Seems to me, deep-deep down, I know Journey Wintergarden is not lying. Same as I know the air is invisible and I am busy breathing it, I know Rushworth L. Wintergarden was good. That he was coming back for me. "How is it he is better? Tell me."

"There is nothing you remember?"

"Small things here and there." I will not confess to him I cannot be completely sure of anything. Of anyone. "The door is opening slowly. Things spilling in," I say. I struggle to keep from looking across the pit at Journey Wintergarden. I want to steer clear of being bamboozled by his ever-changing eyes. *Blue—then grey. Grey—then blue.* The same eyes I remember Rushworth L. Wintergarden having. I stare down at his handsome feet instead.

"Rushworth's heart is open to the world. Mine is sealed. He is better than me in that he is kind. Better in that he is no good at pretending. He is what he seems, Leontyne," he says. "All the things that make him better than me are all the things that failed him as a Lazarus. The lack of those things are what helped me succeed as a Josiah."

Josiah and Lazarus. I think of that back flap of Hushabye Byrd's revival tent. Of all the people coming and going. I try reconciling Rushworth L. Wintergarden was a Lazarus. Thinking on what Avery wrote in his *Book of Jubilation and Woe*, the thing he told his mama. Told her he caught Rushworth L. Wintergarden kissing his daddy. How many folks did Rushworth kiss? "Did your brother love me?"

"Leontyne, he did. He did, indeed. If you remember any part of him, why do you doubt it?"

"Willadeene sneaked away *Jubilation and Woe* for me to take a look," I say. "At all the things Avery says his sister done wrong."

"Acres and acres," Journey Wintergarden says.

Acres and acres. "Except I saw something else that worried me before I could get to Fiddler Crab's list. Something I think very strange." I give myself permission to turn and gaze upon Journey Wintergarden straight into his eyes, but not the permission to say the thing I need to say.

"Go on," he says, running a long finger down Miss Jane Austen's short barrel.

"Maybe you saw it for yourself when Avery was sharing secrets with you in the Pyramid of Giza," I say. "Saw it same as me. Avery's confession. The confession of the Swan Princess, the beautiful Odette."

Journey Wintergarden looks like he might want to smile at me, and I am hoping he will stop himself from doing it. I have no time to count a single one of his pretty, white teeth. "I cannot recall anything such as that," he says.

"It was the thing Avery told his mama. The thing he thinks killed her." My teeth snag my tongue, but I keep on talking. "Avery said he saw Rushworth L. Wintergarden kissing his daddy. Why would your brother have up and done such a thing if it was me he loved?"

Any threat of a Journey Wintergarden smile is gone. "Rushworth is very hard not to love," he says. "My brother spoke of McKinley and Constance Rose Longwood. Spoke of their battle for his attention. Spoke of Blue Heron and Fiddler Crab's obsession. All the things Hushabye Byrd wanted him to come here and do—he did. But he did it without intention. In the end—if it was anyone doing any kissing, Leontyne, it was McKinley Longwood forcing his way upon my brother."

"What Avery told me killed his mama, and what Rebecca told me killed her are not near abouts the same," I say.

"What was it Rebecca said did it? That killed her."

Last thing I want to own up to with Journey Wintergarden is that I might be guilty of murder. *Flitter-flatter....* A thrashing noise comes from the pit. The hysterical fluttering sound of a trapped bird's wings. Then quiet.

"Ewell Day Higgs?" I ask, startled. "Is that you?"

Journey Wintergarden goes stiff. Arranges the gun in his hand on the ready to shoot it.

"Please look down, Journey Wintergarden," I say. "I cannot bear to do it. Is my Ewell Day Higgs still down there alive?"

Journey Wintergarden steps close to the edge. Looks down. Winces. "He is not, Leontyne," he says. "There is not a single part of him living. From the looks of things, it is a tender mercy he is gone."

A tender mercy.... My Ewell Day Higgs. *My daddy.* I turn loose of myself. Spin and spin. Fall down-down perilous through a briar patch of sorrow, the barbed edges slicing me open. Digging out my grief. Out it comes. In sobs and tremors. I let rip a scream. "Idumea ... Idumea...." Is there anyone to save me?

Journey Wintergarden grabs hold. Squeezes and rocks me back and forth. Back and forth until the door creeps open and more Rushworth L. Wintergarden spills in a little at a time. Squeezing and rocking me until I remember Rushworth loving me tender upon a bed of live oak leaves. Squeezing back Rushworth's sweet-sweet whispers. *I am going to take you away from here, Leontyne. To far-far places.*

"I am leaving Good Hope," I say, unraveling myself from Journey Wintergarden. Piecing myself back together. "With Rebecca and Avery. I am done tending that tree. Done making Redemption. There is not a dang-fool thing here for me."

"Listen to me," Journey Wintergarden says. "You are going nowhere with Rebecca."

"What do you mean?" I ask, stepping back.

"She is not going with you, Leontyne. Because she is going with me."

I am having trouble finding my breath. What Willadeene has said is true. "Why do you think she would go anywhere with you?"

"Rebecca has been after me since the beginning, Leontyne. Not in the sweet way Fiddler Crab has been chasing after me. Sneaking love poems into my pant pockets. Under my pillow. A paper star hung with my name on it. But cold and deliberate," he says.

"Cold and deliberate? Like you loved up on Willadeene? Does she know you are leaving with Rebecca? Abandoning her here forever to tend your baby?"

Journey Wintergarden blinks slow at me like he is surprised I know.

"It took two of us to dance that waltz. I told Willadeene from the get-go I had no intention of staying here with her back that night we all had us a drop of Redemption. We both knew what we were doing. It was only a bit of fun."

"You are no-good," I say.

Flitter-flatter.... Another commotion comes from below.

"Cold and deliberate as your Rebecca, I suppose." He holds out Miss Jane Austen. "She gave me her gun. Suggested I might fire it your way, then in Hushabye Byrd's direction." He tucks the gun back down into his pocket. "Rebecca has fooled you. Fooled you into thinking she would go away anywhere with you. The same way she has fooled you into remembering what she wants you to remember."

"Deceiver," I say, stumbling against the basket of bottles. "Why would I believe you? You said it yourself. You are no-good. Not anywhere kind as your brother. You were good at being a Josiah."

There is something true in what Journey Wintergarden says. A feeling like I have been somewhere or done something before.

Leontyne, Leontyne,
Pudding and pie.
Kissed the haints,
And made them cry.

"If Rebecca is so despicable, then why do you want her?"

"I do not want Rebecca, Leontyne. I want to keep you safe from her. She wants to go from here, and I am happy to take her. She could be good for business. She has no idea what I have in store for her. One could almost feel sorry for your Blue Heron."

Flitter-flatter….

"What do you mean? What are you planning on doing with her?"

"Nothing she would not have me do to you. If the roles were reversed."

"Tell me what you have in store."

"I believe I can easily take up where the Singing Prophetess left off. I have the makings of a mighty fine prophet," he says. "And Rebecca. She is nice to look at. During my sermons, she could play the violin. Though, not nearly as well as you. And she could certainly make me a handsome penny. In and out of the flap of my revival tent."

"You are disgusting." I turn. Take off walking fast away from him.

He grabs hold of me. Drags me back. "You and Avery are too good for out there beyond Good Hope. Same as Rushworth," he says, pointing a finger toward the Forest. "Rebecca is plenty enough fit for it."

"When I tell her what you have rolled up in them scheming Josiah sleeves," I say. "She will not be taking off anywhere with you."

Journey Wintergarden takes me by both arms. Pulls me close. "Acres and acres," he says. "There are things you should know…"

Clickety-clack.... Clickety-clack.... Clickety-clack ... Mirabelle knocks around inside her can. *Tell her.... Tell her.... Tell her* ... I can make out Mirabelle clear. Seems Journey Wintergarden hears her, too. He looks over at the can.

Clickety-clack.... Clickety clack.... Tell her.... Tell her....

Over in the graveyard, Babylon stomps back the same rhythm as Mirabelle. Stomps it into dead Baby Girl Longwood's grave.

Clickety-clack.... Tell her....

Another *flitter-flatter* comes from Ewell Day Higgs's pit.

I stare into Journey Wintergarden's eyes. Eyes kind as his brother's. Eyes good looking and shining Moon. "Tell me," I say. "Tell me."

Over across at dead Baby Girl Longwood's grave, Journey Wintergarden glances.

Clickety-clack.... Clickety-clack....

"Dead Baby Girl Longwood is not who is there in that grave," Journey Wintergarden says.

Below in Ewell Day Higgs's pit comes a racket, the sound of a baby squalling.

"Who is there then?" I scream.

"Your Mirabelle," he says. "Your and Rushworth's dead baby girl."

Mirabelle. 'Round and 'round I go. *Spinning.... Spinning....* "That is a lie. My Mirabelle is there in that can. My Mirabelle is a hand."

From the pit, Ewell Day Higgs rises magenta. A little baby puffer fish—a shimmery newborn haint. He squalls. Calls out to his mama. Bellows for Damascus, hungry and raring to suckle a Sarah Fig. He squalls. Carries on. Puffs and puffs.

Crying. There is nothing but the sound of crying babies, the mewling of my Mirabelle. Coppery wisps of infant hair. Those Wintergarden eyes. *I remember now.* I remember Constance Rose Longwood taking hold of my baby, my Mirabelle, keeping her from me.

"You are not fit to have her. This child is too good for the Marsh."

"Give her here to me," I say. "She is mine."

Journey Wintergarden takes hold of me. Keeps me from toppling into the pit. Up into the sky I watch my Ewell Day Higgs drift. Into the Forest toward the Marsh. "Come back here," I say.

Mirabelle, sweet-sweet Mirabelle.... Come back here to me....

The Forest

Chapter 49

A baby girl ... I had myself a baby girl, and her name was Mirabelle. Once I had myself a true-true love, and I had myself a daddy.

I do my best to think about anything else, to keep from remembering. From pulling apart at the seams. I count my fingers. My teeth. Focus on the tingles blooming from my evergreen toe.

My name is Leontyne Skye, and I am sixteen years old. Over and over, I tell myself this. To keep moving alongside Journey Wintergarden through the Forest toward Morningstar. His hand presses into the small of my back, a reminder I am not dead or dreaming.

The bottles of Redemption jostle in the basket hooked to Journey Wintergarden's arm. I try ignoring the *tickety-tack* coming from the coffee can cradled in my arm. Mirabelle keeps telling me she is sorry about our baby. *I been trying to tell you all along,* she says. I refuse to say anything back to her. I am not sure I can trust her. Can I be sure of anything? Why does my hand have the same name as my baby?

"You should know Rebecca and I are leaving soon as we get back to Morningstar. She will be packed and raring to go," Journey Wintergarden says.

I keep walking to the *clink* of Redemption and Mirabelle's *tickety-tack.* "Why can we not all go together?" I cannot let my Blue Heron go. Cannot let her leave out of here stupid to what Journey Wintergarden has in store. No matter the few lies she has told. The truths she and Avery have kept hidden. *My Blue Heron, sleek and tall. I love you best of all.* I repeat this a few times more. Convincing myself to believe it, that this is not some seed of a lie Blue Heron planted inside my head.

"I told you I am no-good," he says. "Listen to me when I tell you there is more trouble for me to get myself into out there than here. And Rebecca is the one of you to help me do it."

"You cannot make me stay, Journey Wintergarden. If I have the mind to go. I will go."

He stops. Takes a hold of me. "There is no world, Leontyne. No living for anyone if you do not stay here and tend this one."

I snatch away. Pull out Eulalee's teeth and rattle the bottle between us. "Tending the dead kills the living," I say. "Why do I have to be the one to do it? To fall apart out yonder in the Doldrums? If I leave from here, there might be plenty of living for me to do before the sky clogs with haints. Before they suck up all the air clear out to China. What do I care then, when I am done living. And the world is through?"

"Perhaps I was wrong, Leontyne. Maybe you are fit enough for living beyond Good Hope. Go on then. Leave. If that is what you have in your head and heart to do. But you are not coming with me." He takes off walking away toward the Forest's clearing, the last bit of way before the path to Morningstar.

I stop myself from turning cruel, from telling him his brother is dead to freeze him in his tracks. "I am telling Rebecca what you have planned," I say. "And you will be going alone." He keeps walking. "I am talking to you."

Journey Wintergarden keeps his pace. I stay put, listening to the bottles of Redemption clatter. To Mirabelle *tick-tacking*. I watch the high-high arch of Journey Wintergarden's feet. The leaves sticking to his heels. Figuring out what to do next.

Here comes another sound. Salome singing Chopin off Morningstar way. Back and forth Mirabelle sways in her can as if she is the one playing, shifting the balance of the coffee can in my arm. As if she is holding and moving Salome's bow. As if she is remembering.

My wrist tingles. And I am remembering, too. Rebecca humming the Nocturne when she was sawing off my hand, Avery begging her to stop.

Off Morningstar way comes pandemonium. A scream. *Agamemnon....* Journey Wintergarden stops. Glances back at me. And the two of us take off running. Running for what seems to be the end.

Running ... running....

Clinkety-clink.... Tickety-tack....

She is killing me.

Agamemnon....

Morningstar
The In-Between

Chapter 50

I cannot gather my bearings. I cannot focus my eyes in this chaos. The bright pool of Moon. Salome singing. Fallen chandelier. *Fallen-fallen.* Obscenities scrawled into walls by crocodile claws. Avery crying.

Rebecca plays Salome standing atop a sawhorse at the entrance to the Pyramid of Giza. She seems surprised to see me, dragging the bow across my violin, squealing a dreadful note across the catgut strings. Butchering all of us here in the In-Between. She lowers the violin from her chin. Taps the bow against her boot, the River running her eyes quickening dark and cool.

"Rebecca is leaving," Fiddler Crab shrieks, his hair wild about his shoulders. "She is stealing our Journey Wintergarden." In circles, he hurries. Covers his ears. Rings his hands. The hem of his pink gown sweeping broken window glass across the floor. Avery spots Journey Wintergarden behind me. Runs for him. Pulls at his albatross arm. "Do not go with her," he says, pointing up-up to Rebecca on the sawhorse. "She is a fiend."

Journey Wintergarden tucks Avery beneath his arm. "I did not come to stay forever, Fiddler Crab," he says, bending down, kissing the top of his head. "I came here looking for my brother."

I holler above Salome. "That is only part truth, Journey Wintergarden. You came here to steal the way to Redemption." I get myself ready to tell Blue Heron what Journey Wintergarden has in store for her. I open my mouth....

"Where is Hushabye Byrd?" Rebecca asks. She gazes down at Journey Wintergarden, then over at me.

Rebecca's eyes. *Those dark-river eyes.* Time and time before I have seen them. Admired them. Watched the current run fast. Run cool. Wanted to float myself inside of them. Only now, something is different. No—familiar. I have seen this look in her eyes before. Moonless and gazing down upon me. Some time, back when—

"There now. It will all be over soon," Rebecca says.

Sawing at my hand.

Her hair drawing midnight curtains over me.

Black moonstone earbobs dangle,

Twinkling black-hearted stars.

Snatched fresh from her dead mama's ears.

Pianissimo. . . .

Here I am again, looking back in my Blue Heron's eyes. Know this: she is surprised. Disappointed to see me alive and standing. Journey Wintergarden was not lying. She sent him out into the Marsh with Miss Jane Austen to murder me and the Singing Prophetess.

"The Singing Prophetess is dead," I announce. Wishing I was a little bit dead, too. Feeling as if I am on the verge. Feeling every bit the fool.

Avery shrieks. Shuts his eyes. Leans himself into Journey Wintergarden.

"What on earth has happened?" Rebecca asks, not blinking.

"A great woe it must be to have lost two mamas," I say. "In such a short time."

A voice tumbles from the Up-Up There. "So little time to grieve the first one properly."

Willadeene. She stands beneath the broken windows of the Cupola. At the place where there is no rail, her sand dollar toes reaching for the edge.

"Be careful, Willadeene," Avery says, panic crackling his throat. "Step back away from there."

I realize I am standing smack in the middle of the mayhaw jelly stain. *Constance Rose Longwood's and my poor Mirabelle's brains.* I shut my eyes. Try to shoo away this feeling I might fall over.

"Do not worry, Avery. I am not liable to jump," Willadeene says. "Regardless of what some other someone might have said. Look at your sister, Avery. She knows good and well I would never do it." She runs her hands over her fast-growing belly. "Is that not right, Rebecca? Even if the father of my baby aims to run off with you."

There is a shift in Willadeene's voice. Self-assuredness. Innuendo. If she does not know she was Constance Rose Longwood, I fear she will know it soon. *I am not liable to jump.* Is Willadeene about to spill the beans? Accuse me of murder?

"Baby?" Avery asks, wriggling his way from beneath Journey Wintergarden's wing. He turns to Journey Wintergarden. Stares into the Up-Up There. "Is it true? Are you having a baby, Willadeene?" Though Willadeene's belly has swole up quick, it is a wonder of wonders Avery just now notices.

"Yes, Avery," Rebecca says. "Seems our poor Mr. Journey Wintergarden has been taken advantage of by your haint. Look how she looks down upon you from the Up-Up There. At all of us."

"Willadeene," Avery screams. "How could you?"

"It was not so very hard. Look at him. He is nearly as handsome as Mr. Rushworth L. Wintergarden," Willadeene says. "Why is it, Avery, you and your sister believe only you should have Journey Wintergarden? Just as you both thought you should each have his brother?"

Willadeene knows. Remembers she was Constance Rose Longwood.

Avery's eyes blink and blink moon shadows on his cheeks. Slowly-slowly, it seems to occur to him. "You never knew Rushworth L. Wintergarden," Avery says. "How would you know what he looks like? How would you know he is more handsome than his brother?"

"I know many more things now than I knew yesterday," she says. "Whenever yesterday was, however long ago that might have been."

The dark-river current slows in Blue Heron's eyes, as slow as she is tapping Salome's bow against her boot. *Click* … *click*…. "How wonderful for you," Rebecca says. "If only Journey Wintergarden and I could stay here until you are done remembering all the way through to tomorrow. But it is time for us to go."

"You cannot go, Rebecca. Until we know how it is I got here," Willadeene says. "How I wound up dead."

Rebecca takes a few steps across the sawhorse, her black riding boots squeaking. Shined up. Raring to go. But there are no pretty horses, Blue Heron. No dapples and greys. No babies to soothe with lullabies. No Mirabelle to cuddle and *coo*. And I can take it no longer. I holler out into a great quiet that is about to follow. "I know about my baby. I know about Mirabelle."

And so it comes. The quiet. And more quiet. Quiet but for the *tick* of Salome's bow. *Ticking* and *ticking* while I lose and find myself again upon this mayhaw jelly stain. Until I have the courage to confess this next thing.

"I did not mean to hurt my Mirabelle. It is not something I could have ever done," I holler out. "And I did not mean to hurt you, Willadeene. It had to have been an accident."

Avery weeps and weeps. "Poor-poor Mirabelle," he says. "Rebecca told me it was best if we never told you Mirabelle was yours. That she is dead."

"That the father was Rushworth L. Wintergarden," Willadeene says. "How very thoughtful of Rebecca to keep the truth from you, Leontyne. To keep your baby and Rushworth L. Wintergarden erased from your head."

Avery blinks more moon shadows. "How do you know about that, Willadeene? That Rushworth L. Wintergarden was the father?" Avery comes closer to me here on the stain, looking into the

Up-Up There. "You have been at it again. Peeking and pilfering *Jubilation and Woe*," he screams.

"My sweet boy. I know because I was here." Willadeene says. "Because once I was living. I am your mother, Avery," Willadeene says. "I was Constance Rose Longwood. Mistress here at Morningstar." Down comes upon us another great quiet. A heavy hush pressing upon us. Until....

"That is a lie," Avery hollers. "A lie...."

"Rebecca has known it for some time now. She told me a short while ago," I say, feeling nowhere near the pleasure I thought I might feel shocking Avery. Paying him back for all the things he has kept from me.

"Acres and acres...." Journey Wintergarden says, a sort of wonderment stirring dreamy in his voice. Another deed of Rebecca's to tally.

"Just look at you, Avery," Rebecca says. "Keeping your very own mother on a leash. You always wanted her for your very own. Miracle of miracles, Brother. You will have her all to yourself once I go away with Mr. Journey Wintergarden."

I feel the shock work its way up through Avery. Trembling the floor—like steam working its way through the Undine's calliope. Building-building. Until he screams. *Holy hell and murder....*

We will all be deaf soon if Avery does not stop his wailing. He wails and wails. Scares the last living sparrows from their nests. Provokes a storm of Willadeene blooms to drift upon us. Azaleas. Daffodils. Morning glories. Wails and wails until the last petal falls. Until Willadeene says this thing she says next.

"Tribulation day. Two years back," she says. "I do not remember all of it. But I do remember who was in the Up-Up There with me. There was Rebecca, and Leontyne. And little Mirabelle. And I know with great certainty, I did not jump with that baby in my arms."

You did not jump, Willadeene. Rebecca says I pushed you.

Avery sops his tears with Rushworth L. Wintergarden's monogrammed handkerchief. "Rebecca said she was here in the In-Between. Watching from down here when it happened." He turns back to study his sister. Rebecca lifts her chin, but not so high the Moon might catch her eyes.

"Do you remember anything, Leontyne?" Avery asks, taking hold of my arm. "Anything at all?"

Heads cracking the floor. "Glints and glimmers. Mostly of me falling-falling," I say. "There are some things we might ought keep forgetting. Is that not right, Willadeene?"

"I am tired of forgetting, Leontyne. I think I am ready to know."

"Acres and acres," Journey Wintergarden says. "I think it best if you try and remember. Before Rebecca and I go."

"I am not sure I give a hoot about yesterday," I say. *Once I know. I know. There is no turning back.*

"You are anything but a coward, Leontyne Skye," Willadeene says.

Avery tugs on my arm. "You are the Great Redeemer."

"I am not," I say. *I am not.* From Eulalee's oyster shell necklace, I hear echoes. As if far off someone calls to me. I reach for Rivière. I think better of it. Drop her. Pull away my hand. Eulalee's teeth churn in my pocket. If I am ever to do it. I should do it now. I lift the necklace. Lick my tongue 'round and 'round in the ancient oyster shells drowning in century upon century of briny Marsh. 'Round and 'round. Until I am back. In the Up-Up There. Tribulation Day.

Two years back....

Morningstar
The Up-Up There
Tribulation Day, Two Years Back

Chapter 51

I am not supposed to be here. But nothing can keep me from it. From peeking behind this door in Avery's Celestial Hall of Books. From eavesdropping on Constance Rose Longwood ambling about on the high-high arches of her bare, pale, pretty feet. Watching her hold and love my Mirabelle, toting my girl up and down rows of books wrapped in her cream silk blanket. Listening to her sing to my baby.

When you wake, you shall have
All the pretty horses
Dapples and greys, pintos and bays....

Constance Rose Longwood has persuaded Eulalee into letting her take my Mirabelle from me. To raise my Mirabelle as a Longwood. She has taken advantage of my Eulalee who is losing her mind. Her teeth. Her hair.

"She is not fit to be a mother, Eulalee," Constance Rose Longwood said before. "She is much too young to care for this child. The Marsh is no place for a girl."

Constance Rose Longwood is a fool. The Marsh only ever has been lived upon by girls. By Eulalee. By all the Skye women come before. Constance Rose Longwood and the rest of her kin would have starved already without us. Sinners long withered away. *Without our crops. Of drops. Of Redemption.*

Listen to me when I tell you this. Constance Rose Longwood is no better off than my Eulalee. She nearly has lost all her ever-loving Longwood mind pretending Mirabelle belongs to her and my

Rushworth L. Wintergarden. Making believe he is coming back to her soon. But it will be my Mirabelle and me who Rushworth L. Wintergarden comes back around for.

Mirabelle *gurgles* and *coos*. Reaches for Constance Rose Longwood's black moonstone earbobs. I shut my eyes. Pretend I am holding my baby, watching her dazzled by and reaching for this blue velvet ribbon her daddy gave to me, the one tied up pretty into a bow in my hair. One of these here days, I am going to teach my Mirabelle to play the violin.

Rebecca calls from the landing just off the stairs beneath the Cupola. "Mother? Where are you? Busy tending that bastard?" *Blue Heron-Blue Heron spiteful and tall. Avery is the one I love best of all.*

"That is your sister," Constance Rose Longwood says to Mirabelle, bending down to kiss my baby on her coppery tufts of hair, her hair pins sparkling-sparkling. "She is a beast," she whispers.

"That baby is not yours," Rebecca says. "You are making yourself look a fool."

Rebecca is here. Standing so close I can smell her. *Black licorice and Christmastime orange.*

Constance Rose Longwood stops. Looks down at Mirabelle. Looks up across the room to the door. "You are only bitter because she is not yours," Constance Rose Longwood says. "Though it was not for your lack of shameless trying."

"You are one to talk," Rebecca says. "The spectacle you made of yourself right here under Father's nose. It is a scandal of scandals. It is because of you—you—that Father sent Rushworth away." Rebecca walks across the room pointing her finger. "You are no better than Leontyne Skye. You are no better than that whore down by the Marsh."

I keep myself still. Chew my lip. Do my best to keep from running out from behind this door to give Rebecca Longwood a piece of my mind. To grab my baby and take off for the Marsh.

Constance Rose Longwood laughs. "Seems your father was quite smitten himself by the charms of Mr. Rushworth L. Wintergarden. That, my dear, is what got your tutor sent away. Not me," she says. "Your father could care less I might try to find myself a little affection. A little affection with anyone living that might come this way. He has long lost interest in me, girl."

"What are you talking about? Explain yourself."

"Ask your brother."

"What would Avery know about anything?"

"Avery saw your Father with his very own eyes, forcing himself upon our Rushworth L. Wintergarden. He kissed the boy.... Kissed the boy.... Beneath the Moon...," she says. "We all know McKinely Longwood wants what he wants. You are like your father in that regard. Both of you are eat pure up with jealousy. And meanness." Constance Rose Longwood takes up singing again to Mirabelle. *Dapples and greys, pintos and bays....*

"Avery is a liar. You are a liar. You know well as I do, Avery is as scheming as you when it comes to Rushworth L. Wintergarden. The two of you could not have him, so you both had him sent away. And you have the nerve to blame it on Father." Rebecca moves closer to her mama. "You two are not happy unless I am miserable."

"We are all miserable, Rebecca," Constance Rose Longwood says, leaning down to kiss my baby again. "Why should you be any happier than the rest of us? What makes you so special?"

Rebecca takes off for her mama. "Give me that bastard child," she says, trying to wrench Mirabelle from Constance Rose Longwood's arms. "Give her here."

"Leave us be," Constance Rose Longwood says, twisting and turning. Keeping Mirabelle out of Blue Heron's reach. "You are frightening the baby. Get away." Constance Rose Longwood slings a hand. Slaps Rebecca's face. Rebecca jerks. Goes still. Constance Rose Longwood takes off with Mirabelle out of the room onto the landing singing along the way.

All the pretty horses

Dapples and greys, pintos and bays....

Rebecca follows after her mama, her black riding boots quick and hard against the floor. And they are all gone, leaving me here alone in the room behind the door.

"Do not run from me," Rebecca hollers.

"Pianissimo...." Constance Rose Longwood says. "You are frightening your sister."

I come out from behind the door. Creep onto the landing to see Constance Rose Longwood and my Mirabelle beneath the Cupola in a wash of Forever Moon. Standing at the place where there is no rail.

"I hate you. So much I could kill you," Rebecca says, her back turned to me.

Constance Rose Longwood looks up to the Cupola, the Forever Moon a glory in her lonesome eyes. "What does any of it matter, Rebecca?" she asks, smiling at Blue Heron. Smiling at me. "We are all dead here on Good Hope."

And Rebecca is running.... Screaming.... Pushing....

And I am screaming. Running. Grabbing-grabbing hold of Rebecca. And Constance Rose Longwood and my Mirabelle are falling-falling. Hair pins sparkling-sparkling.

Rebecca grabs hold my hair. Snatches my ribbon. Shoves me hard. And here I go. Falling-falling.... The long-long ways.... Falling-falling until I am not. Until I am lying here in this splatter of Constance Rose Longwood and my Mirabelle. Until I am looking up-up to Rebecca staring down-down, not a speck of Moon in her eyes. Listening to her whisper this last thing she says.

"Pianissimo...."

Pianissimo....

Morningstar
The In-Between

Chapter 52

Here I stand. Back on this mayhaw jelly stain where the end of me began, my tongue scraped and bloody from licking Damascus's oyster shells. Fresh back here from Tribulation Day. *Two years back….* Fresh from telling everyone here what happened.

"Agamemnon," Avery weeps, collapsed into a delphinium-pink heap. "How could you have done it, Rebecca? Our mother? Poor Mirabelle? How could you have let me think I was the one who did it?"

Journey Wintergarden extends his hand, those long-long Wintergarden fingers to Rebecca, helping her down from the Pyramid of Giza. "It is time, Rebecca" he says. "For us to leave."

"You are still taking her with you?" Avery asks. "After all you know she has done?"

"She is the one best suited, Fiddler Crab," Journey Wintergarden says. "To make the trip with me."

From the Up-Up There comes a Willadeene snow. A shower of magnolia blossoms and forget-me-nots. Next comes down her leash. "I am dead here on Good Hope," Willadeene says. "And I am more alive than you, Rebecca. Alive with this Wintergarden baby in my belly."

Rebecca does not look up at her mama. She does not look up at Fiddler Crab. Or at the skeleton of bricks and beams. She does not look at me. It is certain to me now Journey Wintergarden means to take her, every acre of every bad thing she has sowed. I tell myself this. *If she looks up to the Moon. If I can see it for but a second in her eyes, I might save her from what Journey Wintergarden has in store. Look up. Look up.* But she does not look up at the Moon that beheld all the things she done. *Fiddler Crab, Fiddler Crab, you were the one I loved best.*

Blue Heron keeps walking in her riding boots to the doors. Across broken glass. Across crocodile scratches. Away from her brother sprawled and crying. Away from the Moon.

"Hold on, Journey Wintergarden. Before you go," I say. "I have one favor to ask. Just one favor is all." I hurry. Get down onto my knees. Pry the top loose from my coffee can. Down I gaze at Mirabelle. The poor thing seems shy. A long while it has been since we have seen the other. Or maybe the Moon is too bright. Or maybe she is mad with me. She tries to wriggle and hide beneath the lace. And I remember now. The pain of Rebecca sawing-sawing my hand. A hand every bit still good. A hand strong enough to hold Salome's bow—and I remember calling out for my dead baby. For my Mirabelle. I remember hearing Avery then. Weeping-weeping. Bringing back to me my cut-off hand. *This here is your Mirabelle, Fiddler Crab says. We will put her here. Here in this coffee can for safe keeping. On this piece of wedding lace.*

I reach into the can for my hand, for my Mirabelle. I reach for her dark withered fingers. She has warmed up to me. She is less shy than before. We hold tight to the other. Our fingers lacing and squeezing the longest time. I pull the blue velvet ribbon from my hair. "This is for you," I say, threading it through Mirabelle's fingers. From my apron pocket, I take out my fallen-off toe. Nestle it close to Mirabelle. From the get-go, Mirabelle seems to remember this toe, rubbing herself soft against it.

Next comes Eulalee's teeth, my bottle of black pearl treasure. I give it a shake. Press the bottle to my cheek and kiss it tender. "I love you, Mama," I say. "I always will." Down into the can Eulalee goes. "Keep watch," I tell Mirabelle. "Over my Eulalee. Over my toe." Before I can change my mind, I close the lid back tight. Hammer it with my fist.

Tickety-tack-tack, goes my Mirabelle. *Clickety-clack* goes Eulalee.

"Journey Wintergarden," I say. "Please do this one thing for me. Take this coffee can away from here with you." *To far-far places. To China. Morocco. Rest it beneath a palm tree in an oasis cool with shade.*

Journey Wintergarden kisses my cheek. He presses Pocket Watch into my hand and takes hold of the coffee can. "I will miss you, Leontyne Skye," he says. "And I will miss you, Fiddler Crab. *Woosh*.... I will miss my Avery's Comet."

Face down, Avery lays weeping-weeping. "Why does Rebecca get to go to Cherubim? Why does she get to travel the Ephesians Sea?" Over and over he asks it.

Journey Wintergarden slides off the gold ring from his pinky. "Give this to Willadeene. In exchange for Pocket Watch." This next part he whispers. "To one day give to the baby."

A feeling I will never see Journey Wintergarden again takes hold. Squeezes me by the throat. I know this feeling. The misery of a Wintergarden man heading off to the Out-Out There without me. *Take me with you. I will do anything. Anything, Journey Wintergarden. Let me guard the back flap of the revival tent for you.* I study him as he leaves, deciding if I ought holler out for him to take me. *Why does Rebecca get to go to Cherubim? Why does she get to travel the Ephesians Sea?*

Journey Wintergarden steps careful over broken glass. Over flecks of Uncle Daddy. Over Willadeene's dead honeybees with the high-high arches of his handsome feet. His toes cross the threshold, and I call out to him. "Not every bit of you is no-good, Journey Wintergarden," I say, running my finger over Pocket Watch. "Not every bit. There is some kindness in you."

He turns. Smiles. Right here and right now, I decide not to tell him his brother is dead. I want to see him smile long as he will smile. Long enough for me to count every last one of his Wintergarden teeth.

Sixteen gleaming teeth on bottom. Sixteen gleaming teeth on top.

The Marsh

An Hour, A Week, A Century Later…

Chapter 53

I play Vivaldi's *Winter*. Slow-slow, I tap my evergreen toe. *Bow up. Bow down.* In time, I am liable to grow accustomed to this new, evergreen hand. Accustomed to our new lives here on the Marsh without Eulalee. Without my dented coffee can. Without Rebecca. Accustomed to a life without the Sun.

Damascus sings, and I play this violin. Together, we woo haints across the River as we have been ordained to do. I am not sure we will ever be friends, this haint-trap tree and me. But we have come to an understanding. Possess respect. Managed an appreciation for the other.

Sweet, sweet, are my Sarah Figs.

Lay down. Lay down….

From a high-high crystalline branch, a Sarah Fig turns loose. The poor thing sputters. Moans. Darkly creeps close to sniff it. Mossy hand in mossy hand, my Ewell Day Higgs and Willadeene set off to tend it. They gather the carcass from the Marsh. Rest it careful in Sweet Chariot with the others. Tender, they serenade us with Eulalee's haint-dying song.

On across the River,

To where you ought go….

Ewell Day Higgs does not yet know he is my daddy. He possesses no memory of who he was before. No recollection of dying in a Sinner's pit. There will be time enough to tell him once he collects his bearings, when his garden is fully grow'd. All he knows is that he is like our Willadeene, that he managed to escape a Sarah Fig.

Something else there is I must tell you. We do things here on Good Hope different from how we done before. No Sepulcher. No gutting Sarah Figs. Gone-gone away are bottles filled with and sloshing Redemption. We tend honeybees. The ones snooping and buzzing around Willadeene. Around Ewell Day Higgs. Fussing about our Mirabelle, Willadeene and Journey Wintergarden's child.

We have found our path to a different sort of saving. We make honey. *We make Evergreen.* And what of these fallen Sarah Figs loaded into Sweet Chariot's barrel? Should you bother to follow us up King's Bottom Trail, you will see us set them adrift down the River. Down-down to Kingdom Come. Across Deliverance Sea. A hop, a skip from Galilee.

"Come back here, Mirabelle," Avery says, grabbing hold of the tasseled curtain leash tied about his sister. Fiddler Crab is a good brother, watching always over her. Reaching for her hand. Reaching-reaching. Mirabelle's eyes. I cannot decide. *Are they dusky blue or dreary grey?* They are forever changing like her father's.

Avery pulls the peacock feather from his hair. He tells Mirabelle he gave it once to a handsome boy named Josiah. Swears the boy aims to fetch him. *One day.... Real soon....*

"*Swan Lake*," Mirabelle calls out to me clapping her teensy green hands. "Play *Swan Lake*, Lee-own-teen." I can refuse the child nothing. She is our everything. I abandon *Winter*. I play the finale to *Swan Lake*. Here at the beginning, I play the end.

Mirabelle and Princess Odette take off spinning-spinning down the wetland walk, Journey Wintergarden's ring glinting, dangling on a necklace about Mirabelle's pretty neck, her eyes full-up and spilling Moon.

From the Forest, through the trees, come two puffer fish haints. Squalling. Trembling for Damascus. *More.... More.... More....*

"Where you been? What you seen?" I ask. "Who were you back before?"

Cold air blows restless across the Marsh. Through the cordgrass it whispers, *Idumea... Idumea....* Mirabelle turns loose Avery's hand.

Spins and spins a whirly wind. Charms daisy petals from her garden hair.

Petals rise.

Drift.

Fall down-down upon us. *A Kilimanjaro snow....*

I shut my eyes, twirl along with Mirabelle. I call out to Babylon preening beneath the Moon. To the haints. Damascus. To the Marsh. "My name is Leontyne Starshine," I say. "I am every bit Skye."

The haints call back to me. *More.... More.... More....*

"I beg your pardon," I say. "I am the Great Redeemer, like my mama, and her mama come before." *It is not so very hard being mostly living and only part of the way dead.* And it is not so very cold and so very dark here on Good Hope that we might not one day be happy.

—THE END—

Acknowledgments

Writing is a lonesome endeavor. Without my cherished community of writerly folk and smattering of big-hearted friends, I might never have found my way clear to the end of *Sing Down the Moon*.

A thing you should know: the care and feeding of this storyteller is a thankless, relentless chore. Let me do my best here to tell y'all how much I love and blame the lot of you for turning me audacious—stoking the idea I might have a story flickering in this head and roguish heart of mine.

To Ann Hite, you championed this novel way-back-when. Without your editorial ear and eye, the Forever Moon and I might have drowned in the sea. Donna Everhart, you embraced my peculiar story and me from the get-go, aiding and abetting, turning a Sinner's eyes a gorgeous, golden shade of goat. My critique group: Jef Blocker, Mickey Dubrow, and Marissa McNamara—you endured much, and I thank you for your patience.

Gregory Arial, Kimberly Brock, Jeff Clemmons, Mandy Haynes, Jeffrey Dale Lofton, Bren McClain, and James Wade—I shall never be able to compensate you suitably for your friendship and guidance, for coaxing me safely from crumbling ledges. I am a better writer and human because of you. And less lonesome than before.

Claire Fullerton, my Crocodile, thank you for believing in and guiding me. Mary Martha Greene, we will always have the scandalous, behind-the-scenes tour of Beaufort, South Carolina. Without you, there would be no Chapel of Abundance. Mary Ellen Thompson with sherbert streaks in your hair, I am beholden to you for hosting me during my Pat Conroy Residency, for providing me shelter when I first set out to write this book, and for urging me to look upon the sun setting down quiet and spectacular upon the Marsh. Much gratitude to Babylon, that hussy deer. To the dock. The mirrored sky. To the haints drifting relentless across the River to haunt me still.

Kim Taylor Blakemore (Novelitics Writers Collective), Jeff Clemmons (Marthasville), Joe Davich (Georgia Center for the Book), Darrell Grizzle (Coffee House and Artists), Mandy Haynes (*Well Read Magazine*), Jonathan Haupt (Pat Conroy Literary Center), Zachary Steele (Broadleaf Writers Association), George Weinstein (Atlanta Writers Club), and Georgia Writers Association, thank you for supporting writers, fostering community, and building homes.

Christine Brazil, Tom Eaton, Jon Esther, Lea Harwell, Michelle Johnson, and Zane Shelfer—you are most generous to love this writer the way you do. I sure as heck love you.

Marc Jolley and Mercer University Press (Mary Beth Kosowski, Kelley Land, Marsha Luttrell, and Jenny Toole)—thank you for believing in *Sing Down the Moon,* and for believing in me. I am proud to join the ranks, to have a home. Ann-Marie Nieves (Get Red PR), you give me confidence and forge a trail from which readers might find their way to me.

And to my Timothy—for feeding, loving, and caring for me best. For looking up. For allowing me to behold the dazzle of Forever Moon swimming in your eyes.

It is beautiful here.